The Goddesses Throne

A. Kingsley

DEDICATION

Thank you to everyone who was so incredibly supportive during this process. I am grateful for all of you. Thank you to anyone who is opening up this book with the intent to read it all the way through. You are making my dreams come true.

CONTENTS

PROLOGUE

The palace hadn't been this crowded in years. Though the Pax family threw parties, they were never this large. There were people from all three kingdoms in almost every room of the palace and the large celebration was all for Sage. The sun was beating down hot on that mid September day and the summer days were dwindling. Sage was standing by the large window in her bedroom, the sun pouring in and warming up her skin. She stared out at the carriages pulling up to the place, "I told mum I didn't want a party and she threw me the event of a lifetime," she said.

Her eyes flickered behind her shoulder to the woman who was tightening her corset. "Ouch," she hissed lightly underneath her breath as the tight material synced her ribs.

The woman then helped her put on her hoop skirt, petticoat and dress. The dress she wore overtop of the corset was large, puffy and olive green. The fabric was hemmed with white lace along the collar, the skirt and the sleeves. The outfit was no where close to what she would have chosen to wear on her own accord, but this event meant a lot to her mother. She was turning twenty and in her mother's eyes, she was now an official woman. Leaving her teenage years behind didn't feel like a relief because she would be forced to grow up and for Sage that wasn't easy. She had felt that even her eighteen year old sister was more mature than she was.

The older woman fastened a thin silver chain around her neck and straightened the white elephant charm attached to it flat against her neck. "I know it's not what you wanted, but try and enjoy yourself, you deserve it," she said sweetly.

"Ah yes I will try to enjoy myself as every man around me flushes himself with alcohol and asks me to dance. Pathetic, who even dances anymore?"

Sage and her maid knew the answer to that question. 'Everyone still danced,' yet neither of them responded with that answer. "

1

You should come down and enjoy yourself as well Esmeralda, you could use a break," Sage recommended as she slipped on a pair of olive green shoes with a two inch heel. Normally she would have picked her best pair of flats to go with this dress, but she didn't want to embarrass herself when her mother invited everyone in Pax et Lux to their home.

"I should go downstairs, does my makeup look okay?" The princess approached Esmeralda, their faces were only a few inches away from one another.

The young woman pretended to study Sage's face. "It looks perfect." She ran two fingers through the girl's pin straight, short ginger hair, that stopped just above her chin. "You look gorgeous. Now go, the royal carriages have just arrived."

But before Sage could leave, Esmeralda pulled her back and placed a thin silver crown with tiny white flowers twisted into the metal, on top of her head. "A future queen must never forget her crown."

The princess forced herself out of her room and down the white grand staircase. After a few minutes, she reached the entryway where her mother and sister were waiting. Gracielle, her mother, embraced her older daughter in a warm hug. "You look gorgeous," she complimented, pulling back to get a good look at her daughter's hazel eyes.

Sage directed her eyes away from her mother to her younger sister, Clare, who looked like an angel. "Not as gorgeous as Clare."

She wasn't trying to degrade herself, but everyone knew that Clare was the graceful one, the beautiful one, the one who should have been queen. In the eyes of the people, it was a shame that Clare was two years younger than Sage.

Clare peaked her head around the corner of the stone pillar and fully made her way into the entryway. She was wearing a white, lace dress that had a short train. She looked like a bride without the veil. Instead of a veil she wore a crown that was identical to Sage's. Her loose ginger curls fell neatly against the middle of her back, her makeup was natural, but present. "Sage, don't say that please," Clare whined, pulling at her sister's arm. No matter how much she whined, Sage would never stop and deep down, Clare knew that.

Her mother pushed the two sisters forwards towards the door. Today they would meet their suitors for the first time since the arranged engagements. For Sage it worked out perfectly, for Clare it was a nightmare and she was a nervous wreck.

"Sage I'm nervous," Clare whispered, swaying on her heels. Sage looked over to her sister and shook her head. "Don't be. Everyone will love you, including him. Take deep breaths."

The carriages came to a halt outside the front of the palace. The first carriage to stop was royal blue with red rubies around the edges, it was pulled by four white horses. Stepping out from the high carriage was King Maximus of Deus. His hair was a fiery ginger orange that curled on the top of his head in perfect coils. He had almond sea blue eyes, a tall figure and a sharp face. His eye lids were dusted with golden eyeshadow, his lips bright red. The outfit he was wearing caught the attention of many. A bright red vest over a pure gold button up shirt. His pants were a velvet red and his shoes looked as if they were made of pure gold. On top of his head was a golden leaf crown that fit snugly against his curls. He was only nineteen years old and headed an entire kingdom.

Behind him was his twin brother Prince Julius. A gentler figure, his features were soft and round, blush and fair. His hair was a dusty brown and fell against his head in light waves. Sitting on top of his soft hair was a silver leaf crown. He wore a royal blue suit and simple brown boots. There was no makeup on his young and tired face, just a bright smile as he followed his brother up to the castle doors.

The two guards dressed in olive green armor and white fuzzy hats, lowered their metal crossbows and opened the doors for the neighboring royalty.

Maximus took the lead. He shook hands with the older queen and then bowed to both Sage and Clare. "Happy Birthday Sage and good day Clare." He turned to his brother who had almost tripped on the steps up to the palace.

Julius's face was hot. He shook hands with the queen, waved hello to Clare and then approached Sage with a large smile on his face. "Happy Birthday, you look beautiful." Though the two of them had been arranged to marry one another recently, they both had already been seeing one another for three years.

"Thank you. You look handsome as always." She took his hand and was about to walk away when her mother pushed them both back. "

Not until the Antias's arrive."

3

Sage had to resist the urge to roll her eyes back into her head. Normally she would when she was alone with her mother, but she figured it would be in bad taste in front of a crowd. She turned herself back around and blew the stray piece of hair out of her eyes while she awaited the dreaded visit from the Antias family, who reigned upon the kingdom of Excidium. Though the Queen who had all of the real power was fair and so was her son Cassius, his father, the king, was a wicked man who had caused the kingdom to take a downward tumble. No one got along well with the Antias family, for reasons they often did not speak of, but for peace, an arranged marriage was formed between Prince Cassius and Princess Clare, so they were invited to the day's festivities.

The Antias carriage was dreary yet elegant. The base was painted a solid pitch black, the rim was silver metal and along the carriage were tiny silver stars that sparkled in the sunlight. The carriage was pulled by four black horses and it came to a stop just behind the royal blue one.

As the doors opened, the queen struggled to get herself out with her puffy, black ball gown dress. Before climbing out, she straightened the black metal crown that had white pearls on the center of each thick spike and small silver stars lining the rim, against her head. Once her tall black heels hit the floor, she made her way through the blinding white doors into the palace.

Quickly scrambling behind her came her husband, the king, envious and bitter, as he had no direct control over their kingdom. His skin was a tan olive, but rough and ragged from his years of training. He was older than his wife and looked it too. While she was in her early forties, he was five years older than her. He lacked hair on the top of his shiny head, but he had a large, fluffy black beard on his chin. He confidently sported a pair of black dress pants, and a grey button up collared shirt that was layered underneath a black vest that was adorned with silver buttons. Upon his feet were a pair of shiny black shoes that must have been freshly polished by his servant. His crown was a plane silver with pointed spikes and black jewels. He stuck his large fingers in his mouth and whistled. Like a dog following a command, his eighteen year old son stepped out of the carriage.

Cassius Antias was graceful, he hopped out of the carriage like a cat who always landed on its feet. Even though he was the prince of Excidium, Gracielle, queen of Pax et Lux gave him more credit than his parents. She believed he had a bright future ahead of him and could change the reputation and fate of his kingdom when he ruled. She also believed that he was quite handsome and with time, would eventually make a good match for her daughter, Clare. Cassius had honey gold skin with rounded wood brown eyes. His short, straight black hair was gelled into a smooth combover on the top of his head. He wore a shiny silver suit with black spiral details running up and down the edges, paired with black dress pants and silver boots. His crown was a pure black metal and rose in thin pointy spikes at the top of his head. He also wore a cape over his shoulders that was pitch black in color and dragged along the floor as he walked.

"Forward," the king spat and he and his son followed the queen into the palace.

Upon seeing the Antias family, Sage took this as her cue to leave, but was held back by her mother who had a firm grip on her arm and a fake smile upon her face. She let go once her daughter got the hint.

Both King Maximus and Prince Julius hurried away in haste, leaving just the Pax and Antias family in the middle of the grand hallway.

"Well it's been a while since we have been invited to anything," King Erebus mused as he glanced around the white hallway that was glittering with golden trim and decorated with olive green furniture. "You have furnished it well," he complimented.   Queen Gracielle ignored his attempts to make her feel pity, "well it is Sage's birthday after all and you were invited to the celebration so that Clare and Cassius could become engaged."

From behind both of their mothers, the two met eyes. Clare quickly looked away, putting her focus on her sister's tense shoulders. Sage caught her strong gaze and glanced over to see her nervous face. 'Go introduce yourself,' she murmured, her voice almost unheard.

King Erebus looked down upon his son, his brows furrowed and his lips curled up in a sneer. He grabbed his arm and pulled him out behind his wife, shoving him forward. "Though the deal is done, you will formally propose to her today. You might as well learn to enjoy her company."

5

Cassius moved forward cautiously. "You look beautiful today," though he wasn't lying, under the eyes of many watching, his breath was tight and his words were forced. He had skipped the hello and went straight to the compliments.

Clare put a smile on her dark pink lips, "thank you."

Sage couldn't bear to watch the two of them awkwardly converse anymore and as much as she wanted to help her sister through this, it clearly wasn't her place. She turned on her heels to leave, pushing a short strand of ginger hair behind her ear.

A voice called out to her, dark and cynical, "happy birthday Sage," the voice said. Then the voice that belonged to King Erebus quieted and whispered, "she's going to become a horrible queen if she can't properly greet her guests." Though she was now out of earshot he continued, "I am glad that Clare is your youngest. I don't need a fool like Sage running around my castle grounds."

THE PROPOSAL

Clare had been standing right there when her future father in law declared her sister a fool. Helpless and furious, she felt her palms radiate heat. She had never been great with words, but her face was twisted with scorn, an anger she couldn't put into words. Cassius spoke up, "father, you can not say such negative things about Sage, especially on her birthday. Though you think it may be kind, your insult towards Sage is not a compliment to Clare." Clare's facial expression softened and she took a step towards Cassius. Her eyes then shifted to her mother.

"She's right, don't speak about my daughters unless you have something positive to say Erebus," Gracielle said bitterly. "Now you two go ahead and spend some time together. I don't want to see you both until dinner. Though we don't agree on much. Both King Erebus and I would prefer if this arranged marriage was a happy one," Gracielle said to the two teenagers.

Clare didn't need to hear her mother's words twice. She turned on her heels and headed up the stairs, not bothering to check if Cassius was behind her. With his long legs, he easily kept up with her quick strides. Once they were side by side and out of earshot of their parents, he spoke. "I'm sorry that my father was such an arse. Can we go somewhere and speak? Both you and I were only informed of this engagement a few days ago. I think it would be best if we processed the news together."

The princess stopped walking and paused on one of the stairs that was lined with an olive green, silk carpet. Still angry, nervous and confused, her hand moved to push him away, but she stopped halfway through the motion. Her hand froze, pale and delicate in the air, before she lowered it and outstretched her hand towards him. He gulped and took her hand gently in his. It took him a moment to gather himself before he intertwined her fingers around his own and led her up the stairs, and to the garden that they had played in together when they were just little kids, when his parents hadn't ruined everything.

Silence between them wasn't comfortable, so Clare began to speak. "Cassius, I do not hold you accountable for the wrongdoing of your parents," she told him as she let go of his hand, so he could push open the doors to the indoor garden on the second floor. He let out a sigh as he pushed the door open with one hand.

He made sure that she was safely inside before he let it close behind them. "I know that I am not deserving of you because of my past and because of who I am, but I promise I am not my father. I do not condone what he did when he—"

Clare cut him off, she didn't want to hear him retell that horrific story.

She moved through the humid greenery, her heels clicking against the cobblestone, the sound dying out as she found the marble bench. She sat herself down and smoothed out her dress, letting the only sound be the echo of his footsteps and the rush of the water fountain, until he sat down next to her.

When he took his seat, he left a small space between them. "It would be rude of me if I didn't let you start this conversation. Express to me your worries," he said as he placed his hands on top of his knees and gazed out into the impressive garden.

It all came pouring out before she could choose her words wisely. "I am not ready for marriage. I am still young and I am not sure who I am. I would not be a good wife to you. I would be kind, but it would be hard for me to show you unconditional love, if I am still confused about who I am. I have always dreamed of a romantic love story and sadly, this is not one. Though I think … though I know that I can learn to love you, it is not what I envisioned for my future. If I have to live at your palace away from my sister forever, I will lose myself. She knows me more than I know myself."

He opened up his mouth to reply and she quieted. "I do not want you to be a compliant wife who does not speak her mind. Clare, I want you to feel comfortable around me. If that means you don't live with me, so be it. Though I know I have a temper, I will try not to project my anger upon you. As for your love story," he thought over his words, "I will do my best to give you one. They've called me a charmer for my looks, but that is the extent of it. We must adapt for one another. I will talk to my father about our living arrangements, but your mother has a say in this too, have you expressed your concerns to her?"

Clare placed her hands on the top of her head, "I haven't. She has been so busy planning Sage's party, that I haven't had the chance to express to her my worries about marrying you. She knows I am nervous, any girl would be, but I have not talked to her." She was distracted from her thoughts when he stood up and walked towards the balcony door. "Are you leaving?" Her voice was soft, tender and almost hurt. "Though I am scared, it doesn't mean that I don't want to try."

"I am not leaving," he reassured her. His fingers brushed against the plants until he found a blush pink flower that matched the complexion of her cheeks. "I assume the both of us would rather get engaged without our parents prying eyes."

"Yes I would prefer that," she said.

He picked one of the flowers and twirled it in between his fingers. His eyes flickered to the clear doors that lead to the balcony where the suns was setting. His mum had once told him that women loved sunsets and flowers.

"Clare, would you mind joining me on the balcony?"

He swung open the doors and let the warmth overtake him. Straightening up his collar, he took one good look at the scenery. Large pine trees crowded the Earth, he could hear the river running in between them. The sun was slowly starting to lower itself down into the Earth, leaving behind hues of orange, yellow and pink light. When he squinted, he could pick out their castle to the left and the Demetrias castle to the right.

"Cassius?"

Upon hearing her voice, he turned around to face her. The light portrayed her well, the sun painting a golden sparkle across her skin. He admired her for a moment, standing there in her white dress and then placed the pink flower behind her ear and dropped to one knee. If he could do it here and they could make the first moment of their new life positive, then perhaps their future wouldn't be so bad. He fished in his pocket for the ring and pulled out a black box. Popping it open, he revealed a silver band that had vines carved on the side, topped with one bright, yet dainty diamond.

"I know that our life will present us with many challenges. It is not the life you and I have dreamed of, but it is the life that we have been given. Though you may never be queen to this kingdom, one day you will be a queen to mine. I have learned from my parents who I do and don't want to be. This might be more romantic if you had a choice, but I hope that the way in which it was done, could possibly start the love story that you dream of. It's the only thing that I can give you. So Clare Pax, marry me?"

Though there were no tears in her eyes, the nerves had left her body and instead there was a pearly white smile spread across her face. "I will marry you." She held out her hand and let him slip the ring onto her finger. She then helped him up from the floor. "Oh, there is blood on your finger," she said quietly, her eye's focusing in on his wound.

He gazed down to the small scratch, his fingers still holding onto hers. "Probably a thorn from the flower bush," he shrugged. Then her fingers began to glow.

A RED FLAME

'**Ho**w dare he?' Though she knew not to let what the king had said strike her, she was offended that he had the nerve to put her down in front of her family members. She began to run, not caring who she bumped into on her way up the three flights of stairs to her bedroom.

Prince Julius was awkwardly standing by the doors to her bedroom, gazing up at the skylights in the ceiling. Esmeralada had refused to let him in without Sage's verbal permission.

The woman was polishing the door to Sage's bedroom, when the princess stormed into the hallway. She stood from what she was doing and swung open the door to let her inside.

Julius thanked her with a bow of his head and stepped in after Sage, who murmured a grumpy thank you underneath her breath. The door slammed shut behind them.

Julius tilted his head, his eyes soft and filled with concern. "What's the matter? Did those bastards upset you?" He didn't like to use their names when he didn't have to, at least not anymore, it filled him with disgust.

"That sick wanker thought that he could mumble that I would never make a good queen, in front of my mum. I don't think he is wrong, but how dare he go around spreading such information. I will be the one to make or break that statement, I don't need his help."

Julius knew that touching her was never a good idea when she was angry, so he took a seat on the cotton white sofa in the back of her large room. "You know, Maximus did not think that he would make a great king either. None of us were expecting our mum and our father to die, but you can't prevent death, that's why they call it a tragedy. As the eldest twin, Maximus took the throne, he was so scared, both of us were. How were we going to run a kingdom? But look at him now. Maybe you don't agree, but I think he's done a fantastic job this past year. You know, I trust red heads," he teased. "I believe that the two red flames of Pax et Lux will do a great job leading this kingdom."

"You're wrong. One will and her name is Clare."
"Oh don't be so hard on yourself," he said.

Sage let her guard down, her shoulders slumped and her face
untwisted. She crossed the room and sat herself down next to him.
"I don't want to think about being queen anyways. I would like to
think that my mother has many more years on her throne," she
changed positions and rested her arms against her chest.
"I hope she does too," Julius said as he cleared his throat. Sage's
rule would mean Gracielle's death or her stepping down. She was not
old enough to pass of natural causes, she was too kind to be
assassinated and in Sage's mind, she was too good to abandon her
position. Sensing a heaviness in the room, the subject quickly
changed.
"Well, your sister has been thrown into the world of an arranged
engagement just like we have. Have you told her that miracles can
happen?" He gestured between them and Sage jabbed him in the
shoulder with her elbow, a smile spreading across her lips.
"No idiot. Our story is not hers. The two of us have been eyeing
one another for years. You just so happen to be awkward and
charming at the same time. You are great at leaving me alone when I
need my space and you respect that I tend to be the dominant one in
the relationship. You know we would have ended up together without
my mother proposing the engagement and Maximus only agreed to
her proposition because you told him it was okay. He would fight
demons and Goddesses to ensure that you are happy."
"You are right. He would have never agreed if I wasn't happy with
you, but I am. I just don't think it's right that your sister is going to
have to marry into that wicked family. Clare has always been so nice,
they are going to ruin her Sage."
"She's strong, she will hold her own."
"They are so manipulative."
"She is strong and she won't be manipulated, Julius. Why don't we
just wish her the best and move on. Tonight's going to weigh heavily
on her. Tonight everything changes."
"Do you think your mother will wed us all on the same day?"
Julius asked.
Sage snorted, "No. We will be the first, don't worry your little
heart."
"Will we? Because if Clare doesn't marry Cassius soon, the Antias
family might start a war."

"She's only eighteen and doesn't even know him, if mother marries her, I might have to kill her." Sage said hotly.

"Well let's hope that doesn't happen. Did you want me to propose to you since we are engaged now?"

"Absolutely not."

"Well alright then, just wear the band that matches mine."

The door swung open to reveal Italus. Sage must have missed him when he stepped out of the carriage. A little boy, once an orphan, taken in by the Demetrias's out of compassion when he openly declared love for Maximus during his coronation. He was fairly short and frail for his age, but had put on weight after staying in the castle for a year. He was only eight years old, but sweeter than any kid that she had ever met.

"Did I miss him step out of the carriage and how did he open that heavy door? Did you not teach this young man how to knock?" Sage questioned.

Julius laughed as he glanced at the boy who was running into the room. Esmeralda stared sheepishly at Sage, peeking her head around the door. "I suppose he came in a separate carriage with some of the staff. He came to tell you—"

"I came to tell you that dinner is being served, Princess Sage!" He was bouncing up and down on his heels as he extended a hand to her. She took his tiny hand in hers and stood up. Julius took his other hand. "I appreciate that bud, but next time let's knock."

As they made their way out of the room, Sage slowed their pace to engage Esmeralda. "You should come have dinner with us. Some of the other staff from Maximus's kingdom have come to enjoy the meal, you should introduce yourself."

The maid seemed hesitant. Sage, who still had a free hand, dragged her along with them, but they both knew upon reaching the stairs that they could not make their arrival like this. She let go of Esmeralda's hand and let the woman trail behind the three of them. They took the stairs slowly, careful not to let Italus trip on their way down. The staircase led them straight to the grand hall which was home to two large marble tables, stretching just under fifty feet. Chairs that were white and olive green in color lined each side of the tables. In front of each chair, on the table, was a plate, a napkin and a set of silverware. In the middle of the two long tables was an array of food. Duck, mash, vegetables, berries and tarts for dessert, all fresh from the kitchens.

The room quieted when Sage entered. Her eyes met those of her frightened sister's. She'd have to ask her what had happened later. She then caught her mother's glance, she was gazing at her from the head of the first table. Next to her mum there were two open seats, one for Sage and one for Julius. Italus was next to Maximus a few seats down. Over a hundred guests were standing up around the tables, admiring her dress and her beauty. It was so quiet that Sage thought that they could hear her swallow.

Her mother broke the silence and spoke, "tonight we celebrate my daughter Sage's birthday. Everyone raise a glass."

As Sage walked down the aisle adorned with an emerald silk carpet, her eyes kept flickering to the glasses frozen in the air. When she finally reached the seat to the right of her mother, the glasses clinked and with a wave of her mother's hand, everyone sat down. "Let the feast begin!"

Celebratory murmurs and cheers filled the air as guests began to talk and fill their plates with all of the food that they desired.

Sage did not have to speak, Julius acted. He grabbed Sage's plate and filled it with a large sized helping of all of her favorite foods. He poured apple cider instead of champagne in her glass and then set the cloth napkin on her lap.

"Such a sweetheart," Gracielle commented as she watched Julius pour red wine in his own glass. It wasn't that Sage couldn't drink, she just didn't like the taste. Julius gave the queen a crooked smile, unsure of how to react and then filled his own plate. Sage had a feeling this dinner was going to get interesting, so she figured she would start the fun now. Cutting into the slice of duck on her plate, she plopped a piece into her mouth. After she finished chewing, she looked to her sister.

"So there is a ring on your finger, care to tell the world why?" The front of the table that had been filled with royals gazed her way. "Oh, Cassius proposed. We are engaged," her voice was light and shy. While Cassius looked proud, puffing out his chest and locking eyes with his father, Clare looked timid. "He's quite the romantic," she lied.

Sage caught Julius's questioning eyes and kicked him underneath the table so he would not comment on the matter.

King Maximus who had not received the kick underneath the table and was poor in the skill of keeping his mouth shut, began to speak. "Well I am sure he is romantic. His mother and father romantically killed my family."

Gracielle's eyes widened, her mouth open in horror. Of course they all knew what had happened, but nobody had ever been vocal about it before. Before the Antias family could comment, she interrupted. "Enough. I am sure Clare is right. I am glad it was romantic for you darling."

Sage laughed as she swallowed down a piece of her duck.

"What's so funny?" King Erebus questioned.

"Nothing. Worry about yourself old man," Sage spat.

If it wasn't Sage's birthday, Gracielle would have exploded on the girl. Instead, she gave her a piercing look and quickly changed the subject. For the rest of the evening they talked about the life of their two kingdoms and about how Sage and Julius were also newly engaged. Once the dessert was cleaned off of their plates, Sage watched as Cassius hurriedly pulled Clare off to the side. Her brows furrowed as she watched the two hurriedly disappear. Sage hated ballroom dancing, yet she would participate in just one dance since it was her special day, but Clare loved to dance, 'so why was she leaving?'

Sage was about to go follow after them because she was concerned for her sister's safety. Though Cassius appeared to be a good man, he was an Antias at heart and at dinner her sister seemed rather uncomfortable with him. 'If she claimed his proposal was so romantic then what happened?' Just as she started down the hallway, Julius grabbed her hand and gently tugged to get her attention. Her emerald eyes flickered to his soft blue ones.

"I know you don't like to dance and you know that I miss a few steps every single time, but we must participate, everyone's watching us, everyone's watching you."

He was right. Though she could travel by horse to meet up with him any day, they hardly danced unless they were obligated to and though they knew their love was real, some at this party thought it was just for the politics, so she had to prove them wrong.. She placed her hands in his and positioned the two of them to dance. With one arm around her waist and one around her shoulder, he nodded at her and like always, she took the lead. Whirling them around the ballroom, she was softly counting the steps to him, catching him when he stumbled. She had always remembered him to be clumsy, but recently it had become worse than ever. Clare had suggested it was because he was overwhelmed with helping Maximus succeed in his new position. Sage, just thought it was Julius being Julius.

As they danced, Sage caught the eye of King Maximus, swirling around the ballroom with another gentleman. It was no surprise to anyone that he was only romantically involved with men, but what interested Sage was who he was dancing with. Every time she saw him, he was flirting with someone new. He hadn't found anyone who could satisfy him and Sage thought that he never would. But she was wrong, he had a man in the shadows. He was already nineteen and in his kingdom, citizens got married as young as seventeen.

Julius told her not to fret, "Maximus just prefers to be single, you know, he goes around," Julius said, leaving out a few details. As he broke his concentration, he stepped on her foot and whimpered a sorry. Sage playfully rolled her eyes, at this point she couldn't truly be mad at him for his clumsiness.

When the musicians switched their song, Sage pretended to keep dancing as she twirled Julius out of the room. "Are you sure that was enough to satisfy the guests?"

Though Julius's eyes were worried, hers were clear. "You know that I don't really care. If the guests are satisfied. The only reason that I dance is for you. I don't care what others think, but I know that you do. We can compromise. Dancing is boring and I have more sweets to eat, come on."

As she made her way down the hallway, she heard shouting from one of the doors. It was Clare. She broke her stride and darted off to the side.

MAGIC FIGHT

Dinner was a nightmare and Clare couldn't wait for it to be over. Her hands were fidgeting and she was bouncing her knee up and down underneath the table. Cassius had seen the green glow from her hand and after that, his small cut had been magically healed. She had quickly run out of the room after the incident and he had chased after her, but it had been time for dinner and he stopped his chase in order to avoid drawing attention to himself. Throughout the beginning of dinner she had to hear her sister picking and digging, trying to get someone to snap and of course Sage had succeeded. Maximus with his short temper, had brought up the topic that no one dared to discuss publicly. He spoke of the night of his parents murder. Dinner was awkward from there. Clare had become quiet and Cassius also hardly spoke as he was too ashamed of his father's past to say something remotely positive.

Clare continued to scoop painful bites of food into her mouth, swallowing in bitterness. As soon as the dessert was cleared off of the table, she rose from her chair and began quickly walking out of the grand hallway. Once she was out of sight, she put two fingers on the creases of her dress, lifted up the ends and sprinted. She could hear Cassius's voice down the hallway, pleading and begging her to stop. Panting and almost tripping on her heels, Clare pulled open the door of the storage room and slammed the door shut. She was looking for the key to lock herself inside when someone from the outside began to pull and twist on the doorknob that she was holding onto.

"Just let me in. This won't end well if you don't talk to me Clare. I don't want to have to use my strength or my parents against you, but if you don't tell me what it was that I just saw, I'm going to have to report you to someone," Cassius shouted.

Her eyes were clouding with tears and though she didn't want to face him, she couldn't risk anyone in the hallway hearing his words.

She let go of the doorknob and he swung the black wood door open and slithered his way inside. The heavy door closed behind him and once they were alone, he looked at her with wide eyes. "What was that? We can't ignore what just happened. There are only a few people in all of Europe, only a few thousand people in the entire world who can use magic and we both know damn well there are only two kinds. Don't think about lying to me. What the bloody hell is going on?"

Whoever Cassius had presented himself as earlier was gone. While he may have been scared of her, she was equally as scared of him. The tears in her eyes began to bubble to the surface and fall down her face in streams. "Please, please you have to promise not to tell anyone."

He didn't respond.

"I haven't told anyone," she exclaimed. "Not even my sister." She took a moment to collect herself and started to quiet her sobs when she became aware that someone might hear her. "I realized only a year ago that I had magic. I don't know how I got it because no one in our family is magical, at least not that I know of. I'm not a master at it. I have only performed small acts, but I'm sure that I could do more if the opportunity presented itself. But I healed you, I have to be good, I have to have good magic," she murmured, trying to convince herself.

Cassius's mouth was open wide. "I won't tell anyone, only if you can promise me that you are not a danger to anyone else or society. I can't have you going around and letting this slip to just anyone and I can't have you accidentally hurt someone."

"Hurt someone?" Her voice was loud and filled with anger. "All the pain your family has caused and you are worrying about ME hurting someone." She hardly raised her voice, but she was furious. "AND you think that I have the ability to hurt someone and feel no remorse? I don't belong to Excidium, I belong to Pax et Lux and I am not EVIL. I am also no fool. I don't need a man to tell me to be careful. Watch your words Cassius or you're going to lose the trust of your fiancé and you've hardly established it."

He opened his mouth to speak, but she beat him to it. "No. Don't talk. You have said absolutely enough. How am I supposed to trust you if you're threatening me? You think I feel safe around you?

Your parents are murderers Cassius, let's not forget that. I don't know what you're capable of and I am not going to say anything else about my situation because I'm not sure what you're going to say or who you're going to tell. Your ignorance could have me killed. You've made a horrible first impression."

She turned to leave and when he tried to block her, she knocked herself into him and he tumbled backwards. She opened the door and ran directly into Sage.

Clare wasn't sure what bits of the conversation her sister had heard and though she trusted her sister with her life, she was horrified. She had wanted to tell Sage about her magic herself, this was not how she wanted her to find out. Maybe Sage hadn't even heard that she had magic, but whatever it was that she heard, it hadn't been good because her face was twisted with an undeniable rage. "I'm going to beat him."

Clare's eyes went wide. Though she had given him a good yell, she didn't physically hurt him and she didn't plan on physically hurting him either. Julius went to grab Sage and tell Cassius to move, but it was too late.

"Sage no. Sage NO!" Clare shouted. Her sister had already moved forward and overpowered the boy. She pulled him out of the room and threw him to the ground. Her fist met his face. The sound of her fist meeting his face echoed throughout the hall. He put his hands out to stop her, but she struck him in his eye and then his other eye. Both of his eyes were bruised and his nose bloodied when Julius and Clare grabbed her shoulders and pulled her backwards. "ENOUGH!" Julius shouted, the image of violence tormenting him.

Sage snapped herself back to reality as she looked down at the once gorgeous and stoic face that she had temporarily destroyed. Cassius was staring up at Clare, silently begging her to do what she had done with his cut, but she just stepped back. Not here not now. For a moment, Clare thought nobody had heard, but their shouts and his cries of agony had the security guards running towards them. "Princess Sage, Princess Clare. What has happened in this royal mess?"

"I punched his face. I punched it multiple times," Sage admitted.

"She punched his face many times," Julius added.

Cassius was rather quiet until the guards looked to him for conformation. He was holding his cheek like a small child, there were tears held back in his eyes and his teeth were gritted together bitterly. His eyes hardened when he glanced at Sage, the skin on her right wrist was sprinkled in his blood. "She fucking punched me thats for sure."

If there wasn't a grand party going on in the ballroom, the guards would have notified their parents immediately. "I don't want to disturb the fun of the night and I don't want to get anyone in trouble on such a special evening. You four can work this out yourselves in the hospital." The guard's finger twitched as he beckoned Cassius to get up off of the floor and follow him.   Reluctantly, Clare shouldered her way past Sage and extended her delicate hand out to Cassius. The two of them were in for a wild ride. One night together and chaos already followed them, she couldn't bear to think about what would happen when they got married to one another. Using what strength she had, she helped pull him up off of the floor. He was at least seven inches taller than she was, so she had to pull him down to her height in order to support his weight. At such an awkward angle it would take them at least fifteen minutes to cross the castle grounds and make it into the small building at the back of the palace.

Julius through gritted teeth, offered to help. "I too have been in a time of need, just let me take him Clare. Follow behind us."

Clare switched places with Julius and instead walked by her sister's side. The two of them trailed a few feet behind the boys.

When they had distanced themselves out of ear shot, Clare's eyes were narrowed and sharp. "What were you thinking Sage? What got into your mind? What are you planning on telling his parents?"
Sage looked to her little sister, her eyes crowded with confusion. "I heard you yell at him Clare and you never raise your voice. Not at me, not at the guards, not at Phoebe, not at anyone, even when they have hurt you, even when they have broken you. What would he have had to do to warrant your screams?"

"I can't tell you that," she whispered.

"Can't tell me? There isn't a thing that you can't tell me."

There was a look in Clare's eyes that suggested that her sister was wrong, but she didn't want to hurt her feelings. After all, she had just punched Cassius for her and although she thought the situation could have been handled differently, at least he would think twice about acting like his father again. "Well I can't tell you now, but maybe later."

"I'm holding you to it. There isn't a thing that Cassius can know and I can't, I won't let him hold it over your head."

As they passed the ballroom, the four of them picked up their pace and quieted so the guests wouldn't glance their way. The noise of the violin and cello were so loud that Clare was sure no one even bothered to glance out the entry doors. But just incase, Julius was on Cassius's right side and was the first one that they would see, but unfortunately he was four inches shorter than Cassius and wasn't tall enough to completely block out Cassius who was holding up a shirt to his nose so that he didn't drip blood all over the white floors. "Why do you people not have your prisons in your palace?" He hissed as they continued to walk through the palace and approach the exit.

"We don't want the people who live here to have to hear their screams or cries," Clare snapped.

"So you'd prefer to pretend that hey don't exist?"

"Both of you please shut up," Sage hissed. "Does it really matter? A prisoner's a prisoner. Be grateful that I'm taking you to the hospital. If it were up to me, I would call your carriage and you would arrive at one in about four hours."

At her words, they both quieted. Clare's mind was racing at the fact that she could heal him right now if she wanted to, she did want to in order to save her sisters reputation, but she couldn't. Upon reaching the exit, the guard who had been ten feet ahead of them, notified the other guards that they were on their way to the hospital and that all of them would be back shortly as his injuries were minor. With a look of disapproval in his eyes, the guard by the door, pushed the door open and let them out.

It was chilly in the night with a slight breeze. On top of the large hill the stars seemed so close and so bright that they illuminated the winding path that was curved by dirt and lined by trees. In another five minutes, they reached the hospital that resembled a large cottage.

Clare knocked on the door and it was quickly opened by the head doctor. When she saw the princesses faces, her own face twisted into worry, but relief washed over her when she noticed that they were not hurt.

The nurse was a stern woman with gray in her hair, lines on her face, but warmness in her heart. She had been the woman in charge ever since Sage and Clare were little girls. She had mended injuries as small as scraped knees and as large as broken arms. Whenever she opened her door and had to see their faces, she was always in distress. She had prayed over these girls and had played with them in her free time. To see them hurt was horrifying. But now, she saw Sage often and the girl was usually hauling someone else inside.. "What happened?" The doctor questioned as she beckoned them in.

The hospital was an oversized cottage with three large rooms that housed palace patients, a room for surgery, the living room and a break room that was the kitchen.

"I punched him," Sage admitted as she watched Julius pass Cassius onto Mary.

Mary sighed and took the prince in her grip. She led him to a room dedicated to patients with less severe injuries. There were two people occupying the beds and two more beds open. This specific hospital was only meant for palace inhabitants or visitors so it wasn't often packed. She sat the prince down and had him uncover his nose. "Quite the damage, what exactly did he do to deserve this?"

Clare and Cassius both said nothing at the same time while Sage had said, "everything."

Mary stared at the group with concern before shooing Julius and Sage out of the room. "Surely his fiancé can stay," she grinned at Clare and the girl returned an uneasy smile before kneeling at his side. Of course Mary had already known.

"Surely this room isn't where you house the sick right?" Cassius questioned, trying to hide his disgust as someone coughed. "No, this is where we place people like you who are healing from physical wounds. You are in no place to judge our medical facilities, I believe you are not family yet. I would suggest you learn your place before making another comment." The woman pulled out a kit from underneath the bed. "I can prescribe you with some ointments and some pain killers for the swelling, but I can't do much for the bruised nature of your face other than suggest makeup," she laughed a bit, but Cassius did not join in. "As for your nose, I will take a look to assess the damage."

Clare locked eyes with Cassius, wincing as she watched him hiss out in pain when Mary spread the ointment across his eyes and placed drops inside of them. Her hands twitched, eager to heal him. She didn't want his parents to know that her sister had done this. Sage could lie all she wanted, but they would figure it out.

"How long will he be here for? I was planning on spending some more quality time with my fiancé before he has to go home."

"I am sure the royal families will not leave until the morning your highness, you know this is tradition. He will be here for about an hour but then you two are free to spend the night as you wish."

Cassius's lip quivered, "you want to spend more time with me?"

"Yes," she half lied.

The woman took a look at his nose, wiping up the blood. "It seems to have stopped bleeding. The blood is drying. She didn't punch you hard enough to break it. Congratulations prince, your nose will keep its original handsome shape." She fished inside of the kit and took out a small vial of green leaves. "These are for you. You can take one every five hours. One leaf will numb the pain for a few hours. Go ahead and take one now. I assume your stomach is full."

"It is." He plopped a leaf in his mouth and watched as the woman turned around.

"I have other patients to attend to, one of my three nurses will attend to you in about thirty minutes to an hour. Once we know your condition will not worsen, you will be free to go Prince Cassius." She closed up her kit, gave him a bag of ice, placed a kiss on Clare's head and then made her way out of the room.

The door shut with a small thud and the two of them were left to stare at one another. Clare didn't want to speak first, but it seemed that the prince was a stubborn man. "I know you probably meant well, but you can not threaten me. I shouldn't have to prove that I will be careful with my magic, but I will."

"I shouldn't have threatened you, but your sister shouldn't have punched me, at least not more than once."

"I know, but I am not my sister. You can take your issues up with her. Will you be running to your parents when you're free or will you join me in my bedroom without a word?" There was a moment of silence before he answered her. "I will join you, though I can't promise it will be without a word."

The hour passed by slowly. Clare didn't speak to him much. Thankfully Julius and Sage were allowed back in the room, so the three of them could converse together. Cassius occasionally chimed in to say something. At the end of their conversation, Sage half heartedly apologized and claimed that she didn't regret what she did, but didn't plan on doing it in the future if he behaved. Julius hardly thought it was an apology, but since he also wasn't a fan of Cassius, he didn't argue.

Soon the doctor was back in the room. She took the ice bag back that she had leant him and set it aside for further use. When he got up, she changed the sheets. "You are all set Prince Cassius. If you have any further issues you should go see your castle doctor. Let him or her know that I have already prescribed you a pain reliever to take, eye drops and an ointment for your eyes. Now would you like a sweet or a toy?" She teased, as she guided the four back to the front of the large cottage.

He shook his head, an unnoticeable blush spreading rapidly across his cheeks. "It's okay, I'll just sign the documents." He tried to ignore Sage's laughs as he fumbled for a quill. His hand grasped the feather, his fingers twitching as he scribbled his name messily inside of the patient data log. In order to avoid suspicion, he gently grasped Clare's hand and the two of them split from Sage and Julius. They would both have their own "romantic evenings."

WORDS OF AFFIRMATION

When Esmeralda saw Sage and Julius enter the princesses room together, she exited. "I will be in the maid's quarters if you need me princess." She never used formalities around Sage when they were alone, but when others were present, she did her best to remember her assigned place in the world.

Julius was quick to lock the door, he was too awkward to participate in any sexual activities, but he was keen on privacy. If he was going to snuggle with his love then he would prefer to do it in private.

"Can you promise me that you will not punch Cassius again unless he really deserves it? I don't know what happened with your sister, but I do hope you find out when I leave tomorrow. I'm not sure he deserved four punches though. That was how many punches there were right?"

"I don't think that your family deserved to die either. That deserves a few more punches. I don't really regret it,"she admitted.

"Come on Sage, you know that he wasn't a part of that scheme. When my parents died he was seventeen, the same age as your sister. He couldn't have stopped his ignorant father even if he tried. Do you see the way he cowers in his father's shadow? It reminds me of how Augustus used to treat us. Do you know what he did to Maximus when he realized he had feelings for a boy? He beat him Sage. Even though no one really cares who you like these days, our father was one of the rare people who cared. I'm sure Cassius has gone through a similar experience because like Augustus, Erebus is ruthless."

Suddenly Sage went quiet and her smirk turned into a frown. "I'm sorry. I didn't know your father could be so cruel. He was always cordial with my sister and I, so I assumed he was kind when I shouldn't have. But you never really told me this, you just told me that you two never got along well. Is that why you and Augustus were never as close as you and your mother?"

"This isn't really where I was expecting the night to go, but I am going to spend the rest of my life with you so I guess I should open up a little more. Yes. My father never really liked either of us. He was constantly over training us in hopes that we would grow up to be like him. Though Maximus was extremely strong and I could hold a battle myself, we were not the war lords he wished us to be. Maximus gets his temper from my father. While Maximus shatters things and screams, my father would hit."

"I'm so sorry. I didn't know."

"It's alright, like you said, I didn't tell you. You've never really spoken a lot about your father either."

"Well, he was only around until Clare and I were six and eight years old, so I don't have many stories to tell, but all of the memories that I have of him are well. I tell my mum that she can remarry, that papa wouldn't mind, but she refuses. I suppose that she doesn't need anyone anyways."

"No she doesn't and neither do you or Clare."

"You're right we don't, so you're lucky I like you," she teased.

Julius sighed, a soft smile returning to his lips. His eyes darted towards the royal blue suitcase in the back of her room. "They must have already brought my things in. Saves me a trip back out into the cold, plus I could do without any more prying eyes tonight. Yours are already enough," he teased. He stumbled over his own foot when he stood up from the sofa and then regathered himself. "I brought a book to read while you bathe. I'm patient."

"I was thinking that we could bathe together," Sage suggested, her voice soft.

Julius tensed up, his mouth hung open, "are you sure, you don't want me to just read my book?"

"You can read your book if you'd like, but I thought it might be time for us to finally move forward just a bit. Julius we've been together for a long time."

"It's not that I don't want to Sage, it's just that there are things I'm insecure about and—"

she came behind his shoulders and kissed his cheek. "It's fine. I am going to draw the bath and if you'd like to join me in the large tub that has room for almost five people, then I will be waiting for you."

Julius watched her disappear, his eyes wide. He placed a hand on his chest and drew in a deep breath before racing to his suitcase. He dished out his sleep wear and hesitantly made his way after Sage. The smell of bath water slightly eased his nerves. "Do you put herbs in your water?" he questioned as he peered into the stone room. He placed most of his night clothes on the counter, but left his robe on the floor by the tub.

"I typically don't, but Esmeralda says that I should. Why do you know a way?" Sage responded.

"Do I know a way? Of course I do." He walked over to the shelves that hung over her vanity and grabbed a few jars off of the shelf. "The perfect relaxing bath includes lavender, rose petals and a splash of milk."

"A splash of milk do we even have any milk in my room?"

He pulled open a cabinet to reveal a few equally portioned jars of milk. "Esmeralda is smart just like Antoine, the two of them should meet. He is here tonight."

"Antoine is the one who serves you is that right?" Sage asked as she dipped her hand into the water to make sure that the temperature was alright.

"He is. He came with us."

Once the tub was filled, Julius poured one of the glasses of milk into the tub. He then sprinkled in the lavender salts and a handful of rose petals. He placed all of the ingredients back on the counter and took a deep breath. He could feel the steam coming from the bath, she must have liked to bathe warm and that didn't surprise him. "Should I turn away?"

"No," Sage said as she gestured to her large dress. "I'm going to need your help with this thing. Esmeralda normally helps me get out of these dresses. Julius nodded. His hands went towards the zipper on the back of her dress and he carefully lowered it. He helped her slip the sleeves off of her shoulders. She slipped off her shoes and lowered the dress to reveal a hoop skirt, a petticoat, a corset and her thigh highs.

"They really don't let you girls breathe. Is Clare's dress this complicated?" he asked as he helped her step out of the dress.

Sage laughed, "no, her dress today doesn't require any layers. We both prefer shorter dresses. Well I prefer pants and a cotton t shirt, but during special occasions, I have to wear the hoop skirt and if it was her birthday, she would have to as well."

"I see," Julius responded, his voice intrigued. She guided him through how to remove the hoop skirt and then he untied her corset.

She doubled over in relief. "Finally," she breathed out. "I have it from here." What was left was a tank top, her pantyhose and her undergarments. She quickly stripped. He noticed a few fresh scratches on her shoulder and before he could ask, she informed him that they were from her training. It was good that she had spoken because he had found her body just as gorgeous as her heart and her mind, that he was left speechless. She stood facing him, her hands clutching his. "Let me help you." She helped undo his bow tie and set it on the gray quartz counter, when she was done she slid the suit jacket off of his shoulders. "Sage, you are the most beautiful woman I've ever seen, not that I have ever seen another woman naked." He hadn't.

A blush spread across her cheeks, "thank you Julius." As she fiddled with the buttons on his shirt, he stopped her.

"I have to warn you about something."

She shook her head, "I'm sure that you're handsome."

He couldn't find the words to warn her, so he let her unbutton his shirt until it fell to the floor and she stood speechless. Across his stomach was a large scar, a deep cut from a sword. A wound that could have been fatal.

"Julius," her cold fingers pressed against his stomach and he felt tears fill his eyes. He was a horrible liar.

"I almost died the night I lost my parents." There was a tight strain in his voice. "Maximus would have lost me too."

She pulled him down in a hug and it wouldn't have been so awkward if her naked body wasn't pushed up against his chest.

He gulped and pulled away. "Would you mind just," she could tell that he was freezing up, so she sunk herself into the hot bath water, her eyes were still on him as he finished undressing, his clothes now on the floor. As he walked towards the bath and settled himself inside, she reached a hand out to him.

"How come you didn't tell me? You must be scarred," she said.

"I don't remember most of that day actually," he started to say something else but then stopped.

Sensing how uncomfortable he was, Sage changed the subject. "Well you are the most handsome man I have ever laid my eyes on. I have to admit that I've seen a few men naked, but don't worry, nothing came of it and no man compares to you. You are perfect to me."

He seemed to ignore the last bit, his heart pounding in his chest.

"You think so?" He couldn't really understand why. Unlike most princes, he didn't have abs or toned muscles. Though he was in good shape, he had a pouch on his stomach and a massive scar across the area.

"I know so."

"Sage you are going to kill me with your kindness someday."

"Kindness? That's a special thing reserved for you and my sister," she said with a raise of her eyebrows. "Julius?" She questioned.

"Yes?"

"I'm really glad that I get to spend the rest of my life with you and not some stuck up dick."

"Sage, I am really glad I get to spend the rest of my life with you too. You are the kind of woman that any sensible chap dreams of marrying."

THE SERVANT

She didn't want to have a romantic evening with Cassius, what she wanted to do was save Sage's reputation. "You can head up to my quarters and I will meet you there," she told him, not bothering to look into his eyes. "I have something to do," that wasn't necessarily true, but she needed some time away from him. If she didn't distance herself from him now, then she would end up doing something that she might regret. She let him get a head start and once he was out of sight and ten minutes had passed, she followed one of the guards back into the building. "I'm going back to the ballroom for a minute," Clare told the guards once she was back inside of her home. He nodded and she slowly made her way to the grand ballroom and began to think of what she was going to tell her mother or his parents if they asked where Cassius was. When they had the chance to be together they were now expected to be joined at the hip.

Clare took a deep breath and headed inside of the ballroom. A good majority of the guests were still dancing and she figured that they would do this until the sun came up. A few guests sat in the chairs scattered around the room. Knowing there would be refreshments somewhere, Clare made her way to the back of the room. She wasn't really concentrating, her mind still spinning, until someone smacked straight into her and she hit her head against their chest. The boy was a year older than her, but did not look it. He quickly stepped away from her and his mouth dropped open in horror when he saw who he had just bumped into. "
Princess Clare," he quickly bowed before standing up straight to face her. "I am so sorry, I didn't mean to bump into you."
She recognized him as Antoine, Julius's servant. She had spent enough days with the Demetrias's to know their most trusted staff. He was a handsome fellow, tall and skinny, a bit clumsy with awkward young features and messy, wavy blonde hair that was almost white in

color, only the tiniest hint of yellow present. He wore small silver framed spectacles over his amber eyes.

"May I get you anything princess? Where is your fiancé?"

"He is using the loo. The food made him quite queasy I'm afraid. Would you care to share a drink with me?"

"With you?"

"Yes with me."

Antoine opened his mouth either to agree or object, but he didn't get the chance to respond before Garcielle inserted herself into the situation.

"Antoine is a lovely man, but so is Cassius, so I suggest you get back to him before anyone else notices alright?" the queen said. Clare frowned, "alright."

Her mother was quick to depart, her long dress dragging behind her. Antoine disappeared for a moment and as Clare was about to walk away, he tapped her on the shoulder and placed a glass of champagne in her hands.

"For your troubles," he explained, bowing his head.

"For my troubles," she echoed quietly. She gave him a kind smile and then made her way out of the ballroom and up the stairs where Cassius would be expecting her.

She took her time up the stairs. Phoebe must have already left because Cassius was standing at the doors alone and the room was vacant. "You took quite a bit of time."

"I needed time away from you." She pushed her way past him and went into her room, where she slipped off her white heels. She then went straight to the white canopy bed which was decorated with blush pink pillows and sat down while she waited for him to walk inside of the silent room. "I would just have you go home. I don't want to spend the night with you. But I'm sure your parents would be disappointed in that decision and we need to talk about your situation."

She pointed to his bruised face. He waited for her okay and then sat next to her on the bed.

"I'm sure you don't want to have to explain to your parents that you got your arse kicked by the person that they seem to hate so much. I can fix that. I believe I can make your wounds go away, but you must promise to never threaten me again and to never to speak of my magic to anyone else. It stays with you until the information is made public, or until you die. Do you understand?"

Cassius thought his decision over before speaking. "I understand. Will you tell Sage?"

"Eventually she will know, but I'm planning for it to only be the two of you. I'm going to start my own journey, so I can figure out how I have this magic."

"Was your father magical?"

Clare winced, taken back by the comment about her father, "not that we knew of. My mother knew him far longer than us and she never mentioned anything. He never showed any signs. He was just a military general, if he had magic I'm sure he would have taken a different path."

Changing the subject, Clare gestured for him to remove his shoes and lay down. He did as he was told and she crouched over him. "I'm going to place my hands on your face now."

She placed her fingers around his eye. She didn't have to think or murmur a spell, her fingers instinctively began to twitch. A green magic began to flow out from the tips of her fingers and onto his face. The magic seeped into his skin. Her hands trembled as the magic grew stronger. She felt him groan beneath her as his skin became less inflamed.

After about a minute of green essence, the left side of his face was brand new. She was powerful. She didn't waver or collapse, she went to his next eye and started the process over again. Slowly but surely his face went back to normal

. Finally, she pressed a finger against his nose and the last of the bruises faded away, his nose straightened to its normal position.

Clare took her hands away from his face and the green glow came to a stop. She took a deep breath and told him that he could sit up. "

Did it work?" He questioned, touching his face with his own fingers to try and feel the bumps and bruises. She reached over to her nightstand and grabbed the flowery compact mirror. She held it open for him and he gasped. His face looked good as new. "How did you learn this?"

"I'm not sure," she said honestly. "It just happened one day. I don't even know how I do it. I probably should figure that out, but I don't know where to begin. It's honestly a little frightening." She wasn't going to let him see her crack again, so she held herself together.

"I bet," he whispered. "Most witches don't have a great reputation."

"Don't call me that," she murmured.

"Right, I won't," he whispered. "I figure you don't want to share a bed tonight and I figure my parents are going to leave tonight and send a carriage for me tomorrow. Maybe they'll stay, but I know that they'll want me to spend more time with you."

Clare thought this over. "They won't leave, i'm sure at this point the alcohol has kicked in and they're just as giddy as everyone else in attendance." She gestured to the blush pink sofa across the room, "it's a pull out sofa, let me make it up for you." She wasn't purposely trying to push him away and she knew eventually that they'd have to sleep in the same bed, but it was the first night that they were engaged and there were no set rules. Plus he had already crossed a line today and she would have been a fool to reward bad behavior. Sliding off of the bed, she pulled the sofa outwards until a full size mattress popped out. She fished into her closet and took out a sheet, a spare white blanket and two pillows. Cassius helped her make the bed and when it was ready, she gave it a pat with her hand. "I've had many sleepovers here. I assure you it's comfortable. I hope you don't snore," she said somewhat jokingly. "Was your luggage brought up?"

"I'm not sure if I snore," he admitted as he scratched the back of his head. "Thank you for making up the sofa bed. My luggage was brought up." He moved over to the black suitcase in the corner of the room. "I normally just sleep in my boxers, but if that makes you uncomfortable, I won't."

"It doesn't make me uncomfortable because you'll be away from me and under the covers. Just be comfortable. I don't plan on bathing tonight. I'm too exhausted and I'll do it in the morning, but my tub is across the room and beyond those sliding doors if you'd like a bath." She could tell that he was thinking it over. A part of her wanted to draw him one anyways, but she didn't.

When he said no, she didn't push and instead went behind closed doors to change. She slipped into a white nightgown and had taken off her makeup with a cloth, her face now a bit red and puffy. She ran a hand through her curls and stood staring in the mirror. "Cassius, can you braid hair?"

"Can I?"

"Would you braid my hair please? Sage usually does it for me."

"Am I allowed to come in?"

"Yes."

Cassius slid open the sliding door and took a deep breath. She was always gorgeous, but when she was relaxed and natural, she looked like a goddess. His mother had never taught him how to braid hair, there hadn't been a need for him to do it. He didn't have any siblings and his mum always braided Cisily's hair. He moved behind Clare, gently gathering some of her hair in his fingertips. When she handed him the hair tie he froze. "I can't braid, but I can do a thing."

She laughed at his words, a genuine and bright laugh. He lifted her hair up with his hands and tied her hair into a loose ponytail, he then went around a second time and pulled the hair halfway through so it was hanging in a comfortable half bun. "This is the thing," he said as he gestured to the mirror.

Clare spun and puffed the makeshift bun with the back of her hand. "I appreciate it. Though you'll need to learn how to braid," she teased. "Thank you."

Clare folded up her clothes and set them aside, she then followed Cassius out to the main room. "What's the time?" She asked him as she closed the sliding doors behind her and tiredly slid into her bed.

He sat on top of the pull out sofa and checked the clock above them. "It appears to be midnight. Are you normally asleep by now?" He asked her. He took off his shirt and set it aside, tugging off his pants, he placed them on top of the shirt and then crawled underneath the covers so that he wouldn't disturb her.

Clare pulled her own covers over herself and nodded. "I sleep pretty early. Sage goes to bed late. We are opposites."

"I see."

"Do you go to sleep late?"

"Yes a bit, but I won't keep you up. You should turn off the light."

She reached over and turned off the lights, she thought about talking to him, but her eyes were heavy. "Goodnight Cassius."

"Goodnight Clare."

The morning came quickly. Clare was up before Cassius. She was an early riser and she assumed that he was not by how snugly he was wrapped up in the covers. While she got up at sunset and the sound of birds chirping, she imagined him rising five hours, tired and groggy. She rolled her shoulders back to stretch out her body and ran a hand through her hair to feel how messy it was. Not terrible, he had put it in a makeshift bun after all and that was better than nothing. Sliding out of bed, she let her warm feet soak up the chill of the wooden floors. Summer was soon going to turn into fall in a day. She took a peak out of her window to look at the pine trees, standing tall and still. The sunrise had painted the sky a few warm colors. 'When she saw the yellow and pink sky would she forever have to think of Cassius?'

There was bound to be a royal breakfast, but not even her mother or Sage rose this early. If Cassius was sound asleep, it was safe to say that his mother and father who had danced the night away, were also sleeping. She'd be okay to go downstairs. Of course the staff would be preparing breakfast and there was a chance that Julius was up, but she didn't mind him. She'd take the risk. She pulled her hair out of the bun and pulled a shawl over her nightgown incase of unexpected company. She didn't bother to put on shoes, the ground was cool enough and shoes were restricting. She quietly moved past Cassius. Her hand touched the door knob. She debated on waiting for him to wake up, but she decided against it. 'I don't owe him anything,' she told herself before sliding out the door and gently closing it behind her.

Just as she suspected, the halls were quiet. The sound of a few doors quietly closing echoed throughout the palace. The sound of plates and silverware clanking as they were laid out, overpowered the birds chirping. She caught the eye of Esmeralda, Sage's maid, carrying a large basket of laundry. Since she didn't wish to disturb the workers of the castle, she took the secluded staircase that led down to the kitchens. She'd be able to exit the dining room and go out to the porch from there. Normally she'd sit in the sitting room and read a book with a cup of hot cider, but she didn't want to risk one of the guests finding her. It was too early to deal with those she had to hide from. As she entered the kitchen, the chef greeted her and passed her her favorite cream mug filled with hot cider. She thanked him and asked him how last night was before walking to the porch where the two glass doors were opened for her. She was expecting to sit down in one of the many rocking chairs and think to herself, but someone had beat her to it. Antoine.

He was sitting in the farthest rocking chair to the left, a cup of coffee in his hand. He hadn't noticed her, his eyes were blankly gazing out into the distance, studying the forestry and the deer who were coming out to graze in the grass. Clare cleared her throat and watched his head turn towards her.

His eyes bulged and his coffee almost slipped out of his hands, but he caught it before it could fall and set it on the table beside him. "Princess, I didn't think anyone would be up this early in the morning."

"Me neither," she mused as she sat down a few chairs away from him. She set her drink down and smoothed out her nightgown. Unlike her, he was already dressed and ready for the day. She assumed he would be loading up the luggages and taking care of the horses. "You don't have to leave Antoine, you can stay."

"I'll have to leave soon, but just not yet," he responded, taking another large gulp of the coffee that he had almost dropped. She could smell it, the chef always made good coffee, but it was too bitter for her liking. "Did you sleep well last night?" he asked her, his eyes questioning.

"Yes and no. I didn't do anything you might have thought I did," Clare blushed.

"I didn't assume that, you don't strike me as the type," Antoine grinned.

"Did you sleep alright?" she asked him.

"Not well, but I'm away from home. It's expected."

"They taught you how to read didn't they? You speak well."

"Oh I already knew how. My mum aught me. I'm sure that you already know this Princess, but every family has a destiny and an animal to represent them. My family's destiny was to serve, the animal that represents us is a dog and our colors are brown and white. I was lucky enough to serve the royals. They educated me more when I arrived, but my mum had already prepared me."

"Where is your mother?"

"She serves a rich family in my kingdom and so does my father. I get to see them both whenever I please. Maximus is kind when he's not angry."

"I'm happy my sister marries into his family."

"Are you happy with your destiny?"

She went quiet.

Antoine became stiff. He may have regretted what he said, but this issue was not new, he often said what was on his mind when given the chance. Julius didn't mind it, but he wasn't sure how Clare would feel if a servant spoke out of line. "I'm sorry," he apologized.

"It's fine. Don't be sorry. You didn't make this decision for me," Clare whispered to him as she lifted the finally cool cider to her lips and drank.

"Well I must go feed the horses," he told her, standing up and holding his coffee to his chest. She stood up. "I'll go with you."

"You will?"

"Well sure, I don't have much else to do."

He thought this over, she had a fiancé, but what was the harm? This wasn't romantic. "Follow me then. Actually never mind, I'll follow you, you know your way around here better than I do," he laughed.

She curtsied and gave him a shy smile. She then led him out to the front of the palace, sipping her cider as she walked. The carriages were lined up to leave, but the horses were put away in the stables. The guards raised an eyebrow at her, but they were rather fond of Antoine. Despite his rank, he was a gentleman, so they let her go without supervision. Walking with him in the grassy fields, she looked down to his feet. "Take off your shoes. Feel the grass on your feet. Just for a moment."

He gazed at her as if she were mad, but then he noticed her feet were bare. "Well if the princess insists." He took his boots off along with his socks and placed them in the grass. He noticed her set her drink down, so he did the same. Then she took off in a run and he was chasing after her through the tall fields all the way to the stables where they were both out of breath. "Oh Oralee," he breathed out, doubling over.

"Wasn't it nice to feel the wind in your hair and the grass in between your toes?" she laughed as she poked him in the side so he'd stand up.

He was smiling wide. "It was. "Princess I haven't ran like that in such a long time." He told her as they entered the stables.

She brought him all the way to the end of the area where his four horses were located. "Me neither, I don't run or exercise often, but

Sage is another story. What are their names?" she asked, as he opened the stable and grabbed the brush on the wall. He started with the horse in the corner running the brush through the animal's mane. "These are the royal horses. Maximus and Julius have their own horses at home, Julius's is a gray spotted horse named Procella and Maximus's is a large chestnut horse named Brunius. But these horses here pull the royal carriage. Their names are ivory, pearl, ice and crystal," he explained as he began to brush Ivory's tail.

"They're quite pretty. I'll have to show you my horse when you're finished," she said.

"I'll look forward to it," he replied.

Clare sat down on a bale of hay and watched him brush the horses   manes and fasten the gear to their bodies. She wasn't sure how much time had passed, but she had been gleeful the entire time. He told her stories about each of the horses and explained how much he'd love to have one of his own. In return she told him her own stories about their horses and helped him guide the Deus's horses out of the stable. They each had one horse on each side, holding onto the reins as they walked them out into the grass. On their way out of the stables, Clare showed him her horse. A creamy brown horse with darker brown spots and a gray mane. "I named her Panthera when I was younger, but now I'm regretting that name," she laughed as they walked out onto the field.

"I like Panthera, it suits her. We named one of ours ice, it can't get much worse," Antoine assured.

The sun was high in the sky as they crossed the field. Clare knew she'd have a sunburn from being out without protection for just a few minutes. They stopped to let the horses graze while Antoine put on his boots. Once they picked up their drinks from the grass, they stopped at the carriages. Clare helped him attach the horses and was going to help him grab the luggages when she heard Sage's voice. Her sister had peaked her head out through the door. It must have been late if she was up and dressed. Clare gazed up at the sky and then down in horror at her nightgown.

"Mothers waiting and she's not happy. I'll cover for you, but it'll only work if you hurry," Sage hollered.

Clare gazed sadly at Antoine. In her mind she was hoping for something romantic to happen, but instead he gestured to the door.

"Go on princess, I'm sure we will meet again."

Something inside of her was sad to leave him. She pushed that feeling down, resisted the urge to hug him and held out her hand. His hand was thin, tough and bruised, but recently moisturized. "Till we meet again, Antoine," she said without looking away from his eyes. She let go of his hand after he shook it and then she ran inside and up the stairs so that way she could change into something decent.

DISCOVERY

Julius had slept on one side of the bed and Sage on the other. While Julius was a fan of cuddles, she wasn't a huge fan of physical affection, so they typically compromised. In the morning, Sage had given in and snuggled up close to him while he read her a book. She hated reading, but when he spoke the stories out loud, she did not mind it, he made every story that he read come to life. Eventually the two of them decided to get out of bed. Julius dressed himself in a pair of navy blue slacks, a white button up shirt and a navy blue coat decorated with silver swirls. Sage was dressed far more casual than she had been yesterday. She wore an olive green day dress that cut across her shoulders and stopped at her knees. If it was up to her she'd wear shorts and a knitted shirt, but she would never hear the end of it from her mother if she showed up to breakfast in front of the Demetrias's and Antias's in an outfit that casual.

Julius had placed his luggage outside for Antoine to grab. Sage followed after him and took his hand, they headed down the stairs together. "I'm surprised that Antoine isn't here yet," he murmured to Sage. When the two of them reached the hall, almost everyone was gathered. Cassius and his parents looked quite upset.   'Surely they hadn't found out that she had punched him. Well, wait how was his bruise gone?' Sage thought. She wasn't sure if she was seeing things and it was too early to confuse her mind anymore than it already was. She shifted her eyes to the empty seat, 'Clare was gone.'

"Where is your sister?" Gracielle tried to say calmly.

Julius sat down next to Maximus, leaving Sage alone in the middle of the room. They always lied for one another, so she'd have to think of something good. "She probably went out to plant seeds in the garden. She mentioned it to me last night. Let me go get her." Before her mother could object, she ran out of the hall. She heard noises in the front of the palace and swung open the entrance door. Clare was there and she was with Antoine. Sage smirked, "mum is waiting for you and she's not happy. I'll cover for you, but it'll only work if you hurry." Clare ran straight past her and up the stairs without a word.

Sage was left staring at Antoine. He had turned his face around, but she could tell he was blushing. "Safe travels!" she shouted before slamming the door. She had to wait for Clare, she couldn't let her sister walk into that room full of mad adults alone.

Normally Clare took a while to get ready, they'd spend hours waiting on her. Sage always wondered what she did in there, but this time it only took five minutes for her to come running down the stairs. She was wearing a blush pink dress that rolled down to her ankles and had puffy sleeves. Her cheeks were pink from the sun and matched her natural blush.

"You owe me a conversation later," Sage said demandingly as they walked into the dining room.

"I know," Clare whispered. She met her mother's glaring eyes. "Sorry I lost track of time. There is no clock in the gardens."

Cassius's father scoffed, "and you didn't care to invite my son?"

"Father please," Cassius pleaded.

"He was sleeping, so no. I didn't want to wake him." She sat down next to Cassius and looked over to Maximus, who was smirking. 'Did he know about her and Antoine?'

"It's fine Clare, I was sleeping well," Cassius said with a slightly bitter tone.

Sage raised her eyebrows because she wasn't buying Cassius's words, but she stayed silent and dug into her food. "Did you pray?" Her mother asked.

"Gee mum to which one? There are eight goddesses." Her mother looked upset at her daughter's lack of care, but gestured for everyone else to dig in, since they had done a group prayer while Sage and Clare were away. Clare murmured what seemed to be a prayer under her breath and then took a bite of her potatoes. "So you're going home after this right?" Sage asked as she pointed her fork at the king of Excidium. Her mother looked appalled. "What I'm just asking? I have plans."

King Maximus laughed, answering for the other family. "Well yes. Everyone's leaving today, but my kingdom is hosting a large sporting event in two weeks and I'd like you all to come. Gathering together might further our peace, keep things civil."

"We will be there," Gracielle said delighted.

Cassius's parents debated, then the king spoke. "We will come. Only so you don't think to attack us."

41

"You attacked us?" Julius said in confusion.

"Have you heard of revenge?" The king said as he rolled his eyes.

"We would've already gotten revenge if that's what we wanted," Maximus said.

"Right," Queen Adria said, hoping to end the conversation.

"You'd be stupid to start a war," Clare chimed in, her voice loud.

Sage pointed her fork in the direction of her sister, "what she said."

Breakfast dragged on and Sage had managed to sneak in a few more snide remarks. It was the Antias family who declared their departure from the castle first. King Erebus had a meeting to catch, so they needed to depart. Sage stood up from her seat and reluctantly shook hands with the king and queen. She watched as her sister also had to force herself to be kind and reluctantly hug Cassius. It was forced and quick, barely a hug, more so just their sides brushing together. However, it seemed to please the king as he gave her a soft, yet cunning smile and snapped for his son to get out of the hall and head towards the carriages. "We will discuss Clare's arrangement and living situation through letter Gracielle," he said as he kissed the woman's hands.

She gave him a pained smile, pulling away before kissing Quen Adria's cheeks. "I look forward to it."

The Demetrias's stuck around two hours after breakfast. Sage wasn't sure why, but she was happy to have Julius by her side just a tad bit longer. The two of them went out into the yard to shoot arrows while Maximus stayed behind with Gracielle. Sage assumed that they were going to talk politics. They were the leaders of their kingdoms after all and Maximus was very young. Only nineteen, he'd need all the mentoring that he could get in order to succeed. As Sage and Julius walked towards the back of the palace, she nodded at the guard and he left them alone. There was a large clearing of forest behind the hospital before the palace gate. Far out in the distance were three targets and by Sage and Julius's feet were two sets of arrows. "I brought them out here yesterday, but we didn't get the time. I'm glad I get to shoot with you before you go," Sage said as she picked up the bow. She quickly shot her first arrow and it hit near the center of the target, she then she drew another and another. As she shot the arrows, the tension in her shoulders dropped. "Julius, are you going to pick up your bow?" she asked him as she shot another arrow without care, this one hit the center of the target. Out of the corner of her eye she saw him pick up the bow and arrow.

"You know I'm not great at this, my weapon of choice is a dagger, but I guess I'll give it a go."

Sage wasn't sure why he was suddenly so self conscious, they had shot together plenty of times and though Sage was the better shot, he had never cared before. "I know that and you know my weapon of choice is a sword, this is just a hobby. I know it isn't your hobby, but you've never cared about how much you miss, why start caring now?"

"Oh I don't know, I want to impress you I guess." He steadied his arrow and drew back with the muscle that he had managed to keep after his injury. He almost missed the target, but the arrow stuck out at the very edge.

Sage snorted, not at his shot, but at his comment. "Impress me? I'm not hard to impress and you impress me everyday with your growing confidence, well except right now," she took another shot, this time at his target and landed her arrow purposely next to his. "See even the arrow knows that we are meant to be, there's no need to impress me."

Julius wasn't sure that this was true. Growing up no guy had impressed Sage, but with some luck Julius had. Ever since they were little, guys would run after her, especially before she cut her hair short. They would bring her flowers and ask her to dance, but she would always say no. Maximus and him had come up with a theory that she was a lesbian, but this was not a bad thing, as both the Demetrias's and the Goddesses were accepting of all sexualities and identities. After years of feeling like he had to compete with those who crushed on her, Sage had been impressed by him. At his fifteenth birthday party, he was sitting alone, eating a grilled turkey leg outside their castle temple. She was walking by and he invited her to join him and they shared the turkey leg. Apparently, that had been enough. Things had picked up from there and now, here they were shooting arrows. He believed that it was a coincidence that he was the one to catch her eye, not fate.

He decided to change the subject. "Sage," Julius whispered. "Is everything alright with Clare?" He was aware that someone may be near, so his voice was hushed and low. He cared deeply for Sage, but he cared deeply for Clare as well, just in a different way

. Sage sighed and put down her bow, her shoulders dropping. "I am honestly not sure, I need to talk to her today once you two depart. I'm still confused about what happened last night and how Cassius's eye is now fully healed. I tried not to make any faces at breakfast or even acknowledge what I saw because it was too early. You noticed this as well right?"

Julius pursed his lips and his voice dropped to a volume that almost could not be heard. "I did. Sage, I think your sister might have magic."

THE LIBRARY

Breakfast was a bore and Clare was glad that it was over. She had been kicked out of the dining room after the Antias's had left because her mother wanted to have a private conversation with Maximus. She was going to use this time to talk to Sage, but her sister hadn't looked her in the eye and instead walked away with Julius. She spent a few minutes bored and anxious in the sitting room wondering how she was going to calm her nerves. Then an idea struck her. She waited until the Antias carriage was out of sight and then rushed up the stairs, holding her dress and panting. When she reached the top of the stairs, she saw Antoine holding a large bag. "Clare," he muttered in surprise as she greeted him on the second floor. "Antoine, do you need help gathering anything?"

"No princess, but I appreciate the offer. The horses are tied up and this is my last bag that I need to grab. I am going to wait inside of the carriage for Prince Julius, then I will be on my way," he tried to step around her, but she blocked him.

"Please do not leave, you may put your suitcase away, but then I would like you to come to the library with me, I could use a relaxing hour or two and sitting in the carriage all by yourself must be boring. Would you join me please?"

Antoine was too shocked to speak, so he moved past her and hurried down the staircase. She wasn't sure what that meant, so she stood next to the railing and stared down at him, watching him disappear out of the doors. A young girl, three years older than Clare, came out from the hallway holding a bundle of clothes. "Phoebe!" Clare said in shock. Phoebe was her maid and a kind girl who was a good friend to her. "What did you just see?"

Phoebe had fair skin, pitch black curly hair and dark brown eyes the color of rich chocolate. "I saw you standing alone at the rail?" Her voice was questioning.

"Oh, yes! I was just looking for Sage," Clare told her. Phoebe raised an eyebrow, but she nodded. "I will see you later. I have to do the laundry."

"Okay, see you later." Everyone had left her. She waited about five minutes, she was about to turn around when she saw the blonde almost white headed figure come up the stairs. It was Antoine.

"Since the princess requested my services I will join her, but I only have an hour. It would be inappropriate if I wasn't waiting for Julius upon his arrival."

"Of course," Clare grinned, "follow me."

She brought him around the looping balcony that overlooked the lower floor and into the library. The library was a large room filled with thousands of books on wooden shelves. The ceiling was painted with art of the eight Goddesses. Carved high up on the wall and lining every inch of the room were skylights. Natural light flooded the library, but the windows were so high up, that unless someone scaled the palace there was no way to look inside of the room. Antoine was staring up at the shelves in awe. The Demetrias's had an impressive book collection, but it was nowhere near as nice as the Pax's. He pointed up to the ceiling. "Who did the art of the Continental Goddesses? My oh my look," his finger was pointing at Oralee the Goddess of Europe. She was depicted as a tall woman with blonde wavy hair that went down to her waist. Though quite stunning in her normal form, she could change her appearance at will, this was just her preferred look, she thought it suited Europe well. The Goddess was wearing an aqua dress that was sheer against her sun kissed skin and golden hoop earrings. "She looks just like I imagined her."

"I love that she is our Goddess, she is so kind," Clare smiled. "Oh and I did the art."

He gasped. "You did all of the art?"

She tried to keep a serious composure, but she laughed. "No, no I didn't do the art, I was joking. Though I wish I did. I do art and I think it's decent, but it's not this good."

"Is there any art of yours in this library?"

"There is."

Clare guided him down the long aisle that led to the back of the library where there was a sitting area to read. On the back wall was a portrait of her mother, a handsome muscular man with long brown hair and two red haired children.

"Is that your family?" Antoine asked.

She answered him. "Yes, that is Wade, my father. I used a reference portrait of him, I'm rather proud of this painting." The images were clean and painted in a realistic style.

"You did a gorgeous job. My quarters at home need some spice, maybe you could paint me something?"

"I'll keep it in mind. Do you have your own personal quarters at the castle?"

"Yes. There are servants quarters where a few servants share a large room, but Julius has grown rather fond of me, so I have my own room. I give it up if they need it, but they hardly do."

"I'm glad they're so kind to you."

"Me too," he beamed.

She hammered him with questions about his favorite kind of books and once she knew what he liked, she took him to the section about history.

"I've read up on history at our library, but it's mainly filled with stories about our kingdom. I take it you have a lot of your own history here?" Antonine questioned. His fingers ran against the spines of the books, his eyes fixated on the covers that he thought were the prettiest. "I'll admit, I like your library a bit better than ours. King Maximus doesn't really read, but Julius does. His section is neatly organized, but Maximus just kind of throws his books on the shelves in no particular order."

Clare laughed, "our books are filled with our history, we have some of yours and some from Excidium. There is a variety, but yes most of the books in this section focus on our history. I have a few that I will recommend to you. Take them home. I promise my mother won't notice, neither will Sage. I'm the only one with that kind of eye."

His face was frozen. The princess was going to give him books to take home out of the royal library. He tried to object, but she had already gotten out the step stool and climbed up to reach her favorite books. She pulled out a red leather bound book titled "*The History of Pax et Lux,*" a compact gold book titled "*Oralee*" and a solid white book titled "*Why the Elephant?*" Which explained why her kingdom's animal was an elephant and why their colors were olive green and ivory. They were the symbols of the first leader, passed down throughout generations, the book discussed each leader and their family. "I'll probably see you soon. Maximus said he was going to hold an event at his castle. If you read them, we can discuss them then." She carefully climbed down the step stool and handed him the stack of books.

He took the books from her hands and held them close to his chest. "I'll need something to put them in. This is our little secret. Though Princess, I don't think it'll be great for either of us if your mother or Maximus finds out that we are spending our free time with one another."

Her smile turned into a frown and he visibly became panicked, he had not meant to upset her. "I just am afraid they'll yell at me for not knowing my place in this world and they will yell at you because you're engaged. Even if we are just two pals who enjoy one another's company, everyone always assumes differently these days."   His voice was soft and hushed, tender and gentle.

She gave him a solemn nod. "You're right, but this is my life. I'm allowed to hang out with who I want. Cassius will have to get over it. I'm allowed to speak to other men." Her shoulders tightened. She brushed off her fury and went over to the desk area where there were a row of book bags. She handed him a simple brown one. "They don't let me control much of my life. They can allow me this much."

He nodded, put the books in the bag and hung over his shoulder. "I still have a few more minutes. Any last adventures Princess?"

There were so many thoughts going through her mind. She could have dismissed him so his arrival to the carriages would be less suspicious, but she needed to distract her mind. Having the conversation about her magic with Sage would take a toll on her, she might as well enjoy the last few moments of bliss that she had left. "Yes actually, follow me. You'll need to move quickly. I really shouldn't be taking you here but there is something that I want to show you." His amber eyes flickered with intrigue and a bit of fear. She grabbed him gently by the wrist and pulled him forward. He was following right behind her heels. The princess was touching him. They walked up to the third floor where the royal's quarters were located and his eyes widened as he noticed the other servants wandering the halls with baskets of laundry and trays of food. Clare hid them behind a corner and when the coast was clear she ran to her room. She swung open the door and sighed in relief when Phoebe wasn't there.

Antoine quickly shut the door and dropped his book bag. "This is too far, I shouldn't be here, if anyone sees."

"No one will see, I just wanted to show you my art."

Her room was like he expected it to be. Comfortable and cozy with a girly flare. The decorations of accented pink and creamy white were complimented by the natural light pouring in from the gardens outside. Everything was neat and organized. In the corner was a large white wooden chest. When she opened it, he caught the glimpse of a dozen canvases. After he was sure that no one was following them, he moved closer towards her, but stayed a respectable distance away. His eyes were fixated on the canvases. She pulled the first one out to reveal a magnificent garden scenery. The painting was filled with flowers of all different colors. A large fountain and an area for seating were painted in the middle of the canvas, he wondered if she had been there. Then she spoke. "I like to paint what I see. When I'm sitting alone, nature speaks to me. Or I'll paint Sage when she's calm or my mum when she finally relaxes." She reached into the chest and pulled out another painting. This one looked exactly like her sister, but it also looked a lot like Clare. Though their hair was different lengths and Clare had sea blue eyes and Sage had emerald eyes, their facial features were similar. In the painting, Sage was leaning down over a table, writing something in a journal. "I don't paint my fantasies very often. I'll get my hopes up. I paint what I know is real. It's reassuring."

His eyes were wide with amazement, he was speechless. She could tell that he wanted to take a closer look, so she beckoned him to join her and handed him the painting. He ran his calloused thumbs over the edges of the canvas, "They're beautiful. Who taught you to paint?"

She handed him another painting, this one was of her mother snoozing on the sofa. "My father was always painting. I'm self taught, but I took after him. I would give you one, but these mean everything to me and nothing to you. I promise I'll paint you one that will have meaning in your eyes."

"I appreciate that princess. How long does it take for you to paint something like this?" He handed the painting of her mother back to her and took the next painting in his hands. On the canvas there was an ocean and clouds, they weren't far from a beach after all. "It normally takes me a few hours. They used to take me days, but I've gotten good at it. I do the base and the larger details while I watch the people or the nature, then if it gets too tiresome, I'll finish the smaller details later in the comfort of my bed or the sofa."

Gazing out of the window she noticed that the horses were stirring and the driver had fixed himself up on top of the carriage. "Oh dear Oralee, we need to get you down there." She took the painting from his hands and set it back down on the chest. They both ran to the door, clumsy and frantic.

His glasses almost fell off of his face as he quickly grabbed the book bag and slung it over his shoulders. "Wait why are you coming with me doesn't that defeat the point?" he asked as he pushed open one of the doors and started to run down the stairs. "I'll stay behind you. I have to say goodbye to the king and the prince."

He nodded and waved goodbye to her. She was waiting for him by the railing and once he was out the door, she slowly followed, fixing her hair that had gotten messy from their running.

She met her sister at the door. Sage never looked at her in this way. There was a mistrust, a fear in her eyes. 'What had happened? What had she done?' Clare decided to clear her thoughts, they could come back once she had said goodbye to the Demetrias's. Saying goodbye to them was less formal as the Pax's were close to them. She hugged both Maximus and Julius goodbye and watched them make their way into the carriages after they said goodbye to her sister and Gracielle. Like always, Sage and Julius looked as if they wanted to kiss, but they didn't, they never did. Clare always wanted to ask her sister why, but she didn't because she was afraid that she'd offend her. While Clare was a hopeless romantic, Sage could have cared less for romance until she met Julius.

Just as she had expected, when the carriages were out of sight, her mother grabbed the two of them by their wrists and dragged them inside. Her eyebrows were raised as far up on her forehead as they could go and her mouth was twisted in anger. "Are you serious?" Gracielle said as she let go of their wrists and folded her arms tight against her chest. "You!" she pointed to Sage. "Constantly making comments that nobody finds funny and trying to stir the pot. Do you wish to start a war? You know that they will in a heartbeat. You were foolish and you won't be allowed on our next visit to the Demetrias's until you get your act together." She then turned to Clare. "And you. You had a first impression to make and instead of making a good one, you wandered off to Oralee knows where, frolicking and neglecting time until you were late. You've both made foolish decisions. I wasn't going to embarrass you in front of the other families, but know that I'm disappointed in you. Go."

Clare took off quickly and Sage followed behind her. She was going to run off to her room, but Sage grabbed her sister's arm and pulled her to her own quarters instead. She shut and locked the door, pulling her into the tightest corner that she could.

FIGHTING FLAMES

"You're not getting out of this Clare," Sage hissed as she sat down next to her sister. "Please explain to me what is going on. Why are you hanging out with a servant, not like I care about his status, but why? I'd also like to know what Cassius said to you and how his wound healed so fast. I want you to explain all of this to me. I'm your sister, we are supposed to tell each other everything. I've been telling you everything, but how much have you been hiding from me?" Her eyes were clouded with sadness, she wished her sister had trusted her enough to speak up earlier.

Clare was shaking. There had been multiple instances in her and Sage and Clare's life when things went wrong, such as when someone had broken into the palace and the time that they got lost in the woods, but Clare had never seemed as terrified as she currently was.

Sage softened up a bit, "look. I know that if you're this scared to tell me, this must deeply concern you, but you know that I won't tell a soul, not even mum. Just tell me what's going on Clare, I want to be there for you, but I can't be there for you if you don't let me in."

Clare hesitated. She opened her mouth to speak, but no words came out. She tried again, "It's hard to explain, but it's easy to demonstrate. Cut yourself please," she said quietly.

"What are you talking about Clare?"

"I can't explain my situation, I have to show you. Please just do it and trust me."

Sage raised an eyebrow in confusion, but she extended her arm without question and reached for the sharp key on her dresser. She moved the key across her forearm until the tiniest bit of blood bubbled to the surface. Clare's fingers were twitching and in a matter of seconds her hands were over Sage's arm and a bright green glow mended the cut. The process didn't take very long since the wound was so small. The green glow stopped as quickly as it started and Sage met her sister's frightened eyes.

"I don't know where I would have gotten this power from," Clare whispered.

"I don't know where you got it from either," Sage said as she stared down at her arm in disbelief. Even though Julius had tried to tell her about Clare's magic earlier, she had not believed him.

"Do you understand why I didn't tell you?" Clare asked.

"I do, but you know that I would never think of you less for possessing magic, especially healing magic. You've never used your magic for anything dark have you?"

"No, not at all. But Sage, I wanted to tell you that I feel a weird tingling sensation when I'm around Julius."

"Clare are you infatuated with him?" Her voice wasn't angry, rather disturbed.

"No! Oh my Oralee of course not."

"So you think he has magic?"

"No, I mean not really. I don't know what it is, but he's different too."

"What about Maximus?"

"Different, but not in the same way, Maximus is just Maximus."

"I see. So you healed Cassius's face?" Sage asked, changing the subject.

"I did, I covered for you."

"I appreciate it, are you going to tell mum about your magic?"

"No, I'm going to try and figure this out on my own."

A mutual silence settled between the two of them. Sage was studying Clare's fingers, wondering if she could pick out anything abnormal about them, hoping to find an easy explanation for her magic. There were no markings on her fingers, no scars, no relics, they were just normal and the tips were painted bright pink. Sage had never believed in magic and she had never believed in fairytales. She had never even believed in the Goddesses like her sister did. While her sister would go to the temples and pray, Sage would wonder why she gave into such rubbish. While Clare was studying and reading novels about dragons and magic, Sage dismissed them as fantasy and not history. She thought the reason for this was their age difference. When she told her mother the obscure things that her sister was reading and had faith in, her mother just dismissed her. But her mother had not known about Clare's magic, she was just defending her youngest daughter. Clare had never shown any blatant signs of magic when she was younger, but the more Sage thought about it, she realized this perception was false. Clare had always healed incredibly fast. One day when they were younger and they were playing in the yard, Clare had fallen down and bloodied her knees. Within a moment, she was healed and the blood was gone. Sage had always thought that her brain had gone delusional that day, but it all made sense now, Clare had never been normal. Whenever she got injured she disappeared and came back as good as new. Sage couldn't imagine how frightened Clare must have felt all of those years. Now only Sage and Cassius knew of her magic. Cassius knew. Sage broke the silence. "Cassius knows. We can't trust him. Blimey, we can't trust him at all. We have to kill him."

Clare grabbed her sister by her hands and yanked her forward so that their foreheads were practically touching. Clare was an inch or two taller so they did not painfully collide, but their eyes met. Clare was fuming, there was a venom to her voice that warned her sister not to do anything rash. "You will not kill my fiancé. That is FINAL!" She pushed Sage back, her eyes still glistening with rage. She didn't like to raise her voice at Sage and she didn't remember the last time that she had done it, but it was necessary in the current moment. "I will grow to love him," she said through gritted teeth. "I don't know what it is you hate so much about him, but you have to give him a chance. You can't just write off every person that you see."
"His parents—"
"Exactly, his parents."

Sage pushed back a strand of hair behind her ear and huffed. "So what's your plan? You said you were going to try and discover the reason behind your magic by yourself and from what I can tell you don't have a clue how to do that. Would you like a couple of suggestions from your sister who is constantly dragging you out of your messes? And do not deny me, I have saved you from boys who are gawking over your looks plenty of times and I have saved you from danger. I know I can help you Clare."
Clare didn't seem so convinced. Though she had calmed down quickly, her arms were folded over her chest and in that moment she looked exactly like her mother. "You can't save the day every time Sage, but you are my older sister and I should trust in you. Though clearly I was right about the whole magic thing, tell me, what is your

grand plan?"

Sage leaned forward, she was now sitting in a criss cross position, her hands folded in her lap as if she were back in primary school."You need an excuse to leave, for a very long time. Magic folk don't live close to the palace, you'll have to travel far. You are not going alone, but I can not go with you either. It pains me, but mum would never allow both of her princesses to leave for a long period of time. I say you can not go by yourself because you are a woman and the world is cruel. I know you're capable, but I worry about your safety. I encourage you to read, read lots of books about magic before you go, do your research and then follow the clues you've collected. I really don't know what else you could do. I don't want you to leave, I'll miss you."

Clare leaned her head against the wall, watching as her sister returned to a relaxed position. "I'll miss you too, but it has to be done. I was thinking that at the Demetrias's event, I could talk to Julius. I feel deeply that he knows something. You are not going to like this, but if I can't go alone, I am going to ask if he will allow Antoine to come with me."

"It will never work, mum will contact Erebus and Antoine will be chained to a whipping pole within minutes. You have to take Cassius with you instead."

"I can not. I wish to take Antoine."

"Why? He is a servant."

"Because he is intelligent and I bet he believes in magic. I will ask him to come and since you think it'll cause a fuss, I'll ask Cassius to come as well."

"If word gets out that Antoine is on the mission at all, it won't end well."

"Then he can meet us somewhere along the way and we call it an accident. He can then accompany us on the rest of our journey."

"Alright, if you won't change your mind then I suppose that would be fine, but don't say I didn't warn you. When are you going to ask Cassius to accompany you?"

"Good thinking. I will make sure to ask him first so that way he feels special. Could you ask mum to draw me a carriage. I'll leave in an hour or two. I will stay in Excidium until the event, then I will meet you in Deus."

Sage wanted to tell her sister no, she wanted to scream it at the top of her lungs, she wanted to pull her back into her arms and cradle her so tight that she would never be able to leave her arms, but instead she found herself nodding her head. She couldn't control Clare, she couldn't protect her forever. She was old enough to take care of herself and old enough to marry. Sage was sure that their mum would also love the idea of her daughter spending time with her future husband. "Alright," she said quietly. She stood up from the ground and extended a hand to Clare, "let me help you pack."

The two of them moved around the room and gathered Clare's belongings. Sage had packed her toiletries and her art supplies, while Clare rummaged through her large closet to pick out a few outfits. She had designated three nightgowns, two fancy dresses and six casual outfits for her stay. She was sure that she could guilt Cassius into buying her more outfits if she ran out of clothes to wear, so she wasn't worried. Sage had gathered her a few books about magic and placed them inside of her luggage. She helped her zip up her bag and carry it down the stairs. Gracielle was sitting on the sofa and reading a book. "Mum, Clare wants to go spend some time with Cassius. Do you think you'd be able to call for a carriage?"

Gracielle put down her book and her stern eyes turned loving. All her anger had seemed to fade away, this request had made up for both of their mistakes. "Well of course, some quality time together will bring Clare and Cassius closer." She stood up and flattened out her long, olive green ruffled dress. "What a nice surprise. Tell Clare to go take a bath and get ready. Phoebe will help her prepare and you can help me prepare the carriage."

Word traveled quickly in the palace. As soon as she heard, Phoebe had drawn Clare a bath and laid out a dress for her. It wasn't a color that she typically wore, but it was a color the Antias family loved, black. The dress was made out of a thin satin fabric that would cling to every curve on her body. It had mesh sleeves and would stop just below her knees. After Phoebe had made sure that Clare was clean, she handed her a bathrobe and let the girl dry her hair and fluff out her curls. She then helped her into the tight black dress that made it hard to breathe and a bit hard to walk as it went down past her knees. She felt like a clutz in the tall black heels that her mum had picked out for her. Phoebe had done her makeup smokey and dark, she looked nothing like herself, but if this is what it took for Erebus not to hate her family and let her drag his son into the woods, then so be it. Phoebe helped her down the stairs and to the carriages where her mother and Sage were waiting. Sage looked horrified while her mother clapped. "Mum, you've dressed her like a prostitute."

"I have not. I have dressed her like a lady ready to seduce the man she is going to marry."

"I planned on strolling the gardens with him, not seducing him," Clare said in annoyance as she took her sisters hand and heaved herself into the carriage.

"Well he will like that as well, be safe my darling," Gracielle said as she kissed her daughter's cheek.

Clare pulled both her sister and her mum into a hug, not letting them go until a minute had passed. "I will be safe, I will see you at the event!" she shouted. The guard shut the carriage door and the carriage took off at once.

Sage stood staring as the carriage rolled away. "I hope they treat her well," she whispered.

THE ANTIAS FAMILY

The carriage ride was rather dull. There were only two things that Clare could do and the first was to look out the window and stare at the passing scenery. The pine trees turned into beach coasts and the beach coasts turned into cities built in the middle of the desert as they got closer to the castle. If she got bored of looking out of the window, she could read the books that she had packed. None of these options were too exciting, but reading about the origins of magic gave her the energy to stay awake and distracted her from her nerves. It had been years since she had visited the Antias's in their own home. As they pulled into the main city, she placed the pale floral bookmark in her book, set it down and peered out of the blush pink curtains. The city was darker then she remembered. Almost every building was painted the color black. The trees lining the cities weren't green, they were pale and yellow. The atmosphere of Excidium wasn't village like either, instead there were big cities. The castle was an hour away from the heart of Excidium. The afternoon had turned into evening when her carriage finally arrived. The castle was pitch black and gothic, the gates were black bars with intricate diamond points at the top. There were guards outside garbed in black and holding spears. 'Would there be any color in this city?'

A normal carriage from Pax et Lux, would have been white with olive green accents, but Clare had taken her own. A blush pink carriage with rose gold embroidery and white horses, her presence stuck out like a sore thumb and had the royal family out of their doors in a matter of seconds. The carriage came to an abrupt stop and Clare jolted forward, her hands resting on the guards knees. She carefully removed them and handed him her book so he could put it with the rest of her belongings. Her eyes latched onto Cassius's confused face. He was standing outside, dressed in a clean black suit with a gray wolf fur collar. His hands were relaxed against the front of his body and he was starting to smile as the realization that Clare had arrived sunk in. If Clare had not felt so uncomfortable in her own skin, she would have smiled too, but the dress she was wearing was making it hard to do so. She waited until the guard pulled the carriage doors open and then carefully stepped out, taking his hand for balance. There was silence as everyone took in the sight of the princess who looked strikingly gorgeous, but nothing like herself. The only thing that made her recognizable was her kind face and the crown of silver that was twisted with white metal flowers upon her head.

King Erebus broke the silence. "What a pleasant surprise. Did your mother pick out that outfit?" His gaze lingered too long.

"She did," Clare said uncomfortably.

"Charming. Well, Adria, let's welcome our new guest inside. She won't need a guest bedroom, she can stay with Cassius. Cassius will show her to his room."

If she hadn't been recently engaged to Erebus's son, she would have objected, but she didn't want to be rude, so she forced a smile onto face and nodded. She wobbled a bit in her tall heels, but Cassius was right by her side to catch her. He linked his arm with hers and she leant up against his tall frame. "I am very surprised that you came to see me, especially after yesterday," Cassius said. He didn't say what had happened, his parents were still watching, but she knew what situation he was talking about.

"I thought it would be better for us to mend things, I don't want to fight with you if I have to spend the rest of my life with you." That was true.

"Well I'm glad you came. You know," he whispered in her ear, "you don't have to wear black."

"I wore black to impress you, are you not impressed?" She was surprised by her own words.

"Consider me impressed," he said.

Their banter was interrupted by his parents who were now walking by their side. "Clare you always look beautiful," Queen Adria complimented genuinely. "Erebus and I would like to give you two time to get to know one another further, but we would like you to join us for dinner in two hours. Is that alright?"

Cassius nodded, about to answer for the two of them, but Clare had spoken up first. "It is alright with me." Cassius glared at her as if she hadn't any manners and gave her the look that suggested they'd talk later. "We will see you soon. I'm going to show Clare around the castle," he told his mother.

He waited until his parents were out of sight to speak with her. "My father is strict and though I am glad you speak your mind, he will start tallying up every little thing that you do wrong. Talking out of turn would be one of them. I know our kingdoms work differently, but here, I speak and then you may share your thoughts. Now, would you like to get out of that dress first or would you like a tour around the castle?"

Silence filled the hot air. 'What had happened to the version of Cassius who at least tried to be polite? Was he out of his mind?' "I would like to change into something else, if that is alright with you, or are you going to dictate what I wear as well?" She saw a new anger in his eyes, one she hadn't seen when he was visiting the Pax palace. Maybe he was more like his father than she had thought.

He composed himself as if there was not a prince in the world who could take him down. "You may change and now that you've said it, I'll okay the outfit before you leave. I wouldn't want my father to dislike you any more than he already does," he said, his voice cold.

It was as if a switch had flipped. She hadn't taken a liking to him at the party, but she hadn't hated him either. If she wasn't going to be free in his home, then she would fight to never live there. Maybe they could set up a compromise, or maybe he was only this way because he was being secretly watched. He was two faced and hard for her to read. She was quiet and observing as they walked the castle floor to his room. He had decided to start the tour on their way there as if nothing had happened, as if he was still kind and charming. There was a black skeleton like drawbridge that they crossed to enter the castle. Lit by flames instead of natural light or electricity, it was muggy and warm inside. The walls were all stone and had no color to them besides a cool grey. The castle was one big open space. Little furniture, no privacy. The kitchen opened up to a ballroom and a ballroom opened up to a dining room. Then at each corner of the grand room there was a stairway that split either up into the bedrooms or down into the lower floor of the castles, where she had heard they kept the prisoners. She didn't wish to go see them, but she had a gut feeling that Cassius would take her down there anyways. The Pax family didn't keep prisoners in their home, but she knew the

Demetrias's did. It was an odd way that her family would never understand, but she tried to keep herself open minded.

He guided her to the front left corner and up a set of winding stairs that looked as if they would fall apart on her. She took each step slowly, leaning on him for support as she wobbled in her heels. He was odd, but she hadn't lost complete trust in him yet. At the top of the stairs she noticed that the long hallway revealed over a dozen black doors all leading to private rooms. At the very end of the hall were two large double doors with vultures for knockers, the symbol of his kingdom. She knew just by looking at the door that it was the entrance to his room.

"I don't show many people my quarters. If it were up to me, I would have had you sleeping in the guest bedroom next door, but my parents get what they want. I am just an adult living under their roof. Go ahead, after you." He pulled open the vulture handle and let her inside.

Her eyes landed upon a clean sight. The walls were stone and on the back wall there was a large window. The glass was open and framed by black curtains, but the sight outside was nowhere near as pretty as back at home. She felt sick looking at all the black, but maybe that was how they felt with the Pax's olive green or her blush pink. His bed was large, it must have been a king size and was topped with silk sheets and the fluffiest of silver covers. On his walls were paintings of knights and war. 'Did they have something in common?' While she had paintings of roses and family on her wall, he had paintings of knights and war, but they still both had a collection of art. In the corner of the room she spotted a sitting area with a bookshelf. There was another door that he explained led to the toilet and the bath. Her luggage had been laid down on his bed.

"Make yourself at home. You may read any of the books you would like and come to relax in here when you feel stressed. I must check your luggage though. My father still does not like your sister, they are worried that she might have slipped something inside of your bag."

Clare tried not to look offended, instead she questioned him, "did you tell your parents what she did?" Her voice dropped to a hush and became fierce, "did you tell them what you know?"

"No." He said bluntly, he took the pitch black pointy crown off of his head and placed it on his dresser. The accessory did him no justice, it blended in with his black hair so well, that only the points of the crown were noticeable. He gestured towards her bag and she unzipped it. She had been hiding nothing, she knew she might not get away with it here. He moved closer and fingered his way through the clothes, the toiletries, the art supplies and the books. He undid all the pockets as if he was a guard himself and in the end, he had found nothing, but his eyebrows were still raised at the selection of clothes that she had chosen and the books that she had brought. "I have books here, why did you bring your own? I am not going to take them, I am perhaps just curious."

"Because I want to ask you something, but now is not the time, later tonight."

He eyed her and then shifted his gaze down to the ring on her finger, he supposed he should trust her. "Alright. Well I will have to take you shopping, but which outfit would you like to wear tonight?"

Clare sat down on his bed and undid her heels. Without her asking, he swooped down near her feet and gathered them in his hands. He placed them neatly at the bottom of his closet where his collection of boots lay. "We can share a closet. There is plenty of space, my mum made me get rid of some things, she said they were out of fashion," Cassius said.

Clare couldn't help but smile at the thought of his mother picking out his outfits. He smiled back at her and she thought that she could see his gentle nature slip back, but she knew it wouldn't last long, 'what was he trying to accomplish?' Clare reached back into her now mess of a luggage and looked for something suitable to wear for dinner. She had brought an olive green dress that was dotted with small white polka dots and adorned with frills on the sleeves and at the bottom of the dress. She had a feeling that this would not be fancy enough for his household, but there was not enough space in her luggage to pack a ball gown.

"Your dress is beautiful, but I do not want my parents to be displeased. How about, I lend you one of my cousin's dresses, she will not mind."

"Does she live here?" Clare questioned as she folded the dress and placed it back into the suitcase.

"She does, she will be chuffed to meet you," he extended a hand to her and she took it. She slipped on a pair of flats to wear while they walked around the castle. "Bear with me in your uncomfortable dress for a moment longer. I will finish the tour and then you will meet Cisily. Cisily's mum is Adria's sister and my aunt. While the main kingdom of Excidium is one big chunk of land, there is an island across the sea that my mum's sister and husband govern. There are not many people on this island, but it is still under Excidium rule. My mum could not be there to govern herself, so she sent her sister and her husband who she made the rulers. Though they still had to obey and enforce all of her laws, they were the representatives. Their children were born on the island and raised there until they were ten and eleven years old. Noticing how lonely her children were with nothing to do, my aunt sent her children across the sea to live in the heart of Excidium, here. Though Theo and Cisily were technically a princess and a prince, my horrible father made sure that they were never called such and that no one would call them that because I was to have all of the spotlight."

Clare took his hand and walked with him down the hall.

He stopped at the staircase and gestured upwards. "My parent's quarters are up a flight of stairs. There is no reason to go up there besides for the rooftop deck. I will accompany you if you'd like to see the view sometime. The war rooms, the military planning, it is all up there and since you are not family yet, you may not see it." He guided her away and down the stairs. He showed her where they ate and where the servants slept, fortunately they were nice conditions that did not disturb her. He guided her to the library which was nowhere near as large as hers, but cozy and pretty. He took her to the spa which they had set up in their castle and promised that he would take her there again when she needed to unwind. He took her to the outside gardens and pointed to the outside of the temple that they used to pray. This time the building wasn't black, it was gold with all eight goddesses carved on the outside of the ancient style building. Next to it, he pointed to a small hospital for royal emergencies that was not in the shape of a cottage, but rather a steel building that looked like a prison. He explained to her the importance of staying healthy so that she would never have to have a stay there. Then what she had been dreading, he led her down the stairs, five flights, to the dungeons that were so far underground the temperature had dropped ten degrees.

It was damp and muggy inside and the prisoners had all thrown themselves up against the metal bars to get a good look at the prince and the princess. Their faces were pale and ragged. The place wreaked of death and filth. There were three or four prisoners per cell, each cell was so small that there was no place for the prisoners relieve themselves. Clare had never visited her own prisons. 'How foolish she had been. Were all prisons like this or were these conditions specific to Excidium? Did the people piss on one another because there was nowhere else to go?' They were standing at the entrance and she could only see into one cell. A man in his fifties, naked, scabbed and bruised, a woman clothed in rags, her limbs bony, a man with a foaming mouth and another woman, naked, on the verge of death.

"You may look away," he said gently.

She did, she buried her face into his shoulder and breathed in the sweet scent of cologne, attempting to mask the filth. "What did they do to deserve this?"

He had an arm around her waist, holding her close up against his side. He was staring off into the distance, "Personal or offensive crimes earn public executions, those criminals are killed instantly. We are not alone in that, even Deus still performs public executions on occasion, Pax et Lux is the only kingdom who has outlawed that form of punishment. Minor crimes such as theft, are just public whippings and then they are released. But there are people who keep committing crimes or they are such bad crimes, it is better for them to suffer. They stay here. The reason why some are naked is because they have lost their minds, or their clothes are too itchy and filthy. I am sorry that you had to look at their bodies. No one comes to bathe them. There are people assigned to bring them meals once a day and there are people who collect the bodies if someone passes. They don't get visitors, they don't get to see the light of day, there are no windows, everything is lit by small flames that eventually flicker out. Clare, remember this is not my doing. I did not choose this. Chin up, I was instructed to show you the rest, I promise I will tell you when you can close your eyes again."

She lifted her head up from his shoulder and let her eyes gaze back out into the prisons. Hands were reaching out of the bars in attempts to touch her, to feel royalty. people were angrily shouting at the prince, but he ignored them and focused on keeping Clare out of their grasp. The walk felt like it would never end and whenever someone had passed away, Cassius would nudge her and she would bury her head back into his shoulder.

At the very end of the prison, he pointed out a trap door underneath their feet. "People who commit treason and help our enemies go down here." He pointed to the hole, underneath and very far down there was no light, no food and a silhouette of a man screaming to himself. Even Cassius's face was twisted with disdain. "Let us get out of here, you have seen enough for a lifetime."

She hurriedly followed him up the stairs, practically running. The farther she climbed, the faster she went, hoping to reach the top as quickly as possible. The scent never left her nose, it still lingered and clung to their clothing, the smell of his cologne was now masked with something much worse.

"I am sorry for that, but as a princess and my future wife, you must know the conditions of the people. We will go see Cisily now. She will excuse our filth and then we can bathe before dinner. Come on, she will distract your mind."

Clare wanted to retreat back to his room, huddle in a corner and draw everything that she had seen, but Cassius was right, maybe Cisily would be able to distract her and maybe she could befriend the girl. If they became close she would have an ally in the castle and she could get more information on which version of Cassius was real. They climbed the stairs that led to the row of bedrooms and Clare felt her calves shaking on the way up. She wasn't sure if it was because she was nervous to meet Cisily or if she was still scarred from the prisons. She kept close to his side as they walked. Sure he was a new important figure in her life and he was quite the alarming character, but out of everyone in this castle, he felt the safest. Cassius stopped a few doors down from his own and knocked.

The door flew open to reveal a beautiful woman. She resembled Cassius, but gave off a free and loving energy. She was a fairly tall woman who was Clare's age. She had tight black curls that coiled up like springs. Her hair was down to her shoulders, her jaw was sharp and her face was sculpted. She had the same deep brown eyes as Cassius, but her skin was warmer than Cassius's, a beautiful shade of walnut brown. She was smiling brightly at the sight of Clare.

"She's finally here!" the girl beamed as she pulled Clare in by her hands and spun her around. "She is so gorgeous and look at all of the bright color in her hair," Clare was blushing as she let the girl examine her ginger hair. Nothing this bright had run in the Antias family. Cisily's father had moved from central Asia to Europe. Her mother, Adria's sister, had been from the lower parts of Excidium

65

where the people migrated from South American and were less fair as they were more exposed to the sun. Red and blonde were not common hair colors in Excidium and Cisily was fascinated with all things out of the ordinary.

Cassius let out a baritone laugh. He moved inside of the room and let the door close behind him, he exchanged a hug with his cousin and then sat down on the bed examining the two women. "I want you two to get to know each other, but that will have to wait until tomorrow. Clare needs something formal to wear, she could not pack anything elegant because it would not have fit inside of her luggage. Would you be able to find her something and make it fit?" Cisily was still beaming, she opened up her closet to reveal dresses of all different colors and styles.

Clare was smiling as she came close, finally someone who appreciated a variety of colors.

"Take your pick, I don't have anything formal to do tonight. Oh I can get you ready and all dolled up for Cass, it will be so fun!" Cisily laughed at the horror in her cousin's eyes. "You'll need a bath, you two smell where were you?"

Clare's smile faded as the memories came back, thankfully Cassius had filled his cousin in on her arrival and their tour of the castle including the prisons.

Cisily had put her hands on Clare's shoulders, rubbing them warmly. Clare melted into her touch, leaning against her, she already took comfort in having the presence of another woman near. "I'm sorry you had to go through that darling."

She felt as if she could stay in Cisily's arms for a long time and listen to her babble on and on about whatever she wanted. There was a comforting feeling about having a girl her age near, but Cassius was also near and they had things to do. She gently removed herself from the girls embrace and thumbed through the dresses. Eventually she found one that suited her perfectly. The dress was a shade of deep pink. The dress was cut across the shoulders with white frilly lace attached to the front. It fit the top of the chest tightly and then spilled down into a large puffy gown, with pink ribbons and more white lace trimming the ends. "This one, I will dress in this one."

Cisily took the dress off of the hanger and then turned around to face her cousin with a harsh look. "Well go along now. I am going to chat with your fiancé. Go wash up and I will have her returned to you by dinner."

Cassius stood up and bowed his head, waving to Clare before sliding out of the door and disappearing. Clare would have plenty of time to ask Cisily questions and get a better read on Cassius. He could not hide.

A SERVANTS TASK

Antoine had the entire carriage ride home to think about his experience with Clare. It was lovely and he was foolishly delighted to spend more time with her, when he got the opportunity at the event in two weeks. She would be in front of him again and he would know that it wasn't a dream. He could tell her about the books that he had read and he could see the piece of art that she had made for him. No. These were all terrible thoughts. He was a servant and she was a princess. They could not have any informal relationship, he could not think about her like that. He would continue to keep his thoughts of her a secret, or so he had thought. When they returned back to the castle, he was placing the books that she had given him on his shelf, when he heard a bell ringing in the distance, Julius must have needed him. He got dressed in his servants outfit, a cream pair of pants, a white button up shirt, a pair of white shoes and a frilly blue collar to signal his allegiance to Julius. He raced up the stairs and was prepared to knock on the door, but it was already open.

"You may come in Antoine."

Antoine shut the door behind him and gazed at Prince Julius with questioning eyes. "You needed me?"

Julius gestured for him to sit down, an innocent smile plastered to his face. "Clare," was all he said.

Antoine put his hands over his face, fingers pushing up against his glasses, he took a seat on the bed. 'So Julius knew. How had he seen, what had he seen?'

"I will not punish you and neither will Maximus. I told him that you two had been out together, so he wouldn't get angry at you if anything slipped. Though I'm personally not mad, I wanted to warn you that you're playing with fire, you're playing with flames and I'm not just talking about Erebus. But, keep in mind that king Erebus has a temper too, but one that is violent. If you are in the way of their prince, if one can call him that," he said, "it won't end well for you." Antoine was about to speak, but Julius kept rambling as he often did. "There is something odd about Clare. I feel different around her. I need you to find out what it is."

"What do you mean? Wouldn't Sage tell you if there is something wrong with Clare? You're even close to Clare herself, so couldn't you just tell her your concerns?" Antoine said in confusion.

Julius shuddered and his face went pale. "No, not about this. I am clumsy, I might … well I just can not."

"What do I ask her? We have only met once. I'm not sure she'll trust me."

"Ask her about the green glow. She'll understand."

PREPARATION

Sage was pacing in the sitting room. Her sister had probably walked right into hell and there was no way of reaching her, except by letter, which always took too long. She didn't have Julius to confide in or yell at because he was at home and if she yelled to her mum after already irritating her, Gracielle might scream and send her into another dimension. So instead she went outside and took her anger out on the dummies. She grabbed her trusted sword. The hilt was sleek, shiny and silver, with cross guards. The blade itself was made of steel and had the logo of an elephant carved at the base. She had polished her sword recently, so it would slice cleanly and it did. Each dummy came apart with one hit, stuffing and hay spilled out onto the floor. She didn't expect to be interrupted. She continued slashing and striking until there was nothing left. As she was staring down at her mess, she heard a familiar voice clear her throat. She spun around to see Gracielle, arms crossed against her chest, chin held high.

"Sage it's late. Come inside, we need to talk," the queen said.

Sage and her mother never had small talk. They didn't sit and chat about the weather or how their days had been. Sage put the sword back into its cover on her belt and followed her mother inside. "Why what's wrong? Did I do something else?"

Gracielle shook her head as she led her daughter to the room that was used to strategize for war. Sage couldn't help but feel alarmed as she sat down in one of those emerald green cushioned chairs. Her mother sat across from her. "I don't like to think morbidly, but I'm getting older and the world is becoming increasingly more dangerous. It's about time that we have this conversation. If anything happens to me or I can no longer fulfill my duties effectively, you are well aware that you are first in line for the throne. You would rule our kingdom. I would like to discuss with you everything that you need to know."

"Mum is there anyway Clare can take over instead?"

"No my love, that's not how life works," she reached across the table and took her daughter's hands in her own. "It can only be you."

Sage took her mother's hands and slumped over, she was sweaty from her outburst with her sword, but her mother didn't seem to mind very much.

"I want to teach you how to run a kingdom. How to put the citizen's needs before your own, but first you must learn our complete history. Though you know some of the basics you do not know it all." She let go of Sage's hands and reached underneath the table. She grabbed a stack of five books and set them in front of her daughter, a loud thud followed the motion. "Read them all before the event. These books cover everything that you need to know about the three kingdoms and their history. They also discuss the Goddesses because as a leader you must care or pretend to care about them. They will be vital to your success wether you want to believe it or not. I want the books finished the day before the event. Then I will be able to quiz you. Once you are better educated, I will teach you how to run a kingdom."

Sage couldn't remember the last time that she had read outside of school. She wanted to tell her mother that this was all unnecessary and it would be a long time before she had to take over, but she had a feeling that this wasn't true. She took the books under her arm, wondering how she was going to finish all of them in such a short amount of time, but if Clare could manipulate Cassius in two weeks, then she could read five books. She could feel their bond strengthening even though they were miles apart. "Alright, I will do it, but only because you told me I must. I don't plan on losing you anytime soon and don't even think of stepping down."

Gracielle gave her a soft smile, the new wrinkles on her face deepening as she did so. She was young, yet old for her time and the stress kept piling on. "Good, now off you go. You have a lot of reading to do."

PAINT

Cisily had prepared he bath so over the top that Clare was unsure if it could even be classified as water. The bath water was milky and smelled of roses, lavender and maybe chamomile, she had forgotten the list of ingredients. She hadn't taken a very long bath, but she soaked long enough to get the stench off. After drying off with a soft towel, she slipped into the fluffy bathrobe laid out for her and called for Cisily. The girl flocked to her side and held out the dress with excitement. "You are even pretty when you are fresh from the bath," she complimented. "I'm quite a bit taller than you, so I altered the dress to the best of my abilities to fit your height," she said. She led Clare to the chair by her vanity and began to brush through her wet hair. "If he wasn't my cousin, I would ask you more about your activities with him."

"Well we are just hardly getting to re know each other, so there are no activities. We were childhood playmates, but we grew apart when tensions rose between the three Kingdoms. Now that peace is attempting to be made, we are meeting again. You should tell me more about Cassius, I don't know too much."

"Well..." she said, "he used to be a very bright and happy kid. Then my uncle was continuously unkind to him. Around the age of twelve he became distanced and cold. I'm sure you've noticed that he now walks with his shoulders high and he always stands so stiffly. There are moments, mostly when we are alone, when he is the same boy that I once knew, happy and smiling. Other times he is sly and closed off. That is all I feel comfortable sharing at the moment, but do not be afraid of him Clare, he is a good man, he is just blinded by the shadows." After Cisily finished brushing out Clare's hair, she dusted her cheeks with blush.

"Do you know how he felt when they told him about the arranged marriage? Did he have a past lover?" Clare asked, closing her lips so Cisily could apply lip gloss to them.

"He did not have a past lover, so there is no need to be jealous," she teased. "I don't know if he was glad, but he smiled a little. He has always admired you Clare. When we were younger, we used to tease him about you after parties. He was always blushing furiously during those conversations. He was never upset with his parents about their decision. I don't think he minds very much. If anything I think he is angry for you, he feels bad that you are stuck with him. You know, the two of us never talked much when we were younger, but I was at those parties too. I would hear you talk about love stories."

Clare's face lit up in a blush. She took Cisily's hands as the girl helped her up and led her to the folding screen that she could change behind. "I did not know everyone heard my fantasies. How embarrassing. I can tell Cassius cares for me," she said, "but sometimes he treats me like a doll."

"Men are frustrating. I don't think he is alone in that category."

Clare did not agree with her completely, the men she had been close to all her life had not been this tiresome, but she kept her lips shut.

Cisily turned around to give her privacy while she changed. Once Clare had the dress on, Cisily helped her put the dress on and smooth it out. Clare was impressed, she felt a small smile grace her shiny lips. The dress suited her style perfectly and she felt confident in it. For the first time she felt her heart flutter in hopes that Cassius would like it. She had no feelings for him, but she desperately hoped that they would come. He was an attractive man who kept her mind stimulated, but if she were to be happy in a marriage, he would need to be more than just attractive. "You look gorgeous. I think I did a pretty good job, what do you think?" Cisily asked as she gestured to her makeup.

"I think you did a great job as well. I would love to keep talking to you, you have been so kind to me, but I must get to dinner or his parents will dislike me more than they already do. Thank you once again."

"Of course, I hope to speak with you again."

Clare dipped her head and curtsied. She hurriedly slipped on the pink flats and began to hastily make her way down the stairs. She was hoping that she was not late, but she was sure that she wasn't when she heard hurried footsteps behind her. Cassius was approaching her.

He was wearing a black suit similar to the one he had on earlier, but he was now clean and shining. His half wet hair dried in loose curls and he smelled of vanilla and mahogany. He took her hand in his, "Cisily did you justice. You look gorgeous," he whispered in her ear, sending shivers down her spine. "Now this is an appropriate outfit for dinner. My mum will never admit it, but she loves pink."

Clare doubted that.

As they approached the table, Erebus and Adria stood to greet them. "You're just on time," Adria said softly. "Dinner is just about to come out of the kitchen. Please have a seat." She sat herself down in one of the chairs and Erebus followed. Cassius pulled out a chair for Clare and once she was seated, he pushed it back in and sat beside her.

The duck had barely arrived when the king began to start asking questions. "So, you clearly didn't want to visit my son just because you felt like it. You have better things to do as a princess. Why did you come? I don't like lying," his voice was harsh, his breath hot as he stabbed the duck with his knife and began to cut.

Cassius didn't glare at his father, but he put a hand on Clare's leg and let it rest there. He was on her side. She was going to ask Cassius to accompany her on her journey, tonight, but maybe it was best for her to ask here, so they would trust her.

"Well I wanted to come spend some time with Cassius before the event. I want to know what it's like to live with him and I actually wanted to ask him if he'd like to come on holiday with me."

"Holiday?" The question was echoed by the three at almost the same time.

"Yes. My mum has given me permission to go across the forests and travel for a month. Sage will take on both of our duties." She had not been given permission yet, but she figured that this was the only way she could convince them.

"I would love to go on a holiday. I don't get to do that very often," Cassius said with a wide grin. She hadn't ever seen him that bright. His stern face was adorable and puffed up with glee. His parents on the other hand still looked cross.

"He is a prince, the only prince. We will think about it," Erebus said.

Adria chimed in, "but we are glad that you are here for our son and our son only. We wouldn't want you falling in love with anyone else."

'Antoine.' Her mind began to spin. She was in no means in love with Antoine nor was she in love with Cassius, but the white haired boy had caught her interest and if anyone found out that they hung around one another and continued to do so, she'd be in a world of hurt and so would he. They'd have to do their best to keep their mouths shut. "Right. I would never," Clare said a little too quickly, taking a bite of her food. Cassius's hand left her leg and found its way to his plate. She hoped that they would quit interrogating her and move onto another topic, but her wishes did not come true.

The king kept going. "As you know my son is next in line to take over the throne, though of course neither of us plan on leaving this Earth anytime soon, how will you support my son?"

Clare sighed. She knew that the right answer was going to be something along the lines of stay pretty, feed him and stay silent, but she couldn't bear to play along with that game. "I'm a princess, I've seen my mother strategize through war and tragedy. The people have always said that I would have been fit to be queen, though I'm sure Sage will do a lovely job one day. I will use my skills to help Cassius succeed. I have always been good with my citizens and I'm sure I'll be just as great with his." She felt the tension increase on the other side of the table. "Of course only when he asks for my help. I wouldn't want to interrupt him, how unladylike that would be," she said sarcastically.

Adria began to smile, she interrupted her husband and shifted the conversation in a different direction. "She's only just begun her stay, let her relax a little," the queen said, glaring at her husband out of the corner of her eye.

Clare thought she heard Cassius mutter a 'yeah' in agreement, but it might have been in her imagination.

"What are some things you like to do in your free time? Cassius has classes he must attend to every day, but what can we do to help make you feel comfortable?" Adria asked.

Clare smoothed out her dress and after taking a few more bites of the duck and mash, she answered. "I fancy art. It is something I do rather well. I'm also fond of music, I can't play, but I love to listen. I wouldn't mind spending time with Cisily, if she doesn't have any classes," Clare suggested, knowing the loneliness would eat at her if she didn't have someone to talk to until the evening.

Cassius seemed delighted that she wanted to get to know his cousin. "Oh yes Cisily is available, her brother lives with us as well. Though I may get jealous if you spend too much time with him. His name is Theodore, but he goes by Theo. He mostly spends time in the library. Actually I may not get jealous, I don't think he fancies women. They will be your friends here. As for the art and music, we have painting supplies, servants and instruments to keep you happy," Cassius said confidently. Adria was glad that her son was trying to impress Clare and keep her comfortable. She let him take the lead in the conversation. "If Clare proves herself, will you let us go on holiday?" he asked.

Erebus wanted to say no, but Adria was the one in control of the kingdom, she grinned, "of course, though I believe she won't have much trouble. She's impressed me already."

The rest of the dinner went smoothly. Erebus went on to explain the kinds of training Cassius was put through, both physical and mental. Cassius had invited her to watch one of his fighting practices and Clare had agreed as long as Cisily could tag along. While King Erebus spent the rest of dinner boasting about his son, he stated that Cassius could still sleep with any woman that he wanted and that the kingdom called him the prince of charms. Cassius explained that he would remain loyal to Clare and hoped that she would give him the same amount of commitment back. Clare agreed and realized that this would mean she couldn't be seen with Antoine. If he was jealous of his might be gay cousin, then he would certainly be jealous of the servant. Adria on the other hand had spent the rest of her dinner ignoring her husband and discussing books and fashion with Clare. Once dessert was finished and cleaned off of the table, she gestured for her son to go make sure his bedroom was clean. Once Erebus had left to go resume his work, she pulled Clare aside.   "I know this is hard for you. While my husband may be an ass, I am here to support you. You may come to me if you need anything. Just imagine that I am your own mother. Do not hesitate to reach out to me. I know that this process can be overwhelming. And I hope you do not think that when I was younger I chose him because I did not."

Though Clare had assumed that Adria was the nicer of the two leaders, she hadn't expected for Adria to like her and she hadn't expected to like Adria. Of course she did not trust the woman yet, but she wanted to trust her. If the queen had been in an arranged marriage too, then she must have known the struggles. "Did you grow to love him? The king."

"I did, I grew to love him," her voice went quiet and Clare could tell that this wasn't the complete answer.

Maybe their love had faded over the years. A part of her wanted to keep pushing, but she kept her thoughts concealed, she didn't want to ruin what was beginning to blossom. "Well, I hope to be like you in the sense that I grow to love my future husband. Do know, I am trying my best to open my heart to your son."

"I am sure you are, now go. I think he has a surprise for you," she winked and gestured up the stairs. "I hope you remember your way."

"I do, it's been a while since I've played here, but after the tour my memory has been refreshed. Thank you again."

Clare gathered up her dress in her hands and slowly made her way up the stairs. She was careful in taking her time, she didn't want to trip and make a fool out of herself. Everywhere there were people watching. Anything silly that she did would be seen and the news would be spread quickly throughout the castle like wildfire. As she made her way down the hallway, she noticed Cisily emerging from Cassius's bedroom.

"I was just helping him set things up," the girl said happily, "he has a surprise for you."

Clare noticed that the girl was always smiling, she returned the grin. "He does? How generous. Are you off to bed for the evening?"

"Oh yes, I'm quite tired. You arrived fairly late."

"Right. I do feel a bit tired myself," she looked fearfully to the door, hoping that this surprise wasn't sex.

"Well," Cisily said, "off to bed I go. I heard dinner went well, you can fill me in tomorrow, don't keep him waiting!" She hurried past Clare and into her bedroom, waving to her new friend before shutting the door.

Clare drew in a deep breath before continuing down the hallway, she could only hope that this surprise was something innocent and not something lustful. Cassius opened the door wider for her upon her arrival. She was quick to scan the room, sighing in relief when she saw two sketchbooks and some acrylic paint laid on top of a lilac blanket on the floor. The room was lit by a few candles, the window open to reveal an array of stars.

"I thought that you might want to change into your nightgown. I will change as well. My mum suggested that I do something romantic for you tonight. When you mentioned painting at dinner, I knew that I could set something up with Cisily's help. I thought that we could paint portraits of each other. How does that sound?" he asked.

Her eyes lit up at the expensive paint sets beneath her. "It sounds great, but I'm shocked that you'd want to do this. You don't strike me as the artsy type. In fact, you don't strike me as someone for romantic dates at all." She watched him shrug off his suit jacket and hang it up in his closet.

"I'm not. I don't think that I've ever set up something this nice for a girl. They normally just come back and sleep with me," he gestured to the door leading to the bathroom. "Would you like to go change?"

"I would, but be patient with me. Corsets are a struggle to take off sometimes and I normally don't do it by myself."

"Would you like me to help?"

"No," she said quickly.

She quickly brushed past him, opening the door and closing it as fast as she could. Her heart was hammering. She didn't know that he had been such a sly fox. Constantly sleeping with women, bringing someone else into his bed. She wasn't surprised, 'but would he be able to control his urge?' Clare had never slept with anyone before and she hadn't planned on sleeping with him anytime soon. Maybe her plans would have to change. Sure he was appealing, but she didn't know him well enough. She hoped he'd be able to wait. As she began to unzip her dress, she realized that she had forgotten her night clothes. "Cassius!" she called out as the dress dropped to the floor, the fabric spilling across the entirety of the small room. "I forgot my nightgown, would you please bring me it along with some fresh knickers. After a few twists, she managed to untie her corset, exhaling deeply.

"Yes," she heard him grumble. She heard a thud at the door and assumed that he had dropped her clothes.

While she still had some clothing on, she quickly opened the door and kicked the clothes in with her foot. After fully undressing, she slipped on the pair of strawberry underwear and the soft white nightgown dotted with yellow stars. She picked up her dress and heaved it into the room. He told her to leave it in the corner for now and she did. He was no longer formal. He was wearing a black fitted t-shirt and a pair of black boxers. Apparently he wasn't fond of trousers. She plopped down across from him and took the canvas in her hands. She was about to ask him if he was good at painting even if he didn't enjoy it, but he beat her to asking questions. He picked up a brush and dipped it in the cream colored paint, she did the same, watching as his mouth opened up to speak.

"I can't ignore what happened last night. With the magic I mean. I need to know more." He was splotching paint on his canvas with his brush, but he wasn't looking at the painting, he was only looking at her.

Clare on the other hand was focused on mixing the cream paint with a dark brown to get the perfect shade of light brown. She parted her lips to respond, but went quiet as she painted the outline of his face. Once she had made some progress, she began. "That's why I asked you to go on holiday. Of course I want to get to know you, but I need someone to come with me and help me figure out where my magic comes from. Now only you and my sister know, even my own mum is unaware. If she has noticed, she has said nothing."

Cassius was struggling with painting her hair. His brush was a mixture of cream and orange since he had forgotten to clean it. "I don't know how I would be of use to you."

It was a blunt and cold statement and now that she considered it, 'what could he do?' She took a moment to think about it as she began to paint the base of his neck, fanning the paining with her hand when she was finished so that it would dry and she would be able to add the next layer. It came to her. "I can not fight. I may be able to heal, but I can not fight very well. I can deliver a good punch and maybe stab someone, but that is it. Who knows what kind of magical beings I may encounter on my journey or if I'll need someone to lift something heavy. If magic is real, who knows what else is out there and I need moral support, I know you are a great listener. Normally Sage could be my strength and the other half of my heart, but I guess that's up to you this time." She finally looked up to get another good look at his face. His nose was wrinkled, scrunched up tight to his forehead, focused as he attempted to listen to her and paint her curls at the same time.

"I am a good fighter and sometimes a good listener. I will do you a favor and go if my parents allow it. I am curious what you are capable of. I don't trust magic, you are no exception. I am only keeping my mouth shut because I don't want to get you killed. Magic is a gift from the Goddesses, good or bad, it is desired. Perhaps people are jealous, but they do not like it and if they find out that you have it, they will try to kill you. They'll want what you have."

Clare could not deny him this time, he was right and though she did not want to admit it, she knew this information was true. "Do you notice anything strange," she whispered, "about Prince Julius?" She was contouring his face with a blend of different colors. While she waited for the contour to dry, she painted on his fitted shirt which clung to him so tightly, it was as if a force was pulling the fabric inwards, enhancing each muscle on his chest. Cassius had quickly moved on from the color of her hair to the ocean blue color of her eyes.

"Not really. I don't pay much attention to him considering I don't like him much. Why?" he asked.

"Never mind, I am not sure. May I see your painting progress?" She asked

. He quickly pulled the canvas close to him, the paint dripping a bit. "No. Keep painting."

Clare shrugged and grabbed a small brush so that she could paint his nose. Long and triangular, another perfect feature on his handsome face. She hummed quietly to herself in attempts to fix the silence, but Cassius had already broken it. He was not good at silence.

"Where do you think this magic comes from? It doesn't just come out of nowhere. Why did the Goddesses choose you?"

"I suspect my father had something to do with it. I didn't know him for too long, but it is possible that he was keeping a secret." She had taken another brush out to draw in his well kept, dark eyebrows.

"I remember him vaguely. The Goddesses might have favored him because of his looks. That long wavy brown hair and those bright blue eyes, he was so muscular. A military hero. He is someone to look admire," Cassius said.

Clare laughed, "so you fantasize about my father?"

"No, of course not, I am just rather observant."

She looked up to capture his lips and saw his head tilted to the side in confusion. He moved closer to her and studied her nose, round, small and in his opinion, cute. While he was staring, she caught sight of his lips. His bottom lip was slightly bigger than the top lip, cracked a bit and in desperate need of chapstick. They were so close, she pushed his forehead back a bit with her hands. "You'll see my painting this close," she laughed, her cheeks blushing as she finished his lips and then moved onto his arched eyes. He had long eyelashes that batted as he talked and covered his dark eyes. He scooted back and continued to wave his brush aimlessly around the canvas.

"I can not capture you at all Pax, you are hard to define."

She could tell he was almost finished, but she hadn't even started on his hair. "And you are nosy. Just hang on a while longer while I draw that messy hair of yours." Clare was enjoying herself, she was enjoying time with Cassius, he wasn't so bad after all, at least when he was out of his father's sight. She supposed that this was why they had been close during their childhood, Cassius had still been happy and innocent because his father hadn't ruined him yet.

Cassius finished his painting of Clare and stared at her, she caught his gaze and they locked eyes as she finished painting the strokes of his messy black hair. If she stared too long she would get lost in him, she would lose herself while trying to figure him out. She placed the last few finishing touches on her painting and then smiled up at him. "I am done. Should we reveal our paintings? This was your idea and you seemed to get upset when I wanted to peak early, so please enlighten me on how this should be done."

"We will swap paintings on the count of three. How does that sound?"

"It sounds fine."

"Well then, one." He was thumping his legs against the floor. 'Why was he so nervous?' "Two," she was smiling kindly at him. 'Why was she still giving him a chance?' "Three," they swapped paintings. He carefully took hers and she delicately took his.

While Clare had burst out into laughter, Cassius was in shock, his lips could only mouth the word, 'wow.' Cassius's painting looked as if a five year old made it while playing in the rain. His portrait of Clare looked as if it was melting. Her features were smeared and lopsided, her hair was a mixture of orange, cream and blue which was the result of neglecting the water cup. Clare's painting on the other hand looked professionally done. He looked just as he did in person on the canvas, handsome and stoic. She had almost perfected his features and he was staring at himself with fascination.

"I hope I did not boost your ego that much, you surely lowered mine," she joked. Watching others enjoy her artwork was always a treat, but watching Cassius who was always so picky, grin at his own face, was even sweeter.

"You did boost my ego a bit. I can not hang it up, that would be narcissistic of me, but I will give it to my mum for her room. She will love it." He quickly moved on. "So you had fun?"

"I did," she let out a yawn, her eyes were droopy, she had no idea what the time was, but exhaustion was setting in. "I am also quite tired. How are we going to sleep?"

He set down her canvas and began to pick the paint up off of the floor and move it on top of his dresser. He too was tired, but he didn't want one of them to wake up in the middle of the night and get paint all over the floor, it was a miracle that they hadn't stained the stone already. "Just in the bed. It is large enough for two. I will do my best to stay away from you."

Clare grabbed a book out of her suitcase and set it by the bed in case she couldn't sleep. He left a candle on for her as well and once he was done cleaning, he climbed into the left side of the bed. She climbed into the right and stared up at the ceiling. Her innocence was fleeting. The only people that she had ever shared a bed with were her sister and her parents. She remembered when she couldn't sleep, she would sneak into her parents room. Wade would roll over so she could squeeze in between him and Gracielle. He would put an arm around her and pull her close, he promised to fight off the nightmares and he always did. Sometimes Sage and Clare would have sleepovers. They would spend the evening in one another's rooms, discussing the day's events and their dreams for the future. They would play games until the night turned into day and then they would fall asleep as the sun came up. When Sage had nightmares, she would come into Clare's bed and sleep by her side. Clare often did the same. Neither had to wake the other person up because their presence was enough. Boys had fallen for her when she was a child. She was constantly asked to dance and asked on dates, but she had always turned them all down. She had never shared a bed with anyone romantically. Sure Cassius and her were nowhere near touching, but it was a level of intimacy she had not prepared herself for. She had not kissed anyone and he had slept with many. They were so different.

'No matter how many times they painted would she ever be enough to satisfy him? Would his dim castle fulfill her?'

Her thoughts ceased when he spoke, his voice very low and scruffy. "Goodnight Clare," he said

she blew out the candle in hopes that there would be no need for it and went to sleep.

CASSIUS V.S CLARE

The next morning when Clare woke up, the sky was high up in the sky and Cassius had already left. He had opened the curtains and left a note on the nightstand along with a tray of food. Clare sat up and rubbed the sleepiness out of her eyes. She was glad that he wasn't here to see her, her hair was messy and sticking up in almost every direction. Gazing to the nightstand, she picked up the small note. His handwriting was messy, rushed and loopy. 'Training.' Well that was the Cassius she knew, brief and blunt. She reached over to the side of the bed and picked up the glass of orange juice. She took gentle sips, the tang of the juice helping to wake her up. She was halfway through a muffin when Cisily bursted into the room.

"Clare!" she beamed, shutting the door behind her. The girl had already gotten dressed. Cisily was wearing an emerald green day dress that complimented her skin and her eyes nicely. Cisily plopped herself down on the other side of the bed. "Oh keep eating, I was just wondering how the surprise went. Cassius would like you to come see him train and I was told you wanted me to come! You are so kind! Would you like me to pick out your outfit?"

Clare swallowed another bite of her muffin. "Oh well sure, you can pick it out, you did a good job helping me yesterday."

"They agreed that I could take you out to the city for some shopping later today, would you like to come? Cassius will be tagging along, but not to shop with us, he'll be shopping with Theo. Aunt Adria feels bad that her sister's son, my brother, is alone a lot, so he's coming with us. You can meet him then."

Shopping was right up Clare's ally, she agreed to the suggestion and stuffed another bite of the muffin in her mouth. "Did he bring all of this in here? How long have I been sleeping?"

"I am not sure when he brought it in, I know Cassius begins classes and training quite early in the morning, before the sun comes up. As for you, it is still the morning, do not worry. Do I have permission to search your clothes for an outfit?"

"Yes you do, it wouldn't be the first time." Clare leaned back and finished her food as Cisily went to work. The girl had a lot of energy for the morning, but she did not mind. "Do you have a lover?" Clare asked her as she watched her go through her clothes.

Cisily had chosen Clare's classic white day dress. It was long and would go down to her ankles and flow to the floor behind her. It hugged her snuggly in the chest and had two puffy sleeves. There was a corset type stitching at the waste and lace trimming the bottom of the dress.

"Oh no, I don't have a lover, but this is quite a lovely dress, you should wear this one today."

"It is one of my favorites, you made a good choice," Clare grinned.

Cisily laid the outfit down on the bed and paired it with the plain white flats that Clare had brought. "I don't mean to rush you princess, but we really do not have all day. Though I am sure the longer we take the longer Uncle Erebus will make my cousin train just so that way he can show him off."

Clare took one last sip of her orange juice. When her feet hit the cool floor, she stretched her arms above her head and twisted her torso in attempts to wake herself up. "I will meet you by your quarters in twenty minutes. Will that be alright?" she asked the girl.

"That will be alright, I will pick out some jewelry and gloves for you, you did not seem to pack any." She waved to Clare and then headed out the door, shutting it gently behind her.

Once Clare was alone, she gathered up her clothes and headed over to the mirror. On the counter, she noticed that Cassius had left his brush, cologne and gel scattered about, he must have been in a hurry. She moved his things to the side and brushed out the knots in her hair. Her loose curls began to puff when she brushed them, but she reversed the damage with a hair cream to smooth them back into place. She quickly shed her nightgown and replaced it with the white long day dress. After she made sure that her cheeks were rosy and her eyelashes were curled and darkened, she set her laundry on top of her luggage, slipped on her flats and headed back to Cisily. She only had to knock once.

The door was flung open. The girl took Clare's hands in her own. "White looks so gorgeous on you and so will silver." From her hands dangled a thin silver chain, at the very bottom was a small butterfly charm. She clipped it around Clare's neck and then reached beside her. "Would you like a pair of gloves?"

Clare peered past her and to the window. The sky was fairly sunny and she did not expect it to be cold just yet. "I am alright, thank you."

The two of them took their time as they made their way outside of the castle. Cisily explained that she could not ruin her good outfit by rushing. Clare didn't mind, the stroll through the castle grass was nice and the sun warmed her up. The grass eventually opened up to a grey, large, dome shaped building. She assumed that this was the arena. A pair of guards let them inside. There was a long stretch of dirt, Cassius stood in the middle of the arena, a black hilted sword in his left hand. He had a sparring partner across from him. He was a lengthy boy with not much muscle, his skin was the same shade as Cisily's, his hair was short, curly and well combed.

"Oh my gosh!" Cisily exclaimed, "that is Theo! This should be good, come on." She grabbed Clare's hand and rushed her to a seat in the front row. Clare smoothed out her dress and sat down on one of the black folding chairs. She scanned the arena for Erebus and when the coast was all clear, she sighed in relief.

"From what I heard, I didn't think Theo fight," Clare said.

"He does fight, but he does not like it. He probably filled in, the other boys must have been too busy."

From across the arena both boys stopped their sparring. Theo was panting hard, he had his hands on his knees as he shifted his eyes over to the crowd. "Cis? What are you doing here?" he shouted, setting his sword down on the ground, so that he could fully recover himself.

Cassius was dripping with sweat, but he appeared to be in much better shape. "Clare, you made it." His voice was warm and raspy from how tired he was. "You said you're not much of a fighter huh? I don't believe you. Once I am done with Theo, I would like to see you fight."

Cisily turned to her in shock. "Clare is he seriously asking a lady to fight? If you'd like me to I will go grab my aunt."

"No it is fine," she told the girl, Sage had taught her a thing or two about fighting. "Fine!" Clare shouted.

"I can not believe that you are going to fight in the dirt in your white dress, surely you are something else Clare," Cisily told her.

"You clearly haven't met my sister," she replied. Clare knew that if Sage were here, she would never let Cassius beat her in a fight. She would be cheering her sister on and shouting at the top of her lungs. At the thought of her sister, she frowned. It felt as if they were further apart then a few hours, she sincerely hoped that Sage was doing alright. She let the thought go, she would see her sister soon.

Theo and Cassius commenced their training. Their swords raised in the air and clashed together. Clare was surprised that nobody had gotten hurt. Cassius seemed to show no mercy as he swung fiercely at Theo. Though Theo was not as well trained, he was still swift and agile. Even if he did not care for training, it was clear that he had been forced to endure it. Eventually Cassius had his sword pointed right at Theo's stomach, an attack his cousin couldn't block. Clare could feel an odd sensation bubbling through her, her fingers began to twitch and she shoved them under her leg. Her body was waiting for blood to be spilled, but Cassius stood still and Theo backed away from him. Theo dipped his head in defeat and the two of them shook hands after concealing their weapons. The horrible sensation stopped and Clare snapped back to the present when a voice called out to her, "Come on Clare! Let's see what you've got!"

Clare stood from her seat and moved down to the dirt field. Before she greeted Cassius, she greeted Theo who was heaving for breath. She placed her fingers around his torso and gently straightened him. "You know, in order for the air to flow, you must stand straight," she told him.

"Must I?" he stammered out, as he straightened himself up. He towered over her, he was a few inches taller than Cassius and he hadn't grown into his body. He swayed on his feet as he spoke, "it's nice to finally meet you again Clare, it has been a long time since you have been here."

"It has," she agreed. "It was nice to meet you Theo. Go keep your sister company, I have a man to beat."

Cassius greeted her with an extension of his hand. She gripped his sweaty palm and shook it before pulling away. His hair was almost covering his eyes and she had an urge to fix it, but she didn't, she stood still, staring up at him. "Did you like your breakfast?" he asked her.

"I did, thank you."

"It was nothing," he turned to face the stands. "Will you two go fetch me some water please? I will meet you both afterwards."

Cisily stood up in outrage. "I guess, but how dare you make us miss the fight! I will see you later and I want all of the details."

When the two had cleared the arena and it was just Cassius and Clare, Clare clenched her jaw. "Why did you make them leave?"

"Something in me doubts your magic is just healing." He unsheathed his sword and it around in circles. "Would you like a weapon or would you like to do this without them?"

"Drop the weapon, I am afraid one of us will get hurt if we use them."

"Fair enough." Cassius put his sword away on a rack that held about five other swords. His was by far the most elegant and personalized. A black hilt with a large diamond in the center, the blade long and shiny, the words, 'life or death,' carved into the metal, in cursive.

He held his fists out close to his body. He wore all black while she wore all white, they were two halves to a whole. She held her fists up to her chest. She was unsure of when to attack, but she wanted to be ahead of him, so she settled on swinging first. He quickly dodged her punch, dropping low, before popping back up and striking towards her stomach. She twirled away from him. He got closer and her body began to bubble again. A fighting response building up inside of her, ready to explode. When his fist went to strike her face, an overwhelming sensation took over her and she couldn't fight it off. A glowing bubble of green exploded around her and his punch hit the green magic wall.

He pulled back and yelped, holding his knuckles to his chest, his eyes wide and watery.

She was standing there, fists clenched at her sides, a shield of green glowing bright around her. The shield dropped and she felt dizzy. She was swaying on her feet, her vision blurry, he was saying something to her, but she couldn't hear him. The world faded around her and she collapsed.

He caught her in his arms and lowered her to the ground. His hands underneath her, holding up the fabric so that the back of her dress wouldn't drag against the floor, her head was in his lap. He knew that he couldn't call anyone to help, there was no explanation for this, so he waited. A minute later her eyes opened and she stared up at him. Her face was pale, her lips parted, but no words came out. "We need to find out what this magic inside of you truly is Clare. Maybe defensive magic comes with healing magic," his words were hushed, barely a whisper.

"You bastard, you knew that this might happen," her voice was lighter than normal.

He held her head close to his chest. "I didn't know you would faint. Has this happened before?" he asked as he helped lift her up despite the pain in his knuckles.

"No."

"Can you stand? Can you go again?"

She glared at him, 'what would Sage do?' "Yes I can."

She placed her hands on the floor and used the ground to help get herself up. When she stood the color seemed to rush back into her face, quicker than it would the average person.

He stood up after her, he held his right hand to his chest, his knuckles looked twisted.

"Come here," she said softly.

He did. She let her fingers close over his hand and the green glow returned. She watched his jaw unclench as the magic worked its way to his bones and they restored.

"You are so incredible," he said.

"It's scary, I don't know about incredible. Hand me a sword," she demanded.

"I don't think that giving you a sword is a good idea anymore," he removed his hand from hers quickly. Despite his initial thoughts, something inside of him told him to give her a chance. He grabbed his own sword and impulsively tossed her the sword with a flaming red handle and a sleek short metal blade.

She grabbed it by the hilt and held it close. "I do not like to fight, but I am no innocent girl. Sage has taught me well."

"Right, I forgot about Sage," he joked.

Before she could think to begin, Cassius had brought down his blade and sliced her arm. She let out a howl of pain, dropping her own sword and cursing him. He did not look apologetic, he looked amazed, he stared at the arm that he had cut. The blood was slowly evaporating and the wound had stitched itself up quickly. Her skin was normal. The pain ceased and she glanced down at her arm. "You bastard stop testing me!" she shouted at him.

"I believe that is enough for today anyways. If the Demetrias's were not having some stupid event I would suggest that we leave on our trip now. Your magic is not weak, it is powerful and I don't want it to hurt you or anyone else, but I promise that we are done for today." He put both of their swords back on the display. When he was by her side, he reached out to hold her hand, but she moved away. She was about to lecture him when Cisily and a much more steady Theo, came back holding two glasses of water.

"Well who won?" they asked. Clare had dirt on the bottom of her dress and at the points of her shoes, she was sweating and she was a little bit out of breath, but that had been the extent of her condition. Cassius also looked well, her magic had refreshed him.

Cisily raised an eyebrow, shoving the glasses of water into their hands. "Did you even fight or did you just make out the entire time?"

"Cis!" Theo scolded.

Cassius opened his mouth to speak, but Clare, afraid of what would come out, chimed in, she had gotten good at lying. "We did fight, but both of us were so well skilled, that we decided to call it even. You promised to take us all shopping, so we could not get too sweaty."

Cisily looked as if she wanted to believe her, but was struggling to do so. Cassius confirmed her lie, "she is right. Though I don't necessarily want to go shopping, if I stay here, my father might work me to my death."

"Right, well then let us go shopping."

The shopping trip had gone well. Cisily had paid for the trip with her mother's money since Clare's currency did not work in Excidium. They had left the main city with many shopping bags. Clare piled her bags into the carriage, she had been focused on arranging them neatly, when she felt a hand on her waist. She turned around to glare at whoever it was, but when she saw Cassius, she relaxed. 'This was unlike him.' She glanced past him to see that his people were lining the streets and chanting, she now understood. They were ecstatic to see her, of course the people had been informed of their partnership. She moved closer to Cassius and waved at his people. The clouds had started to move in and a breeze swept through the warm air. Though it was currently windy, Excidium would be the last kingdom to achieve the true climate of fall, the desert stayed warm for a few months longer. Deus changed with the normal seasons and Pax et Lux got cold quite fast.

Cisily distributed bread and water that she had bought from the bakery across the street, while Theo helped pass out the slices of strawberry tart that Cisily had bought. Clare understood the art of good publicity, she took Cassius's hand and moved with him towards the crowd. "Mama, look she is so pretty!" one of the little girls shouted as Clare approached them. "We have never seen the princesses up close! Where is your sister?" the girl's mother asked.

Clare's lips were curled into a gentle smile. "My sister is taking care of the duties at home while I visit my fiancé."

"Do you love her Prince Cassius?" another girl from the crowd asked.

Cassius grinned and shook his head in disapproval. "Our relationship has only just begun." His hand tightened around Clare's. "And there is so much more for us to discover."

THE WORLD'S TEST

The days that led up to the event were some of the hardest days of Sage's life. She had not felt this empty since losing her father. She could not remember the last time that she and Clare were apart for more than a night. She knew that she had to get used to it, considering her sister had a journey to begin, but this was not easy for her to accept. She spent the nights in Clare's room, sleeping in her bed as if she was a child in need of comfort. She would occasionally stare at her paintings in hopes to feel connected to her. "You are so far, I hope that they are treating you well, if not I will rip Cassius's head off the next time that I see him," she said to Clare's wall once. Phoebe would come to clean up Clare's room and Esmeralda would check in on Sage.

"Are you still reading? How far have you gotten?" Esmeralda would ask.

It was the day before the event the Demetrias's were going to hold. Sage had done nothing but read, train, eat and sleep. Esmeralda walked into the grand dining room to see Sage slouched over on top of her book, drooling, her soup completely abandoned. With a sigh, the girl sat down in the chair next to her and gently tapped her shoulder. Sage didn't budge, so she tapped harder. The girl shot up from her sleep and wiped the drool from her mouth. "Huh is it time to leave"? Did I forget to pack?"

"No," Esmeralda said as she messed with the end of her long braid. "You must pack today, but you leave tomorrow morning. It is mid afternoon. How is the reading coming along? Your mother wanted you to be done soon." She passed her a napkin and Sage wiped the rest of the sticky spit off her face. She pushed her now cold soup back in front of herself and forced it down her throat. "Well," she said between spoonfuls. "I am on my last book. I have am trying to retain as much information as I possibly can, but these damn books are filled with information. I can't possibly remember all of it. I can only hope that mum doesn't quiz me just yet."

"Well I did hear she was going to give you a test," Esmeralda said honestly. She took a look at the book titled, *"A History of War,"* and then pushed it back to her. "Well at least this one seems interesting. I suggest that you finish it up so we can pack together."

"Our packing will have to wait until I finish this book and do my outside training. I'm only staying the night so it shouldn't take long. You know what, you can go ahead and pack an outfit or two for me and pack a few more for Clare. I don't really need to be involved, I trust your judgement."

"Why am I packing a few more outfits for Clare?"

"Oh, well she might want something new and fresh to wear, just ask Phoebe to help you pick something out."

Esmeralda's face went hot and a mild blush spread across her cheeks. If Sage or Clare had blushed, it would have been noticeable, but Esmeralda's complexion had hid it well. "Right, Phoebe," she whispered.

Sage shut the book and put down her spoon. She leaned in close to talk to the girl. "Did Phoebe do something to you?"

"Oh no. I quite enjoy Phoebe's company."

Sage smirked and folded her arms folded against her chest. Though she was tired, this situation gave her energy, there was finally something amusing taking place at the palace. "You enjoy her company huh, how so?"

"The same way that you enjoy Prince Julius's company." She hid her face in the bright red scarf that she was wearing.

Sage gently bumped her arm with her knuckles, a friendly gesture. "I see, I see. Well I am happy for you Alda. Have you kissed her?"

"Last night I kissed her. She is quite gorgeous, I am glad that you support us. Do you think your mother would mind if the servants dated?"

"If I pass this test my mum will not mind anything. But in all seriousness, no, she will not mind," Sage said. "Go see Phoebe and pack please, I will see you shortly."

"Yes, see you shortly!" Esmeralda exclaimed as she dashed out of the room, leaving Sage alone with her book.

Sage hated reading. As she continued to turn the pages of the book, she gradually lost interest. The farther she read the more of her day was wasted. She was trapped in another world that made no sense to her and the only way she could escape was by shutting the book. And she would have shut the book in a heartbeat if her mother wasn't waiting inside of the war room, waiting for her to declare that she had finally finished something that didn't involve swinging her sword furiously in the air. Another hour of sitting in the chair and she finished, she finished that damn stack of books. She left the copy of the book she was currently reading on the table and dashed out of the dining room. The door to the war room was already wide open, her mother was thumbing through about a hundred documents, her thin framed reading glasses were tilted against her nose. She didn't have to look up to know that her daughter was there.

"I was waiting for you to tell me that you had finished reading," she said. "Sit down, so we can discuss what you've read. Then you can go do whatever you do with that sword of yours all day."

Sage sat down across from her mother, her fingers anxiously tapping against the desk. "Well I did finish them all. I didn't think I had it in me, but I knew Clare would have been able to finish them and once I realized this, I knew that I could do it too."

"You girls amaze me, it's always what would the other person do, not what you yourself would do," Gracielle said.

"We look up to one another and I trust Clare more than I trust myself."

"I admire that," Gracielle said honestly. She reached into her drawer and pulled out three pieces of parchment. She paired the paper with a quill and then pushed the materials across to Sage. "Well here is your test. I have had this prepared for a while. I didn't know when to start training you. You are physically fit, but a queen must be more than that. She must know more about her kingdom than anyone else and she must have proper etiquette. Oh and Sage please remember for future reference, our kingdom doesn't send those important to the political system into battle. You could always break that rule, but I would rather you not," she said as she cleared her throat.

"Well go ahead. I'll leave you be so you can fill out your test," the queen said. Sage stared down at the page, her heart beating fast. 'How could she possibly remember everything that she had read?' She picked up the quill, dipped it ink and then gestured to her mother. "Do you think you could give me a bit of space please? I can't think when you're hovering over me."

Gracielle stood. She brushed against her daughter's shoulders on the way out of the room and gave them a tap for good luck.

Sage was left alone, with a test. She would complete every single question, even if it meant making up the answer. Everyone doubted her. Everywhere she went there was talk about her younger sister. 'It's a shame Clare isn't the next queen, she's much more fit to hold the throne. Clare would do well even at a young age. She'd have her older sister as an advisor. Sage is a good princess at best, nothing more.' The conversations that she had heard throughout the years encouraged her to keep pushing forward. She would pass this test. If she concentrated hard enough then she could remember everything she had read, even when she was exhausted.

It took forty minutes for her to finish the short answer questions. When she was finished she called her mother back in the room. Gracielle sat down in the seat across from her. She was smirking at the exasperated expression on her daughter's face. "You remind me of myself sometimes. Hand over the test and let us see what you've got." She took the test pages from Sage's hand and set them down on the table. Just as Sage had feared, her mother started to read the questions aloud.

"How was our kingdom founded? Your answer was correct. Our kingdom was founded by the great Serenity Pax, one of your distant relatives. In our kingdom the woman keeps her last name and the kids take her last name. That is how it got down to me and you. Your father is no Pax, but I loved and do love him dearly."

She moved her thumb down the page to keep reading. "On what beliefs was our kingdom founded? You said, on the foundation of peace and you were correct again. As the last kingdom founded in Europe, we hoped to keep peace between the Demetrias and Antias family."

"Which brings us to our next question. State the notable European wars. You listed the war between three kingdoms and the war between wolf and vulture. You were correct."

Gracielle continued this process until she had read through and discussed each individual question with Sage. They discussed foreign affairs and how emigration and immigration were the only main issues that the continents had to work together to solve and how the continents have never gone to war with one another and do not plan on doing so. They also discussed what to do in case of emergency and what would happen if there was no one blood related to take the throne.

When they had finished discussing, Sage had only missed three questions and her mother was quite proud of her progress. "If I would have handed you this test before you read, you would have failed it no question. Is that correct?

"It is."

"Now you will be able to speak upon matters confidently tomorrow. You know what our kingdom values and what our citizens want and need, but I still have to teach you etiquette. You can not keep stirring the pot at the dinner table. Someone is going to strike you out of anger some day. You must keep yourself calm and bite your tongue. Those silly comments in your head do not need to be said aloud. Go ahead and have some time with your precious sword, I will see you at dinner and there I will teach you proper etiquette."

Sage stood up, a prideful smile just barely gracing her lips. "Mum?" She caught Gracielle peering up at her out of curiosity. "My sword's name is Amicus," she told her.

Her mother replied back to her with the word, 'companion.' "At this point, I am surprised you did not name it Clare."

"I thought about it, but Clare would never hurt someone intentionally." She bit her lip to keep herself from spilling any of her sister's secrets and then made her way out to the back of the palace. With Amicus by her side, she felt powerful. Her mother didn't carry a sword on her dresses, but when Sage became queen she would. True happiness and relief only came when both Clare and Amicus were as close to her as possible. When she swung and hit her targets, she was told not to think about people, but thinking about people was the only way that she could swing accurately. She didn't like Cassius, mostly out of jealousy and only a little bit out of rationality. She also didn't like his father, King Erebus, for obvious reasons, so when she swung, she swung thinking of them. The dummies leaked stuffing and hay. She hit them over and over until her arms grew tired. Eventually she had severed their heads and there was nothing left to hit. If she killed her dummies, then she would never be tempted to kill someone real, someone human. She felt bad for the servants who had to keep making her targets. The more they made the quicker they went. When she saw more were available, she increased her training. Sage thought about going inside to see if she could grab another one, but she remembered that her mother was going to be waiting for her. She sheathed Amicus and made her way inside of the cool hall. She nodded at the guard on her way inside, wiping the sweat off of her brown as she walked. There was no time to bathe, she would have to face her mother like this. Brown cargo pants, an olive green tank top that was soaked with sweat and brown boots covered in dust and filth. Even her face was dirty. She had a habit of touching things and then proceeding to touch her face.

Upon her entrance to the hall, Gracielle sighed. "For future reference, a lady does not show up to dinner like this."
Sage began to unwrap the white cloth on her left wrist. She had injured it the other day and while she practiced and now she was required by Gracielle to wear the tight cloth when training to keep everything in place and 'prevent further injury.' She didn't dare to roll her eyes, but she was desperately resisting the urge. After she dropped the wrap into the trash bin, she joined her mother on the other side of the table.

"What? A lady does not show up to dinner both late and covered in sweat? How odd." She was about to sit herself down, but her mother grabbed her good wrist.

"As the queen you must gesture for everyone else present to sit down, once they are all seated, then you sit. For tonight you are the queen, so go ahead."

Sage raised an eyebrow looking at her as if she were mad, she then shrugged her shoulders and lazily waved her hand up and then down.

Gracielle sat and then Sage sat promptly afterwards. "Next time move your hand with grace. Not so lazy and quick."

Sage took a deep breath. Preparing to be a queen was a lot of work, she could hardly imagine what it would be like to take over the position entirely. Clare was already so graceful, she wondered how her mother allowed her oldest daughter to be this 'rude' for so long. Gracielle gestured to the knives and forks beside her plate. "You know this well, but a reminder. The big fork is for your main course, the little fork is for your appetizer. The big spoon is for soup and the little spoon is for dessert. The big knife is for meat and the smaller knife is for your butter. Make sure to keep your napkin on your lap.

You hold the fork in your right and you hold the knife with your left, no elbows on the table, but keep your hands visible at all times."

As she looked down at the food in front of her, a cut of meat with some vegetables, Sage delicately cut her steak with the big knife and used the big fork to take a bite of the broccoli. If she had been on her own, she would have tried to eat the steak with her hands, but that was only when no one was watching.

"Now what sort of conversations do you think are appropriate at the dinner table? Not the ones you like to make, but the actual conversations you should be having," Gracielle asked.

Sage spoke between chewing a mouthful of steak, "I don't know, politics and pleasantries."

"Yes, subtle politics, nothing that will get anyone heated, the state of the kingdom, what the weather is like, the little aspects of your day, speak of nothing that will get emotions high. Chew with your mouth closed please."

Sage sighed and swallowed the bite in her mouth. "Seems rather dull, but alright. What else is there to learn?"

"You are the queen, you are allowed to interrupt if you please. Others still find it rude, but you are allowed to do it. You always offer and have dessert ready for your guests. Even if they say no, you must bring it out anyways. No talk of sex at the table. Though I doubt you would do that, it is a rule to keep in mind when you are in a formal setting. Other than that, smile, look happy and enjoy your meal respectfully."

The rest of dinner Sage had to practice what her mother had taught her. They talked about the music that they fancied and the changing weather outside. It was a nice change of pace, but something she didn't wish to do often. When they had finished the lemon tart, Gracielle dismissed her daughter up to bed. "Go make sure Esmeralda took care of all your things, we leave early tomorrow. Do not stay up too late, tomorrow will be a busy day and you will want to make a good impression. Bags under your eyes won't impress anyone."

Sage waved goodbye to her mother and then headed up the staircase. At the top of stairs and around the corner, she saw Esmeralda and Phoebe holding hands. The two of them were whispering, their faces touching. Sage didn't wish to ruin their moment, so she waited until they went their separate ways to continue. Esmeralda turned the corner to see Sage, her dark brown eyes wide. "Oh, Sage! Don't worry I have packed all of your things, you are not behind schedule, in fact you are ahead. I drew you a bath with eucalyptus and laid out your clothes. Earlier I made conchas, I know you might have had dessert, but have another one, you deserve it."

Sage grinned at her, "I will have another dessert, thank you, go along for the night. If my things are already packed, then you have a free evening to yourself." Normally Esmeralda might have protested because she wanted to spend more time with her, but Sage could tell that other plans had been made.

"I will see you in the morning!" Esmeralda said happily, she grabbed the bottom of her flat, long cream dress and then took off in a sprint.

Like Esmeralda had promised, the bath was set. The water was cool and refreshing against her skin. Of course she was glad to be able to spend time with Julius tomorrow, she always was happy to see him, but she was more happy to see her sister. She needed to see her, she needed the reassurance that she was alright, that she wasn't bruised and that she didn't have markings along her skin Sage hoped that tomorrow Clare would look relatively happy with Cassius and not miserably upset. If Clare was going to run off with Cassius in an attempt to find out where her magic came from, Sage needed to be sure that he was of no true threat. She also wanted to study Antoine. Though Clare had taken a liking to him, she wanted to see for herself. 'Would her sister and Antoine meet again?' If they did, it certainly would not be good. Their appearance together would create a large danger for Antoine and a reasonable amount of trouble for Clare as well. Sage hoped that there would be downtime at the event to talk because she had so much to tell her sister. Such as how many books she had read and how incredibly boring they all were, along with the fact that Phoebe and Esmeralda were now either hooking up or dating. It would all have to wait until tomorrow. Sage sunk her head below the water and focused on the soft flow of the bubbles instead of the weight of the world crashing down on her.

THE ARENA

Clare had spent the past weeks navigating a maze of emotions. While Cassius was off training, her and Cisily would spend most of their mornings and afternoons together. Cisily had been fond of taking her out to the city to shop and it had gotten rather tiring. Whenever they were out in public, Cisily usually picked out a dress so large that Clare could not see her feet. The guards would follow them as they walked the streets. Her prior perceptions of the city had been debunked. She thought the people were unhappy, suffering, drowning in a pool of no color, their lives bleak and bland, but she was wrong, those who were in the middle class seemed happy. The conditions in the poorest areas of the three kingdoms had gone down recently, it was not just Excidium. Cisily had made sure to pass out food at the end of each outing and Clare had done the same. By the time that Clare and Cassius would have to leave for the event, the people would fall in love with Clare. It was a feeling that she had been used to at home, but was surprised to receive inside of Excidium. She wondered how Sage would have been perceived by these people. 'Oh Sage. How was her sister doing?' Hopefully well, but if not she would see her soon. When the two girls would arrive back at the castle, Clare would change out of her large dress and then sit on Cisily's bed. During their time together, she taught the girl how to paint. It might have been an excuse to finally paint something for Antoine, but Cisily had gotten a good amount of fun out of it.

Clare objected at first because the girl might get paint on her white covers, but Cisily insisted they paint there anyways. Clare taught her the different brush strokes and how to blend her paint, then they set off to make their own designs. While Cisily had painted what appeared to be a dog, Clare drew the stables and the horses that she and Antoine had taken care of when they met. Clare had finished around the same time as Cisily and Clare's was far more put together. Though their skill level was quite different, they enjoyed painting together.

Then after she spent time with Cisily, she had a few minutes of alone time before Cassius burst into the door, his hair sweaty, his clothes soaked. He would always greet her with a hello and bring her a snack before heading to the bath without another word. Her evenings were spent with him. They would walk the gardens, mostly in silence, a few words about their day here and there. He would then accompany her to the library where she read and he pretended to. Dinners were reserved for time with the queen and the king. Every day King Erebus had more questions that she had to answer. Cassius was often chatty at the dinner table. He seemed to ignore his father whenever he could and strike up a conversation with his mother. After dinner, they would retire to his bedroom. There were no more cute dates. Cassius would fill out documents that he would not let her see while she would read and then they would fall asleep on opposite sides of the bed. Thankfully in the mornings they remained separated. Every now and then something out of the usual would happen, Cassius would become over protective of her or the green glow would spark from her fingertips. Her magic was so uncontrollable that he now made her wear gloves when he was not there to hold her hand. They avoided the topic of magic in public and limited it to the bedroom where he would theorize and she would quietly hush him, explaining that soon their entire life would revolve around magic, so why not take a break from it.

As Cassius had promised, Clare had a day at the spa a few days before their departure to Deus. He took a day off from the spa to join her. The two of them woke up early that day and headed to the part of the castle where the spa was located. A woman greeted them at the door and guided them to separate rooms. There she instructed them to strip of everything but their undergarments. She gave them a robe to cover their bodies. The two of them rejoined in the middle of the spa, Cassius hesitantly eyeing Clare. Though one might assume a prince would keep pampered and have the occasional spa day, Cassius did not. His father thought it was too girly of an activity for his son to partake in. Secretly Cassius had always wanted to go, but he was still nervous, he had never done something so relaxing, so freeing.

"It'll be alright," Clare told him as she followed him into the room with the two massage tables.

The massages lasted sixty minutes. The two of them talked occasionally, but they mostly enjoyed one another's silent company as they laid face down on the cushioned tables. Then they had gotten facials and finally, they relaxed in the sauna with their robes still on.

" I'm glad you kept your promise, I needed something like this," Clare said honestly as she leaned against the hot wood.

He was admiring her from a few feet away, his fingers running over the space next to him. "Yeah, I'm glad I could keep my promise to you. I needed this too, I'm sure you could sense that. You seem to be pretty good at reading my emotions whether I want you to or not."

"Sadly I do know that you are more than the stoic prince you try to be perceived as," she said.

"Whatever," he grumbled. "I'm just glad we can get along with one another. I'd hate to end up like my parents. One day I want to love you, I don't just want to tolerate you." He slowly inched closer to her and when she didn't move away, he relaxed by her side. Close company, the two of them could manage this. Of course they slept close in their sleep, but that was a necessity, it wasn't necessarily a choice. This was different. To sit close willingly, was a step in the right direction. While Clare still thought of Antoine day and night, her dreams filled with the image of his blonde hair and spectacles, Cassius was only thinking of the girl beside him.

"Yeah, I'm glad we get along too," she smiled at him. Her hands folded in her lap and she closed her eyes to savor the one of the few last normal moments of her life.

The morning finally came to leave for Deus and they left the castle before the sun came up. King Maximus would be awaiting the arrival of both Excidium and Pax et Lux before noon. Clare woke up that morning anxious to see her sister and Antoine's sweet face. She packed up all of her belongings including her new paintings and a brand new handbag. She handed her things over to the servant who trudged her bags down the stairs, and then she got ready for the day. She had chosen a royal blue dress for the occasion. The colors of the Demetrias family were ruby red and a midnight royal blue with the wolf as their symbol, it was only appropriate to fit in.

Cassius handed her a pair of gloves to match, she slipped them on and helped him straighten his tie. He had been wearing a red suit jacket with a black tie to match his dark hair that was gelled into a comb over. His boots were the same dark shade as his hair and his sword was clipped onto the leather black belt that was resting on top of his silk red trousers.   Clare took his hand. "I can not believe that after tonight I am basically running away with you," Cassius said.

"It is quite bonkers, but at least we finally know where to start our journey," Clare mused, but she quickly changed the subject.   "What does Excidium do when all of the royal family leaves at once? We personally keep our flag raised so it appears as if we are still there and then we increase the guards. Incase of emergency, my mother's advisor takes over."

"Same here, that is the basic foundation of running a country in Europe. Did you eat breakfast or should I grab you something to eat before we leave?"

"I ate," she said shortly. Her eyes rolled in response to the way that he talked to her. Just because he was a man did not mean he knew everything and it did not mean he had to make her feel stupid. It was simply one question that she didn't know the answer to.

"Good, come along then," he said as he led her out to the carriages. Clare hugged Cisily and Theo goodbye and then joined Cassius in the first carriage. It was just the two of them.

Clare leaned her head back against the plush, velvet, black cushion. She moved her long hair out of her face and sighed. "What is it?" Cassius asked. He was sitting criss cross in his seat to avoid the fluff of her dress.

She looked over to him, her eyes half closed. "I am not in the mood to interact with anyone today. I am drained. I would like to see Sage, but I don't need two sets of mothers watching me with prying eyes."

Cassius scoffed, "prying please, I am sure they will be too busy watching the fights and won't pay too much attention to you. If anything you can sit between your sister and I and say nothing. I am rather good at talking for you remember?" he joked.

"My sister will not want to sit next to you," she said honestly. "Plus I have business to take care of."

"You do? What sort of business awaits you? Surely not another suitor? Should I keep you close today?"

Clare felt her heart sink. "No," she choked out, "Sage and I just need to take care of some things together, that is all. Now are you going to let me nap on the ride there or are you going to chat my ear off?" She watched his smile falter, he looked like a hurt puppy and though he annoyed her at times, she felt bad. She placed a hand on his leg.

"Sorry."

"It's alright. Sleep and I will wake you when we get there."

The carriage arrived hours later. Clare did not need Cassius to wake her. She had woken up half way through the ride and he was the one sleeping now. She decided to sketch him on her notepad. When the ink dried she shoved the picture of sleepy Cassius away and decided she wouldn't tell him about the doodle. The carriage jolted to a halt outside of the large castle. The Deus castle was built out of a sandy brown stone and had lots of towers. The stone was adorned with gold along the exterior and a large flag that was half red and half blue with a wolf head in the middle, flew from the tallest of the many castle towers. Clare noticed that the white carriages from her home had already arrived. She watched as Cassius's eyes fluttered open but she didn't bother to wait for his hand. She rudely ignored him and leapt out of the carriage. Her sister was facing the other direction, but she bounded for her. Upon hearing her distinct footsteps, Sage whirled around and embraced her sister in the tightest hug that she could give. Sage had been wearing a long olive green dress, but it was simple and nowhere near as big as Clare's. She held her sister close and examined her skin, once she was deemed okay, she spoke. "What is up with the ball gown and gloves?"

"It is their way of dressing and well I'm sure you can predict the reason for the gloves. I've missed you Sage."

"I have missed you too," Sage said as she peered her head around Clare's shoulder and saw Cassius sauntering towards them, his hands in his pockets.

"You act as if I have killed her Sage," he called out.
"Anything is possible. Now don't talk to me," she replied.

Gracielle appeared behind the two girls and wrapped her arms around their shoulders. Gracielle grinned at Cassius. "Sage has learned so much recently, she will be kind to you."

"I will?" Sage asked in shock.

"She will?" Cassius echoed in confusion.

"She has?" Clare asked.

Sage grabbed her sister's hands when Gracielle let them go and walked away. "When we have a moment, I will tell you everything. Mum worked me like a dog while you were away and Phoebe and

Esmeralda kissed," she giggled as they walked up the steps of the castle.

King Maximus stood at the front entrance. He was serene and god like, Clare could have sworn she saw Oralee herself in him, but it couldn't be. As someone who harnessed magic, she felt connected to the goddesses and when she was around Julius she felt a deep tug, when she was around Maximus she felt a godly shimmer. If only it were an appropriate matter to bring up, then she could express to them how she felt. She had a feeling that maybe she was not the only one with a secret. Maximus's ginger hair was gelled to perfection. His eyes were dusted with gold eyeshadow, his lashes painted and elongated. He was wearing gold jewelry that decorated his neck and his wrists. His suit was that same gold and she was sure it was almost all real. He was wearing rose red trousers. There was no weapon clipped to his belt, but on his head there was a large glittering gold leaf crown.

While she wore flowers like her sister, Cassius wore spikes and the Demetrias's wore leaves.

On Maximus's arm was a man in his twenties who was groomed well, smiling and leaning onto the king of Deus's shoulder. Julius stood next to his brother and waved to Sage. But after he waved to Sage, Clare and Julius caught eyes.

Instead of looking away, Clare caught herself staring. It was as if a magnetic force was keeping their eyes locked on one another. 'What the hell was going on?' Both of their eyes were wide, unblinking, struggling to pull away.

Sage had pulled her sister's arm, she staggered on her heels and her eye contact broke. "Clare are you alright?" Sage whispered. Julius looked dazed himself, he had to turn around to rub his eyes before standing at attention once more. Clare rubbed her own.

"I'm fine. There is something strange going on here, but I can not figure it out."

"I feel nothing. I don't feel any danger. Everything is okay, you may just need to eat more," Sage explained.

Clare had drowned out half of his words, but Maximus had explained what was going to happen today. They were all going to travel to the grand arena and there they would sit in the booths and watch fights between people and animals, then they would feast back at the castle for dinner. The group turned around right where they stood to get back into their carriages. Their luggages had been taken inside of the castle. "I am going to ride with my sister, I will see you there," Clare told Cassius, quickly running off so he would not be able to stop her. As soon as the two climbed into the white carriage, Sage slammed the door shut and they squealed. "So, tell me all about what mum put you through," Clare said as she leaned back against the cushions. She took off the gloves and let her fingers run against the soft fabric that she knew so well.

Sage rolled her eyes "She made me read more books then I have read in months. Five books to be exact and then she made me take a test on all of the material. I did pass in flying colors and I was quite shocked. Then she sat me down at the dinner table and scolded me for creating drama and told me how to act properly. She is rather boring in that sense, but I did get a good meal out of all this. She expects me to talk like a queen and impress the others today. Though I may have already disappointed her as I ran off with you squealing like a little girl. But how was your time with Cassius and how is our plan going? I wanted to write to you more, but I was afraid that any letter I sent would be read before it was handed to you. Erebus would like to see me ten feet underground, so I wouldn't put it past him to use information against me."

Clare sighed, she leaned forward. "Erebus would like to see me ten feet under ground as well. He interrogates me at every dinner, I don't know if it will ever stop. I am proud of you Sage. I don't care if everyone doubts you, I have always had faith in you, in fact I think you would make a better queen than I would."

"What?" Sage seemed shocked.

"It is true, you can fight well and you are more than willing to say what is on your mind even if it is a bit offensive. Sure I have poise and grace and a bit of sass, but you would be a passionate leader. You are fearless, you are bold and you were born for the spotlight." Clare could tell that her sister was speechless, she was frozen still, so Clare kept talking. "I'll stop attacking you with compliments and change the subject. Cassius is confusing. Sometimes he is mean to me and sometimes he is nice to me, it's as if he is flipping a switch. His cousins Cisily and Theo are nice. His mother is kind, but you know Erebus is a nightmare. They are going to let Cassius leave with me tomorrow. Oh and we also had an incident with my magic."

"An incident? Clare please tell me nobody saw you." Sage was suddenly able to speak again.

"No, I do not think so, all the guards were outside, his cousins were gone. I was able to do something else besides heal. Defensive magic. I created a shield. Cassius is worried about what I can do and though I do not trust him fully, I trust him not to hurt me. However I do not trust him to keep his mouth shut, which is why he must come with me. Oh and a cut from a sword healed on my arm within seconds."

"Why did you get cut by a sword?"

"Cassius did it, but do not worry, it was just a test."

"A test that could have failed and could have broken our kingdom's heart. He was reckless, I should cut his dick off."

"Well I'm not sure you have to do that," Clare replied.

They did not have time to discuss much else in the carriage. The arena was only a few minutes away from the castle itself. Citizens wearing their family colors and symbols packed the streets. It was a big day, it was not everyday all three families came together to watch people and animals fight to the death. Some citizens had been privileged enough to buy a seat in the large arena. Of course they would be rows beneath the royalty, but they would be honored to be in the same open space as them, enjoying the same festivities. Both Clare and Sage shared a breath before they made their way out of the carriage.

The switch happened fast on the side of the carriages unseen to the public. Maximus led the way, the gorgeous man still attached to his hip. Behind him, Julius and Sage. Then Gracielle, accompanied by a handsome guard so that she would not be left alone. Behind her Adria and Erebus and then finally Cassius and Clare, who were hardly in front of the servants.

"So they think we are the scum of the lot hmm?" Cassius said.

Clare looked back, sure enough she had locked eyes with Antoine. Their gaze was strong for a moment, before she forced herself to look away. She took Cassius's arm in order not to seem suspicious.

"I doubt that is what they think, though the Demetrias twins don't seem to like you very much."

"You seem to find them odd yourself, I saw the way you were looking at them Clare, what is it?"

"Honestly I don't know, but you need to smile," she told him. When they stopped talking, a soft and kind grin spread across Clare's lips. The citizens cleared a path for them to get through. Cassius had put on one of those smug and tight grins. Though Clare could tell it was fake, from afar it looked real.

The games had not started yet, no one would dare to begin the show before the king arrived. Suddenly Clare grew uneasy as she began to remember what this event would entail. "There will be blood," she was talking under her breath, but Cassius was so close that he could hear her.

"Right," he said, he hadn't thought about that, he checked to make sure that her gloves were on and they were. Leaving the event would be rude if they had no excuse, but he could not imagine what might happen if somebody died and Clare were there to watch. 'Surely she could not revive the dead, that was dark magic right?' "Try and control yourself and if you can not, then I will think of an excuse to make sure we can get you out of here," Cassius said.

"Alright," she told him.

The booth was not big enough for all of them so they had to take two. Julius, Sage, Cassius and Clare were in one booth with Antoine as their servant and Erebus, Adria, Gracielle, Maximus and his man were in another. Sage was partially relieved because she would no longer have to impress her mother, but she would be sure to stay formal and try to integrate politics into the conversation if she could because Gracielle always seemed to be watching. Clare on the other hand was horrified. She would have to navigate her way between Cassius and Antoine all while trying not to lose control and attempting to figure out the mystery that was Julius. Antoine and Julius exchanged an acknowledging glance upon their arrival to the box. Though Clare wanted to sit with her sister it was frowned upon and they were encouraged to stay seated with their partners. Clare and Cassius took the seats to the left and Julius and Sage took the seats to the right. In the middle there was a gold table.

Antoine was dressed in all white, holding a platter of food, standing awkwardly at the back of the booth.

"So," Julius started as they waited for the 'fun' to begin. "Do you feel more acquainted?" he asked Cassius and Clare.

Cassius spoke first, "yes," he said bluntly. Clare shrugged, he wasn't wrong, she did feel closer to him.

Clare was burning up in her gloves. There was hardly a breeze and it was clear she was sweating, even in the booth's cool shade.

"Antoine, would you mind taking her gloves. I do not want her to be uncomfortable, it's hot," Julius said, smiling innocently at Clare.

She could not tell if he knew or if he was being genuine. It would have been odd to object. She felt her face go hot as Antoine kneeled to the ground.

He looked up at her, his shiny white was hair glistening, his pearly white teeth were glimmering.

Cassius tensed as he watched Antoine pull her gloves off with ease and precision.

Antoine did not say anything to her, he just neatly folded her gloves and set them aside. He ignored anything between them and darted back to his spot.

Once the royals were comfortable in their seats, the event quickly commenced. The first man to enter the arena was large and tall with lots of muscle, he was decked out in solid black armor. There was the crest of a moon on the front of his chest plate and he held a black sword in his hands. "He is fighting for the Goddess Mallory of South America. She is the Goddess of their continent and the Goddess of the moon and death, my family worships her," Cassius said as he leaned forward to get a closer look at the man down below. His hands were on his chin, he was eager, practically bouncing in his seat when they released the tiger.

Sage looked over to him in disgust. Most people worshiped the Goddess of their continent, most people in Europe worshipped Oralee, the goddess of Europe, light and happiness. But people worshipped the Goddesses for different reasons. In Sage's mind, she figured that the Antias family was fond of the moon or death and it was not hard to figure out which one considering their history in murder. But what Sage was unaware of was that his family had descended from South America and that was why they worshiped Mallory.

Clare noticed Julius tense up, his eyes filled with tears. Her fiancé was excited about the Goddess of death even though Julius's parents had been murdered in front of him. She elbowed Cassius in the gut and he groaned, glaring at her in annoyance. But it had worked, he hushed himself. Sage on the other hand kept talking through the fight to sooth Julius. "Well, I do not like Mallory very much, but I have always liked Visola, as she brings good health and Africa is a very beautiful continent after all, or so I have heard, I have never had the good fortune of going."

The fight was quick, the man must have been well experienced. The people sighed at how fast the battle was over. The man had sliced the tiger with his sword. The animal's head rolled off of its body and landed several feet away. A group of people came to collect the tiger and bring in the next competitor. Clare could not comprehend what had just happened or how quickly he had managed to kill. Her hands were itching and her brain was clouded. She felt heat spread through her fingertips and she shoved them quickly under her dress. Cassius stood in recognition and extended his arm out to her. "What?" she murmured, her voice was hot. She could feel Sage's stare and she could feel Julius's energy growing brighter than before. She wanted to yell out loud and scream because of the overload of emotions. Cassius had distracted her by pulling her up by her feet.

"We are going to dance."

"Now? Surely that can't be appropriate."

"Yes dance, it's good publicity," but that was not his true intention. He pulled her into position and grabbed her hands as tightly as he could, the instant harsh sensation, washed away the prickling rush in her fingertips. Her eyes refused to look at the tiger and Julius must have calmed himself down as well, as his presence faded in her mind. She breathed Cassius in deeply, the smell of cologne was comforting and soothing. His hands entirely covered hers and though he could feel a weakening beam of her magic, he showed no signs of shock. He twirled her around and then dipped her low to the floor.

People were cheering, not for the fight, but for them.

King Erebus and Queen Adria were smiling just as bright as the citizens down below, but Cassius wasn't doing this for his parents, he was doing it for Clare. He sat her back down when the clapping began to slow and she felt much more calm.

Julius who could not dance for the life of him groaned, "nice job showing off."

"What can I do? I love the attention," Cassius shrugged. He gave her hand one last squeeze before letting go and relaxing back into his chair.

'How much more blood was going to spill today?' If the fights got worse, Clare and Cassius would have to leave the event, which would damage their public image. Clare assumed that Cassius thrived in situations like these, his home life must have been tense when she was not there, a chaotic space must have been what he was used to. Both Maximus and Julius had witnessed murders and neither seemed to be enjoying the event for its intended purposes. Maximus hadn't been watching the games, he was making out with his date right in front of Erebus just to piss him off. Clare doubted he radiated the same tense energy as Julius. She could not navigate her sister like she could the Demetrias twins and she was not sure why.

When the tiger was cleaned out from the arena, another fighter took its place. 'No,' Clare thought. She immediately stood up, her eyes squinting. The fighter wore the armor of the Goddess of North America, Olive. A bronze armor, shiny and engraved with the symbol of a leaf. Clare knew she would not be able to control herself if human blood was shed.

Cassius was gazing at her from the corner of his eye, he knew he had to get her out of there. "Sit down," he commanded and she did. He looked back to Antoine, hardly acknowledging his human presence, but beckoning him forward as a servant. "A glass of water please. Clare is faint."

Clare caught Sage's eyes, sparkling with concern.

Antoine had hid the blush on his face with his sleeve as he handed her a glass of water and then dipped away.

If she wasn't so nervous she would have graciously thanked him or asked him how he was doing, but her heart was shaky and her mind was cloudy. She truly did not feel well and she had no idea what was happening to her body or how to control it.

Sage cleared her throat, watching as Cassius took the glass of water and gently held it to Clare's frozen lips. She took tiny sips.

Sage tugged on Julius's arm. He turned his head innocently, his eyes shining.

"What is it?"

"Will you draw Clare a carriage? She does not look well. I can go with her so that way she is not alone."

Julius squeezed Sage's hand. "I will, do not worry, but you can not go with her. One of the daughters of Pax et Lux must be present, or it will bring bad publicity. Italus is at home with one of the sitters, he would be good company."

"Do not be silly, a tiny boy can not take care of a woman."
Cassius who was still holding the glass to her lips raised an eyebrow,
"Why are we arguing? It is clear that I will go."

"You can't. As much as I don't enjoy your company, you have to
represent your kingdom." Julius glanced over to Antoine who had his
nose buried in a book, a book Clare had given him. "I will send
Antoine." He smiled as he waved his good pal and servant over. The
blonde hurried over to the royals, his eyes fearful that he had done
something wrong. "Will you please accompany miss Pax to her
carriage? She does not feel well. Make sure that she lays down and
has something to eat," Julius said.

Cassius and Antoine met eyes. Cassius tore them away and glared
at Julius, his eyes sharp and pointed. Antoine quickly looked away
from the group and turned to Clare. He extended his hand out to her
and she gratefully took it, her head pounding as she heard a yell of
pain from down below. "She likes sweet fruity teas and desserts!"
Sage hollered out to Antoine who was guiding Clare into the tunnel
that would lead the two of them out of the arena. Clare smiled a bit,
resting her head against his shoulder when they were out of the
public eye.
"It is a shame that you are ill," he said solemnly.
"I will feel better once we are out of this arena."
"Does the sight of blood nauseate you?" he questioned.
"It does."

As soon as they were in the carriage and away from the arena,
Clare doubled over in relief. Antoine gently held her up by her waist,
letting go when she was properly sitting up straight. Clare broke the
silence between the two of them, "I painted you something. It is in
my luggage. I think you will like it," she said hopefully.
Antoine smiled, his smiles were always genuine and sheepish, as if
he was embarrassed to be having a good time. "I can not wait to see
it. You saved me as well by the way. I hate that bloodshed is a form
of entertainment, I try to bury my head in my book and ignore it all,"
he said.
"I don't blame you," there was a sad smile on her lips. "Antoine, I
need your help."

Now he was terrified. "As much as I would like to help you. I am a
servant, but I am not your servant, I can't do much for you unless it

is a simple task. Princess, how many times do people have to tell you that being seen with me is a death sentence to the both of us?"

"Antoine please, we were just seen walking out of the arena together. What are people going to think? You were just helping me through a hard time."

His voice was steady and calm. "They are going to think I am in love with you. This is how the world works. They will believe that I am trying to steal you from the prince. Now princess, what is it?"

"I feel strange around Prince Julius."

"And he feels strange around you." As soon as Antoine saw that shocked look spread across her face, he put a hand over his lips. "No, no, no. I should not have said that. You know, I did not even mean that. Sometimes I lie. Oh I am actually such a liar," he was rambling in attempts to fix his mistake.

"He does? I know you are not lying. Why does he feel that way?"

The carriage came to a halt and the two of them crashed into one another. Antoine quickly pulled away from her, pushing his glasses up to his nose.

"I don't know, you two need to talk to one another. I refuse to get involved. Now please I beg you, get out of this carriage and please princess do not talk about this again until we are alone."

Clare huffed. She got back out of the carriage and one of the guard's escorted her up to the spare bedroom, Antoine trailed a few feet behind them, cradling his book in his hand like he would a newborn child.

On their way to the bedroom, a little boy ran up to them. He didn't look like the Demetrias's. He had olive tan skin and dark wood colored hair. His eyes were a deep hazel green and freckles dusted his small face. He was short and scrawny, but bursting with energy. "Italus," the guard greeted. "The princess does not feel well, you must excuse us."

"She looks like Maximus!" He said as he pointed to her hair. "Rest well princess!"

"Thank you Italus," she beamed, smiling just for him. Once the little boy left, the guard continued their journey to the bedroom. "Prince Julius will not mind if Antoine accompanies you. If you need me, I will be just outside your door. I will remove him at any time," the guard told her.

"Thank you, but I assure you that won't be necessary," Clare said as the guard shut the door, leaving her and Antoine alone.

"My luggage must be here, let me find your painting."

"No," he whispered. "I don't want you to change the subject, not yet. What do you need my help with? It was rude of me to refuse out of terror. You are a princess, I am me, I over reacted, I should help you, it's my job to help not only Julius, but everyone he cares about."

Clare rolled her shoulders back, "you can still refuse me. I will not obligate you to say yes. Tomorrow I leave on a retreat with Cassius to learn valuable information. I do not fully trust him. I want you there as well, I want you to meet us on our trip a few days after we've started."

"I can not help you if I do not know what information you are looking to discover. You have just met me, you're being silly."

"Magic," she whispered, her voice barely heard. "But I trust you, I can just feel you are a good person. We had an instant connection, there is no denying it."

His mouth opened when he realized she was talking about the green glow, Julius had been right. "Maybe we did, maybe we do, but no, Cassius would be furious."

"He'll only be upset at first, I promise after a while that he won't mind. Surely there is something out in this world that you desire, that you want to discover. Your family serves, but what is it that you want?"

Antoine tugged at the ends of his blonde hair, "it does not matter what I want. Cassius will kill me if I show up and if it is not Cassius then it will be some monster and if it is not some monster, it will be the people when they find out that I have been accompanying you. I want to survive Clare. I want to continue serving the prince and continue to bring back money to my family. But I want to help you too. Magic is a dangerous thing, especially for a young woman to carry. I will help you, but I beg of you, to help me come out of this alive." He was pleading to her in the quietest voice that he could manage. Clare was a young girl, only a year younger than him, but she was a princess and any man would be foolish not to care for a princess. They'd be an even bigger fool not to care for a tender and kind soul like Clare. She had been right, there was an instant connection when they first met, something that he had never felt before.

Clare took his hands in her own. They were warm and overworked, "I will do my best to bring you out of this alive, though I don't see that as an issue. If I may ask how do you know about the danger of magic?"

"My cousin had magic. One day I saw her slip, from an innocent young girl, to someone frightened and afraid. She told me and I was a coward. I stayed away from her. I am alive and she is not. She was hung for the power she possessed by a group of evil people and when she was gone, they extracted the magic from her. I am afraid that they could do that to you. As much as I want to live and how much scared I am of death, if it is my assistance that keeps you from suffering a cruel fate, then I will help you. But you still need to talk to Prince Julius about what you are feeling, that is not my conversation to have with him princess."

"Antoine?"

"Yes?"

She pulled him in towards her chest, he awkwardly froze, his hands sticking out near her sides. "Thank you," she said sweetly.

He let his arms relax behind her as he rested his head against her shoulder. "You're welcome," he said quietly.

THE UNDEAD

Sage had not been enjoying herself. Julius's company was nice, but that was the only good thing about the event. Her sister was gone once again and out of her sight and men were being killed before her eyes. At least Cassius had left her sight, he had left their booth to sit next to his parents. Gracielle struck up a conversation with him. Though Sage had tried to talk to Cassius's parents, Erebus had not been fond of talking politics with her. He dismissed her and turned back to his wife who had given her a tender look as an apology. Towards the end of the event Sage had almost fallen asleep. The event was scheduled to last all day, but when Maximus got bored, they were allowed to leave. Eventually he and his lover got tired. Maximus and Julius stood and waved to the crowd. The people cheered and as they applauded, Maximus gave them permission to leave.

"I have to talk to your sister when we get back to the castle," Julius said awkwardly as he grabbed Sage's arm.

She pulled away from him, her eyes hot. "You don't get to be mysterious and pretend to be sweet. I hope you know whatever you say to her will come back to me. Don't you dare try to hide anything from me."

Julius winced, that fire in her eyes scared him. "Well then I guess I will talk to both of you when I get back home. I hope you are both very good secret keepers."

"I do just fine," Sage said, she walked in front of him to avoid talking to him. She heard Maximus laughing up front, his eyes staring at the two of them, "oh shut up," Sage scolded. She got in the carriage with her mother and slammed the door.

Gracielle raised an eyebrow. "What did a man do to upset you, this time?"

"You say that as if it happens all the time," she said as she watched her mother smirk. Sage groaned out in frustration, "okay, so what if it happens a lot? Men are irritating. You should have put me in an arranged marriage with a woman, my life would be less infuriating."

"If that was an option I would have, but there are no other princesses in Europe besides Cisily and according to Adria and Erebus, she does not count. Aren't you happy with Julius?"

"Typically, just not right now."

"Well that does happen sometimes, your father and I didn't always get along."

Sage did her best to think back to her early childhood, to remember a moment where her mother and father fought, but she couldn't remember a time and it infuriated her. Their relationship always seemed so perfect. Wade would kiss Gracielle on the cheek when he returned home from work, they would eat dinner together every night, bathe together and sleep in the same bed. Whenever he had the chance to be, he was attached to her hip. They took their space when they needed it, but most days they were together. Her memories of her father always included her mother. She had one distinct memory of him alone, when he handed her his sword, the blade was covered and it was placed in a clear box with a lock on top of it. "I am giving you this because I have to go away soon, so I can protect our kingdom. Just keep it in your room until your mum lets you use it and unlocks it for you. Treat it well." Then he kissed her on the cheek. That was the last time she had seen him. She opened her mouth to speak, to tell her mother that she missed him or that they seemed perfect together, but she didn't wish to upset her, so she stayed quiet.

When they arrived at the castle, Sage had calmed down a bit. During the carriage ride her mother had started up an odd conversation about the different kinds of frogs she had seen down by the moat and Sage listened with intrigue and concern. At least it had taken her mind off of things. When she stepped out of the carriage she rejoined Julius. They hurried up the stairs of the castle, avoiding the adults. The guard showed them both to Clare's guest bedroom. When the door opened, Clare and Antoine were laying on the bed, admiring a painting. She noticed her sister and jolted up, shoving the painting back into his hands.

"Julius do you need something?" Antoine asked, clearing his throat.

"No, but you may stay for this conversation."

Julius sat at the end of the bed and Sage sat down on the other side of Clare. The two sisters exchanged confused looks.

Julius was quiet at first. He seemed to be formulating his thoughts, wondering how to phrase what he was going to say. "Clare. I know you have magic. You didn't have to tell me, I didn't have to overhear it, I just knew." He took another breath. "Oh Oralee, Sage please promise you won't run away after hearing this."

He met her eyes, she didn't seem happy. Her arms were folded over her chest, her lips dropped in a pout.

He continued despite her lack of acknowledgment. "The reason I could figure this out is because there is magic inside of me." Audible gasps escaped the sister's lips. He kept going in a panic. "I am not a user, I can not use magic. Please let me explain. The night that Cassius's father and his guards broke into the castle. I died. Maximus is my twin and we can not live without one another. He took me to a man in the mountains and asked him if there was anything that he could do. He was a man with good magic that had turned dark and because he cared for his king, he brought me back to life. He had already revived one of his own family members. I guess once a healer revives there is no turning back. It took a week for me to come to, but I did. I am normal, just a bit clumsy and a little robotic at times. I've lost nearly all of my childhood memories before the age of twelve, Max has had to talk me through them. I promise I am no ghost, no spirit, but I was once dead. Any questions?"

Sage's fists were clenched tight, her knuckles curling inwards, she was a ball of rage.

Antoine seemed rather calm, just nervous. As Julius's servant, this was something he had been entrusted to keep a secret, he wondered how the two girls would take it.

Clare's face had brightened a bit, though she wasn't smiling, the answer to her questions had presented itself. "So the night of the murders, you said that Adria wasn't present. Yet she is roped into the mess as well? And now not only did he murder two, he murdered three. Speaking of Cassius and his family where is he and do the king and queen know you've been revived?" Clare asked.

Julius shook his head. "Maximus said he'd distract Cassius, so I assume they're downstairs. Adria wasn't present the night of the murders, yet she is roped into this mess because she didn't try hard enough to stop him. But no I do not hate her because even if she tried harder, I'm not sure that she could've stopped him anyways. Though don't get me wrong, I still am not fond of her. To answer your other question, they do not know that I died. They think I was just badly injured." He self consciously moved his hand over his shirt, where his scar lay underneath. He looked away from Clare and turned his attention to Sage, "please say something," he pleaded.

Her anger had turned into hot tears that she wouldn't let fall. "How dare you not tell me. You lied to me, you told me that the scar was from a bad wound. Do you not trust me? Don't you think it's a bloody good idea to tell the woman you're supposed to marry that you have been artificially remade? Or that your heart doesn't beat as fast as it once did?" She stood from the bed ready to storm out the door, but Clare pulled her back down and held her sister in her arms. She rested her head on Sage's shoulders and rubbed them in hopes to comfort her. If she left now in fury, it wouldn't look good to the rest of the royals.

"Hear me out Sage. I didn't tell you because I didn't want you to fall out of love with me."

"Are you even in love with me Julius?"

"Can we have this conversation later?" he pleaded.

"Yes, please let this be a private conversation, but let's also focus. You know more about magic. Obviously you and Clare feel connected because you share this similarity. What can you tell her to help her? What do you and your brother know?" Antoine asked.

Julius forced himself not to look at Clare or Sage, instead he focused on the back wall as he spoke. "I know that once a healer revives a human soul they're lost to the dark. I know that magic is something that certain evil minded folks are trying to steal. That it can be dangerous. I could have woken up scary and malicious if the magic was not performed properly. I can not be certain how, but I know the Goddesses are real. After my experience, my faith strengthened. I thought I saw Oralee while I was out, but I may have been delusional. Clare must be careful. My secret is contained within this room and with Maximus. The man in the mountain sadly passed a year ago, he could not live with the darkness anymore. The knowledge of my secret died with him. Where does your secret lye Clare?"

"With everyone in this room and Cassius."

"Cassius, really? If he tells his father you are done for!" Julius exclaimed.

Sage shouted back at him. "Watch your tongue."

"I'm sorry but it's true. I have no doubt King Erebus would use magic for something cruel if it came into his possession. I'm sure he supports those trying to acquire it. He would try to take over our kingdoms again if he got a hold of magic, I just know it," Julius whispered. "We can't stay in here much longer without Cassius getting suspicious. Sage, please, please talk to me later. Clare, I recommend you visit our temple tonight and pray with anyone accompanying you on your journey, Sage told me a little bit about it."

"Cassius and Antoine will be joining me," she told him.

Julius raised an eyebrow as he looked over to Antoine. "Oh is he now?"

"I was going to run away, but I suppose telling you is a bit better isn't it? I won't be leaving for a week or so. She convinced me to join her on her journey today."

Sage fell out of her sister's embrace, looking rather proud. "Of course she did. Who's going to watch and make sure Cassius isn't doing something stupid," Sage added.

"Right, well I suppose in the meantime I'll have to make do with another servant," he teased. "Now I think we have to go back down to the main floor."

Clare stood and waited for her sister to link arms with her. Sage had hesitated between staying behind to speak with Julius or going with her sister. "We will talk about it tonight," she told Julius. Sage linked arms with Clare and walked down the stairs with her. When Cassius saw the sisters, he immediately broke out of conversation with Maximus. "Oh Clare, there you are. Maximus was chatting with me on and on about eyeshadow and I don't know if I can hear it any longer."

Clare raised an eyebrow at him and smiled at Maximus who looked rather offended. "I would love to talk about eyeshadow with you while my fiancé does something else." She sat herself down in front of the king. Sage sat beside her. Both of them had just sat through something difficult to hear. Maximus radiated a vibrant energy, it was nothing like Julius's. They were twins but opposites. It was odd that Maximus knew this secret and was acting so normal, but this was his brother and he would conceal their secret with his life. He was the one who had sought out dark magic after all.

Cassius scoffed. "Well alright then, I see how it is."

Erebus emerged from behind the corner, Queen Adria by his side, Gracielle trailed shortly behind. "Or, we could refrain from talking about makeup and discuss the important political matters which you have truly brought us here to discuss," Erebus proposed, his voice haughty.

Maximus stepped down from the table he was standing on, his lips drooping into a frown, "party killer, fine."

Julius had re emerged, clearing his throat. "I was going to show Clare and Cassius something, is this a conversation that they need to be involved in?"

Maximus looked over to his brother, his smile returning. "No. Though a shame I did not get to talk about eyeshadow with Clare, she does not have to be involved. Your partner," he teased, pointing to Sage who still looked cross. "Will stay, she is a future queen after all."

The two groups split. Julius took Clare and Cassius somewhere undisclosed while the rest of the royals took their seats. Sage had followed her sister with her eyes until she was out of sight. She assumed Julius was going to take them to pray like he had promised. She still trusted him with Clare's life, but it did not take away from the fact she felt betrayed. Such a large secret, she didn't know how to feel about it. In a sense, Julius was a walking ghost, not meant to be on this Earth. She shuddered, her eyes settling back on to the people in front of her who had just gotten comfortable in their seats. This time her mother would expect her to participate. Her silence would be valued as ignorance in a setting like this. Maximus started. "The tensions of the world are high right now. Africa has been peaceful for centuries, probably thanks to their kind Goddess, but the rest of the continents have been suffering through war. We are in no financial state to help them. I believe we are teetering on a war of our own. Ever since the incident has happened, we have remained quiet, but I would like to address the elephant in the room and no I'm not referencing Pax et Lux. King Erebus you and your guards killed my father and my mother that night, though her body disappeared. You horribly injured my brother and yet you act as if the air is clear and peaceful. What were your motives?"

Sage had not expected Maximus to be so poised and proper. She had seen him during his worst outbursts when he stood on tables and threw things everywhere. He was the type to snog in public and he flaunted his fashion like a king would his excellent battle strategies. But he could command a room when he needed to. At first his people hated him. When his father Augustus, a cruel man, but a powerful leader had died and left Maximus to rule, the people were in outrage during his coronation. Little Italus had stood up and voiced his allegiance to the new king. After hearing his speech and seeing him in the village, they took a liking to him. Though the people would miss Augustus, more than his sons ever did, they were now fond of Maximus and she could see why. He felt so real and human, yet he could act a royal when he needed to be one. But what he had said about Julius, how smoothly he lied, discomforted her. 'It is for Julius's safety, you love him so you should understand,' she thought to herself.

She looked to Queen Adria and King Erebus as this was their turn to respond. Adria spoke before her husband could, "my husband is at times irrational. He hated your father with a vengeance and so he attacked. I gave him my blessing because I did not think he would kill anyone." She awkwardly took a sip of the strong red wine from the glass that sat beside her.

Maximus tilted his head to the side. "Really? Are you sure that's why? Are you sure King Erebus wasn't just hoping that by killing the old king, the new king would be so clueless that he would give up his kingdom and Europe would become two kingdoms instead of three? I had a lot of little spies tell me that," he smirked. "I don't think it was because my father upset you, I think it is because you have a lust for power, don't you think so?" Maximus asked. Erebus was gritting his teeth. It was clear Maximus had hit the nail on the head, but of course Erebus would never admit to such a disastrous thing. "I don't wish to start a war, but if you attack anyone in my kingdom again, I will not stop the war until we have won it," Maximus said.

There was a horrible silence in the air. Gracielle looked over to her daughter, she had something to say, but her hopes were high that her daughter would be able to say it first.

Sage leaned forward. "Well if I may speak." She tried to remember what Clare had always said. "War would be disastrous. There would be death, we'd have to employ young soldiers, our people would fall into poverty. These are all things that we can avoid on a large scale if we don't go to war. Our citizens will suffer and turn on us if we go to war twice in a hundred years." She could feel her thoughts slipping away, so she hurriedly continued. "We do not want to get involved, but we are allied with the Demetrias's. If you attack in attempts to take over their city, we have no choice but to back them."

Gracielle nodded proudly, "she is right. Our kingdom does not like to go to war, but it would be foolish for us to sit and watch. Europe is meant to have three kingdoms. Oralee herself has said it and spoke it into existence, we will not fall to your reign. So do not attack and we have peace."

While Adria sipped her wine, Erebus fumed in his seat. "Then you must promise never to give us a reason to attack you. If you wrong anyone in our family then we will start a war. If everyone could govern like us then I would see no worry about having three kingdoms, but the liberties some of your people have are disturbing at best."

Maximus licked his lips. "Right because freedom of speech is such a   cruel thing. Treason is one thing, but talking bad about your government should not land you in prison Erebus. Adria wouldn't the world be so much happier if your husband knew how to shut his mouth?"

The woman looked up from her wine glass. "Perhaps, but I don't make new rules, I just enforce the old ones. If one day Cassius would like to change our kingdom then he may, but for now, my passive ways will stay. So if my ancestors believed it was criminal, I will stand by them."

"You are an odd woman, but it is settled, as long as no one does anything to set off your short fuse then there will be no war."

Sage bit down on her lip, she would have to tell Clare to be careful around Cassius. "There should be no war," Sage echoed.

The king of Excidium looked over to his wife and smiled mischievously. In his eyes she was a toy that he could play with, wind up at his will and then dispose of when he was done. "Then perhaps there will be no war," he told them.

NO RETURN

As the trio walked out of the castle and towards the temple, Clare turned to Julius who looked solemn. His hands were shoved in his pocket and his eyes were pointed towards the ground. "I am glad I understand why I feel connected to you now," Clare told Julius in hopes to cheer his spirits.

He shrugged.

Cassius wrinkled his face in confusion. "What is there to understand? Why do you feel connected to him?"

Despite his low spirits, Julius was quick to lie, "she was curious about my religion. She was unsure if I believed in the Goddesses and I told her that I did. That is why she feels connected to me because there are not a lot of true believers in her family."

It only took five minutes of walking to reach the temple. The temple was a building made purely out of gold and each goddess was carved onto the roof. Each individual took their shoes off before entering the sacred building. To Clare's left was a pile of stacked offerings, she grabbed an apple off of the platter. Her voice was hushed, "I wish our royalty had built something this magnificent."

"We did get lucky. Our kingdom name does mean God after all. I'm sure it made the Goddesses a bit mad that our founders didn't choose Deas, but if they were angry they have forgiven us now. Maximus has always said he felt close to the Goddesses and I feel it too, but not in the same way."

Clare raised an eyebrow, 'could this be another secret?' She chose to ignore the comment and move on.

Cassius came up behind Clare and picked up an orange. "Which Goddess protects travel?" He asked her as he gazed at the eight full body statues that were distributed throughout the temple. Clare looked back at him in surprise. Cassius had just asked her for her knowledge, there was a first time for everything.

"Well, it depends on where you are traveling. We are traveling in the European woods, so we will pray to Oralee as she resides over Europe and the beaches and we will pray to Olive because though she is the Goddess of North America, she is also the Goddess of the woods."

Cassius seemed surprised to hear this explanation. "Oh alright. My parents only taught me about Mallory and Oralee because they had to. They didn't explain much else to me." He looked over to Julius. "You look like a hurt puppy. Just come pray with us so we can get out of here please." Cassius waved Julius over, a small gesture, but one that held a lot of weight. Julius grabbed an apple and stood on the other side of Cassius.

"I will lead us in prayer," Clare suggested. "You are coming on this trip because of me, so please let me pray for us," at her words Cassius seemed relieved, he had no idea how to phrase a prayer.

Clare knelt down by the large statue of Oralee. Clare's long hair touched the ground and spilled out like liquid as she bowed. "Dear divine Goddess. Thank you for blessing us with the ability to lead your three kingdoms. There is something I must discover so that way I will be a good princess to my home and a good queen to Cassius and his kingdom. Please guide and protect us along the way." She set down her apple, got up onto her feet and then moved to the statue of the Goddess Olive. "Cassius you can try to lead this next prayer?" Clare asked as she nudged him.

He knelt next to the statue and dipped his head. "Goddess Olive. I am sorry that I have not visited you before. Please protect us on our journey through your woods. We can not do this alone." His words sounded forced. There was a hint of something genuine, but it was clear he had not done this before. Clare deemed it good enough. She kissed the statue's feet, set down Cassius's offering and then stood up. "Do you feel a connection with the Goddesses like Julius?" Cassius whispered. He had heard a rumor that the Goddesses chose who had magic.

"I do, I'm not sure my connection is the same as his but I know that they're supporting us," she said.

He seemed skeptical, but his face pulled into an awkward smile, "if you say so. Oh and Clare, did you tell him about your magic? Does he know?"

She thought about lying, but in the end she told the truth, "he does. Don't worry, he's a good secret keeper."

Julius had spent his time praying only to Oralee. Cassius was watching him from afar.

"Is he okay?" Cassius whispered to Clare.

Clare grinned, "so you care about him?"

"No I don't care about him," he snapped. "But I'm not dumb, I notice when people's behavior change."

Clare shrugged. "He and Sage got in a fight. I'm sure he will cheer up when they make up."

Cassius laughed. "We seem to get in little fights every single day."

"We do, but we are not the same as them," she said.

Julius stood up from the floor and walked back over to the two of them. "Alright. Let's go back into the castle. I'm hoping that dinner will be ready. I don't know if I can take any more awkward tension. I'm already awkward enough."

"And I hope at tonight's dinner I don't get interrogated," Clare added.

"And that Sage doesn't punch me," Cassius murmured.

Clare glared at him. "Oh please. She doesn't punch people for no reason. She will behave today, she's under my mum's eye."

"Well," Cassius said as he thought over his next words carefully, "I won't let my father attack you anymore, especially not here. I promise." He extended his hand out to her in hopes that she would take it.

She considered it for a moment, then took his hand. Not for the public, not for image, but just to hold it. "Only because you promised."

The kingdom leaders and Sage had moved from the sofa to the table. Antoine was wiping the long table off with a cloth, preparing for the meal to be served. Wherever Maximus's lover was, he was nowhere to be seen. Julius filled in the open seat by his brother and Cassius and Clare took the two open seats near the end of the table. The conversation started off fairly light. They talked about the fights that took place at the arena and Clare's health since she was away. But then King Erebus just couldn't help himself. "My son is going on a trip with the princess tomorrow. If he doesn't have her pregnant when they come back from his trip, I'll be highly disappointed." He took a sip of his wine. There were agitated looks from all parties at the table. Gracielle couldn't find the words and before either Cassius or Clare could speak, Sage stood up and pointed her finger at Erebus.

"You fool! She doesn't need to produce a child as long as you two are alive and sadly you are. You will not sexualize my sister and pin her as someone who is only beneficial to your kingdom because she's able to reproduce! Shame on you and she's only eighteen you sick fuck!" she shouted. "Clare is wildly intelligent and kind. Why do you hate her so much?" Sage questioned.

Now Gracielle stood. It had been a while since she had raised her voice in front of other royalty. She looked over to Erebus and Adria while she spoke. "Sage is right. You will not talk about my daughter in that way. You of all people Adria, should know how difficult life is inside of an arranged engagement. Since you've been in my daughters shoes, you should quiet your husband."

Maximus stood. He debated quieting them, but instead he added fuel to the fire. "You really should learn how to respect women, Erebus. At least the men who I sleep with want to sleep with me."

Julius stood up, his fists clenched. "I agree that nobody should not speak like that to Clare, but this is not going to end well if you all keep yelling at each other."

Adria was in the middle of bickering with Gracielle and Erebus was shouting at Maximus. Cassius and Clare were the last two to stand. Cassius was pointing at his father. Clare was glaring at him waiting for him to say something, but he was frozen, unable to speak. Clare's face had gone bright red, her fists clenched. "YOU COWARD!" she screamed at him. "You can never grow the courage to stand up to him can you? And the rest of you, enough! King Erebus doesn't need to be reminded of how horrible of a person he is. I'm sure he already knows."

The room quieted, the sound of a fork dropping in the kitchens could be heard. It was the type of tension that could start a war. Erebus grabbed his wife by the arm. "We are clearly not welcome in either of your kingdoms. Clare is always welcome in ours, but her stay will never be as lovely as it once was. We are leaving. Put one more foot out of line and my wife will send the armies after you." Adria leaned over the table to give her son one last kiss on the cheek and then was pulled by her husband out of the castle.

When the door slammed, Gracielle spoke. "I think we just started a war." She looked to Cassius desperately. "Can you convince him not to do anything?"

"No." He was glaring right past Clare to Gracielle. "He will manipulate my mother to start a war. When I cross him it is not good and it does nothing. But have faith in him, he can take a few insults."

"Does he hurt you when you speak up?" Gracielle whispered.

Cassius glared, he looked offended. "No," he lied.

Clare spared him a look of pity before commanding the room. "A family dispute is something stupid to start a war over."

"You did call him a horrible person," Cassius murmured.

"I did, but If he can't thicken his skin then he shouldn't be running a kingdom. I don't fully believe he will start a war over this, but he won't be kind to us if we make any more mistakes."

Maximus crossed his arms. "The Antias family has been planning to take over our kingdoms for centuries. They've tried countless times and failed. They will try again, but this time we will prepare. I suggest making plans now. Which side of this fight are you on Cassius?"

"Neither," he spat. "I'm running off into the woods with Clare. It doesn't matter what side I'm on if I'm going to pick berries for the rest of my fucking life."

Sage clapped her hands together. "You're lucky then. One wrong move and we will destroy your kingdom. Hide in the woods while you can and try to be of use while you're at it. That's why you're going to be there after all. She needs your help, she doesn't love you. Though I'd be better to go with her because I could beat you in a sword fight, unfortunately I'm not allowed to go."

That seemed to catch his attention. "You think you could beat me in a sword fight?"

Gracielle interrupted. "ENOUGH!" she shouted, finally losing her temper. "I lost my husband in a war, I won't lose my children to one. And thank you Clare for informing me about this trip with such short notice. I suppose, you have permission to go," she said in annoyance. "I can't prepare to win a war with all of this endless bickering. If you'd like to go have a childish duel then by all means go ahead, but take your screaming matches outside and leave the king and I alone." She glanced over to Julius who was awkwardly shuffling his feet in the corner. "You too."

Clare shook her head. "I'm sorry I didn't tell you sooner mum, or even ask you, but I promise I will talk to you about it later tonight. And Cassius, I would love to watch my sister kick your ass, but I am going to change out of this horrible dress and into something more my taste. Plus I'm still thinking about the fact that my fiancé's father might start a war." She turned on her feet and started to speed walk away from the group.

"Wait!" Cassius said. "Let's all get in our night clothes and meet back outside in thirty minutes. I think there are a few conversations waiting to be had and my sword is upstairs." He caught up to Clare and walked by her side.

Sage had hollered after them. "You're just too scared to fight me now you coward!"

Cassius rolled his eyes. He wanted to murmur something under his breath, but Clare wasn't in the mood and neither was he. "So you are upset because you would have liked to see my father slap me in front of everyone?"

Clare sighed, she opened the door to their guest bedroom and slammed it once he was inside. "I am upset that you didn't at least say how you feel and I am also upset that you don't know how to apologize. I am so young that I don't wish to have a kid until I am older than Sage. I am sure you are not dying to romance me either."

"That last part is a lie, but don't worry, I don't want kids either," he said, sending a pink blush across her cheeks. "Next time I will try to speak my mind to him, though I doubt there will be a next time for a while. How long do you think that this trip is going to take?"

"However long it needs to take, Cassius. I don't plan on coming back home until I know what is inside of me and how to control it. So you might be picking berries for the rest of your life," she said angrily. She dug into her luggage and pulled out a white nightgown dotted with flowers. "I need you to help me take off my dress," she said bitterly.

He gracefully moved towards her and undid the zipper. His hands were warm, his head leaned over her shoulder as he worked. His hands pushed down the sleeves of her dress and trailed down the rest of her body until the dress hit the ground.

She was still clothed in her undergarments, hoop skirt and corset. "Thank you, but I have it from here," she said.

When he turned around, she looked back to get a glance at him. He was furiously taking off his suit as if it was suffocating him. He threw each expensive piece of clothing onto the floor until he was almost naked, the muscles in his back expanded as he drew in a deep breath. Clare forced herself to turn around and she worked on removing the rest of her outfit.

"Are we going to be mad at each other our whole lives?" he asked her as he pulled on a pair of soft gray pants.

Clare had just pulled the nightgown gown over her body. "Probably. Will you put my hair up? You did it so well on our first night together," she lied. It was just another excuse to feel his touch. She turned around and stepped over the large dress on the floor. She could easily do it herself, but even when she was mad at him, she wished for him to subtly touch her. Though in different ways, both Cassius and Antoine made her feel as if she was turned inside out.

"Seems like an odd ask for a girl who just called me a coward, but I suppose that I have to start proving you wrong. My skills have improved I assure you." He took the hair tie from her wrist and pressed his body up against hers, leaning his head to the side so he could see her face while he put her hair up. He felt the tight breath in her chest and his hands lingered before he pulled away. "You lose your breath when I am against you. Good to keep in mind." His voice was soft and hushed. "At least I know I'm not completely worthless to you."

Down the hall, Sage wasn't sure what Julius could possibly say to make their situation any better. He had lied to her and expressed no interest in telling her the truth. She had asked about his scar and he had lied, but Clare had lied as well. Why did everyone in her life not trust her? She was good at keeping secrets as long as she could tell Clare and in both of these situations that wasn't necessary.

Julius was too awkward for silence, "are you really going to duel him?" he questioned.

She sighed, trying to let go of her anger. Disappointment would be much easier to control. "I am, but you don't just get to escape this Julius. I have questions and you are going to answer them."

He nodded, politely pulling the door open for her. "Of course I will. Any question you have I will answer it for you. You should not have to keep wondering. I'm a bit curious though, did you not notice anything different about me since that night?"

Now that she thought about it, she had never made the connection. His hair was duller and he did not sparkle with the same charm that he used to. He tripped more often and his heart beat slower, even his voice had gotten slightly higher. When she asked him questions, he had to think longer before answering. She blamed it on drastic puberty, but that had not been the case. "My sister lied to me out of fear, so I understand why you may have been too scared to tell me. It feels odd to know that I am engaged to a man who is supposed to be dead, but somehow I am into you all the same. I would be with you through hell and back. I really would."

"Sage, it's been a while. Do you love me? You've never um, well explicitly said it. I'm just guessing that you do." He noticed her eyes go soft.

"Yes Julius, I love you, I'm just really bad at expressing it. I love you revived from the dead or not." She cleared her throat and sat on top of his lap. "I would still like to ask those questions." He gave her a soft 'of course' and she started, quickly changing the subject from their love, something she was horrible at expressing. "You said you forgot most of your early childhood. What memories do you still have of us? I want to know what you lost. I want to be able to restore your memories like Maximus did for you."

She stood up from his lap and slid her day dress off, she picked up a baggy burnt orange nightshirt and pulled it over her chest. She paired it with a pair of soft, cream shorts. Julius changed as well. This time he was less embarrassed. She had bathed with him once, this was hardly as intimidating. But she had no desire to make him the slightest bit uncomfortable, so Sage still turned around to give him privacy as he slowly took off his suit and began to put on a navy blue T-shirt and a pair of gray night pants. "I remember when we were little, Gracielle would force us to hang out when we had the opportunity. You and Clare normally only hung around Max and I at the gatherings. I remember a lake we went to. I remember having sword fights with you. Then I remember nothing up until I was fifteen and we began to get close. Our childhood memories are sadly distant. Something I can hardly reach." He had finished dressing and plopped down next to her on the bed. He extended his arms open and she fell into them. She rested her head on his lap and gazed up at him. "You used to color with me. I remember I wanted to do nothing of the sort. I wanted to play outside in the dirt and the mud, but you'd drag me inside and sit me down so we could color. You'd read me your essays for your classes as well. You'd ask me for my opinion and I would always give you an answer even though I was nowhere near as smart as you. You used to pick me flowers in the garden. You were so sweet. We would play games with Clare. I'm surprised we never got lost in those woods, we probably would have if the guards didn't follow us. And I remember your mother. With her brown hair and her sparkly blue eyes. I remember she loved me and my sister with all of her heart. Clare always spent so much time with her. I'm sorry you lost her," Sage sighed. She could see the pained sadness in his eyes and that look on his face brought tears to her own eyes. "And then I almost lost you." She closed her eyes, squeezing them shut as tight as possible.

He pulled her in close to his chest and instead of wiping her tears, he let her cry. "You did, but I'm back now and I love you. I'll never truly leave you." He kissed the top of her head gently with his lips. "Do you want to cancel that fight?"

She sat up and turned to face him, she wiped her tears and caught her breath. "No, let us go. Cheer me on."

Sage was surprised to see Cassius and Clare had already made it outside. They seemed to be in better spirits. Clare sat down on a stone ledge, her feet dangling in the air as she watched Cassius swing his black hilted sword in the air. They weren't talking, but she didn't look as if she wanted to kill him. Sage hollered out a hello, cupping her hands over her mouth to project her voice. Clare smirked at Sage who began swinging her own sword to mock Cassius.

Julius kissed her lightly on the cheek. "Good luck," he told her, before skipping off to join Clare on the ledge. He gave the girl an awkward, nervous lopsided smile and she gave him a bright one to show that she wasn't upset with him or his secret. Now that she knew and he wasn't holding the weight of secrecy, his energy felt calmer. Clare didn't mind being around his aura when it was calm. It reminded her of a running waterfall. Serene, rushed and loud, but calming. Cassius turned to look at the two of them.

Clare caught his eye and shouted. "Just know neither of us are rooting for you! I'll always pick Sage!" She watched as he rolled his eyes. He presented himself so cooly, but he was hot and tempered like his father deep down and he had so much trauma shoved far underneath the surface. "Don't hurt each other please," Clare shouted as they both raised their swords into position.

Sage stood with her right foot forward and her left foot back so when he clashed his sword against hers, she could hold her ground against him. Though he may have been physically stronger, she was a close competitor and was much more agile and swift than she was.

Shorter than him by at least over nine inches, it was easy for her to duck when he broke his sword away from hers and swung. She heard Clare and Julius cheering and clapping, her name was the fuel that kept her quick on her feet. Before getting up from her crouched position, she swung at his leg, but he was quick and blocked her attack with a jump. She rose back to her normal height.

"I didn't think you would be this good," Cassius admitted as their swords met above their heads, his words were breathy from their fight.

Sage smirked. "Is it because I'm a woman?"

"No, it's because you're Sage." He smirked as he watched her brows furrow in pure fury. He was stumbling back now as she ferociously swung at him. His sword twirling to block her. "I have a feeling you actually want to hurt me. You heard the rules," he said.

"I do want to hurt you, but you're right I heard the rules." Their swords parted in the air and they both drew them down to their sides. She had to get him to the ground in order to win the fight, but there was a solid chance he weighed fifty or more pounds than she did because of his height and muscle .

Sage twirled around behind him while he wasn't looking, changing the direction of their fight. She heard Clare scream something along the lines of 'kick his ass', and she was more than happy to do so.

When he pointed his sword low for her ankles, she hopped over the blade and threw her own to the ground. A risky move. She saw him reach for it, but while he was distracted, she had pushed herself onto him and knocked him to the ground. Her hand fumbled for the sword and once she had it, she held it over him. But he was quick. His sword pointed up in the air, he clashed it against hers, she couldn't get him to drop the damn thing.

They were both grunting in frustration, their muscles shaking. Sage found the strength deep within her core, she pushed and pushed until his arms dropped and his sword tumbled beside him. Before he could grab it, she crawled on top of him and pointed her sword against his chest. 'One, two three,' she had won, she had beat Cassius in a sword fight. "

Take that Cassius, hah!" she shouted as she got off of him. He looked rather embarrassed and ashamed of himself. If his father hadn't stormed off in a rage, Sage had a sinking feeling in her gut that he would have beat his son. There was that undeniable look of fear in his eyes, one she couldn't shake easily. For a moment she thought she might pity him. She extended a hand to him and helped him up from the ground.

"Nice one Pax, but I'll get you next time." He shook that look out of his eyes, though she could still tell he was uneasy. They shook hands and he looked over to Clare and Julius. Though Julius was smiling brightly, Clare wasn't. He tilted his head at her, 'shouldn't she be cheering for her sister?' There was a half turned, thin smile upon her lips. She wasn't looking at her sister, she was looking at him. He didn't need her pity, so he turned away. Sage turned away from him and made her way to the two of them.

Clare's smile brightened and the two sisters embraced in a hug, "good job, you're going to make a great queen. Mum says they shouldn't send royalty into battle, but they should send you," Clare said.

"You think so?

"Oh I know so."

Julius was grinning. "I know so as well."

For once Sage let her ego fall away, she glanced over her shoulder to Cassius and then looked back to Clare. This was her signal to go and make things right.

Clare walked to Cassius and brushed against his shoulder. "You put up a pretty good fight." Her fingers trailed across the hilt of his sword, studying the metal so she could get to know its features better, there may be a day when she would need to use it.

"Though I hate to admit it," he said through gritted teeth, "your sister is wildly talented. My father always had me training with my damn sword. No one trained her and yet, she beat me. I'll admit I am jealous."

Clare sighed, "she was dedicated, nothing stops a dedicated woman. But Cassius, what would have happened if you lost and your father was here?" She took her hand off the sword and watched his entire body tense up.

"That is nothing you need to know. I would rematch your sister, but it is getting late and if you wanted to leave early tomorrow, we should go to sleep, or at least we should try. You're not as delightful when you are sleepy."

"Go upstairs, I will meet you soon, I want to talk with my mum and my sister alone before I go."

Clare and Sage met Gracielle in the grand room a few moments later. Maximus had paused his conversation with the queen to give her privacy with her daughters. He explained that he would come back when they were done as there was much more to discuss. Gracielle sat down on the sofa with a large sigh, she was still in her puffy day dress, her eyes tired, her ginger hair streaked with new gray hairs. "I am glad we could meet. I guess we have a lot to discuss don't we." She smiled tenderly at her daughters who were sitting on both sides of her. She pulled them in close to her body. Clare breathed deeply, she shut her eyes as she relaxed against her mother. "Our little girl is going to journey to Oralee knows where for months on end. The palace is going to be lonely without you." She squeezed her hand. Clare reached over with her other hand to hold Sage's.

"And Sage is training to be the next queen, though promise nothing will happen to you when I'm gone," Clare said.

Gracielle smiled down at her. "You know I can't do that, but I can try my best. You know our security is well." She looked to Sage who was still quiet. "Cat got your tongue?"

Sage's eyes were watering, her lip curled up. She had to compose herself before talking or else the tears would start to flow. "I could barely withstand two weeks? How can I get past more?"

Seeing her sister so vulnerable had Clare twisted with emotions, her own eyes began to water. "I'll write to you guys I promise. I'm going to be okay."

Gracielle took off her golden necklace that had a heart attached to the end, embroidered with flowers. Wade had given it to her. She clipped it around Clare's neck. "You will be safe. You have two delightful men going with you."

"You know Antoine is going?"

"I do, you are not very good at whispering, but I don't mind. I also have picked up a few clues and I know that you are in possession of magic, Clare." Clare and Sage's faces were frozen in horror until Gracielle spoke again. "Don't worry I'm not mad or upset. I still love you dearly. I can see why you two hid this from me. It is scary and it is intense. I don't know much about magic either, so I am glad that you are going on this journey, Clare," Gracielle said.

"Thank you mum," Clare cried, "I was so scared to tell you."

"You two should never be scared to tell me anything, I am your mother, I am here to protect you."

After a shared moment of silence. The two girls told their mum about the duel. "My oh my, maybe Clare will have to only rely on herself," Gracielle half teased. She kissed them both on the forehead. "You will both be okay, you have your father's perseverance. He had a brother. They were close like you. Unfortunately, his brother died in the war a few years before your papa. You two never got the chance to meet him. But the two of them reminded me of you two. If they could get through whatever life threw at them, so can you. I promise."

"They sound like an awesome pair," Clare said, trying to ignore the fact that their fate had been death.

Sage curled up closer to her mum. "Tell us a story about them."

So Gracielle told them a story where Wade and his brother attended a ball, the one where Wade had swooned her off of her feet. She explained how charming he was, but how much he hated to dance and how clumsy his brother was. She told them how at the end of the night, the three of them were the only ones left in the ballroom. They were sitting in a corner of the large room, shoes off and exhausted, drinking the rest of the alcohol. The boys told her about their trials of becoming soldiers and she explained to them how exhausting the life of a princess could be. Then she went on about how her mother had found them at the end of the night and was in a rage. At the end of her story, she had two sleepy princesses by her side. She walked each one to their rooms and kissed them goodnight, but they did not go to sleep. That night Sage and Clare had found another guest bedroom and stayed up all night talking to one another, reminiscing and discussing the journey to come. Eventually they had fallen asleep a little before the sun came up.

Clare left that morning with Prince Cassius. Everyone waved them goodbye as they rode off on horses into the woods. Clare wouldn't see her sister for quite some time.

A SERVANTS JOURNEY

Antoine had just finished folding away the last of his clothes into a large bag. Now that Julius knew of the journey, there was no need to run away. To avoid any suspicion, Maximus was told that Antoine was going to visit his family and in his place there would be a new servant in training. So Antoine went to pray and pack his bag. Clare's letter had arrived the night before.

Dear Antoine,

After traveling for five rough days, Cassius and I have made it to our first location where we will be waiting for you. He still does not know about your arrival and it is best that we keep it a surprise. Throughout the week, I have felt no strange pull to magic until we arrived at this tiny cabin in the woods, home to a woman named Fran. She has promised a maximum week nights stay in exchange for our labor in her gardens. By the time you arrive I am certain we will have enough information to guide us in the right direction. Hopefully with the correct address you should arrive quicker than we did. I believe Cassius and I just went in circles. We had to stop to let the horses rest and then we could not find the direction we had started in. So we argued and screamed at the top of our lungs in the middle of the forest. In the end, we did not know where we had come from and we headed off in an unknown direction. This may have happened several times. I look forward to your arrival. Cassius is not cruel, but he can be rather boring. He doesn't enjoy literature and I have this strange, but strong urge to hug you when he is not looking. It is hard not to think of you. Please hurry and come soon, I miss your light blonde hair and happy amber eyes, rich like the sunshine.

(The cottage that lyes on East Pulcherrimus road under Deus rule)

Love, Clare

After reading her letter, Antoine had packed up the rest of his belongings as quick as he could, vowing to leave the next morning. The letter was stuffed into the pocket of his leather brown satchel, he would need the address in order to find them. On his way out of the castle that had sheltered him from the unknown, he stuffed three apples, two loaves of bread, a container of water and a chunk of cheese in his bag. Julius met him at the door.

"You are allowed to take one of our spare guard horses. The fawn colored horse with chestnut hair will be yours. Her name is Vita. I saddled her for you. I'm going to miss you when you are gone, no one serves me as well as you do," he smiled sadly.

Antoine returned the gesture, his eyes widening when Julius placed an arm on his shoulder.

"It is my job sir, but I will miss your companionship. You've treated me like a good mate." Antoine gently removed himself from Julius's grasp. "Also thank you for lending me a horse," he grinned.

Julius walked him to the horses and helped Antoine up onto the saddle. He helped strap his bags down to the horse. When he finished, he looked up at Antoine and did not break his gaze. "Be careful with Clare, I wouldn't want anyone to get the wrong idea. The kingdom's citizens are well aware of the arranged engagement, you don't want to be caught up in the middle of their relationship especially when it's unintentional."

Antoine nodded in agreement, but his heart throbbed, it was intentional. "Well, I'll be off then. Make sure Princess Sage is doing alright for Clare's sake and as always, keep yourself safe, I want to come back home to two Demetrias boys."

Julius smiled. "I want you alive as well Antoine. Be safe. Thanks for pissing off Cassius for me."

Antoine kicked the horses side and the animal began to trot away. "Anytime!" he shouted over his shoulder.

Antoine traveled through dirt pathways, through villages, he crossed a river and continued his journey through the forest. Instead of five days, it took him three to reach the small cottage in the middle of the woods. It had a grey exterior built of stones, two windows made of pink and yellow stained glass and the roof was painted a pastel yellow. The cabin was flanked by two massive gardens that were filled with flowers of all colors and an assortment of vegetables. There was a dirt pathway leading up to the cottage that was lit up by lanterns. The sound of people chatting inside could be heard and Antoine thought he heard the sweet softness of Clare's voice. He noticed behind the home, a few horses were hanging out in a fenced area. He led Vita over to the area and once he got a good look at the two horses already occupying the space, he knew he was in the right place. He recognized Clare's horse from the stables and any strong pitch black horse was a good indicator that Cassius was also here. There was another silver horse he assumed belonged to the lady named Fran. He led Vita inside of the enclosure and removed the saddle and load from her back. Once he closed the fence, he carried his things up to the blush pink door and knocked.

The door swung open to reveal an old woman in her late fifties. She had a heap of long black and gray hair thrown up in a bun at the top of her head. She wore a pair of pinstripe trousers and a bright purple blouse. She was wearing no shoes, there were wrinkles along her face, prominent when she smiled at him. There was a fluffy cat by her feet, snow white with bright blue eyes. "You must be Antoine, the librarian, they told me all about you."

He raised an eyebrow, but nodded in agreement. He peered past her to see Clare and Cassius sitting down at an oak table, two mugs of coffee in front of them. Fran moved aside to let him in and took his bags, he thanked her and smiled as Clare rose from the table, her eyes mesmerized as if he was the most magnificent person she had ever laid her eyes upon. They could not hug now. He waved to her and then waved to Cassius, pushing down that hurt feeling he felt when he saw the sadness flash across Clare's face. He sat down next to Cassius, who moved his chair further away from him.

"I'd ask why you are here, but Clare gave in and told me that you are here because you are intelligent apparently and can connect clues. Seems like something I could do, but apparently you do it better and apparently you are emotionally supportive, though I'm not sure how she would know that," Cassius said.

Antoine shrugged and decided to stay silent.

Fran took the empty seat at the table and brought over another cup of coffee, she placed it in front of Antoine. "The conversation was just getting good dear," she told him. She brought her cat up on top of her lap and gave the furry creature a few good strokes.

"Well what did I miss?" he asked.

Clare answered, "I was asking Fran if she knew anything about magic since we had read her name somewhere in a magic book. She does not have magic herself, but her sister does. Her sister lives up in the mountains and she gave us her address. She was just about to tell us what else she knew about magic and then you came inside. We had been too busy with the garden to ask her beforehand, but it is no trouble," she added, "we enjoy the work," she lied. The look on Cassius's face was a clear indicator that he would rather have done anything else. The image of him pulling up weeds made Antoine want to burst out into laughter, but he kept it to himself.

"I'll be sure to help while I am here, but you should continue your story. Though tired, I can listen well."

The woman took a sip of her coffee. "Terrible kids, interested in learning about magic," she waved her finger in disappointment. "Magic gets you killed. Knowing about magic and disclosing that information is a crime in itself. Why do you think I live in the middle of nowhere? I was interrogated once, I will not go through that torture again. Be careful with what I tell you. I am only helping you because your friend is a princess, she's not just any girl." She pointed to Clare. "My sister was once young and scared. Magic is something created and used by our Goddesses and given to individuals who they deem worthy enough to use it. The only Goddess who openly enjoys creating chaos is Mallory, so oftentimes her magic falls into the wrong hands. Magic users will feel a strong connection to the Goddess who chose them, this Goddess does not have to be their continental Goddess. For my sister, she felt a connection to Evangeline of Australia. It is not known for sure, but we believe that this Goddess chose my sister. Clare, do you feel a strange pull to a certain Goddess?"

"This might not be related, but I feel a strange pull to Prince Julius and his family, one I can not describe, but I have always prayed most to Oralee. I can not put my finger on why his family feels so close to me."

"Maybe Oralee has granted one of them magic or magic lyes within one of them. Magic is always inside of the user, but they have an awakening when they truly need it. I will leave my sister's story for her to tell, but Clare, when did you have your awakening?"

Clare tucked a piece of hair behind her ear. "Just last year. I'm not sure if that's quite normal. Apparently the signs have always been there, but it hit me then. I was walking down the stairs when I realized there was a large piece of glass in my shoulder. I had pain for such a short time, that I thought it might have been a headache. I took the glass out like I was invincible. I remember feeling another sharp pain when I withdrew the glass, but it quickly went away. I told no one about that day. Then after that discovery it was as if my powers awakened. I could sense when someone was hurt, something drew me in. I couldn't stand blood because I just wanted to fix it," she gulped. Antoine stared at her with pity in his eyes. He wanted to fix her pain. If he had a power, it would be to protect those he loved from emotional pain.

The woman reached across to take her hands. "The Goddesses decide when your powers are ready to be awoken. They chose this time for you because they had a feeling you'd need them. Can you think of why?"

The princess darted her eyes between the two boys sitting next to her. They were from two different kingdoms and seeing their contrasting faces brought one reason to mind. 'War.' She felt her heart skip a beat at the sudden realization. Cassius peered over at her in concern. "What is it?" he questioned.

"Well," her eyes flickered to Fran. "War was the first thing that came to my mind."

"Oh don't be silly. My mum would never start a war so quickly," Cassius said.

Antoine managed to speak up, he was not a servant in this home, "but your father would and he's a manipulative man who happened to look pretty upset when he left the castle. Clare is right. The Goddesses must have thought a war was surfacing. I'm not sure how one girl's powers could help, but Clare, she is special."

"There is not much else I can tell you, I'll send you off to my sister in the morning if you are ready," the woman said, ignoring Cassius's attitude. "But I know that magic is a dangerous thing. Something that the evil people in this world want to acquire for themselves. They wish to extract the magic from its users and use it for evil. For revival and for war and destruction. You must not get caught using magic around anyone you don't trust. Though I assume it's not something you can control, you must try. I am sending you to my sister as soon as possible. My sister is wise, she will be able to help you control what you feel. Go rest up. I'll have breakfast ready for you three in the morning." She gave them a kind smile and gave her cat a few more pets.

Antoine turned to her, "where should I stay?"

"With them of course, there are two beds. No need to be shy."

"Obviously Clare and I will share a bed," Cassius said as he stood up from the table. "Thank you for the coffee," he told the woman. Clare stood up and gave him a glare. She could defy him all she wanted, there was no one here to be furious with her.

"Yes thank you for the coffee. We will make sure that everything is cleaned up before we leave," she told Fran.

The three of them headed off to the spare bedroom in the back of the cottage. There were two full sized beds. One was done up neatly and the other was messily thrown together. There was an array of bags on the floor and a few items discarded throughout the room. There was one window on the back wall covered by cream curtains. The covers on the bed were quilted.

"Clare and I will take the bed closest to the window, you can take the one by the door."

There was an innocent smile on Antoine's face. He set down his satchel by his nightstand. "Alright, I'll make sure to protect you both," he winked.

Clare giggled and his smile only grew brighter. "Well I'll bathe and join you shortly. Don't wait up, get some sleep."

By the time Antoine had grabbed his bags from Fran and finished cleaning up, Cassius was sound asleep.

Clare on the other hand had the curtains open, using the moonlight as her guide to scribble in the pages of what appeared to be a sketchbook. At the sight of Antoine, she carefully set down her book and rushed towards him.

He put a finger to his lips in an attempt to quiet her, but she ignored him.

Her hands wrapped around his waist and he lowered his finger to return her hug. She was warm from the heater vent above their bed, her skin soft from the rose moisturizer she had been using. "I forgot to pack some of my toiletries, I might have used your soap," he whispered, his smile spreading from ear to ear. He rubbed his hand against her back. "I didn't expect you to miss me so much. Should we talk in the garden? I don't want to wake him."

Clare pulled away from the hug and took his hand.

The two of them moved silently out of the room and outside into the cool night air. The stars were so far away, but they appeared to be dancing just above their heads. The large pine trees rustled gently. Every so often, a pine cone fell to the ground.

Antoine had brought a blanket from the sofa outside. He sat down on the cement leading up to the doorway.

She sat next to him and he wrapped the blanket around the two of them.

"We absolutely should not be doing this," he said nervously.

Clare shrugged. "It'll be fine. Cassius sleeps like a rock. If he notices us, I will just say that we were discussing tomorrow's plan. Don't get too worried okay?" She relaxed her shoulders and leaned against him. "How was your journey? Was it boring? Did you eat enough? Should I go get you something to eat?"

"Clare, I'm fine. I can wait until the morning to eat. My journey was well. No injuries and surprisingly a decent amount of sleep. I'm here now like you asked me to be, I'm still a bit nervous, but I'm here. How was your journey with Cassius? Was he good to you?" he asked.

She adjusted her position to lean further against him, surprisingly, he did not move away. "It was long. We got lost like my letter said. After a few screaming matches in the woods, we eventually ended up here. Cassius is fine, he isn't my favorite person, but he is fine. I feel like I have my sister's temper these days, but without the violence. I miss Sage already. I hope she's doing well. Are things escalating between the kingdoms? I can't get the post out here."

Antoine was scratching his chin which was free of facial hair, aside from a tiny amount of stubble peaking through. "I haven't heard anything that seems out of the ordinary. King Maximus is a tad bit more stressed. He's preparing for the worst. Which I understand, I wouldn't put it past Erebus to convince Adria that war is the best option. Maximus is still seeing the same bloke. Usually he switches them out every few days, but this one has stuck around. He needs someone stable in his life anyways. They're happy together and I'm very happy for them. I was also happy, but nervous to see you. You and the royal family mean a lot to me. You treat me so normally, I know in some places that is frowned upon. I come from a serving family and we don't get much respect. You're so kind to me, too kind to me and we have a lot in common."

"We do have a lot in common, I'm glad things don't seem bad back at home. I can't imagine how stressed my sister is. I wish I could feel her pain like I feel magic presence, but I can not. I am nervous to go see Natalia. I'm afraid my magic will hurt someone."

"It will not. Your magic is defensive and it heals, anything dangerous I'm sure she will be able to tame. That is why we are visiting her after all."

"You're right." Clare let silence fill the air for a few moments. "I wish I could fall asleep out here with you"

"Yes me too, but we should get to bed. We have a long day of traveling ahead of us tomorrow. Especially you, I'm sure all of this new information is draining to hear."

"You're right. Antoine, may I have one more hug?"

"Anything for the princess, but more specifically, anything for Clare."

She embraced him so tightly that he thought he was going to vanish in her arms.

THE DEATH NOTE

It had been a little over a week since Sage had last seen Clare. King Maximus had been sending letters to the Pax palace everyday. Queen Gracielle would sit by Sage in the war room and guide her through writing a response. Her mother was training her to speak eloquently when it came to political matters. One wrong word or a snotty phrased sentence and a war could start. King Maximus was rational enough not to do such a thing, but this was practice for if she ever needed to communicate with King Erebus as well. In the letters they discussed what the kingdom's response plan would be if the Antias family declared war. Queen Gracielle, who usually preferred to stay neutral in times of crisis, knew she could not use this act much longer. 'If he attacks your kingdom. We will fight on your side. I am not opposed to a united Europe, but I will not let that unity be under his rule,' she had Sage write. Sage had just finished filing away the letters and the prepared battle plans when her mother burst into the room with another letter. They had been coming in nonstop. She was too anxious not to read it, the envelope had already been discarded, the parchment was crumpled, she slammed it on the cherry wood desk in front of Sage. "Read this. It is not good."

To the Pax family,

Have you ever heard of spies? I fear if you have then you are not good at detecting them and neither are the Demetrias's. I would like to gladly inform you that there was a spy at both Sage's birthday celebration and the Demetrias's sporting event. I will not tell you what they look like. That sadly takes all the fun away. This little spy reported to me some very useful information about your daughter, Clare. It seems that she has a little crush on a servant named Antoine. Unfortunate, especially for my son. I invite you to attend Antoine's public execution. It will take place whenever I catch him. I am so nice to spare Clare. I hope to see you in attendance.

King Erebus

Sage set down the letter, her face frozen. Gracielle moved over towards her and sat by her side. The two of them had gotten a lot closer. Instead of spending time with Clare, Sage spent time with her mother. It wasn't ideal because she couldn't gossip with her or tell her anything that crossed her mind, but she was good company. They did have a few things in common, their urge to be lazy at the end of the day, their sweet tooth, their love for food and their love one another and Clare. Clare was in danger because she was with Antoine and if anyone harmed him, then Clare would crumble into a million pieces. "Is that even legal? Can he do that?" she asked her mother.

"Unfortunately because he is a servant, if he is not on Demetrias property then he is not doing his job and he can be executed for that alone. That hardly happens because no one usually minds, but we know Erebus does. If he manages to catch Antoine outside of Demetrias territory, he's a goner," she said solemnly.

"We have to send a letter to Clare immediately," Sage said.

"And what if Cassius reads it?" Gracielle asked as she handed her daughter a quill, she seemed more frail than she had been before. Sage knew she wasn't skipping meals, but her mother was silently stressed. 'Could her mum take any more pain?'

"Then good. Maybe he will stop his father."

Gracielle shook her head. "Handsome boy, but gullible. If his father has written to him and told him he believes Clare fancies Antoine, I imagine he will throw a fit of rage. You need to get this letter out to Clare first so that way she can convince him otherwise before he is even told."

Her mother was right and she was giving that boy more credit than he deserved. Sage still hated him, but he was going to be family some day, she'd have to make room for him in her heart. "Right, well what am I waiting for?" She opened the desk drawer and pulled out a fresh piece of parchment. Smoothing it out on the desk, she wrote.

Dear Clare,

You know that I miss you dearly, but I do not have the time to write such things. I am in a hurry to send this to you, so I will send it to your last location and hope that Fran will point our guard in your direction if you have moved. You have been caught. I do not know if you love Antoine, I mean you have not even fancied him for that long, but I know a spark is there and so does King Erebus. That damn bastard had spies at our recent events. Protect Antoine with every ounce of magic you have if that is what you must do, they are coming to find him and when they do, they plan to execute him. In the meantime shower Cassius with affection. This is all you can do to prove them wrong and save his life. I love you lots and I believe in you.

With Love,
Sage

Sage neatly folded the letter and stuffed it into a cream envelope. She pushed it frantically to her mother who wrote the address in neat handwriting. She then called for a guard who took the letter and ran down the hallway and out the door as fast as he could. He was told to ride his horse as fast as the animal's legs would take it and not to rest for a second. Sage's face now twisted in anger. "If they manage to kill Antoine, we can't stand down, we have to go to war." She told her mother, her hands raised in the air.

Gracielle frowned. "I thought I told you, you must be level headed about these things. But you are most likely right, only because the Demetrias's would declare war first and we would be obligated to follow. Antoine is very special to Julius, you know that. If Maximus sees his brother upset, he will scorch the Earth and kill as many people as it takes, to make sure Julius smiles again one day. For him, he'd kiss the sun to soak up the rain." She pushed a strand of hair behind her ear. "It is time that I show you something, come on." She stood up and helped her daughter stand from the chair.

Gracielle guided Sage down a few flights of stairs and gave her a lantern, They arrived at an old cellar. The room was large with no windows and was only lit by flames. She shone her own lantern light against the wall and illuminated a row of armor, swords and daggers.

"This place is where you will run incase of an explosion or attack. It is your best chance of survival if you can't get out of the palace and it is where you will suit up for war. A queen should never fight on the front lines, but I have a feeling if something happens to me, my ghost wouldn't be able to stop you from joining your soldiers." She smiled at her daughter's soft laugh. "This place was your fathers. Somewhere to store his armor. We didn't have room for it in our closet since my dresses took up a lot of space. These weapons and armor belonged only to him and his brother. He'd want you to have them. Just like he wanted you to have Amicus, he told me someday, this would all be yours. And don't fret, Clare has some of his clothes and old sketchbooks, she gets her artistic skill from him. She will not be jealous." She slipped Sage a small note, "this is the code to open the door to this place. I hope you never have to use any of this, but with a tyrannical king in power, I believe that you might."

"You know, you always said papa died in the war, but you never told us how." Sage ran her finger over the bright white metal armor. Gracielle bit down on her lip. She hated this story, she wished she could take it to her grave, but her daughter had the right to know. "Right. Well, I was not there, so I truly do not know, I only know what Jesse and their higher ranking officers told me." Her lip quivered, her mind trailing off to that horrible day. "I had been sitting on the sofa, reading a book, it was a romance novel, one Wade had recommended to me, he was a big reader as you know. Then there was a knock on my door and I thought he was coming home." Her eyes began to water, "so I opened the door and there was his mate Jesse, he was crying, sobbing. The man next to him I had never seen, he was wearing all black and he was holding up a certificate. He told me he was sorry to inform me, but my husband had died in battle," she began to cry. Sage pulled her mother close, her own eyes watering at her mother's distress. Once Gracielle had collected herself, she continued. "He showed me the death certificate and said that they had already cremated him, like I had asked in case something happened. The man left and Jesse came in. He was sent home from the war because they feared he was not capable after Wade's death. A man stabbed your father in the eyes, he went blind. Jesse tried to pull him to safety, to a medical tent, but the knife had hit his brain and he had passed on."

There were a few moments of quiet understanding as   Gracielle cried and Sage held onto her tight. Once her tears had stopped, Sage whispered, "what happened to Jesse?"

Gracielle shrugged. "I don't know. I never invited him back to the palace because I would have been reminded of Wade. I should have kept him in our lives and I regret it. I don't know where he is darling, but if you ever find him, bring him back to me, so I can tell him I'm sorry. I was grieving and I was foolish."

"It's okay mum, you were going through a hard time. I'll do my best to find Jesse. I'm glad you showed me this place. You are right, no ghost can stop me, not even yours." Her watery eyes flickered up to the ceiling. "I hope Clare gets that damn letter soon."

"She will darling," Gracielle said.

And as they slipped inside of bed that night, Excidium was preparing for the dead.

A WISE WOMAN

They arrived at Natalia's a day later. The mountains were only a few hours from Fran's place in the woods, but getting the horses to climb up the steep hills to the large cabin added more time onto their trip. After the Deus guards recognized their royal status and Antoine's citizenship, they were allowed to cross the border without official documentation. The three of them and their horses managed to arrive at the home an hour before sunset. The cabin in the woods was larger than the previous one that they had visited. The exterior wood was painted white and the royal blue roof was sloped, curving out into triangle shaped points. Natalia stood in front of the smoky gray door. She was similar in age to her sister, but she had aged less visibly. In fact, she looked as if she was only in her early forties instead of her late fifties. Natalia had pitch black hair and high cheekbones. She was a lot tanner than her sister, but they shared the same dark brown eyes. She wore a long, royal blue dress with puffed out sleeves. Underneath the dress was a grey button up top and on her feet she wore gray flats. She smiled upon meeting the three of them. "It is so good to see you Princess Clare, Prince Cassius and Antoine. Welcome to my home, come in please."

"How do you know who I am?" Antoine asked.

"I'm a Deus citizen, I've seen you around," she said.

The three travelers left their dirty shoes at the door and followed her into the kitchen. On the oak counter she had laid out three pastel blue tea cups on neon blue saucers. The cups were already filled to the brim with a light tea. On the table there was a bowl filled with sugar cubes and a bowl filled with cut up lemons. She made them each a sandwich and then sat herself down. Once the three of them sat beside her, she wasted no time getting started. "I assume you have come to me for help with your magic, so I will help you. I am going to train Clare and help her control some of her powers. But what exactly are you two doing here?" She raised the cup to her lips, her eyes flickered to the two boys.

Cassius was the first to respond. "Well I'm here for protection and comfort. I'm not sure what he's here for." He glared at Antoine who was smiling warmly while he sipped his tea, his leg bouncing up and down.

"I'm here for emotional support and problem solving. I suppose we thought we'd be running into monsters and criminals on our journey, but fortunately that has not been the case. I hate to ask more questions, but how did you know Clare has magic?"

"I can sense it in her. And a lady can defend herself, Prince Cassius, you are not needed, but I'm glad you two are accompanying her. Magic can be emotionally draining. Having two people you trust by your side is good, even if they might corral." She turned to look at Clare who was attempting to be as polite as possible while ignoring Cassius and downing her tea, she was extremely thirsty from the day's travel. "Clare, I would like you to change into something more comfortable and meet me in the back of my home. As for you two, you may have some free time or come watch us train, but since there is still some sun in the sky, I'd like to get in an introductory session. I'm not sure how much time you have and I want to send you back home to your kingdom or to continue your journey as quickly as possible. I heard you planned to be away for months, but that is not necessary. I want the princess to go home as quickly as possible."

After they had all finished their tea and sandwiches, Clare changed into what Natalia had provided her with, which was a loose pair of mesh, royal blue pants and a white button up, short sleeve top. Clare pulled on a pair of her own white boots and tied her hair up into a messy bun. Cassius had gone outside to take in the view, leaving her and Antoine alone. "I'm nervous," she whispered to him. His hands found hers and he held them gently. "I bet you are and it's okay to be nervous. If anything goes wrong, I'll be a few steps behind you and your fiancé will be too."

Clare nodded, her voice tight, "I trust you." She raised their hands up and gave his knuckles a quick kiss before breaking away, there was a bright blush on his face.

"Let us go," he said.

Clare and Antoine met Cassius and Natalia outside. Cassius was laying on the ground staring up at the sky and pointing out the

151

different types of butterflies to Natalia. He didn't seem like an insect lover, so she was a bit put off, but she went along with his excitement anyways. "Yes, I do get a lot of butterflies out here, Cassius," she said. She then turned her attention away from him and waved to Clare. Maybe she should have continued to call them by their royal titles, but she was in the middle of the woods and they were teenagers who were now guests in her own home. She decided she could do whatever she wanted.

Cassius sat up from the floor and waved as well. "You look quite ravishing. I hope I get a piece when you're done," he told Clare teasingly. He watched her go still, at first she was stunned by his joke, but once she comprehended it, she rolled her eyes and shrugged. She moved towards the center of the clearing where Natalia stood. Antoine walked away from her and sat by Cassius. "I think you made her uncomfortable," Antoine said shyly.

"I was joking," Cassius said grumpily.

Clare met Natalia at the center of the clearing. When the woman bowed, Clare followed. "I feel honored that you want to train me."

"And I feel honored that you are accepting my help. We are going to start off by grounding ourselves. Magic takes control. You must know that you are in control of your own body. Take long and deep breaths."

Clare squared her shoulders back and drew in a deep breath, she gently exhaled and repeated the process until she cleared her mind. The thoughts began to leave her one by one like leaves falling from a withering tree. She forgot that Antoine and Cassius were watching her and she stopped thinking about her sister's absence, instead she focused on relaxing. She opened up her eyes to see Natalia smiling at her.

"Now think about your magic like water. Your magic has a constant flow and is surging within you. Think of this magic as a stream of water that you can control. You must believe that you are in control of yourself to manipulate your powers to do what you want them to do." Natalia closed her eyes and together they concentrated. After a moment, she opened her eyes and put something in between them while Clare was drawing in deep breaths. She had placed down a wounded bird with a broken wing. "Now I want you to open your eyes and look below you."

Clare looked to the ground to see a small gray bird, one wing flapping, the other hanging sadly by its side. The bird let out a distressed chirp. Her eyes scanned the small bird and then she saw it, blood, crimson and sticky.

Natalia noticed her eyes go wide. "You have to learn how to control yourself. We will help the bird, I promise, but pretend you are in public and there are eyes all over you, you are a princess, you can not have an outburst, you must stay calm. I am not itching to help this bird, nothing is drawing me in. I am holding back the energy inside of me and so can you." She watched Clare's fingers twitch and grip the side of her pants. Clare ripped her eyes off of the bird and instead focused on Antoine who was picking flowers from the grass, twisting their stems into one another.

The bird made another noise and she turned her attention back to it. Instead of thinking of the blood, she let her mind wander, she was sitting in a flower field with Antoine, counting the petals of a flower, he was smiling and telling her about the novel that he had just finished.

"Very good." The strict voice broke her train of thought. "Now we are going to take the bird to a remote location so we can heal it in private. Pretend the two gentlemen observing us don't know you have magic. Go ahead, pick up the bird."

Clare knelt down and the urge returned. The closer she was to the blood, the harder it was to push the urge away. As she scooped the bird up in her hand, her fingers twitched and closed in tightly. Before she could ground her magic, her fingers began to release an emerald green mist. Within a second, the bird's wing healed and her shoulders dropped in relief. The bird chirped and then flew out of her hands and into the woods.

She caught the eyes of Cassius, he was amused and staring.

"I failed," she said bluntly as she looked to Natalia.

"That is alright. You can not expect to succeed at everything the first time. Life is a game and you must play to win it. Most inexperienced players do not win on their first try. Plus, your magic seems to be stronger than mine. Most healing magic glows blue, when someone's magic has turned evil it turns black, I have never seen green, I am not sure what it means, but it must be harder to control. We will try again. Cassius, bring me something wounded."

The prince stood up from his place on the floor and peered behind the tree. There were a few wounded animals lined up, she

153

must have injured them for the training. He placed a squirrel with a broken paw in the middle of the two women and stepped back. "You are strong Clare," he said reassuringly, before retreating back to his spot next to Antoine.

"You should pick some flowers and help me," Antoine said to Cassius as he continued to weave the stems together.

"Fine," the prince murmured, his voice annoyed as he began to pull the flowers growing in the ground out in fistfuls.

Antoine shook his head, "I guess that works, but I am not so sure why you ned to go about it so aggressively," he said.

There was no blood on the floor, but it was clear that the animal in front of Clare was injured. Though she had the urge to help, she felt relatively at ease. "Blood must pull you forward," Natalia concluded. "Now let's try this again. Pick up the animal and move it out of sight. Imagine a wall, a damn, and behind it the magic, trapped, unable to escape."

Clare knelt down and picked up the squirrel. When she felt the wounded flesh, her hands began to tremble, instead of focusing on something else, she focused on her magic, she wouldn't let it escape. She hurriedly walked behind a tree and when she was out of sight the imaginary magic damn burst open and her magic poured into the small creature who then scampered away.

"You did it," Natalia said proudly. "Did you know there is a way to perform magic without your aurora spreading, in other words the glow. It is something that I have just recently mastered, but seeing as you are powerful, I think it is possible for you to pick it up in a few days. Would you like to see it in action?" She looked at the girl who was still stunned from her own abilities and grinned, "very well then." She headed off to the same tree Cassius had picked up the squirrel from and brought forward the last animal, a cat with a broken tail.

Natalia placed the gray tabby on the forest floor. She then knelt down and placed her hands just above the creature's tail. She focused and then pressed her hands down, the cat let out a hiss as her hands touched the tail. The damaged bones snapped back into place and her hands retreated, there had been no blue glow. "How did you do that?" Clare asked in bewilderment. "I need to learn how. If I'm able to remove my aura then it will be easier for me not to get caught with magic."

"Months and months of practice. But like I said, I think you can learn it quicker. It takes an immense amount of willpower and strength, but you have that Clare, I see it in you. Just know that this trick does not extend to all situations. It is easier to perform without an aura on minor injuries like a cut or scrape, but it is draining to perform on broken bones. I feel a bit winded. Controlling your magic's visibility is almost impossible when it comes to a person you love. If my sister was ever in danger then I wouldn't be able to control the way my magic looks, in fact, I am not sure if I would be able to control my magic at all. It just might burst out of me to help save her. Your magic is connected to your heart. That is why we can differentiate between good magic and bad magic. If someone is truly in your heart, then your body will attempt to do anything that it can to save them. Would you like to try controlling your healing magic on a person? I don't expect you to be able to hide your aura, I just want you to resist temptation."

The information was a lot to take in at once. Clare was sure she must have heard this somewhere in a magic book she had read, but had forgotten. Magic books were banned in most public places to help protect magic users safety, but there were plenty of magic books locked away in the royal library. Most of the magic books in the royal library focused on stories where magic had been used for better or for worse, they often didn't go into detail on how magic itself worked because only those who used magic truly knew and a lot of magic users had been murdered. Only a few remained.

When she had finally processed the information, Clare made a mental note to write what she had learned down in the sketchbook she had brought on their journey. "Yes, I would like to try," she looked over to Antoine and Cassius who were messing with the flowers. "I can't hurt either of them." She wouldn't be able to control herself if Antoine got hurt, he was soft, fragile and she swore to protect him. As for Cassius, she wasn't sure if he would impact her as much, but she had a feeling she would protect him with her life too. He had a place somewhere in her heart, but figuring out where that place was, was the hard part.

Natalia offered herself instead. "I'm sure you care too much for both of them, so you wouldn't be able to control yourself. Let's start with me. We need to see if your compassion is stronger with humans or animals." She took out a small switchblade and cut the back of her hand, she showed no signs of pain. "You need to control yourself. Imagine I am a stranger and you can not heal me in public or you could possibly expose yourself to a dangerous person who wants to steal your magic. I'll take care of healing myself, in fact my body is going to heal this cut when I let it. For now, your mission is to walk away from me and go sit with the boys on the opposite edge of the clearing."

The burning, hot sensation that rushed through her body at the sight of blood, amplified when the blood belonged to a human. When she saw animal blood, her fingers would twitch and her skin would go warm, but now, Clare felt like she was on fire. She forcefully turned her head to the boys, but something inside of her turned it right back around. She closed her eyes and tried to think of the magic, behind a damn, but it wasn't working, she needed something stronger. She thought of her sister's voice, her sister calling her name from afar. She imagined Sage sitting near Cassius, yelling at him for existing, her foot moved in the opposite direction. As Sage's voice became clear and more distinct inside of her head, she turned away from Natalia and walked towards the boys, she began to sprint.

The two looked up in alarm. "Is everything alright?" Antoine asked as he saw her running towards them.

"Did that woman hurt you?" Cassius questioned angrily. She fell to her knees and brought them both into a hug. The burning sensation left her body and the smell of blood faded, the sweet smell of flowers and the tang of Cassius's cologne filled her nostrils. Cassius peered down at her awkwardly, moving his body off of Antoine's, to ensure that the contact he had was only with Clare.

She pulled away from the both of them and her lips spread out into a smile. "I'm alright. I did it, I walked away." The two of them gave her a high five and she turned to Natalia who was giving her a thumbs up. The blood had disappeared from her hand and she was walking back towards the group of teenagers.

"The urge is stronger when it comes to humans isn't it? I experience the same thing myself, but I have had more years to practice concealing what I feel. Some magic users feel a strong connection to animals, but I was not sure if that was you. It wasn't. What helped you turn away? You'll need to remember that thought for the next time you are in a troublesome situation and you know you can control yourself."

"My sister," Clare said triumphantly. "She was calling me and I ran to her. I ran as fast as fire spreads."

"Good job," Natalia replied.

"How did your skin not heal within seconds?" Clare asked. "When I get injured my body doesn't wait, it heals me immediately."

"I didn't let it heal me right away," Natalia said, "magic is all about control."

Through the trees the leaves rustled and there was a frantic shout. "Mrs. Pax, Mrs. Pax!" came a voice from the trees. Clare stood and ran towards the noise, Cassius followed after her, he didn't plan to lose her anytime soon. Clare darted through the trees until she reached the voice. A man on a horse who looked half dead, extended his hand out into the air, there was a letter dangling from his grasp. Clare took the letter in her fingers and turned it over to see the wax seal that belonged to her kingdom.

"Thank you," she smiled. "Finally a letter from mum and Sage," she told Cassius happily.

Cassius faked a smile and then turned around to roll his eyes. "Why did you have to make such a big fuss about it?" Cassius said angrily to the man who was turning his horse in the other direction. "Your highness I was told that the contents of this letter were important and to deliver it as quickly as I could."

Clare was still smiling, "well thank you, I appreciate your service. Maybe it has to do with Sage and Julius's wedding, they might want us to come home for it. I will open it up later," she told the horseman. "Tell my sister that in a few days a letter will reach her."

"But your highness—"

"She said she would read it later, you prick," Cassius said angrily, "you are dismissed."

Natalia and Antoine emerged from the trees. She dipped her head towards the royal guard. "Now, we can not let this handsome man embark on a large journey without a cup of tea can we? Why don't you three go clean yourselves up. We are done for the evening, the sun is almost set. I will continue your training tomorrow if time allows me to and I'll let you know who may help you on the rest of your journey as well. There is a room for each of you, so do not fret, my home is plenty big. I will fix this dashing man up a meal. How does that sound?" The man jumped off of his horse and followed her into her home.

Antoine moved forward, a flower crown in his hand. "I know you already have a crown, but we both made you another one. Well I made you one and he sort of helped," Antoine said as he extended the crown to Clare.

Clare beamed, "It's lovely! A letter and a crown all in one day, I am so spoiled!"

Clare and Cassius took one bedroom and Antoine took another. Clare was going to get undressed to bathe, but instead she decided to open the letter. "I should probably open it now," she told Cassius. Though they didn't have to share a bedroom, they had chosen to, to strengthen their bond. Clare sat down on the royal blue bedding and carefully lifted the tip of the envelope up from the wax seal. After pulling off his boots, Cassius kneeled down and unlaced hers.

"Go ahead, I'm just trying to treat you like the princess that you are." He looked up and smirked at the bright blush that appeared on her face.

While she read the letter, he removed her boots and set them by the door. On his way back he noticed a change in her facial expression. She seemed panicked, she had one hand placed over her heart and her other hand gripped the letter tightly.

"Is the wedding that soon?" Cassius asked her as he joined her at the foot of the bed.

She turned to him, a lump in her throat, she was unable to formulate the words, her hands were trembling and a chill up her spine sent shivers down the rest of her body. She pushed the letter in his hands and he took it, quickly reading over what was written on the page.

"No," he whispered in denial. His thoughts were running wild, 'did she fancy Antoine?' No. That wasn't important. What was important, was that his father was going to send a man hunt to look for the three of them and once they found Antoine they would try to kill him. He angrily set the letter down and tugged at the strands of black hair falling in his face.

Clare had finally found the words to speak, her voice shaky and almost numb. "Why would he do that? And before you get angry at me, Antoine and I were just hanging out as close mates. There is no reason for your father to kill him. Please write your father Cassius, please," she begged. She stood up from the bed and began to rummage through her luggage. She pulled out her dusty brown sketchbook and ripped out a page, handing him a quill and a sealed pot of ink.

He bit down on his lip and set the items down. "I will write to him, but first I need to hear the truth. I know the truth doesn't seem urgent when you hear something like this, but it is something that I need to know. I will write to him either way, but please tell me first. What is it that he saw that made him so angry?"

"I don't know what he saw because nothing we have done justifies his death. On the day of Sage's birthday, we went down to the stables to look at the horses and then we went to the library. On the day of the event, he escorted me back to the castle and that is when he found out about my powers, but there was no way a spy could've been in the castle, they could've only seen what happened outside. The event and the stables."

"Is Antoine here with us because you fancy him?"

She was quiet and unable to answer.

"Right, well I believe I have my answer. I am going to write to my father. I don't like this situation, but I would never wish death upon someone who makes you smile so big." He grabbed the quill, pot of ink and parchment. "If you'll excuse me, I would prefer to be alone."

"Cassius, I'm sorry," she called, but he was out the door.

Cassius went to Natalia's office and set down the items. He messily tossed his hair around and let out a disappointed sigh. 'How was he to ever win her over?' Maybe her heart did not belong to him. After all she was sad when they were told to get engaged, he wasn't the love story that she wanted, but Antoine could give that love story to her. He could give her flower crowns and paintings and poems. He was sweet, intelligent and caring. 'What was Cassius besides good looks and anger?' He had always thought so highly of himself, but Sage had proven he wasn't that great with a sword and that he wasn't a prize to be won. He was damaged goods, that's what he was. The product of a child who was verbally and physically abused, a child who constantly tried to one up any other boy. He attempted to put his arrogance aside to make Clare happy, yet still she refused him. 'Maybe this was what he deserved for being a dick all of those years.' He shook the thoughts from his head and dipped the quill in ink. He pushed away his selfish desires and wrote in defense of the boy who stole from him.

Father,

Your anger has gone too far. Keep it directed towards me and me only. You can punch me when no one is looking or call me worthless, or botched, but keep your wrath far away from my fiancé. If you kill the boy, who has done nothing wrong, then you slowly kill her. She is to be my wife one day whether she is in love with me or not and I want her to be happy. So call off your guards and your troops or the next time I see you, I won't hesitate to release years of pent up anger. I'm done bowing to you.

Cassius

He set the quill down and folded the piece of parchment up into a tiny square, placing it in one of the spare envelopes lying around. He addressed the letter to his father and then carefully peered down the stairs.

Natalia and the guard were bonding over a cup of tea

. He cleared his throat and the two looked his way. "I'm sorry to interrupt, but this is an urgent letter that must get sent out immediately. Do you know of anyone who could take it?" His eyes flickered to the guard who seemed intrigued. "I will pay you greatly for your sacrifice if you choose to take this letter to my kingdom." Cassius moved closer to them and set the letter down on the table. The guard frowned at Natalia. "I would hate to leave you, but I need more money and," she placed a comforting hand on his shoulder to let him know that it was alright.

"It is okay darling," she said kindly. "Just let me pack you some food to go." She stood up and paused to stretch out her limbs and then made for the kitchen. "You three may start a fire out back if you wish to. I have plenty of wood."

Cassius nodded and then turned to the guard. "Thank you and please go as quickly as you can, this letter is urgent."

He made his way back up the stairs, he would have to go back and talk to Clare. She was waiting for him in the hallway, he sighed, it was hard to stay mad at her forever. "She says there is a fire out back that we can sit by, I would prefer it if it was just you and I, but we can invite him too." He peered down the hallway to Antoine's room. "We aren't telling him this, not yet," he said stubbornly, thankfully, Clare agreed with him. "I will go just with you if that is what it takes to fix things between us, I don't want you to be upset with me forever."

Cassius pondered the idea, "no, I feel bad leaving him alone, just try to look a little more interested in me." He stalked past her and knocked on Antoine's door.

The blonde stumbled out in his night clothes and laughed when he saw Cassius, "what exactly do you want from me? Don't you despise me?"

"I never said that," Cassius scoffed. "Clare and I are going to build a fire, we want you to come." His eyes flickered away from Antoine who looked rather cheerful.

"Well if I am invited, then I will be there, count me in." He turned around and slipped on a pair of boots before walking out with Cassius.

Clare was smiling, she stood at the end of the hall, "well come on then."

The three of them went down the stairs and out the back door where they wouldn't disturb Natalia. There was a cluster of logs around a pile of wood just outside of the house. Cassius found a box of matches on the ground. He carefully took one out and struck the match, bringing light to the night sky. The match fell from his fingers and hit the wood, sending the wood up in flames. "How easy, we didn't even have to use your magic," Cassius pointed out, taking a seat on one of the logs. Clare sat next to him, figuring after his reaction to the news, she should bond with him. Antoine sat across from them.

"I don't have fire powers," she said, half annoyed.

Cassius shrugged, "anything seems to be possible with you, so I am just leaving our options open. Who knows, maybe you'll discover that next."

"Natalia said she would point us in the right direction, but she got too busy with the guard."

"Well that shouldn't be a problem considering I sent him off."

Antoine tilted his head, "why?"

Both Clare and Cassius met eyes, trying to hide the shocked

expressions from their faces. "I had to write back to my sister," Clare lied. "Cassius gave it to the guard to deliver."

Antoine leaned closer to the fire and pressed his hands together for warmth. Third wheeling with a couple when he had feelings for one member in the party was rather awkward, he had to think of something to say. He had an idea. "I want to get to know you guys better, so let's ask each other some questions, or at least let me ask them." He laid down on his log and looked up at the night sky. He didn't give them a chance to say no, he went down the list of questions in his head and picked one at random to start with. "Favorite color?"

"Blush pink," Clare said.

"Black," Cassius said bluntly.

"What's yours Antoine?" Clare questioned.

"Orange cream, it's odd, but I love it. Okay next question. If you could live in any kingdom, which one would you live in? I really like it with the Demetrias's, but think I would live in the kingdom of Kōun. The king, Akira is so nice and it is one of the happiest kingdoms."

"That's a good answer. I think I would live somewhere in one of the African kingdoms because I love their goddess and I have heard that the people are kind and that they can practice magic more openly there," Clare said as she laid herself down on Cassius's lap. He seemed surprised, but he made sure that she was comfortable in her current position and didn't move.

"I would pick somewhere in South America to get in touch with my routes," Cassius grinned. "I guess something in the family tree twisted, I wish I would have been a prince in one of their kingdoms instead."

Antoine acknowledged both of their responses and then moved onto the next question, "favorite dessert?"

"Strawberry tart," The two of them said in unison. Cassius and Clare raised an eyebrow at one another, they finally seemed to have something in common.

"Ah look at you two," Antoine smiled softly, knowing that this was how it was supposed to be, "mine is a lemon tart."

Before he could speak again, Clare interrupted, "I think it is my turn to ask the questions if you don't mind."

"Well of course not, go ahead princess."

"Favorite hobby? Mine is painting."

"Reading," Antoine said and Cassius went next, "fighting."

"Come on, fighting can not be your favorite hobby," Clare pouted.

He shrugged his shoulders, "I didn't really have a childhood where I was allowed to pick another hobby. Anyways, next question," he said awkwardly.

So she moved onto the next question and then the next. For a moment it seemed as if they were just normal teenagers. As if they didn't live in castles and palaces miles apart from one another. They were not trying to impress anyone out in these woods, they didn't have to hide who they truly were, they were allowed to be unique, to express themselves and relax, to let their guard down. They laughed and shared their interests for a while, losing track of time.

Clare had fallen asleep on Cassius's lap, he was stroking her hair and watching the woods, he didn't want to wake her, so instead he made sure nothing would hurt her.

Antoine on the other hand was pretending to sleep.

Natalia came out from the house with three blankets. She draped one over Antoine and then another over Clare and handed the last one to Cassius, who put it around his shoulders.

"I came out here to tell you where to go next, but the person who needs to hear it most is sleeping, so I will tell you. A man named Jesse, he lives somewhere in these mountains, he's in hiding, he's wallowed in sadness. He was good mates with Clare's father, he will know who Clare is. He is a good place to start, I don't think he has magic himself, but he will know about her father's lineage. I'm not sure what he knows, but I think it will be of use. I'd head out in the afternoon, after another training session, but don't worry, I'll make you kids some breakfast."

Cassius barely smiled, he just muttered a weak 'thank you' and she frowned.

"You seem to be the protector kid, what's going on? Can I help you with anything?"

He shook his head. "We got some bad news today and of course my father was the one who had to initiate it, even out here I can not escape him. I need to protect them from him, especially Clare. I don't like to let her know just how much I am hurting inside."

Natalia sat down on the other side of them, her frown deepening. "Men should speak about their emotions too, this girl is plenty brave, I am sure she will let you lean on her."

"I know she is strong, but I don't want to lean on her or anyone. What I went through was tough. My way of coping is just bottling it all up inside. I don't know when it'll finally leave me, or when I'll finally break, but I'm scared that when I do, it'll be worse than just a few tears." He gritted his teeth together. "I don't know why I am telling you this."

"Perhaps you are telling me because it feels good to talk about it," Natalia suggested. "We all go through horrors, some worse than others. Bottling it up will do you no good Cassius, you can entrust this information in another person, just one."

He thought about her offer, mulled it over, eventually, he told her just a little bit, "I put on an arrogant front because I don't want anyone to think I am anywhere near soft or compassionate. I was raised to be apathetic and uncaring. If I wasn't, if I was too soft, I would pay for it. I will not describe how he abused me, but I know he would still do it if he had the chance," he shivered. "He just doesn't take his chances these days because he knows how strong I have become. I don't feel any better talking about this, I'm done with it."

"I understand," Natalia gently placed a hand on his shoulder. "I am sorry you had to go through that and I am glad you confided in me. If he wasn't a king, I would have a word with him, but there would go my head. You are strong Prince Cassius, you will prevail. You don't have to have magic to have strong strength and control," she said.

He flinched away from her sudden hand movement, but stayed still when he realized that she just wished to comfort him. "Right, thank you." He cleared his throat, his cheeks burning and then coughed when a gust of the fire's smoke hit him right in the face.

"I'll put the fire out," Natalia said as she stood.

"I don't want her to wake and you should get some sleep," Cassius suggested.

"And so should you," Natalia said softly, splashing out the fire with a bucket of water she had kept nearby. "Rest Cassius, let your mind go off to a place where your father can not follow."

Natalia disappeared back into her house and Cassius saw Antoine shift in the darkness. His breath hitched at the thought of him overhearing the conversation he just had with the woman. He screwed his eyes shut and laid himself down on the log, Clare's head still on his lap. Sleep came when the sun began to come up.

Clare woke Cassius up that morning, she had not meant to, but he was a light sleeper and any small noise often disturbed his slumber. His eyes fluttered open to see her shining blue eyes staring at him. Once she registered he was awake, she sat up and stretched. Her mouth fell open and she released a loud yawn. She stretched her limbs and as she adjusted to moving, his hands lightly trailed down her sides. Her hair was quite the tangled mess, but it didn't seem to bother her. She was content with her situation, waking up in the woods in Cassius's arms. It was something she would have to get used to and though royalty were not allowed many vacations when they were in charge, she would suggest that they go every so often. She turned so that she was facing Cassius and let her hands grasp his fingertips that were warm from holding onto her all night. "Did you sleep alright?" She asked softly, her voice soft and groggy from being unused for a while. Her eyes flickered to the log where Antoine had once been. Her eyebrows furrowed, her head spinning with questions, she didn't necessarily remember falling asleep last night.

Cassius let his fingers fall out of her grasp, he gently pushed a stray strand of hair behind her ear. "Not really," he said. His dark eyes were tired and sunken, she placed a hand on his cheek and he flinched, but quickly forced himself to relax.

"I'm not going to hurt you Cassius," she whispered, "you just look tired and I wish I could magic the sleep into your body."

"Well, sadly you didn't get sleep inducing abilities," he said, ignoring her comment about hurting him. He had caught her eyes flicker over to the other empty log. "He was here last night, I'm sure nothing bad happened to him, he's probably inside with Natalia. Speaking of Natalia, she came out here last night while you were sleeping. She said she knows where we should go next and that we should leave soon." Mixed in with the smell of the pine trees, he caught the smell of pancakes in the wind, "I think she is cooking breakfast, so I'll let her explain what she's said, she knows the information better than I do."

Clare broke away from him and slid off the log, she held her hand out to him.

He debated on pushing her away or letting her lead him. In the end his hand gravitated to hers and he let her pull him up and to his feet.

She stood on her tiptoes, reaching up as far as she could to the top of his head where she pulled out a few leaves that the wind had left in his hair.

He gulped, holding his breath until she was done, she made his heart stir and he wasn't sure what to do about that feeling, besides desperately hope that it would go away. When she was flat on her feet, he thanked her. "I appreciate you saving me from looking like a disaster." He was still holding onto the hand that she had used to pull him up.

The two of them crossed the grass to the front door that was wide open. At the sight of Antoine, Cassius squeezed her hand tighter, partly to reassure her he was still alive and mostly to assert his protectiveness over her. He let her hand go so they could sit at the table and ignored Natalia's sensitive gaze, choosing to forget that they had spoken last night.

Natalia flipped a pancake over the furnace in a medium sized pan. "Clare, I wanted to speak to you, it looks like you slept well," she laughed, her eyes scanning the princesses ruffled hair.

Clare blushed her cheeks lighting up, "I did, thank you. Please go ahead and tell me what you wanted to tell me." She had taken a seat between the two boys. She picked up the forest green mug in front of her and poured some coffee from the pitcher inside, she wasn't a big coffee drinker, but she would need the caffeine to keep pushing through the day. She greeted Antoine with a wave and he smiled warmly at her, not letting his eyes linger too long before going back to reading the book he had borrowed from Natalia.

"I know a man named Jesse, he was friends with your father. He lives up here in the mountains. I have taught you some things about control and I don't want to keep you here longer then needed. I will give you one more lesson, but keep practicing what I taught you on the rest of your journey. Jesse will be your next best hint as to where your magic came from. After your stomachs digest, I will write you a letter to take to him. It's been a while since I have spoken to that cynic, he used to be so lovely. I hope you will deliver it for me."

"Of course," Clare smiled gently, her interest piqued. "Do you know anything else about him?"

"Not much, I'm sorry. He moved into the mountains after your father passed away. He was friendly at first, but he suddenly turned dark, he told me he didn't want to talk to anyone, so I left him alone.

I'm sure he will welcome you, he should recognize your name. He has to," she assured.

Natalia finished making a stack of pancakes and set the plate that held the large stack down on the table. She put down a jar of fresh maple syrup and a few berries that she had gotten from her garden to top the pancakes. She also had made a few eggs for protein. She sat down across from the three of them and passed them the silverware. Before she let them dig in, she spoke, "thank you Oralee and Abilene for blessing us with this food," she smiled up at the sky. Abilene was the Goddess from Asia, where her mother and father had come from. Once they had come here, she and her sister had changed their names to defy her parents and blend in, she became Natalia and her sister became Fran.

Once the small prayer was finished, she gestured for them to dig in. They each took a reasonable sized portion, doing their best to fuel their bodies for the day of travel ahead. Antoine was eagerly digging in, smiling warmly as the first bite slid down his throat. "Thank you, this meal is very good," he said as he continued to eat.
Clare and Cassius echoed their thanks. Cassius had a smaller plate than Clare and he was barely picking at his food.
Clare frowned. "Are you okay?" She whispered to him.
"Yeah, just not that hungry," he told her half honestly. Though he wasn't starving, he hadn't felt compelled to eat after spilling his emotions last night, but Clare's concern and the fear of being impolite was enough to make him eat what was on his plate without any complaints.
"Is there anything else we should know about our journey to Jesse or anything else that we should know about him?" Clare asked, attempting to make conversation as she finished her pancakes.

"Your journey should be short," Natalia told them, pointing her fork at Clare before taking another bite of her egg. "He doesn't live far from here. You'll need to cross the border and then keep going straight through the mountains. Then you should reach him shortly, you should be there just after the sun goes down. I've heard that his place is a little out of shape, so don't be surprised if it doesn't resemble this one in the slightest," she said honestly. "And don't worry, I have already packed you kids a bag. I put some apples and some pastries, some bread, cheese and a few other things along with three containers of water in your bag." She seemed rather proud of herself. Clare finished up her plate and tilted her head.

"Do you have any children?" she asked. Natalia seemed like the type to nurture and to love.

"Oh no, I never found the right man. I was disowned for not marrying," she twisted her face into a frown. "Fran left with me and we lived together for some time, making our living off of our crafts. We eventually separated so she and I could live our separate lifestyles. My magic was too much for her and her cats were too much for me. So no, no children. Though I do like them very much," she admitted.

Clare returned the frown, "I'm sorry to hear that. You've been so kind to us, I want to let you know that you are welcomed as a guest at the Pax palace anytime. Even if you wanted to live with us you could, there is plenty of space."

She seemed touched to tears, "oh I couldn't live there, but I might make a visit in the future."

Antoine grinned, "I'm sure Julius would be happy to have you as a guest as well."

Cassius awkwardly finished the last bite of his pancake, "I would offer you a place at the Antias castle, but I'll do you a favor and not give you that offer."

Antoine quickly filled the silence that followed. He knew Cassius was unaware that he had heard everything last night and he preferred to keep it that way, if they kept talking about his home life it was plausible that he might let something slip. "I am going to go take a bath so that way we can be on our way, thank you again for this breakfast, you really know how to cook." He wiped his mouth with a napkin and stood up, pushing in his chair. "You should really consider visiting the local villages, bring your cooking, there are always orphanages there, so many kids without homes, I know you could make them very happy with your food." He gave her a comforting smile before disappearing up the stairs and into the guest bedroom where he could freshen up for their journey. Cassius was next, he stood up and looked over to Clare.

"I'm going to get a head start and freshen up okay? I smell like a fire. Thank you for the breakfast Natalia." He bent down and for a second he contemplated kissing the top of Clare's head, his lips puckered and froze. 'Were they there yet?' Clare glanced up at him and nodded. At her permission his lips gently grazed the top of her head and he jogged up the stairs into the other guest bedroom.

168

"I take it that is the first time that has happened," Natalia said as she looked up the stairs and winked.

"Oh, yes, he hasn't done that before. I'm not sure why. I understand his hesitation though, the two of us have needed to strengthen our bond. He is so different when he is away from his father. He's fragile and kinder, I like him this way, but I don't like when he hurts. Anyways," she said, "we haven't even kissed yet. Natalia, can I have some motherly advice?"

The woman leaned forward on her elbows, eager to help. "Of course darling, what is it?"

Clare drew in a breath and lowered her voice to a whisper. "I am attracted to both of them. I love different things about both of them and my heart is so torn."

Natalia frowned sympathetically. Clare wondered if she had been in a similar situation herself. Natalia didn't speak, she waited for Clare to elaborate because she knew sometimes all one needed was a listening ear. Oftentimes after talking it through they would come to the conclusion themselves without any help.

"Cassius is kind underneath. We don't have much in common, but he tries so hard for me, harder than he should have to and he is very attractive," she lost her breath and had to recompose herself before continuing. "There is definitely some flickering spark between us, but then I compare him to Antoine. Antoine is my fairytale, he would be my happily ever after. He loves to read, he appreciates the arts, he is cute and would cuddle with me. He is soft and gentle while Cassius is the opposite. I am supposed to be with Cassius, I will be with him, there is no escaping it, but how do I get these feelings for Antoine to go away?" she asked.

Natalia finally opened her mouth to speak after some consideration. "Feelings can not just go away overnight. You know what is morally right, you should be with Cassius, for everyone's safety, but we are always drawn to the dangerous unknown aren't we?"

"We are," she whispered sadly. Her eyes began to fill with tears and Natalia stood up and crossed the room to sit in the chair next to her.
"What is it darling?"

"Natalia, I am going to get him killed," her tears were slow and hot, falling down her face in streams of regret. The woman placed her arms around the young girls shoulders. She wasn't sure what she meant, but she doubted that this information was true.

"King Erebus sent a letter," she was choking on her tears now, "they are going to execute him because they saw us together and they think that I'm in love with him. I should have stayed away from him, I should have never brought him here. Is he doomed to the eternity I have made for him?"

Natalia rubbed gentle circles in the girl's shoulder blades, her heart ached for her. "There is still time my dear, you can still reverse whatever mess you may have accidentally made. Love has no bounds, you couldn't control it. He agreed to come with you didn't he?" At her nod, she smiled. "See? He wouldn't have done this if he didn't trust you. Think good thoughts."

They sat there in the kitchen for a few minutes, Clare did her best to quiet her tears. Once she regained her composure, she turned to Natalia. "Can I hug you please?" Natalia nodded and welcomed the girl into a warm and tight embrace. If Gracielle and Sage weren't here to comfort her, then she would be. She would always be here for Clare no matter how far away she ventured, she felt connected to this girl, it was probably their ties to magic that caused her to feel this way.

"If you need me, Jesse's isn't far. Write to me anytime and I promise that I will visit you like you want me to," she stood the girl up and slowly let go of her arms. "Let's have one last training session and then you should go freshen up okay?" She ran a hand over the back of the girl's hair, "I'm going to pack you a few extra goodies while you're cleaning up, you deserve them."

Natalia had told Clare their training would not be too intense and that she could complete it in her nightgown. The two of them, full from breakfast, made their way back to the clearing. The birds were chirping in the trees, the sun was beating down, but the weather was still cool and slightly chilly. "I wanted to show you something that I can do with my magic that don't have to do with healing. I'm not sure if it's the same for you, but if it is, then I'd like you to be able to use these skills," Natalia said as she outstretched her hands. Clare watched carefully as the woman focused. A ball of blue light appeared in her hands and she held it gently like an egg, afraid to break the energy. She lifted up her palm and then passed the blue ball of energy to Clare. The girl held the ball of light, a tingling sensation rushing through her body.

"What is it?" Clare whispered.

"It's a ball of energy and energy creates light. If you don't have a flashlight on you and it's dark, you should be able to use some of your energy to create light. However much energy you expel, is how big your ball of light will be," she reached out and took the blue ball of energy back from Clare. "Go ahead and try," she encouraged her.

Once her hands were freed, Clare took a deep breath. She tried to think of that magic damn inside of her, she attempted to picture the energy flowing through her magic. For a while she stared intensely at her palms and nothing happened. She groaned in frustration, upset that this was a gift she did not have.

Natalia interrupted her groans, "try to think of your energy as a staticky thing, picture how much energy you have stored away. Picture yourself knocking on the door and asking your body for the energy, imagine your body handing it over to you."

Listening to her words, Clare sorted through the mental images she had been instructed to picture, her fingertips began to twitch and as she opened her eyes, she noticed a small green ball of light, it was brighter that Natalia's.

"Well done!" Natalia congratulated as she watched the girl's look of concentration turn into a smile. "So you can leave the ball of energy out as a light as long as you'd like. Eventually that ball of energy will fade away into nothing. How long it lasts depends on how big the orb is. But, if you need that energy back," she gestured to the blue orb in her hand, she pressed it to her stomach and the orb passed right through her. Natalia jolted up and her head twitched to both sides. "You can put it back in. It's not terribly painful. Just a little cramp, a tiny shock."

Since there was no need for the ball of light in the middle of the day, Clare followed after Natalia. After some hesitation she held the green glow to her stomach and pushed it back towards her body. The energy was sucked back into her stomach with a small shock and a painful cramp. She doubled over a bit nauseous, but once the energy had settled back in, she stood up and felt restored to normal. "How odd, I never imagined I could do such a thing. Is there anything else?" she asked excitedly.

"There is something else, but it's a bit more dangerous, I don't know if I should teach it to you," Natalia said honestly, chewing on her bottom lip.

"Please Natalia, what if I need it someday."

"Fine, but please don't use this skill unless you really have to, or you can't control yourself."

"I promise I won't."

Natalia moved ten feet away from Clare. Once they were an appropriate distance apart, she took a deep breath. "This is a fight or flight response of magic users, this skill, is the fight response. Normally if you're in danger, you can use a defensive shield, a bubble to protect you. If someone rams into the bubble, then they fall down."

"Yes I've discovered that," Clare said.

"Well this is a little different. When your body breaks down and believes it's in danger, you are capable of many great things. This is a defensive tactic, but it's a little more intense than a bubble and this often happens when you are in extreme pain. In a response to this pain, your magic damn can burst and you will become a ball of heat. Everyone around you will feel the warmth of a fire. It's meant to make them back off. This magic hurts, it's not dark magic, but it burns. Normally this response happens out of instinct, but you can perform this skill on command if you're well practiced. Now that I'm thinking about it, I don't wish to test it out. I don't want to hurt you and I don't want to make you hurt me."

"Well how does it work? How will I know?"

"You'll know if it is happening. You'll feel the magic damn burst open inside of you like someone is stabbing your stomach. Then the world will spin and you'll feel your skin become as hot as a burning flame. Let's not practice that. In fact that was all I wanted to show you, you should probably go upstairs and get ready to begin your journey."

As Natalia started to walk away, Clare followed after her. "Did something happen Natalia? I understand why you don't want to show me, but you sound a bit regretful that you shared this information with me."

"Forget about it please," the woman said as she walked into her home. Clare was unaware that Natalia's cousin had been killed because she accidentally used this skill. The people found out that she had magic, they thought she was dangerous so they imprisoned her. She died in prison from starvation. Though this skill could possibly protect Clare, was it worth it? She shouldn't have said anything. Clare shouldn't have been performing this skill unless it wasn't a choice, but a reaction. Maybe if she hadn't told her Clare wouldn't have made the same mistake as her cousin.

Cassius was getting dressed when Clare walked into the guest bedroom, before she arrived she had taken some time to sit and think outside. Her thoughts spiraled and she was soon thinking of Antoine, dead. She had let herself cry before wiping her tears and heading inside. Cassius's hair was still wet, he hadn't done a very good job drying it with a towel. He had only gotten his boxers on, he was pulling a pair of black trousers over his toned legs. His face turned to meet hers and she gasped, quickly shutting the door behind her. "I guess I should have knocked," she admitted sheepishly, heading to the corner of the room where her luggage was. She took a deep breath and started shakily looking through her clothes.

Cassius had pulled on a plain black t-shirt over his head. He spun around to help her pack and pick out an outfit, but when he got a glimpse of her eyes, he noticed something was off. "Clare, look at me." His voice was demanding and rougher than he intended it to be. She looked up from her luggage and gulped.

"You've been crying. Why?"

She bit down on her lip and blinked away the tears, she didn't want to break down all over again. She picked up the training uniform that Natalia had washed for her and said she could keep. She folded it in her arms along with her under garments and looked up at the ceiling. "I don't want him to die and I almost lost you. I know you're mad at me for thinking about other men, but I am sorry, if I could control it I would."

He sighed and thought about his next words carefully while pulling her in close to his side. "I am jealous that is all. Though I would love to have a home in such a beautiful soul, I don't own your heart. I will do my best to stop my father I promise." He held her there against his chest for quite some time. "I'm going to start you a bath, finish packing up your things okay? There is a man who wants to meet his best mates daughter."

He moved out of the room to start her up a bath. She was like a rose, beautiful and kind on the inside, but she caused those who loved her to suffer because of her thorns. She made a distraught noise as she fought back more tears. If only she had Sage now, to pull her through this, to threaten to kill the demons inside of her. She folded the rest of her things and put the rest of her belongings away, aside from the outfit that she was going to wear for the day. She placed her luggage next to Cassius's bag. She met him by the bath with the clothes in her hands and their eyes met, lingering and staring for quite some time, before she broke their gaze. "Thank you."

"Of course, are you going to be alright?" He bunched up some of his hair in his hand and scratched the back of his head awkwardly.

"Yes, I'll be okay. Will you take my clothes back please?" Just turn around."

Once he was turned around, she stripped of her night clothes and undergarments. She tossed the bundle of clothes behind her head and he caught them instinctively. He didn't turn around, he made his exit once she was submerged in the bath and didn't look back.

Clare was rather quick. She wanted to start the rest of her journey and the only one holding her back was herself. Once she had gotten the filth off, she quickly dried off and got dressed. She didn't bother to do her makeup or wait for the bath to finish draining. She got dressed in a day dress and boots and threw her soaking wet hair in a bun. She walked back into the room where Cassius was, she tossed him the brush and he caught it, tucking it in the front pocket of her luggage.

He admired her for how she looked and she noticed a small smile tugging at his lips, attempting to poke through his stoic expression. He picked up both of their luggages and gestured towards the door. The two of them walked down the stairs. Antoine was waiting for them. He had the bag from Natalia that was filled with food and goodies, clutched in his right hand and his luggage in his left. Natalia had added extras as promised. The extras included a handwritten note and a fantasy book, a token of her love. Clare had not seen this yet. All three of them thanked Natalia and gave her a hug, Clare's was long, Cassius's was awkward and Antoine's was brief but sweet. It was the woman's turn to cry, she held back her tears as the three of them stepped out her front door and went to go grab their horses. "I promise to see you again," Clare shouted. She waved to Natalia until she was out of sight.

The three of them mounted their horses and departed, hoping to arrive at Jesses before the sun came down.

A BROKEN MAN

Jesse wasn't expecting a group of royal/royal related teenagers to come knocking on his doorstep at eight in the evening, actually, he wasn't expecting anyone to come knocking on his doorstep. It had been years since he last had a visitor. After Gracielle, his last tie to Wade had cut him off, he vanished. From then on he became more and more anti-social. Natalia had reached out to him when he initially moved into the cabin. He kept their friendship up for a while, but he ultimately pushed her away. He was afraid of letting anyone close again because he was afraid that they would die, he was afraid that he had become a curse. Since then he locked himself away in his old cabin. He wanted people to think that he died, that like Wade had, he too had fallen in the war. The cabinets in his home were falling off the hinges and his curtains were outdated and frayed. He had an old hound dog in his home, the only bit of life other than himself in the dreary scene. But even the hound dog was on its last limb and soon he would truly be by himself. At the sound of knocking on his door, he grumbled. Though shocked, the first emotion that he felt was annoyance. 'Who would come to visit him and why now after all this time?'

He swung open the door, not bothering to peer through the peephole. He was too impatient after all of the time that he had spent alone. Though he had isolated himself, he knew who the current royalty was. He had to go down to the village market to get his groceries and when he was down there, he often picked up the news. His eyes scanned over Clare, ignoring the boys. She had the circular face shape of Wade and his same kind eyes. Jesse opened his mouth to speak, but no words came out. He pulled on the sleeves of his green button down and pushed up the oval shaped glasses that he had grown to need with age.

"Clare Pax?" 'Was he seeing this right? Was this one of Wade's daughters? Where was the other one? Had she tragically passed away? How did Clare remember who he was?'

Jesse looked nothing like Wade. His skin was the shade of the midnight sky, his eyes were a wood brown, there was a curly tuft of hair on the top of his head and a large scar on his neck. The girl he assumed was Wade's daughter spoke with the same sweetness that her father once did.

"Yes, I'm Clare and you must be Jesse." She fished in her bag for the letter Natalia had written and extended the note out in front of her. "This is a letter from an old mate of yours, her name is Natalia. I hate to meet you without my sister, but I'm on a journey and I need to know more about my father."

Jesse sighed at the sight of the letter, but took it firmly from her hand. He debated slamming the door on them, but instead opened it wider. Before he let them in, he had a question or two. "Who is that and why is the prince with you?"

"Oh, Cassius is my fiancé and that's Antoine, he is just a good mate of mine," she told him.

Jesse glared at the two boys, but welcomed them into his home. "Shoes off," he prompted, letting the door slam behind them once they entered. The old gray and brown hound dog clumsily stumbled over to the trio and sniffed curiously at their legs. "This is Bella," he grumbled, a smile escaping him as he looked at the old dog and fixed her pink collar. "She's friendly. Also, your mother is a fool for having you engaged to that man. You're too young to be engaged."

Clare sighed, she decided to ignore his comment and instead bent down to pet the dog, Cassius stepped away. "What, don't tell me you don't like dogs?" she questioned as Antoine bent down to pet Bella as well.

Cassius shook his head. "That's not it, these are just good trousers." He looked to Jesse who was rolling his eyes at him.

Jesse sat down on his torn cream sofa. He crossed his legs and raised his eyebrows. "It's good to see that Wade still lives on, but can we get on with this a bit?" He had a bit of resentment for Gracielle, so seeing a girl who looked a lot like her caused him a little bit of pain. Clare moved to the sofa across from him and the boys flanked both of her sides.

"Right, well I don't really know much about you, but I would like to know a little bit about you and your relationship with my father. I know you two were basically like brothers. I'm sure it hurts to talk about him, but I need to know more about him and I mean everything about him. I am afraid my mum was holding back some information or that you know more about him than she does. I don't want to keep avoiding the true subject, so I guess I will tell you. I have healing powers and I need to know where they came from. I know you know Natalia has powers and that you won't hurt me, so please, tell me what you know."

Jesse sighed and slouched back against the sofa. "Right, well I guess I'll start from the beginning. I wasn't expecting to share my life story today."

"Sorry," Clare winced.

Jesse stood up from the sofa to go fetch them some water. When he moved, he dragged his left leg behind him as if it were dead weight.

Clare hadn't noticed this before. She wanted to ask him if his injury was from the war and she wanted to ask him if she could heal it. She had a strong urge to heal his leg, but from what she had observed, this would be pushing her luck with Jesse.

Jesse returned with three glasses of water and set them down on the oak coffee table in the middle of the two sofas. "Your father and I were both drafted to fight in the previous war, the one against your folks." He pointed to Cassius who stirred uncomfortably at the mention of his kingdom. "But there is a difference between your pa and I. He was training to be a soldier when he got drafted, he planned to fight in whatever war was next, so it didn't make a difference to him, but me, I didn't want to be involved in any war. I joined that damn thing against my own will because the kingdom forced me to fight on their behalf. Empires can do whatever they damn please. Anyways your pa was a good man," his throat was beginning to strain, he didn't remember the last time he had spoken of Wade. He couldn't remember the last time he had spoken to anyone besides his dog.

"I didn't have a good relationship with anyone at the base when I first joined. I was a scrawny kid who was made fun of for the way he looked and acted. Most people who live in Europe are white. Some people like Prince Cassius, are of course descendants from other countries, but still I've hardly seen anyone here who looks like me. I grew up poor, but at the base I was getting money for my family, so that was a plus. Our symbol is the blacksmith, the worker. Our colors are gold and black and our symbol is the husky. My parents died of disease while I was at war, but that's not too important to this story. Anyways, your father made it his mission to become good mates with the boy who spent all of his free time after training, reading instead of going to pick up chics. We shared a room with two other boys. It was easy for him to wedge his way into my life. He was constantly asking what I was reading, though I'd never seen him pick up a book. He chose me for any partner activity. Eventually, I gave in and I decided that I wanted to be his good pal too. He became a good mate of mine pretty quickly. I accepted him because though I didn't want to admit it, I hated being lonely. We ate meals together and were practically attached at the hip. Some rumors flew around that we were romantically interested in each other, but that wasn't the case. Wade was one of the straightest men I knew. We had Sunday's off for prayer, but we never spent them that way. Wade had more of a status than I did, he was well known around the base and his family had more money. I'm sure you know this, but in case your mother left out the details, I'll explain. He came from a family of soldiers, their colors are white and olive green like the kingdom and their symbol was an elephant. If a family's status matches the kingdom's, they're well known, they're liked in society, they're allowed inside of the castle at any time as long as the queen grants her permission. That's where Gracielle comes into play, I'm sure she never talks about me," he said.

"We were invited to a few balls before the war started. Wade had known Gracielle from a young age, he'd been invited to these types of events all his life, but I hadn't. I became mates with her because he was seeing her. I supported their relationship, but I knew it wasn't plausible. I warned him of the dangers of war and how their love might fade, but he always told me I was wrong. I met both of his parents before we were shipped off to fight. I'm sure you've never met them, they were older and lived a bit far from the palace. His mother died of disease when you were two and his father passed on quickly after. Not only did the war bring murder, it brought disease. This was a quick war, they shipped us out and we came back shortly afterwards. Your parents were quick to have Sage and then you almost two years later. But little did they know, they'd have six more years with you both before another war started. I was your guys's uncle, your protector. But I didn't do a good job. I am sorry I wasn't around much after you were little." He paused to see her nod that it was alright and then he continued.

"We got the call that we had to go back to war after years of living comfortably and training new recruits. It was a sad goodbye, but we departed. That was the war that took your father's life and caused the problems in my leg. I'm not going into the details of that with you, but just know we did everything we could to save your father's life after his eye injury, but the weapon had hit his brain, there was nothing we could do." Jesse placed his hands on his ears as if the bullets were firing at him and he was trying to block out the noise. "Ask your mother if you want more details than that. I had to deliver the news of his death, she pushed me away after that. She couldn't bear to look at me. Instead of asking for my help in raising you two, or keeping me as a memory, she forbade me from entering the castle. So I ran off. Eventually I ended up here and met barmy Natalia. But, I cut her off too, I'm a curse."

Clare took a deep breath as she processed the information. She had learned some new things and had heard some things she already knew. She looked to the boys who were silent with nothing to say and then spoke. "I doubt you're a curse Jesse. But his parents, do you know anything else about them, anything unusual?" Her fingers began to twitch thinking about her magic and his leg, but both boys reached out to hold her hand and both looked crossly at one another. Ultimately, Cassius won and his hand held onto hers tightly.

"Yes. His mother was always an odd woman. She moved with an ease that was graceful and kind. I remember that she always had herbs in her house, but I'm sure that is useless information. There was one night that I saw a glow of blue erupt from their windows. I never knew what that was, but it looked like an explosion," he said.

Clare leaned forward, letting go of Cassius's hand, her eyes shimmering, "I know what that was. His mother had healing magic!" Clare was in pure delight. She finally had a lead and though her grandmother was gone, her home might have more clues. This was something her mother didn't know, something that Clare's grandmother had kept hidden for her own safety, Clare was dying to know why.

Jesse squinted and scratched the scruff on his face, "I don't believe in the whole magic thing," he said bluntly. "They say people die from it, but I don't know, I've never seen it."

Clare stood from the sofa. "If you let me come closer, I can show you. Please let me heal your leg, I promise I can do it and it won't even hurt that much." She extended her hand to him, hoping he'd allow her to come closer. Jesse eyed her skeptically and then looked over to the two boys who were nodding eagerly. If more people trusted her than just herself, then he didn't see why he shouldn't trust her as well.

'What would Wade think if he turned his daughter away? And surely he'd like to be mobile again if there was a painless solution.' "Fine," he told her, motioning her forward with his own hand and patting the open space next to him.

She crossed the space between them. Her eyes flickered over to Cassius and Antoine, she could see that they both believed in her. The lessons with Natalia would help her as well. She sat herself down on the sofa, sitting rather closely to him. She showed him her hands, a sign of trust that she wasn't pulling any tricks on him. When he nodded the signal to begin, her hands flew to his leg and she had to draw in a breath to steady herself, she wanted to look in control. She thought of the magic bubbling inside of her, but she held it in. She counted to ten to test herself and when she succeeded, she let the magic pour out from her fingers in an excess of green mist. The inside of his leg shook as the magic poured into every cell. The feeling in his leg began to slowly come back. Her hands stopped moving, but the magic kept working until a pop sound echoed and everything was back in its place. He had only felt the tiniest bit of pain when everything slid back into place.

Clare instinctively removed her hands from his leg and looked up into his eyes with hope, there was no way that he didn't believe her now. The proof was there. Jesse parted his lips to speak, but no words came out. They sat there in a minute of silence before he strung together the right words. "So it was magic that night at the house. Wade had no magic, I mean he was as un magical as they come. I'm not sure exactly how it got passed down to you. The Goddesses must have chosen you to be next in the family, that's the myth hmm? Or maybe it's not, I'm not very good with this whole magic thing." He scratched the back of his head and then shook it back and forth. "What do you want me to do about this? I don't know much, all I can do is give you the address to that house, but I don't work for free. I want an invite back to the castle. Gracielle has surely pissed me off, but I need to see Sage now that I've seen you."

"Done!" Clare beamed, "I'll write my mum a letter as soon as possible."

"Right." Jesse stood up from the sofa and when he went towards the kitchen counter, he was surprised to see that his leg wasn't dragging behind him. He was walking with both feet, one step at a time. It was incredible and beyond anything he had ever seen, but he would never admit such a thing aloud. At the counter, he wrote down the address and slapped the piece of parchment to signal that he was finished. "Well if that will be all, please be on your way."

Cassius frowned. "You aren't going to offer us shelter for the night? I don't want to pull the royal card, but that is one good reason to let us stay and another good reason is because you shouldn't want your niece to be roaming the forest at night."

"Okay, she can stay and head out in the morning, you two can leave."

"I'm royalty and Antoine is with us."

"I don't care."

Clare frowned. "please Jesse?"

He must have seen a bit of Wade in her because he softened. Rolling his eyes, he agreed to their pleading. "Fine, but you better be gone in the morning, it doesn't seem like you have time to waste anyways. I'll see you at the castle. There's only one guest bedroom in the place, so have it, someone can sleep on the sofa if they'd like, or both of you can. I don't know what's really going on in this trio even though it might have been explained to me," he scratched his head in confusion. "Help yourselves to whatever is in that pantry, I'm done for the night." He waved his hand to the three of them and headed back towards his bedroom. At the end of the short hall, he turned back to Clare. "Good to see you kid." Then he was gone, that was all they would see of Jesse for a while.

Antoine patted the sofa. "I'll sleep on the sofa, you two can take the bed in the guest bedroom." He stood up from the sofa and the three of them went into the kitchen. They all pulled up a chair and took out the rest of the food that Natalia had packed them. It would have to be enough until they reached the market because Clare didn't want to eat Jesse's food, she seemed to annoy him enough. Her fingers ran over the letter Natalia had written her, she hadn't read it yet and she didn't plan to until she was far away or she'd have the urge to go running back to her and ask more questions.

Clare ripped off a chunk of bread and bit into it with little expression. "I suppose that was successful. Magic does run in my family and we have the address to this home, but there will be no one to talk to there and Jesse didn't seem too thrilled about my presence."

"He was just in shock Clare, I'm sure he was delighted to see you," Antoine reassured as he took a gulp of water.

"I'm not so sure, maybe the memories were too bad." She looked over to Cassius who was staring at Antoine with an odd look in his eyes. She was going to kick him under the table, but Antoine had already asked him what was the matter.

"Hey you okay?" His voice was soft and had the same amount of concern that he held for any human being that he met.

"Yeah I'm okay, but you're not," he said before he could stop himself. Clare's mouth dropped open and before she could recover their secret, Cassius let the words slip. "My father is sending men to execute you and I tried to stop it, but I'm so sorry Antoine I doubt he will back off."

Antoine sat back in shock, once the initial hurt flew over his head, he stood up and walked out of the door.

"Antoine!" Clare called out. She stood up from her seat, glaring at Cassius, she was back to yelling at him. "Crikey! Can you not keep your damn word? You were literally the one who said that we weren't going to tell him. What happened to that? Now you have the poor bloke living in fear, this panic could have been avoided!" Her voice was harsh and tense, if she could have screamed at the top of her lungs she would have, but she held it in.

He held out a hand to her and she spun away from him, storming out of the door to find Antoine.

Antoine was stalking away from the cabin, his arms crossed against his chest. He wasn't sure where he was going, but he needed time to process the information that Cassius had thrown at him. When he heard Clare call out his name, his brain spun, wondering if he should keep going and he did. But when she called for him a second time, he stopped in his tracks to let her catch up to him. She was running, her feet barefoot, they were covered in dirt, her hair was falling out of the bun that she had put it in. "You won't die, I will do my best to keep you alive," she panted out when she was finally by his side. She stepped in front of him, scanning him up and down, as if the executioner had already killed him. "I promised didn't I?"

"You did, but I'm not holding you to it anymore, forget your promise, forget it all. Because you are going to feel really horrible if we acknowledge that you made this promise. There is no escaping a king's wrath, believe me on that."

"Please don't say that Antoine, if you say that then you are creating a scenario where you died because of me. Because I was foolish and couldn't stay away from you because part of me loves you and I don't know how I fell that fast for you. You were just my fairytale prince on a white horse, ready to give me the romantic love story that I deserve like in the romance novels where they run through the fields and watch the sunsets together. That was you. That is you."

It was his turn to scan her over. She was beautiful and gorgeous in his eyes. He was a fairly short man standing at around 5'6 and she was three inches shorter than him. Her hair was the color of fire and messy, pieces of her loose curls blew in the night breeze. Her face was round and soft, her cheeks rosy, her nose small and bulbish. If the Goddesses existed, he bet they all emanated Clare's beauty, she should have been one of them. No girl or guy had ever liked him in this way. If anyone had, they had never expressed this to him. He was starting to believe that he would die before acquiring a grand love story, but now he had one of his own.

"This is going to sound silly. I don't want to die and I have faith that we can prevent this, but if at the end of the day, if my life has to end, I would be glad that the reason was for love. I feel a strange connection to you. Is it love that I feel? If it is, I don't want to say," he glanced towards the cabin. "It would be disrespectful of me to do so. But if this is something I could possibly die for, would you allow me one kiss? Please?"

Clare moved closer to him and placed her soft hand on his cheek. "Of course," she whispered. It was wrong to kiss him when the person she was engaged to was sitting inside. They were far enough in the wood's darkness that Cassius wouldn't be able to see them, but she knew morally that she probably shouldn't go through with this, but she wanted to. If there was any risk that his life might be taken because of her foolishness, then her let be the biggest fool of them all. She didn't have to go on her tiptoes when she kissed him, she leaned her head up and he bent his down. Their lips barely brushed against one another, debating, waiting. But the hunger soon took over and Clare pressed her lips firmly to his. For two people who had never kissed anyone before, they were making do. Both pulling each other deeper into the kiss, their hands trailing against one another's skin.

Antoine pulled away for a breath and whispered something inaudible before pressing his lips back to her blush pink lips. 'I think I love you,' he whispered, but in a language she didn't know, so it didn't feel so wrong. The words were so quiet and inaudible that he hoped it would make himself less of a horrible man.

Clare seemed to understand his hidden language, his words fueled the fire to keep her lips pressed tightly to his. She never wanted to let go of the boy who lit her flame.

The kiss had lasted longer than either of them had expected it to. What was supposed to have been a single peck had turned into fiery and passionate deep kisses. Finally Antoine broke the king string of kisses and the two of them were left to stare into one another's eyes, completely speechless. 'What was there to say?' This was the exact reason Erebus wanted to execute him because for as long as he lived, Clare would always want to kiss him just like this. Antoine pressed his forehead against hers and gave her lips one last soft kiss to affirm that he did not regret this, that he was sure of his actions.   "I don't understand how either of us fell so fast," Clare finally whispered, her forehead pressed against his. Her hands were holding onto his.

"Sometimes, the soul just connects and there is no divide." He pulled his forehead away and rubbed his thumbs over the back of her hand. "I need to go write a letter to my family, I won't tell them of my situation, I just want to tell them that I love them, just in case, but I have faith that we can escape this." He placed a gentle kiss on her hand and then let her go.

"You need to go inside first, make it seem like you calmed me down and that I'm coming inside soon. Well you did calm me down, I feel more hopeful and certainly more alive. Your existence has sparked life inside of me. I'll be sleeping on the sofa tonight in case you need me. He can't stay mad at you forever, he seems like a harsh man on the outside, but he is hurting on the inside."

"What do you mean? Is it the things that he has gone through with his father that have made him this way? How would you know?" She was interrupted by the light outside the house flickering off. She reluctantly broke away from their conversation, not wanting to be caught and went back inside.

Cassius was waiting for her. They moved in silence to the bedroom. "How is he?" Cassius said awkwardly. Clare had a ball of green light in her hands, she froze it in place like an orb and set it on the table while she undressed. Cassius was looking the opposite direction as she traded her traveling clothes in for a strawberry colored nightgown. She told him when he could turn around. She shook her hair around to feel light and free.

"Not well, he doesn't want to die, but I promised him that we would find a way to stop it."

"You promised? I … never mind. Please don't be angry at me. He would have been angrier the longer we kept it from him and I am sure the last thing you would want is for Antoine to be angry at you."

"You're right, but I wish we could have come upon that decision together." She picked up the orb of light and moved to the bed that was fairly well kept. She placed the orb on her nightstand and crawled into bed. "And Cassius, if something ever does happen to him, we are going to raise hell upon your kingdom."

He gulped. "Though I hope it doesn't come to that, I agree. No more innocent suffering." He climbed into bed with her and turned the opposite way. "How did you conjure that light?"

"Natalia taught me while you were getting ready," she told him, her body turned away from him. Clare continued to keep him guessing. His life got odder every day he was with her. He supposed odd was better than what he had before.

"Goodnight Clare."

"Goodnight Cassius."

THE DEAD

Jesse had not lied, he wanted them out of his home. That morning he was nowhere to be seen. His coffee mug was left empty on the table and his shoes by the front door were gone.

"He must have gone to speak with Natalia," Clare said as she finished up her breakfast. The tension was higher than it had been the previous mornings. Cassius and Antoine weren't speaking to one another and both of them were rather quiet when addressing her. Antoine was quiet in hopes to hide what they had done and Cassius was quiet because he felt bad for letting the news slip the night before. Clare on the other hand was in no mood to sulk. She had woken them up early that morning, right as the sun came up, despite the lack of sleep they had gotten. Jesse had a stack of parchment on the far side of the kitchen, she took two sheets from the pile and began to write out two letters. One to Jesse and one to her mum and Sage.

Dear Jesse,

Thank you for letting us into your home. I am glad that I got to meet the man who made my father so happy. I will write to Sage and let her know that I have met you. I bet you'll have an invitation in the mail soon. I owe you more favors in the future. I trust you to keep my magic a secret. Thank you once again.

With love,

Clare

Dear Sage and mum,

Please read this letter in private. I met papa's mate Jesse today and a kind woman named Natalia. Please allow her access to the palace anytime that she wishes, she has done so much for me. Thanks to Jesse and Natalia I have discovered the source of my magic. Papa's mother had magic. I was given the address to her house that is now under your name. I hope to arrive there today if it is not too far. I am elated to go home after all of this, but I won't be coming alone. We must hide Antoine within our palace walls. Cassius let the news slip to him last night. He seemed rather upset and he has every right to be, there is a chance that they may kill him. I love you both, I should hopefully be home soon. Jesse and Natalia should be writing to you soon, please respond to them as quickly as possible. Keep up the good work at home, I'll see you shortly.

Love,

Clare

She left Jesse's note on the counter and then folded her letter to her mum and Sage into a tiny square. At the next market place she would be able to send the letter off. The sun had just touched the top of the sky when the three of them mounted their horses and headed back towards Pax et Lux. Clare's grandmother's home was located in one of the villages on the outskirts of their kingdom. Jesse had laid out an old key on the counter in hopes that they'd still be able to get into the cottage. The cottage was now in the hands of the royal family, so Clare assumed they would have no trouble getting in.

Autumn had finally arrived and with the dried leaves and bright colors came the chill. Clare had packed one cream cardigan for her journey, but it wasn't doing much to provide her warmth. Her pale cream dress blew with the wind and she had to keep one hand steady on her thigh to hold it down. She shut her eyes and braced the cold that was moving in.

The beginning of their journey was quiet. At first the boys were too tired to talk to one another, but as the weather got warmer and the day dragged on, the silence became unbearable and Antoine broke it. "So, what do you think we are going to find at the cottage? Cool magic wands and pointed hats?" he asked.

Clare grinned, she was reading over Natalia's letter. The horses were at a slow, so she was able to take her concentration off guiding and instead focus on reading. Natalia had wished her well and said that Clare had felt like the daughter she never got to have. Clare folded the letter away and tucked it into the pocket of her cardigan. "I'm not sure if that is how magic actually works, but it would be quite funny if that's what we found," she said in a light tone.

Cassius bit down on the bottom of his lip, his eyes focused straight ahead. "Yeah, I'm sure we will find something out of the ordinary," he said weakly.

The rest of the ride to the marketplace consisted of small conversations to fill the time. Antoine told Clare and Cassius about his family members. His mother Angelique, was a hard working woman who was stern towards her children, but out of love. He explained that she looked like his opposite. Though they both had fair skin, her hair was the darkest shade of brown and her eyes were the color of the trees. His father on the other hand, was his look alike. His name was Gaius. The two of them not only looked alike, but shared a love for reading. Antoine told them about his father's skills on the violin and how Maximus and Julius often invited him over to the castle during special events or holidays so that he could play for them. He told them about his two siblings, the first was his younger brother Adem, who took after his mother in terms of looks. He talked about his thirteen year old brothers love for animals and how Adem often worked with the hurt or dead animals at the arena. Then he introduced his little sister Gabrielle, who looked exactly like him. She was only a year younger than him with the same white blonde hair and a pair of ocean blue eyes. She served a wealthy family in Deus and was treated very well. To appease Clare he talked more about his family, he went on about the dinners that they would have together and the games that they would play when they got bored. He told Clare more about his siblings and how kind they were, he urged her to meet them some day and she happily agreed to his pleads. Cassius listened quietly, a knot in his stomach.

They arrived at the nearest marketplace before sunset. They left their horses to graze inside of a fenced in area meant for traveler's animals, and then walked on foot into the village. They attracted a handful of stares from the citizens who were quietly admiring the royalty. It only took a few glances around the area to realize that they were heading in the right direction. They were in Pax territory once again. The white and olive green flags stamped with the elephant crest hung from each cottage along with the owners own family flag and crest. Clare was welcome here and by default so was Antoine and begrudgingly, so was Cassius. The villagers cleared the way as the three walked through the market place. The vendors waved their hands excitedly, in hopes that royalty would promote their small businesses and hopefully purchase something from their shop. Clare greeted a few of the villagers and then made her way to a vendor who was selling fur jackets.

"Princess Clare! It is so good to see you!" the vendor shouted. His Paxonian accent, which was sweet and delicate was strong and made her feel at home after traveling for so long. He looked at her thin cardigan and shook his head, "this is no good, it will not keep you warm!" He shuffled to the back of his tent and picked up a fur jacket that was white and lined with fur on the inside. He handed it to her to try on.

She placed it over her cardigan and snuggled into the big sleeves. She had brought the coins from her horse's saddle bag and was counting them out when the man stopped her, "royalty doesn't pay," he said surely.

She smiled at him and shook her head, "you're too kind to me, but please take this as your tip." She placed three large coins in his hand.

Antoine came up next to her and asked for the gray coat that matched hers. He put it on over his button up shirt and handed the man a tip as well. He had been refusing to let any of them pay, but that did not mean that they couldn't tip him.

Cassius had walked past the coats, but he stopped at a black tent covered in stars where a woman was selling long cloaks. "I'll take that one on the far left please," he said pointing over at the black cloak that had silver clasps. She grinned at him and handed him the cloak.

"Prince Cassius, handsome young man, do enjoy your cloak."

"You don't hate me?" he asked in confusion as he fastened the cloak around his neck and dropped a handful of coins into the tip jar. There were enough coins to pay for the cloak and then some.

"Why would I hate you?" The woman was upset by his comment.

"No one really likes my kingdom around here, the only reason they tolerate me is because I am with Clare," his eyes flickered over to his fiancé. She was standing close to Antoine at another tent, the two of them were admiring classic books that had newly painted covers.

"They hate your father, but they do not hate you. You are not him and you are much more handsome," she grinned. "Thank you for the tip, you're very generous."

Instead of rejoining Clare and Antoine, he left them alone for a few moments. He was the one with the travel bag that Natalia had given them, so he got the food and hoped that he did a good job picking out what they needed. He paid again and tipped generously. In Cassius's mind he deserved to pay, in his mind he deserved to overpay. He had gotten three apples, two loaves of bread, a wheel of cheese, a few pastries, three meat pies and a container of vegetables. He was given a jar of butter and a jar of milk as extras to go along with his purchase.

With a bag filled to the top and heavy with food, Cassius met Antoine and Clare at the book tent. "Hey Cassius look at this one," Antoine said cheerfully as he picked up a book from the table. The book had a pitch black background and painted on it, was a picture of Cassius, holding a sword high in the air, a triumphant smile on his face. "It's a book about a man on an adventure and I guess you are the main character, some sort of fiction."

Cassius picked it up in his free hand and twirled it around, his eyes sparkling. He flipped through a few pages, trying to find the line where the story revealed that he was the villain, but he found nothing. "I'm touched," he choked out, placing it back on the table. Someone had admired him so much that they had written about him. He looked over to Clare, who had purchased two books, one with a floral cover and another with a woman on the cover in an elegant golden gown. Antoine had purchased one that had a painted landscape on it. He paid for all three books and then left with Cassius and Clare.

After leaving the book booth, Clare stopped at the post and deposited her letter. The horsemen would deliver the letter as soon as they arrived back into the village, which according to the woman running the booth, would be later that evening.

"I'm ready whenever you are," Clare told the two of them after the letters were properly deposited. She scanned Cassius once and then grinned, "nice cloak, it makes you look mysterious."

"Thank you, that is the goal," Cassius told her half jokingly.

By the time they had left the market and were back on their horses, the sun was almost set. Clare had asked for directions from a few villagers and she was told that her grandmother's old home was only thirty minutes away from the village. The ride was rather relaxing. With new clothes to keep them warm and food to look forward to when they reached the home, they were in much better spirits. The home appeared in their line of sight quicker than they had expected. The house was on the end of the village street, It had been abandoned for so long that one might have thought it would look out of shape, but since it was royal property and the flag was raised rather than standing at its normal height, the people came by to sweep the leaves off of the doorstep and polish the handles of the door and the glass on the windows. Though they may have not been allowed inside of royal property, the people did their best to make sure that the home was well kept just in case the Pax's ever returned to it.

There was a frail old woman outside, putting the finishing touches on the fall decorations. Her contribution to the home was an autumn wreath. When she spotted the royalty, she half smiled, her eyes glazed as if she were dreaming, she then scampered off to the right and walked to her home on the row.

The three travelers put their horses in the fenced in acres behind the cottage and then moved back to the front of the home. The cottage was warm and bright, similar to Fran's and nothing like Jesse's. The door was painted a bright red, the rest of the house a warm yellow. The plants were still alive and the flowers blossomed. A few people left notes on the small coffee table on the porch, in hopes that the royals would read them. Clare picked them up on her way to the door and tucked them inside of her pocket, she promised that she wouldn't read them until she was with her mum and Sage. She took the key out from her other pocket. It was old and rusted, Jesse hadn't cleaned it in years. The heart shaped handle was faded and worn, the key itself was dull. She placed the key into the door and turned it, relief flooded her when the door popped open. She wouldn't have put it past Jesse to have tricked them.

191

The interior of the home looked nothing like the exterior. The furniture was dusty and cobwebs scattered the creases of the walls. The curtains blocked any light from coming in and there was no sign of human life. Any plants that had once been nurtured were now dead. The family portraits on the walls were the only reminder that this house had once been a loving home. Clare shut the door behind them and moved towards the kitchen counter. Cassius blew the dust off of the stone and set their things down. "Is this where the explosion happened?" He pointed to the glass window in the kitchen, the only window that was not covered by curtains. If Jesse had seen a green puff of magic, he would've seen it here.

"I guess so," Clare murmured. She went to the sink and turned the nozzle, she was surprised to see that there was running, clean water. "They keep the outside of this home clean for us. It's sweet, but I wish my mum would come and clean the inside of this place up. It was once my papa's home," Clare said. She left the kitchen to stare at the paintings that lined the yellow walls. The family had taken great care in getting a new family portrait done for each year Wade and his twin brother aged. They paintings stopped the year that they went off to war for the first time. They had only been eighteen.

"I'm just curious, but what do you think we are going to find here?" Cassius asked as he took a glance around the place. The home seemed so ordinary, 'how could the home of a dead person possibly help Clare on her quest?' he thought to himself.

"I'm not sure, I don't mean to be invasive, but I'll need to check the drawers and the cupboards for any documentation of her powers. I'm sure she would understand if she knew my situation. She was always described to me by mum as a protective, but understanding mother," Clare said. She cast her gaze over to the two. While Cassius was standing there awkwardly taking the groceries out, Antoine had grabbed a rag and was beginning to wipe the dust from the countertops. Clare hid her smile in her sleeve.

The search began. After the food was unloaded, Cassius helped her go through the cupboards and the drawers in the kitchen. They found nothing out of the ordinary there, except for a fine set of porcelain glasses with Wade's families last name engraved on the bottom. Wade was not born a Pax, he was born a Cadell. It was odd for Clare to catch a glimpse into her father's life before he met Gracielle. Though his family had been respected, his lifestyle had been nowhere near similar to the royal life. Clare set the teacups aside to bring to her mother and kept searching. The kitchen presented her with nothing special, so she moved onto the small sitting room.

There was one piece of furniture in the sitting room that piqued Clare's interest. There was a large brown chest in the corner of the room. She knelt on the ground and carefully opened the chest. She had been expecting something that a witch might own, something magical, something symbolic that she might recognize, but there was nothing of the sort, or so she thought. The contents consisted of a few childhood stuffed animals that must have belonged to the children, a pile of blankets and then a smaller black box. When she opened the box she was surprised to see a shiny golden ring with a large emerald on top. 'Why wasn't the ring inside of a jewelry chest in the woman's bedroom? Why would she hide such a beautiful piece of jewelry under heaps of blankets and toys?' Clare thought. She carefully closed the box and slipped the ring on her finger out of curiosity. The ring was much too big for her small hands, in fact it hardly fit, but she had a feeling from how worn the metal looked, that it had fit her grandmother like a glove.

The emerald began to glow. A bright glow strained against the emerald, struggling to escape. The stone could feel the magic in her bones and wanted to be of use to its user, but that user was Clare and not the true owner, so it could not escape. Clare brushed her finger over the stone and the magic quieted. The stone began to grow frigid on her hand as it recognized that she was not the rightful owner. Clare slid the ring off and placed it back inside of the black box, she rubbed fingers together for warmth. This was a magic ring.

Magic jewelry was not common. Natalia did not own a piece and neither did Antoine's cousin. Magic jewelry consisted of metal and a special stone that helped its user control their magic. The legends that Clare had heard, had said that users with magic stones could contain all of their magic in the stone for easier control. When they needed the magic, the stone would release it. "It's not mine to keep, but I would like one of my own, so I can better control my magic, but I'm not sure where she would have acquired such a thing," she said aloud.

Antoine, who had just finished dusting off the sofa, cocked his head to the side, "well, legend has it that here is a cave not too far from here filled with gems. If one glows when you approach it, the

Goddesses have destined and blessed you to have it. However, not too many people know about this cave or necessarily believe in it because not every magic user is granted a stone. I mean, I didn't even believe in it until right now because my cousin was never granted one."

Cassius who was now helping Antoine dust, looked up from the sofa he was attending to, "would it be worth a try to go to the cave to help her better her control? I mean if magic is real, I suppose the possibilities are endless."

"I think it would be worth a try," Antoine agreed.

Clare shook her head, "though it might be worth a try, I won't go now. We need to keep moving because Antoine is in danger." She caught their sorrowful gazes and frowned. Though a good idea, she didn't want to risk dwelling in one area for too long, she'd go another time.

"We will be quick," Antoine promised. He put his hands together and turned his lips into a pout, hoping he could convince her. He was on this mission for her and if he had to risk his execution to help prevent hers, then he would.

Cassius agreed with Antoine's promise and Clare stood. "Only because you two said it's alright. We'll go tomorrow. We'll have to stay here for the night. Let's go check out the bedrooms, maybe we will find some more evidence there."

Antoine and Cassius stayed behind to give her some space and instead focused on tidying up the rest of the home.

Clare started with what appeared to be a teenagers room, what she assumed had probably been father's room. There was a bed with navy blue sheets in the middle or the room and a dresser filled with clothes and nicknacks that he had collected throughout the years. Her eyes turned to the corner and then she saw him. She had never seen a ghost or spirit before. She had felt off around Julius because he had once been dead, but she hadn't been able to pinpoint what it was until he had said it. The room turned cold and she tightened her jacket, a shiver went down her spine. In the corner of the room was a spirit, defined and whole, but silver gray in color. It was Wade. He didn't look hurt or injured like he might have been in battle, but he looked how she remembered him. He was tall with lots of muscle, he had curly hair that fell to his shoulders. He had a soft chin and gentle eyes, small ears and a pronounced nose. Though his scars didn't show, he was wearing heavy armor with the Pax crest on the chest plate. He seemed shocked, his face blank. Clare let out a loud scream.

His spirit rushed to her in attempt to calm her and another cold wave hit her. He held out a hand for her to take, but she backed away from him afraid of the cold. He spoke before she could. "Sage? No, no I'm wrong. Clare is that you Clare?" he whispered, his voice soothing and warm, exactly how it had been before his death. Her eyes were wild, not with fear, but with amazement. "Papa?" she whispered back, her voice broken, her eyes teary. She could see him, he was here, his spirit was real and still alive after all these years.

Their reunion was interrupted when Cassius flew through the doors, his arms immediately wrapped around Clare's waist. "You screamed. Are you alright?"

She turned to face him, her eyes were slightly teary. She patted him on the shoulder, but let herself stay in his arms. "I'm okay." She turned to look at Wade who had his head tilted in confusion. "Can you not see him?" she questioned as she pointed at the space in front of her.

"See who? No there's nothing there, should I go check outside?"

"No, no. Wade's spirit is here. I see him now and he speaks to me."

Cassius bit his lip and debated on how to respond, ultimately, he decided to believe her, "I was wondering why it felt colder." He kissed the top of her head and let go of her. "I'll be back in the sitting room. Shout if you need me okay. We were worried about you."

Cassius eyed the corner skeptically before he left the room, he left the door open. Clare took a deep breath and looked out towards her papa.

"Who is he?" Wade eyed the doorway, though he could see everything, only Clare could see him. His nose was scrunched up and his eyebrows were pointed.

"Prince Cassius of Excidium, I am engaged to him, blame mum for that one. I'd love to chat, but let's please leave the small talk for later. Why are you here? Why not come home to the palace if your spirit lives on?"

"You're too young to be engaged. I would've said no, I guess your mum has gone bonkers. But anyways, I couldn't find the palace. I searched and searched, but I think I went in the wrong direction, so I settled here. It's lonely, but I get to watch the people come by and clean it up. Please can we talk about you? You've grown up to be such a beautiful young girl."

""Thank you, I guess you have a lot of life to catch up on and a lot to learn. I'm headed back towards the palace, you can come home with us."

"You're the first person who has seen me, so I doubt that Sage and Gracielle would be able to. Why can you see me?"

"I have magic, I guess I can see spirits, but I didn't know that I could do that until now. I'm here because I was trying to find out more about my powers. I found out that grandma had magic and I found her ring as well. And now I found you," her eyes filled with tears again.

At her tears, he melted deeper into his soft nature, "I'll come home to see you three, to watch over you, until my spirit fades, but I don't want to come with you now, I don't want to ruin the rest of your trip. Just draw me a map and I am sure that I will be able to find my way back to you. I know I can as long as I have a visual. The tricky thing is, that all of those years I had no idea my own mum practiced magic. I promise if I knew, I wouldn't have hid that from you girls." He stuck out an arm to comfort his daughter, but when it went right through her, he quickly stepped back.

Clare rubbed her tears on her sleeves and looked for something to write on. Wade was quick to point her to the drawer where he used to store his journals. She drew him a map and wrote down the addresses of important places in the area, including the palace. "Life is a little bonkers right now, so I might not be able to introduce you to everyone, but if by the time you get to the palace in Pax et Lux and we aren't there, we have gone to the palace in the royal territory. Head there, I promise that you'll find us at either one of those places. You have to find us because you have to see Sage."

"I miss her like I've missed you. Does she still have that sword by chance?" Wade asked.

"It never leaves her side. Papa, is there anything else in this home that I might need?"

"I don't think so love, but stay the night, rest up and go look for a ring of your own in the morning when it is safer. I overheard your voices talking about the ring in the sitting room, but I did not want to make a scene. I'll make it home eventually. I love you okay?"

"I love you too."

His spirit went out of the window and she was left alone. She took a few moments to collect her thoughts before walking out to the sitting room where Cassius and Antoine sat. At the sight of her, they both rose, their eyes were clouded with worry. "Clare, are you alright? What happened in there? I heard you scream and Cassius said it was a spirit but," Antoine said in a panic.

"It was a spirit, it was my papas. I understand if you two don't believe me, but I know what I saw."

"Of course we believe you," Antoine spoke for the two of them. "It's great that you can see spirits, at least I know if anything does happen to me, I'll still get to see you," he said with a lopsided smile.

"Please don't think like that," she frowned. She moved closer to him and gave him a hug, his warmth sent the chill away and instead sent life back into her body.

She looked at Cassius over Antoine's shoulder. He stood awkwardly, his hands in his pocket, he swayed back and forth on his heels. "Yes, please, don't think like that," he said quietly. "I'm sure this will all be fine, let's just eat and then get some sleep."

THE GODDESSES CAVE

Their time at the cottage was short. There was no time to linger. They couldn't risk Erebus's guards finding them and Clare needed to get home and help her sister out with their duties. The cave was the last stop on their journey before she could go home and tell her mother and Sage about what she had found. Before they departed for the cave she said her goodbyes to her papa. He promised that he would find her again. She took his word and left the home. It only took the three travelers an hour to get there and upon first glance, there seemed to be nothing special about the cave. The entrance to the cave was dome shaped and the walls were stone gray.

"Are we sure this is actually real?" Cassius questioned as he leaned forward to peer inside. From where he stood, there appeared to be nothing but bare space and the unknown on the other side. "I'm sure that this is the right one and I have a feeling that this is real," Clare said as she stared at the cave. She trusted Antoine's judgement and she did not want to second guess him. If other myths about magic had been proven true, it was likely that this one was real too.

The day was bright and the cave was lit by the sunshine that poured in from the entrance and the cracks in the rock. Clare walked in with Cassius and Antoine behind her, Cassius was equipped with his sword that he held out in front of him and Antoine held onto his book that he had been reading. It had the map to the cave inside.

When they first walked in, there appeared to be nothing in the cave but cold air and stone, but as they kept walking and the light began to fade, the stone led them to a pile of gems that filled the cave like a river. Gems of all shapes and colors littered the floor and stacked up high. There were gems the size of pebbles and gems the size of boulders, there were stones the darkest shade of black and gems the colors of the rainbow. They were all dull, barely seen in the light. Clare hesitated ready to turn around, no stones were glowing.

Antoine placed a hand on her shoulder, "it's okay, don't give up, there are thousands of stones here, just walk on top of them, move your hands through them, I know one will glow, I feel it," he assured. He turned to Cassius and gestured for him to put his sword down just in case his hostility disturbed the energy.

Reluctantly, Cassius agreed and clipped his sword back onto to his belt. He crossed his arms over his chest and watched carefully, his eyes lingered on the stones nearest to the floor, just in case an animal erupted from the ground and tried to swallow Clare whole. They hadn't seen any odd creatures on their trip yet, but it was better to be safe than sorry. If magic was real, then who was he to say that a giant slithering worm wasn't.

Clare took off her shoes and shivered as her feet touched the cold stone floor. This was not a necessary step, but Clare had an idea, if the stones could feel her energy, then maybe they would respond to her magic. She quickly stepped onto the pile of gems, wincing at how rigid and sharp they felt beneath her feet. Even though they hurt to walk on, she was glad to be away from the cold floor, the gems were warm and heated up her feet like a pair of socks. Unlike her grandmother's ring, these gems had no active magic and therefore they could only accept her, not reject her. Clare took a deep breath and slowly walked forward. She bent down slightly so her hands could go through the gems on the top of the pile. She took the path of winding gems down to its end and sat down in defeat. As she reached her hand into the pile one last time, a bright glow appeared at the end of the cave.

At the very end of the gem trail, there was a shiny rose quartz gemstone, the size of a dime. The light it illuminated was blinding. All parties covered their eyes.

Clare painfully opened her eyes and crawled through the pile, her fingers grabbed the stone and as soon as it was in her grasp, the light faded into a dull glow. "This is it," she whispered to herself. She heard a few cheers at the other side of the cave and looked back to see

Antoine jumping up and down, a bright smile across his lips. Cassius was smiling, he couldn't bring himself to jump or scream, but he didn't have to, Clare knew he was proud of her.

The princess slowly rose from the pile of gems and made her way back through the stone river with the rose quartz buried tight in her palm. When she stepped out from the trail and her feet hit the frigid floor, her brain began to process the pain, the cold had stung her cuts.

Cassius looked appalled and she looked down to see exactly what he was looking at.

Cuts in all different shapes and sizes decorated her knees and feet, blood dripped down from her knees and painted the floor. The gems had cut her. Her body acted before they could speak. She felt a warm sensation in her stomach and the cold sting on her knees and feet quickly faded away. The blood on her skin dried and vanished. Her cuts folded themselves back into her skin and left her skin smooth and new. The warm feeling subsided and she put back on her socks and boots. As she looked back up from the ground, she began to process what had just happened. Her mouth hung open.

"Why do you look so shocked? Remember when I hit you?" Cassius recalled.

"You hit her?!" Antoine yelled out.

"Not like that idiot, with a sword, when we were dueling. Her skin healed immediately."

"Well yes, I do remember that, but I was attempting to actively use my magic against you, I was focusing. I didn't think about it this time, it just happened," she whispered. "Just like my initial discovery with the glass in my shoulder. I didn't think about it, my body just healed me."

Antoine relaxed, he placed a hand on his chin, "maybe you don't have to focus when it comes to healing yourself, or maybe," he winked, "it's the stone."

"Yeah maybe it's the stone," she said warily.

As they walked out of the cave, she continued to think back on what had just happened. The Goddesses had deliberately placed a stone for her to find in this cave. They knew that she was capable of greatness. In addition to that, her body had healed itself without her focus. It didn't sit right to her. 'Would she be immortal? Could something eventually kill her?' She hoped it would, she didn't want to be on this Earth forever. She was tempted to stab herself in the stomach just to test the theory, but that was an impulsive theory and a dangerous one. Once they were on horseback and were riding back to the palace, she couldn't take the unknown any longer. Antoine had to have known. His books must have told him. "Antoine, please don't tell me that I'm immortal," she said dreadfully, her eyes did not dare to meet his. She heard Cassius laugh at her irrational thought, but she shut him out.

"Don't worry princess, you won't be stuck on this Earth forever. Old age will take you or sickness. Your body might be able to fight off man made poison and cuts, but it can't fight off old age or disease," he said. He changed the subject in hopes to make her feel better, "when I'm home and safe," he said positively, "I'll make you a band for your stone, so you can have a ring. Would you like that?"

"Do you think you could make a necklace?" she asked, her voice soft and quiet.

"Of course, in fact it's easier, one necklace it is," he said cheerfully.

With stops to rest, eat, sleep and relieve their bladders, the journey back to the palace took almost seven days. When Clare got bored, Antoine and Cassius would take turns telling her stories. While Cassius's were about made up wars and duels that took place on the other side of the Earth, Antoine's were romance stories and they often involved a princess and a servant. He never said this explicitly, but he left subtle clues for Clare to pick up on.

They made it to the palace just in time, unaware that the Excidium guards were right on their tail. At the sight of the group's three horses, the door to the palace swung open. Sage sprinted at them. As soon as Clare climbed off of her horse, Sage embraced her in a large hug. The two of them embraced for a minute, before Sage pulled back to see Antoine.

"Good, he's here, as long as he is inside of the palace then they won't be able to take him." Her eyes flickered to Cassius who she greeted with a wave. She would have made a joke that went something along the lines of, 'sad to see you came back,' but she realized it wasn't fitting for the current situation and held her tongue.

Antoine hopped off of his horse and gave the animal a pet, "thank you for being such a good horse, you can finally rest now." He turned to Sage who was holding her arms out to him. He was a bit shocked by the gesture, but he embraced her anyways. "I'm just going to take off the horse's gear and then I'll be inside," he promised.

"No, no, someone else will do it. Whenever you are outside, they can take you, but they can't come inside our palace doors. My mum has sent out an order forbidding it. Cassius is the only person from Excidium allowed in the palace right now. Please go inside, my mum is waiting for you, we will all be there in a second." Her eyes searched his frantically, in hopes that his positivity would shatter and he would finally understand the severity of the situation, but his smile didn't falter. He happily jogged up the steps, the door shutting safely behind him.

Sage let out a deep breath and turned to face Cassius who had just got off of his horse. Her smile returned, "thank you for putting away the horses and bringing everything inside, Cassius," she winked as she grabbed her sister's wrist and pulled her inside.

Gracielle had already greeted Antoine and made him take his shoes off. She had the curtains closed so that no one would see that he was inside. She had put a warm blanket over his shoulders and made him a mug of hot tea. She offered to get one of the servants to rub his feet, but he politely refused. When her daughters walked through the door, the rest of her worry went away. She pulled them both into a tight hug. "I am so happy that you are home, we have missed you so much. I'm sure Sage told you all about how I've been making her write and how I've taught her to dress like a queen."

"It's been so much fun," Sage groaned sarcastically.

"I missed you guys," Clare whispered. When she was let out of the hug, she took off her shoes and went over to Antoine. She sat near him and he wrapped a blanket around her shoulders.

"I'm sure your mug of tea is coming soon," he told her.

"It is," Gracielle said. "With your mug of tea you are going to tell me everything that happened, right? And oh, where is Cassius dear?"

"Well, maybe not everything," Clare laughed, "he's putting the horses away."

"Alright, I'll prepare him a mug too."

By the time that Gracielle returned, Cassius was still outside. She brought back three mugs, one for Sage and Clare and then one for Cassius when he came back inside. She sat on the sofa with Sage, so she could face both Antoine and Clare. "I want to hear all about your journey, believe me, but first I need to go over some safety rules. We are hiding Antoine. I am sure that they will figure out that he is here, but they are not allowed inside. As soon as he steps out from our gates, he is vulnerable. The gates are going to remain closed, but there is the chance of an attack. If they see you, they could create a plan to steal you. From now on, all windows and doors will remain closed and locked, unless I have cleared you to leave and the curtains will not be open on bedroom windows. The only visitors allowed inside are the Demetrias's. The plan is to hope that Excidium gives up, so that we can all return back to a normal life, or that we can get Antoine back to Deus, where is he completely safe. Whatever comes first. Are you alright with this Antoine?"

Antoine looked over to Clare, "of course," he smiled. "Thank you for keeping me safe."

"Of course, now tell me everything that happened," Gracielle said.

Clare told her mother almost everything. She told her about Fran and Natalia, she told her about Jesse and the origins of her powers and she told her about the cave of gems. But she left a few details out. Her conversation with her papa and her kiss with Antoine. She felt as if her mother was not ready to hear that she could see spirits.

Right after she had finished explaining their journey, Cassius came in with their things. He set the bags down on the floor, his honeyed skin was pale from the cold, his lips were chapped and slightly blue. Though he was trying his best not to show that he was cold, he was shivering.

"My oh my," Gracielle gasped as she stood up from the sofa. She gave the boy a hug and brushed back the hair that was starting to cover his eyes. "Thank you for putting everything away. I'm glad that you're back safe." She grabbed a blanket, wrapped it around him and forced the warm mug into his hands.

He was overwhelmed with her love, his heart swelled with joy. He thanked her and then sat on the other side of Clare. The girl reached for his cold hand and he took it, he squeezed her hand in hopes to warm up while he took sips from the tea.

Before anyone could bring it up, he did. "I'd like to apologize on behalf of my father. I understand if I am not welcome here while Antoine stays."

"You are welcome here anytime," Gracielled said, there was a frown on her face, she was sad that he would say such a thing. "In fact, I don't trust your father, he's a bastard. Why don't you stay with us for a bit? He legally can't step foot inside of this palace, there is no way that he can get to you here."

"Yes please stay," Clare urged.

Cassius searched the room and when he found that Antoine

looked content with this and Sage didn't look furious, he decided that he would stay. "I'll write to my mum too, but can you write to her please? She'll only believe I'm safe if you write to her too. I've done a shit job remembering to contact her," he admitted.

"Of course, one letter declaring your safety coming right up."

"Thank you," he whispered. Cassius felt rather content, he was under a mother's wing now. There was no man looming over him, ready to raise hell if he moved in the wrong direction.

While Antoine and Cassius were shown up to their rooms and Sage left to continue her training, Clare stayed behind to talk to her mum. She had gotten the porcelain glasses from her travel bag and placed them on top of the stained glass table. "On our journey, we visited grandmother's home. I found these in the kitchen. I didn't want to let them sit there and waste away, when I know you'd value it." She looked over to Gracielle, who was holding one of the glasses in her hands like one would hold a baby. Delicately, carefully and with lots of love.

"Thank you for bringing this home to me," the queen whispered. She was not going to cry here, but her eyes filled with tears and Clare could see them watering. She decided to avoid the topic of Wade's ghost to save her mum the pain and instead, moved on.

"I really appreciate you letting both Antoine and Cassius stay here," Clare said as she reached a hand out towards her mother. Once she set the glass down, Gracielle took it.

"Of course. I'll never say no to expanding my home, not anymore. Not after what I did to Jesse. Clare I want you to know that I'm not mad at you for catching feelings for Antoine and before you object, I can tell darling. I threw you into an engagement too young, I should have let you choose, even if who you chose was a servant. I can't help but feel a little responsible for his possible execution. If I'd never engaged you to a man then it wouldn't have mattered as much if you liked Antoine. Maybe to the public it would've seemed odd, but there wouldn't have been consequences like this."

"It's okay mum, you were just trying to prevent a war."

"I failed," Gracielle said. She was right, she had failed.

A NEW HOME FOR THE HOLIDAYS

Antoine stayed at the Pax palace for six months. The end of October flew by rather quickly. Both Cassius and Antoine had adjusted to life inside of the Pax palace. They got used to the times that the family ate, bathed and went to bed. The two of them adapted new routines. Antoine felt empty without serving Julius, so he tried to offer his services to Gracielle, but she refused him. Antoine decided he'd help her anyways. Whenever he got the chance, he would fold the laundry before the other servants got to it. He would also show the cooks new recipes to try so that the kitchen wasn't serving the same meals over and over. While Antoine helped around the home, Cassius trained by himself most days and occasionally he trained with Sage. After Sage had shown Cassius, Antoine and Clare the weapons room, Cassius's drive to become a better fighter only increased. When he wasn't training, he occasionally read. He had finished one book by the start of November and it was about war and military strategy.

In November the boys repeated the same routines, but Clare had a new one. She helped Mary take care of the patients at the royal hospital. Though the knowledge of her magic was contained within the palace, her skills were now of great use. Clare learned how to heal consistently heal broken bones and mend tremendous gashes, she learned how to help soothe a bad cough and a fever. She couldn't cure illness, but by experimenting with her magic, she found a way to make the symptoms tolerable. She spent long days and nights with Mary, they would check on the patients every few hours. When Clare had downtime at the hospital, she would study the different parts of the body and their different functions. After her long nights, she would return back to her bedroom where Cassius was sometimes waiting for her. She'd sit down and he'd take off her shoes and rub the soles of her tired feet with his tired hands. They'd exchange stories about their day and then Cassius would depart so that she could take off her white, hospital dress and change into her nightgown. Most nights, once Cassius was asleep, Clare would crawl into bed with Antoine. He'd wake up from his slumber to wrap an arm around her. Sometimes he would talk to her, other times he would pull her in tight and kiss her on the cheek before he drifted back to sleep. Occasionally, they would stay up late and talk to one another and then they would kiss and kiss some more. Their nights together were kept a secret.

December came with the worst of the blizzards and because everyone had been staying inside and had little chance to get sick, Mary only called Clare when she was especially busy. Mary had proclaimed the princess a good nurse, so whenever her help was needed, she would be called upon, but there was no need for her to work at the hospital preeminently. Clare's feet could finally rest and so could she. The snow piled up so high that the royal family could hardly go outside even if they wanted to. Antoine spent a lot of his time reading in the library. There were a lot of good corner spaces to sit in that had no windows, so that way no one could see in. Though Clare had duties to preform, she made time to sit with Antoine in the library every day. They would each read their own book while curled up on a shared blanket. She'd lean her head on his shoulder and when no one was in sight, he would pepper her lips with sweet frosty kisses.

Clare also spent part of her day with Cassius. He would help her with her magic and occasionally to relieve their stress, they would paint. The rest of her time was spent with Sage, just like the good old days. They would have sleepovers in each other's rooms and gossip about Clare's love life. Sage was a good secret keeper. At the end of some nights, all four of them would sit by the fire with a mug filled with hot chocolate milk. Antoine was fond of telling the stories that he had made up in his head and they would listen. Sometimes Cassius and Sage would inform them on their practice duels and occasionally Clare would present the group with a painting. If Gracielle wasn't already asleep, she would occasionally join them, but she preferred to listen rather than to talk. The queen always left the gathering early and kissed each person on the head before she made her way up to her room. Clare split her December nights up as well, some nights she slept alone, other nights she slept over in Sage's room, sometimes she snuck away to cuddle next to Antoine and occasionally her and Cassius would enjoy each other's company for the full night.

Towards the end of December, there was a day dedicated to the day that the Goddesses created Earth. It fell on December 20th every year and to celebrate, loved ones exchanged gifts, feasted on food and worshipped the Goddesses. In preparation for the holiday season, Clare had a lot to do. Occasionally Julius would stop by throughout the month to check on Antoine and visit Sage, so she'd have to take a break from her projects to spend some time with him. It was not safe for Antoine to return to Deus in a blizzard, so instead, Julius visited him. During his visits, Clare and Julius grew closer as she explained to him the new tricks that she could perform with her magic. She told him how she had learned to heal large bones and how while she was working at the hospital, the head nurse had let her fix a pair of broken ribs.

When Clare said she had duties they were almost always in the hospital or war room. Now that she was home, she took over writing the letters because her penmanship was neater.

Julius admired her hard work and they discussed her accomplishments every time that he visited. She even showed him what she had been working on. A series of paintings, fifteen in total. Three for Antoine, Cassius, Sage and her mum and one each for Maximus and Julius. Finally there was one combined painting for Phoebe and Esmeralda. The two servants still fancied one another and they'd only need one couple painting since they lived in the same quarters. Clare refrained from showing Julius his own painting and instead showed him the sketches and themes of the other various paintings that she had been working on. He was always amazed by her work.

Once she had finished with her weekly story and shown him her painting progress, he would share the news about his life. He would usually explain that he had to help Maximus with military plans incase a war broke out. He also explained how he went into the village with Italus, to feed those in poverty. He told her how hard it was to travel to Pax et Lux during the storm and how grateful he was to have Sage and Antoine both safe. He refused to risk moving Antoine during such hazardous conditions.

Julius, Phoebe and Antoine were the only ones willing to help Clare decorate the palace for the holiday. Sage was too busy training in order to take over her mother's position and Cassius had simply never decorated before and he claimed he had his own gifts to work on and that he wouldn't have time. So the four of them made new decorations and found some old ones in the large storage bins located throughout the palace. Each Goddess was granted a section of the home and their colors adorned the various rooms. Tinsel, ornaments, plastic stars and whatever else they could find in that Goddesses color, were put up proudly. A few days before the holiday, the palace was complete and filled with hundreds of decorations. For Oralee of Europe, the decorations were gold and teal. For Abilene of Asia, they were blush pink and light purple. For Mallory of South America, they were black and gray. For Evangeline of Australia, they were gold and white. For Kalani of Oceania, they were ocean blue and orange. For Jenara of Antarctica, they were white and lime green. For Visola of Africa, they were red and black and finally, for Olive of North America, they were yellow and orange.

Phoebe had developed a close friendship with Antoine throughout the month, as they bonded over their servitude. Phoebe began to confide in him about Esmeralda and in return, he confided in her about Clare. They swapped stories and they both always encouraged the other to pursue what was in their heart. Whenever Julius came to visit, Antoine would always spend a lot of time with him. He felt bad that the Prince was worried sick over him. He always made sure to give Julius a large hug and a letter to take home with him before he left. The Prince greatly appreciated this now, but he'd come to cherish it later.

The eve of the holiday was just as celebratory as the day itself. In the morning, everyone spent the time with themselves, in order to finish up their gifts. By the afternoon, all of the gifts were stacked up high in the sitting room. They came in all different wrappings and sizes, some were neater than others, but everyone had chipped in and used the materials at their disposal to create or buy something memorable. That afternoon, Sage and Cassius had another sparring match, but this time, they invited everyone to watch. Gracielle despised sword fighting in her sitting room, but since Antoine couldn't watch outside, she allowed it. Sage and Cassius were still not that close, they didn't hug or talk about their feelings, but once every few days they came together to either polish their weapons or practice their skills. Though Sage would never admit it, it was nice to have a partner to duel with, even if that partner was Cassius. That day for the first time, Cassius had beat Sage. He felt rather victorious with a large grin upon his face and though he was expecting to be booed, his audience cheered for him. Antoine tackled him in a hug and though he felt the urge to recoil, he embraced the affection. Next in line to hug him was Gracielle and then finally Clare.

Clare smiled up at him with her big and compassionate eyes. "I'm proud of you," she said.

With his hand on her chin, Cassius thought about kissing her, she was so clearly in love with the servant, 'but would one peck hurt? Did she love him as well?' His heart was beating fast, she had fulfilled him with a few words, that he rarely heard, 'i am proud of you.' He decided those words were better than a kiss and moved on from his thoughts. Though Clare would always advocate for Sage, she would never look down on Cassius's accomplishments. He held her close. "Thank you Rose," he grinned.

He had taken a liking to calling her that name over the past few months and she didn't mind it. The first time that he had called her Rose was in October, when they could still sit in the gardens. She was painting and he was sitting by her side, he noticed her bright ginger hair and red cheeks made her look like a rose, it slipped out foolishly, but she didn't mind it. He didn't plan on keeping the nickname, but it came out again and again and eventually it became more frequent. Becoming his delicate rose was something that she could get used to, as long as he realized that she still had many thorns.

"Of course, Cassius, anything for you," she said. She poked him in the ribs and when he laughed with a bright smile on his face she knew she had succeeded in her mission to make him happy. Roses could make men melt too.

They didn't read or paint that day, instead the makeshift family gathered in the sitting room to play a few games of charades and Pictionary. Sage and Clare made a wicked team and were hard to beat as they practically read one another's minds. Phoebe and Esmeralda were rather good as well. The last team consisted of Gracielle, Antoine and Cassius. They were an odd bunch, but their size gave them the strength that they needed to be an equal competitor. Gracielle, Antoine and Cassius, won one round of charades, while Phoebe and Esmeralda won two. Sage and Clare swept clean on Pictionary. After the games, it was time for them to eat a meal together. Normally Gracielle didn't let them feast when others were starving, but today and tomorrow, she would let them indulge. It was tempting to retire to her bed, but Gracielle wouldn't allow herself to depart from her family just yet. "We don't have to go to the temple right now, that is reserved for tomorrow, but we will each say a prayer tonight. Let's go around and thank the Goddesses."

Sage went first, mostly because she wanted to get it over with. "I would like to thank the Goddesses for bringing Clare, Antoine and Cassius home safe. I would also like to thank them for keeping peace among our kingdoms, even if it may not last much longer."

Clare went next, "I would like to thank the Goddesses for guiding me along my path of discovery and granting me a stone, I would also like to thank them for keeping everyone safe."

Antoine was next, "I'd like to thank the Goddesses for guiding me on the right path and giving me another home with the Pax family. I love you all very much," he said. "My family greatly appreciates you keeping me safe here."

Cassius cleared his throat, he wasn't very good at the whole prayer thing, but he'd give it a try. "I would like to thank the Goddesses for giving my mum peace of mind, she knows I'm safer here than I ever would be at home. Maybe I'm really just thanking Gracielle for her kindness," he admitted.

Gracielle was pleased, she had tears in her eyes, she reached across the table to squeeze his hand. "I'll always be here for you," she told him. He had to resist the urge to cry, he let go of her hand as quickly as he took it and looked away so he could gather himself.

Phoebe was next, "I'd like to thank the Goddesses for a nice place to work. My years with this family have been wonderful. Some servants get treated poorly, but not me, I have it good. I'd also like to thank the Goddesses for bringing me Esmeralda, my girlfriend."

Esmeralda was choked up from the previous statement, so she just echoed a 'same', which provoked a few laughs.

Gracielle went last, "I am thankful that the Goddesses expanded my home this year and kept my family safe. Not only did they help Clare, discover herself and help Sage, adjust to her training, they brought Cassius and Antoine into my life and home. They are like the sons that I never had." She raised her glass and everyone clinked their glasses together before rejoicing in a large feast.

Once the feast was over and the kitchen staff was beginning to clear the table of dessert, Gracielle claimed that she was going to retire to her bedroom early, but Cassius knew where she was truly going. Before he left the room to go join her, he held onto Clare's soft hands, "I'm also really tired, I didn't sleep well last night, so I think I'm going to head off to bed." He kissed the tips of her fingers delicately, scared he would ruin them, they were soft like petals. Once he pulled away from her touch, he headed off without another word. Gracielle had not gone to bed, she had gone to her study, where Cassius often saw her retreat on long days. Sometimes he couldn't sleep and when Gracielle was stressed, he noticed she didn't either. He knocked on the door and when it opened, Gracielle was not smiling. "You should be near the fire with them," she told him.

"I'm alright, I know Clare likes alone time with Antoine. I don't think I'll ever be him."

"She'll come around," Gracielle frowned. "Love is an odd thing. I know she loves you too. You don't have to be him, it's impossible to be him. It's good to be you Cassius. She is a young girl, she is confused because she's met a man who she believes is perfect for her, Antoine, but she must be with you and she loves you in certain ways too, I can tell."

"But she loves him more, like you said, he's perfect for her. But anyways, I didn't come to talk about that. May I come in?" he asked.

She opened the door wider for him and he made his way inside. The sound of the door shutting behind him was soft, almost silent.

He sat down in one of the leather chairs and crossed his legs. "Holidays are hard when you're away from the people that you love. I was just thinking about my mum. I had a feeling that you might be thinking about Wade or Jesse."

Gracielle sat back down in her chair. "You would be correct in your assumptions. I'm sorry that you won't be going home for the holiday, but know that you are always free to leave, please know it is not you we have to keep here."

"No, I won't be leaving, my mum has already said she feels it's safer for me here. He has been getting more violent, she doesn't want me at home right now. I do worry about her safety though, I hope she's alright."

"I hope she's alright too, but she's a very strong woman, she can handle him," Gracielle said. "I thought about inviting Jesse to the palace for the holiday, to make things right, but I made a promise to Antoine. I don't know if he is truly trustworthy or not, so I held off on inviting him for the boy's safety. I always miss Wade, but times like these are harder. I think about when you know ... never mind, I don't need to bore you with my stories."

"No please tell them, I could use a distraction."

She told him about the holidays that she spent with Wade and how he would spend hours making the girls presents. He always mixed together the rarest paints for Clare and made the perfect cleaning solutions and sharpeners for Sage's blades. Of course he sharpened and cleaned them for her, but she enjoyed watching. For Gracielle, he would always knit her a dress. He never bought anything too expensive or lavish, his gifts came from the heart. She told him how on the night before the holiday, Sage and Clare would sleep in between them and when the sun came up, the children would pester them to open gifts. Once they had their coffee, they all sat by the fire and exchanged gifts. They'd feast and play games all day and when the girls napped, Wade would give her extra kisses and snuggle up against her. She explained to Cassius that Wade was always so warm, he was the perfect person to snuggle up against and that every holiday after his death seemed cold.

It was refreshing for Cassius to hear such stories. His holidays were nothing like the ones she had described or the one he had already begun to experience. He hoped that she wouldn't ask him about his times as a child, but she did. Though she said he didn't have to answer, he explained to her what his holidays were like. He explained how his father hated gifts so they never exchanged any, not all three of them anyway. He explained how there were no decorations and how his father practically ignored the day. There were only a few things that made the day special. Erebus required him to get down on his knees in the middle of the castle and pray out loud to Mallory and Oralee. If it wasn't good enough, he'd strike him until he was satisfied with the contents of the prayer. Later on, his mother would come to draw his bath, there she would clean up his wounds if he had any and then they would exchange gifts in private. Normally he wrote or drew her something and normally, she bought him some candy from the marketplace, something his father never allowed him to have. He'd offer to share some of the candy with her and she would always decline. She would tell him holiday stories that were much brighter than his own. Then she'd have to leave him there when his father knocked on the door saying that she had duties to fulfill, he always found a way to interrupt. Cassius would finish the bath himself and then he would make his way to Cisily's room in the new night clothes that his mum had hidden in his closet. The two of them would talk and then Theo would join them, dressed in his own new clothes. They'd all read holiday stories and pretend they were in another castle that was much more loving. It was always fun to pretend. The tradition continued for years, up until the current year because Cassius had left them.

Gracielle didn't know what to say and she usually always knew just the right thing to do. It was hard for her to imagine a world where a child was treated so poorly. She had a feeling that there was something to blame for Cassius's hard and sometimes cold behavior and this was it. Once she got the okay from him, she wrapped him in a hug and he stayed there, this time he was not even a bit uncomfortable. She apologized to him and he shrugged it off, he knew that there was nothing for her to apologize for. Leave it to Gracielle, to believe that she could have stopped the abuse.

"You're here with us now, in a much better place, if only your mum could be with us."

"I know ... thank you."

Clare and Sage normally had sleep overs the night before the holiday, but Clare had a new idea. "We should invite Cassius," she suggested.

"Why would we just invite Cassius?" Sage asked.

"Because Antoine already told me that he had to add the finishing touches onto his gifts, so his room is off limits for the night. Plus, Cassius doesn't get to do many fun things, so I'd like to include him," Clare said as she stood up from the floor of Sage's room.

"Fine, go get him," Sage said.

Clare was surprised to see that Cassius wasn't in his room. She was peering into the closet in an attempt to find him, when he came into the room, his face solemn.

His sad expression disappeared when he saw her check under the bed. "You really thought that I would be under the bed huh?" When she turned around to face him, he couldn't help but laugh at her winded expression. "Why aren't you near the fire?" he asked.

"We all had our own things to do I guess, but ... Sage and I are going to sleep over in Sage's room and we want you to come!"

"You mean, you, want me to come."

"Well, yes, I want you to come."

"What's in it for me exactly?" he asked. "Having to endure your sister when she's not holding a sword isn't exactly easy, you should pay me."

"Well, you get to spend all night with me and rumor has it I might kiss you."

"So you just get to kiss two blokes at once while you are engaged to one?" He hadn't meant to say what he was thinking, but it just slipped out.

"Cassius…"

"I know, I'm only joking. You love me too or some other rubbish saying. Just know that I only let this whole thing slide because you were forced to be with me and I want you to be happy. But I guess I'll accept a kiss."

"I am happy," she told him, though she was a little hurt.

"Eventually you'll have to make a decision because I can't handle you loving us both forever," he said, putting air quotes around the word 'loving.'

"I promise to do better."

Cassius followed Clare to the sleepover despite their serious conversation. Clare promised herself that she would do her best not to kiss Antoine anymore. For Cassius's sake, she would try to hold those feelings down and be loyal to him, forced engagement or not. He wasn't like the typical man from her stories, the kind that she often fell in love with, instead he was the villain in her story, the third member of the love triangle, the one that typically lost. The loser would have to be enough to satisfy her.

The two of them were tense when they walked into the room, but Sage didn't plan on keeping that mood up for the rest of the evening. "Well I had plans to paint our nails," she said. There was a smirk on her face as she looked at Cassius, "can your masculinity handle that?"

"Obviously, Pax. I grew up with my cousin, Cisily, this isn't the first time that my nails will have been painted." He left out the part where he had to remove the nail polish immediately afterwards before his father saw it.

Sage and Clare painted each other's nails, Clare had chosen pink for herself and Sage went with a neutral cream. Clare painted Cassius's nails a solid black. Though he would never admit it, at least not in front of Sage, he liked the nail polish, he'd have to ask Clare to do his nails again sometime, she was awfully good at it. She had even insisted on clipping them and massaging his hands with lotion and he agreed.

After all of their nails were dry, they took out a deck of cards and played card games until exhaustion hit them.

Sage was the first to go to sleep in her own bed. A small cot was made on the floor for Cassius and Clare, they stayed awake a bit later. They spoke in whispers, until Cassius had a better idea.

"How about we go to the garden?"

"Seriously? If Sage hears me leave our sleepover she will be furious."

"Come on, that's where this all started right? I feel like we have some work on our relationship to do."

"Well, alright then."

The two of them snuck up to the garden. On the way there, they stopped inside of Clare's room to grab two coats, both belonged to Cassius, he had left them in her room as a sign of affection. When they were snuggled in the warm bundles of fur, the cold of the garden was more bearable. They didn't have to whisper there. Clare's heart pounded as she thought over the self made promises that she had made just a bit earlier. She decided to share them with Cassius. "You know, it's very unfair that I am doing this to you. It would be different if you were also unfaithful to me, but you're not. Everyone says it's just because I'm young, but I am foolish. I am your fiancé and though you might not share my love of books or grand romantic gestures, I want to be faithful to you, I need to learn to be faithful to you. I can't promise to you that my feelings for him will go away quickly, in fact I know they won't, but I want to spend more time with you. I don't want to break off our engagement, I truly believe it is for the good of our kingdoms. I shouldn't kiss Antoine, I should be doing that with you." She studied his eyes, hoping that he was relieved to hear her news. It was not his eyes that gave his thoughts away, but the slow rise and fall of his chest.

"If that's what you want, then I am happy to hear it. I know we haven't really kissed, but if you want to sleep with him, if he pleases you, then go ahead. You know, that sort of separation between partner and lover does exist, so I wouldn't be mad."

"Oh no, I haven't slept with him and I don't plan on it either. I wouldn't do that to you. You'll be enough for me when the time comes." She noticed him smile just a bit and she relaxed.

"I'm glad you're choosing us and for this to work out. I want to be happy with you, I want you to be happy with me even if it'll take years. I know I can be an ass and I started out as one, but you make me … not want to be an ass."

"I'm glad to hear it," she said softly. "Can you tell me about your previous relationships?" Her hand found its way inside of his.

"So you are jealous?" he teased. "Sure, but only if you tell me about yours, deal?"

"Well, I would, but I can't. I don't have any past relationships." She watched him try to hide his smile which was growing bigger.

A part of him wished he had lied, so that way he could have told her nothing, but now he had to explain. "Well, I didn't have any serious relationships either. I mostly slept with people after events. Mostly girls, but a few blokes. My father encouraged that behavior, of course he didn't know that a few of those experiences were with men, but that wasn't his business. My mum didn't like it, it didn't matter the gender, she didn't want me sleeping around. She wanted me to find someone who I loved, not desired. She tried setting me up on some dates with a few girls, but that didn't really seem to work for me. Then she decided that she would make my love life into a political strategy to get someone else on her side. I guess she failed considering that it's now my kingdom versus Deus and Pax et Lux. But anyways, she thought you'd be a good fit for me. It was you or Maximus. Even though she secretly knew that he would probably refuse me, she let me pick. I picked you, I just thought we'd get along better, I guess I was both wrong and right about that one. My father agreed because of course you were a woman and you weren't Sage and eventually, your mum agreed too. So now I'm with you. At first I thought you were a handful, well you are a handful, but I like you anyways," he teased. "Does that satisfy you Rose?"

"I suppose it does. The law says we can marry at eighteen, but I am hoping for nineteen and if fate allows it possibly even twenty. How about you?"

"Twenty is good, it gives us time to work out some of our flaws. Maybe by then we will both be in love with one another. Believe it or not, but I am pretty lovable."

"I don't know about all that, you give people odd nicknames," she giggled. "I'm just kidding, I don't mind it when it slips."

"Whatever. Do we really have to go back in there?" he asked.

"Do you want a black eye on a holiday morning?"

"No."

"Then let's go," she told him.

They went back into the room and both of them managed to get a decent amount of sleep. Like a child, Sage woke them up bright and early that morning. "Come on, Julius and Maximus are going to be here soon," she urged, as she ran out of the room and down the stairs. Clare stirred, sitting up, her hair frizzy. She rubbed her eyes and when her vision cleared, she looked to her left, Cassius was still there. He too was just sitting up, stretching his limbs. "She takes this rather seriously doesn't she?" he asked tiredly,

"Oh yes. She'll do anything to feel like a child again, funny how girls are expected to grow up so quickly. Told to be dainty and soft, but they can't be childish and they must marry young and keep their virginity until they're married. It's all a whole whole bunch of rubbish and Sage knows it. I'm glad she doesn't care, I just wish I had her mindset."

"One day things will change Clare," Cassius said, as he glanced at the engagement ring on her finger that she had forgotten to take off. She hadn't pulled it off as soon as she had the chance and he took that as a step in the right direction. He stood up and helped her up off of the floor, he watched her mumble a 'maybe' underneath her breath.

The two of them fixed up their hair before heading down the stairs. Gracielle was already in the sitting room with a cup of hot coffee in her hand, Antoine was sitting beside her and Sage was sitting on the floor, shoveling down biscuits. The door rang and when the guards informed Gracielle that it was the Demetrias brothers at the door, they were let inside. The usual hugs were exchanged. The two brothers emptied a sack of presents onto the pile and took their seats on the sofa. Stellan, who everyone had thought was just for display, but had been Maximus's boyfriend all along, was coming as well, but the guards had stopped to search him. When he was clear, they let him inside. Antoine would be safe around Stellan, after all they had lived together before the death note was sent. Gracielle greeted the extra company happily and beckoned for Phoebe and Esmeralda to join them. Once they were all together, Maximus stood up.

"I know that the gift giving is about to commence, but I wanted to make an announcement. I'm sure that you have all been guessing about my relationship status, so I am glad to inform you that I am settling down, hopefully, for forever. Stellan is my official boyfriend. I haven't told the citizens yet, but we have been dating for a while and we finally want to put a label on things and become public because we love each other. He is family now and I hope you'll welcome him with open arms." He looked over to his left where Stellan stood. The two of them were smiling at the happy reactions and cheers. With a kiss on each other's cheeks, they sealed the news and then sat back down.

"We are so happy for you and on that good note, the gift exchange can commence!" Gracielle exclaimed.

Clare decided to go first. She had spent hours working on all of her paintings. She handed out her gifts which were neatly wrapped in brown parchment and told everyone to open them. At the same time each person opened the paintings.

Maximus and Stellan opened one together as it was a joint gift. Their painting was a portrait of themselves, where Stellan was hanging onto Maximus's shoulder, the painting was so realistic, that it looked exactly like them. The background was a bright red and would look great in the royals home.

Phoebe and Esmeralda got a joint painting of the two of them kissing. Since they shared quarters, there was no need to make two.

Julius got a painting of him and Sage shooting arrows together.

Gracielle's set of three included one of her, Wade and the girls when they were babies, one of Wade and the girls when they were six and then finally one of Gracielle and the girls at their current age. She was a mess of tears.

Sage's paintings varied, one was of her and her sword, the other was of her and Clare and the other was of her and Julius.

Cassius who had never been given such thoughtful gifts was also full of emotion when he opened his. One was of him and his mother and one was of all three of them on horseback during their journey, the other one was of Clare curled up next to him.

Antoine's gift also included a painting of them on horseback, along with a painting of their adventures in the library where they were both reading and finally, one that pictured them running in the grass the first day that they met.

He pushed up his spectacles to get another look, his smile bright. "I love them," he said happily.

Antoine was the next to give his gifts out. He apologized in advance for not having a lot of materials available and everyone hushed him, his situation was by far the most difficult. For everyone except Clare, he had made a card with his dearest thoughts in cursive and a few doodles that reminded him of them.

Clare too got this card, but along with the card, was a thin, dainty chain with a hook on the end. Attached to the bottom was her gem that he had borrowed from her room. Her magic necklace was done. He helped fasten it against her chest, smiling warmly at her ecstatic reaction, which was to embrace him in a warm and tight hug. Everyone else thanked him for the letters, most vowing to read something so sentimental later, when they were alone.

Gracielle, had bought everyone sweaters in their favorite color, Maximus gave out personalized mugs, Julius had gotten everyone books and Sage had bought them adornments for their favorite weapons, aside from Antoine, Phoebe, Esmeralda and Clare, who she gave handmade jewelry from the marketplace to.

Phoebe and Esmeralda did not have time in between their duties to buy or give gifts, so they did not give, only receive with thanks.

Cassius, who claimed himself the worst gift giver, went last. "I've never really given out real gifts before. I had to ask Gracielle for some ideas." He pulled out a cloth bag and asked everyone to open their palm. He dropped a few pieces of candy from the local marketplace inside each palm. Candy was a rare delicacy in the winter even for royals, yet he had managed to acquire it. Antoine wasn't allowed to leave the castle, but Cassius could, he had gone out a few weeks back when Clare was busy with nursing. "My mum would give me candy every holiday, I hope you enjoy them," he said shyly. They certainly did, they thanked him greatly.

The candy was gone in seconds.

After the candy was given out, everyone but Cassius and Antoine traveled to the temple to pray. It was outside, so Antoine was not allowed to go and Cassius felt bad leaving him alone, plus he hated to pray, so he stayed inside. "Thank you for the letter," he said when they were alone, both lying on separate sofas. "I don't deserve anything from you. I'm part of the reason that you're trapped inside, you were too nice to say that I reminded you of a wolf, hard around the edges, but loyal with a big heart that just needed to be unlocked. Maybe it was an insult considering I come from the family of vulture's and the Demetrias's are the wolves," he laughed, "but I'm grateful anyways."

"Stop blaming yourself for your father's actions, Cassius. I'm actually enjoying my time here despite missing my family. And thank you for the candy, I've actually never had a piece of hard candy, I've only had handmade desserts. Oh and it wasn't an insult, but am I really doing my job if I don't annoy you just a tad?"

"Really you've never had a piece? Well I am glad you got to try it and that I could bring you some. You're right though, everyone seems to like to poke fun at me. All in good spirits of course, so I don't mind. Are you upset that you can't visit the temple today?"

"Not really, I've never been big on prayer, I only did it because my mum told me to," Antoine admitted.

"Same, but it was my father," Cassius groaned.

"Common ground!" Antoine said enthusiastically. Having Cassius as a good mate was something that he had always wanted, ever since he had become close to Clare. Now they were finally becoming closer. Even if Cassius wouldn't admit it, Antoine could tell that the prince cared about him.

The rest of the holiday went swimmingly, there was lots more eating and conversing. With a few more days of December to follow, the same routine ensued, except this time Clare and Antoine did not kiss as she tried to focus more on Cassius. The makeshift family rang in the new year together and all was well. For now.

WINTER AND A CROSS

The weather in December had been tolerable, but the weather in January was almost unbearable. Snow piled up so high that the residents of the Pax palace could not see out of the windows or the doors on the first floor. If they wanted to leave, it would be hard to do so. Cassius had been missing Cisily, he thought about asking Gracielle if her and Theo would be allowed over, but he knew for Antoine's safety, the answer would be no.

His time training with Sage had got cut short because they could only duel inside due to the snow and they had to make sure that Gracielle wasn't around to scold them.

Training with Clare wasn't really safe either as if the girl's magic erupted, the blast would wreck the furniture. But every day her control was getting stronger, especially with the necklace around her neck. She was able to look at blood without her insides burning and she was able to see death without her brain spinning and her fingers itching. Between her work in the hospital and her work with Cassius, blood and injuries hardly triggered her and she was now able to perform her magic discreetly, as long as she had the rose quartz necklace on. It was usually always on her neck, except for when she had a long or stressful day, she claimed it weighed her down.

Once she had gotten in the habit of self control, she wrote to Natalia and the woman wrote her back quickly. Natalia expressed that as soon as Antoine was safe, she would be glad to come visit to see the girl's self control.

The members of the Pax palace did their usual activities to keep busy, more letters went in and out, but due to the snow, company was less frequent and letters often got delayed. Antoine was beginning to itch to feel the sun on his skin. He would let the sun burn him if it meant that he could freely go outside.

As January dragged on and the middle of the month arrived, Clare had an idea. She couldn't stand to read the local newspapers, that were filled with the news of poverty and death. She skipped into the sitting room one morning, fully dressed in her warmest, fanciest, winter clothes. Antoine, Sage, and Cassius stopped to stare at her. Two layers of white cloth hugged her legs. Over the white cloth was a blush pink ruffled dress that stopped just at her covered ankles and covered her arms until it reached her wrists. She wore her travel boots, which were white with pink ribbon. The rose quartz was tucked into her dress. To go over her dress, she was wearing the warmest white jacket that she owned. Her hands were gloved in pink satin. She wore pink fluffy earmuffs and her ginger hair was pulled into a tight ponytail at the top of her head, two strands of hair framed her face. Her beauty was almost blinding, but her kindness outshone her looks. She held a picnic basket in her gloved hands. "Cassius get dressed. We are going into town!" Clare exclaimed.

"No you're not," Sage said defiantly as she stood up. "One, I'm offended that I'm not invited and two there is a blizzard coming. You're not leaving, you'll get frostbite."

"Well the last time that I checked Sage, you're not the boss of me, mum has already given me permission. And you're not invited because this is good publicity for Cassius. Our people will take a liking to him if they see him with me and just me. They'll get to see his kindness," she looked over to Cassius who seemed shocked that she would call him kind. "You'll get to keep Antoine company." She gestured to the boy who had his head buried into the book that he was reading.

"Yes, he looks like he could use my company," Sage said sarcastically as she nudged him with her foot. He looked up startled. His eyes glanced around the room and eventually they landed upon Clare. "You look beautiful Clare," he said. A grin spread across her face and she mouthed a sweet 'thank you'.

Cassius was convinced, she didn't have to beg him. Though he wasn't a big fan of going out into the cold, her people needed to like him too. Especially incase a war broke out. It was best for them to know that he had nothing to do with it. He thought of his mother, when she begged for him not to go out into the cold. He knew that for her, he would dress as warm as he could. It wasn't nearly as snowy in Excidium, but Cassius had bought appropriate clothes for the cold weather while he lived in the palace. He knew his mum would have been weary, but if Gracielle thought it was safe, then he knew it would be alright. He got dressed in his warmest winter outfit. A pair of tights, which he was ashamed to wear, were placed underneath his black trousers for warmth. He wore two layers of socks and the warmest black boots that he owned. He wore a pitch black sweater and overtop, a fluffy black coat. He fastened the cape that he bought at the market around his neck and placed his crown on the top of his head. When he walked out into the sitting room, he raised an eyebrow at Clare's peculiar facial expression.

She looked at him in amazement, she was going to compliment him, but instead, she dashed right past him. "I forgot my crown," she shouted. Royals didn't wear their crown upon their heads when no one was around, so it had been a while since she had worn it.

Upon her return, the white and silver flowered crown was placed on the top of her head and her engagement ring was on her finger. She checked to make sure that his ring was on his finger and when she was sure that he had remembered, she handed him his picnic basket which was stuffed to the brim with food. "I'm leaving now, goodbye mum!" she shouted.

The woman hurried from the kitchen to say goodbye to the two of them. She squinted her eyes, she noticed that Cassius had grown a bit of scruff. "Oh how grown up my babies are," she said as she kissed Clare and Cassius on the tops of their heads, she had to go on the tips of her toes to reach Cassius's hair, he had even bent down to help her. "You two be safe and if the storm gets to the point where you can't see, you wait it out in the town. You understand me?"

"Yes mum."

"Yes Gracielle," Cassius said. He looked past Gracielle to see Sage, she glared at him. He laughed and then waved goodbye, specifically to Antoine, before opening the door for Clare.

The snow that had once blocked the door, was cleared and a path was made for them that lead from the door to the gate. Only one pitch black horse waited for them on this occasion. Cassius helped Clare mount the horse and once she was seated comfortably at the rear, basket in hand, he hopped in front of her. She leaned comfortably against him, her arms around his waist. His hands were gripping the reigns, his basket was in between his thighs. He looked back to see Clare and smiled at the white flakes of snow in her hair. "What are in those baskets anyways?" he asked.

"Bread, cheese, a few helpings of cooked duck and some sweets."

"You had a bloody brilliant idea you know. I'm glad I am engaged to someone kinder than I am."

"You would have done this too," she said.

"Not without my mum's encouragement. No one told you to do this Clare. Your kindness isn't artificial. It's true and blossoms more with each passing day."

The nearest village wasn't too far from the palace. Cassius kept a lookout for any spies from his kingdoms. If the spies wanted to come, then they would welcome them with open arms because they spies would see Cassius and Clare together and happy. Then after their realization, they would call off Antoine's execution and retreat from their mission. But there were no spies present.

Their arrival to the closest village was welcomed. As her bright orange hair came into sight and the face of the princess was visible, hungry villagers, skinny and weak, scrambled out from the warmth of shelter and stood hopeful, their hands out in hope for food. This winter had been worse than others and the poorest villages had been struggling the most. "Hello everyone, it's good to see you! We've brought food!" Clare announced to the people.

There were happy smiles and cries of excitement from those who hadn't eaten in days. Clare caught a few uneasy stares looking at Cassius.

The two royals dismounted the horse, each holding a basket in their hands. Cassius greeted the people with a wave of his free hand and the softest smile that he could muster. The food was dispersed between the crowd as evenly as possible. The bread and cheese were divided into quarters and the dessert and meat were cut up into small slices. As the crowd grew, the two royals couldn't keep up with the demand. The food was gone faster than they had anticipated and Clare's heart broke as she stared out at the hungry faces of children, who were still holding out their empty hands.

She looked down the street to see the nicer houses on the hill where the wealthy lived, they must have been cozy, thriving in the time of hunger and famine. She wished that she couldn't relate to that feeling. Though she didn't wish to suffer, she felt awful for having been born with a golden spoon. The Princess turned her head back to the crowd and as she scanned the area, she noticed a restaurant down the block. "We will be right back, please don't leave," she called out to the villagers.

Cassius took her hand and followed her through the crowd, "Clare what are you doing?" he asked her, his voice warm.

"I'm getting more food. I'm not just going to let our money sit in its place when it could be of good use."

"And what if Gracielle is mad? What if she notices it's missing when she needs it?"

"Then I'll accept her punishment, but she's a pretty understanding woman. I don't think she'd mind me doing this. If Adria could come over one day, I bet you they would get along well." She noticed his face go blank. She leaned up and kissed his cheek. "she'll be okay, Cassius."

A woman stood at the door of an almost empty shop. Each table inside of the restaurant was wooden, with silverware and a menu, but no customers. The restaurant had been slow because of the storms, not a lot of people were leaving their homes and when they ate well, they bought from the market because it was cheaper. When the shop did get business, they received a lot of to go orders. Clare could see the worry of going out of business disappear from the woman's eyes when she registered that the princess and the prince walked through her doors. She scrambled forward and dropped to her knees, her head bowed in respect.

"Save that for the Goddesses please. I appreciate your praise, but you may rise," Clare said.

The woman stood up from the floor and handed them a menu. The items listed were not extravagant dishes, but they were cheap and from what she had heard as she walked in, delicious.

"We will take two of each meal please," Clare said.

"Are you sure?" the woman asked, she had tears in her eyes. This purchase was going to save her business. She had almost offered for them not to pay, but her business needed the money. Clare and Cassius would have refused her anyways. They had ordered forty eight dishes in total.

"'I'm positive about this purchase. Do you have any staff to help us carry the dishes out? They are for the people," Clare said.

"A few. Let me get them out here." The woman ran into the back room and came back with four young boys, they were all around the age of twelve or thirteen. They were fairly skinny, but not as skinny as the other villagers outside, they were allowed to eat all of the kitchen's leftovers at the end of the night. The boys stared at the royalty in shock.

Clare and Cassius waved to them.

"Can I hug you?" one of the boys blurted out. Clare nodded, but Cassius looked hesitant, afraid he may be carrying sickness, but when he saw the enthusiasm on Clare's face, he nodded. He was surprised when the young boy ran past her and hugged his waist. He had not been expecting it.

His hand moved to the boy's hair and he ruffled it. Clearing his throat, he spoke, "you're going to be a lot of help to us. Thank you," Cassius told the boy.

The boy pulled away and gave Clare a hug for courtesy, he moved back to the others who were still in shock. The room's silence was broken by a chef yelling orders in the kitchen. While they waited, the owner handed them each a hot mug of tea and some of her home made biscuits.

The boys joined them while they ate. They were pretty quiet until the one with the dark mocha hair, who had hugged them, spoke. "I hugged you because you reminded me of my brother. He passed away this winter," the boy said as he chewed sadly on his biscuit. One of the other boys put an arm around his shoulder for comfort. Cassius's mouth hung open. After he chose his words carefully, he began to speak, "I'm sorry to hear about your brother. What is your name? They say not to talk to strangers, but if you are lonely, you can write to me. Address it to the Pax Palace, I'm staying there right now. I don't mean to replace him, but if you ever need some advice, I'll try my best to help." Cassius had a soft spot for children, he always wished to give them all the things that he never had. One day, far away, he hoped to have children of his own.

"My name is Cruz," the boy said shyly. "Thank you Prince Cassius. Maybe I'll write to you."

Clare leaned across the table, her eyes watery, "what can I do to help the people in the village? I don't want them to suffer."

"You could bring food packages and maybe do some home inspections if you have enough guards. It would help us fix some of our broken appliances. If you could also spare any blankets or warm clothes everyone would appreciate them. Thank you for asking Princess Clare," the oldest boy said.

"Of course, I'll tell your ideas to my mum at once. I assure you that more blankets will be coming your way as soon as possible and as for the other ideas, they'll take more time, but I think we'll be able to implement them." 'No more promises,' she told herself. 'You can only promise blankets because that's something that you can do yourself even if everyone else bails.'

Cassius and Cruz continued to chat with one another. The boy asked about the prince's life and he told him about his old daily routine at Exicidum, leaving out the horrors that he faced there. He then told him about his new routine at the Pax palace. The boy told Cassius his routine on their farm that was currently covered in snow. He had two siblings who he helped take care of so his mother would be able to work. He helped retrieve the eggs and wash the animals, he made food and bathed his siblings everyday. Cassius was quite impressed with the boy and he complimented his strength. The two of them moved onto talking about Cruz's school crushes. Cassius did his best to give him advice while Clare chatted with the other boys about the condition of the village.

Their conversation was interrupted by the owner. She came out of the kitchen with a smile on her face. "Some of the food is ready. Let's get it out to the people while it's hot. Boys, you grab the plates, I'll grab a bucket of silverware." She looked to the prince and the princess, while she didn't want to command them, they had a job to do as well.

"We will take some plates, I'm going to make an announcement once we are back out in the snow," Clare said.

Once they were back outside, she stepped out into the middle of the square with a hot plate of pork and potatoes. The people's eyes were dripping with hunger, following her as if she were prey. If she wasn't a princess, there would have easily been a fight over the food in her hand. "If you have already eaten, please do not take this food. I know it may be tempting, but I want everyone's hunger to be somewhat satisfied today. Please only take what you need."

There were nods from the crowd. Cassius, Clare and their crew of boys began to hand out plates of food for the families to share. The boys were young, but she was glad to see that they were happy to help and she was even happier to see that they weren't in the army. Though the legal age in her kingdom to go off to war was sixteen during pressing times, there were always captains who managed to recruit kids as young as twelve and not get caught.

"Here you are," she said to a family of four, she handed them the biggest plate of food that they owned and a couple sets of silverware.

The family said thanks and then ate the food slowly. If they ate fast, the food would come back up later. When there was hardly any food, most argued that it was better to eat slow and savor every last piece.

All of the plates went quick. As the remaining families ate and the families that had already finished left, Clare stood back in the middle of the square. The snow was coming down heavier and even the warm clothes couldn't stop her from shivering. "We will have to be off. Thank you to those who talked to me, I love hearing your sweet voices. I hope you enjoyed the food. I will do my best to get more blankets out to you soon and have more food come your way. In the meantime, please try to stay inside to avoid the winter storms. Stay warm!" She shivered against Cassius and he wrapped his arms around her waist, his smile lingered as he found Cruz in the crowd. Once the people began to disperse, Cruz ran up to him. "Please respond back to my letter when I write to you, Prince Cassius."

"Of course," Cassius told him. He gave the twelve year old a high five. The boy was called back by the restaurant owner.

Cassius would never hear from him.

Back at the castle, Gracielle had already arranged everything for their arrival. Two hot baths because she did not want them bathing together and two hot mugs of cider. Cassius and Clare both went their separate ways. When they were both warmer, they met up in the sitting room. While they discussed the tales of the day, Sage couldn't help but feel defeated. No matter how hard she tried, her sister by nature, would always be a better queen.

The next day, Antoine's family came to visit him for the first time. They were well aware of the news, but had not gotten the chance to be relieved from their duties to go visit their son. They were also afraid that in the earlier months, it was too dangerous for them to make an appearance. They arrived with hoods covering their faces, but dropped them once they entered the door. Angelique, was a tall woman with brunette hair, brown eyes and cream skin. Her husband Gaius, had hair as white as snow and light blue eyes, he was scruffy and tired, but he smiled brightly throughout his entire visit. Adem and Gabrielle each took after different parents. While Gabrielle looked like Gaius and Antoine, Adem looked exactly like his mother. Upon their arrival each family member smothered Antoine in hugs.

Cassius did his best to stay away during their meeting. When they arrived, he didn't go downstairs. Perhaps he was behaving like a coward, but he didn't want Antoine's family to be reminded of why their son was locked up and suffering. Instead he stayed alone in his room. When he heard the laughter and the giggles, he felt tears form in his eyes. Even this family could laugh while his own could not. He was staring up at the ceiling and twiddling his thumbs when Antoine came into the bedroom.

"Cass ... are you okay?" Antoine asked. It was clear he had been smiling brightly, but when he came into the room, his smile faded.

Cassius couldn't help but feel like the killer of joy. He sat up and rubbed his eyes. "Yeah don't worry about me Antoine, I'm fine. You can go away now," he said awkwardly.

Antoine moved closer and sat on the edge of the bed. "I want you to come downstairs please. I already told my family and they know you have nothing to do with this situation. Please just come have dessert with us. Have you even eaten at all today?" His eyebrows dipped almost touching his glasses. He was bursting with concern and Cassius couldn't take sympathy when he felt like he didn't deserve it.

"Yes I ate," he lied. Phoebe and Esmeralda had been too busy and he didn't want to bother them with an order for food. Just then his stomach rumbled and his lie was exposed.

"Come on Cass ... I mean Cassius, you need to eat and I want you to have fun with us. My family is staying the night, so you'll be stuck in here for the rest of the night if you decide to stay," he said.

"Fine, I'll come. Thanks for caring about me."

"Yeah, of course. How could I not. I love you. You're my friend."

Cassius's mind froze and then sped up again. 'Antoine loves me? He values me as a friend? He actually values our friendship? Someone cares about me who doesn't have to?' Cassius thought. He felt as if he could break down, but he didn't. He couldn't manage to say the words I love you back. They had been hard to say his entire life, the only person he could speak the words to was his mother. So he settled for something that would get the message across, "Yeah you're my friend. I would make sure you ate too," he choked out, before dashing past him and out of the room.

The two boys appeared in the kitchen. Cassius waved shyly, expecting to be met with glares. Clare was elated that he had joined them, Sage looked neutral and Gracielle was pleased. He hesitantly let his eyes fall on Antoine's family. Gaius was grinning from ear to ear, just glad to have his son safe and near. "Come join us son," Gaius said. He wasn't aware of how much that statement meant to Cassius. A soft smile crossed Cassius's lips and he laughed a little when Antoine playfully hit his back. He sat down at the table and listened to Adem speak about his adventures with the arena animals and he listened to Gabrielle talk about the books that she had read. The idea of family was starting to become less intimidating. He was not revolted by these set of humans. While the rest of humanity, his father at the core of this belief, concerned him, he felt nothing but joy sitting inside of the Pax palace and eating a large helping of apple tart. He felt overwhelmingly loved.

January came to a close quickly. The rest of the month the royals spent their time making arrangements to help the poorest village towns. Clare, who took on organizing the project, was slouched over in her chair on the last day of the month.

Cassius approached her and crouched down. "Clare," he whispered, his voice was strained from crying and his eyes were still puffy no matter how many times he had wiped them.

She looked up from the stack of parchment on her desk. When she saw the sadness in his eyes, she collected his scruffy jaw in her hands. "What is it Cassius?" Her tired eyes swam with concern. Her mind immediately jumped to the worst conclusions. 'What if something had happened to his mother? What if while she had locked herself away in this room, they had taken Antoine?'

Somehow the news he told her felt just as bad. "I haven't heard from Cruz and I heard the guards discussing their trip to the village to hand out the blankets. They said that on a farm they saw a mum, kneeling down next to a dead body that belonged to a little boy with shaggy brown hair. I think Cruz died." He was doing everything in his power not to cry, not to break down at the thought of the dead child, but he couldn't. He let a tear fall down his face and then another, his chest rapidly rose and fell, on the inside he was panicking, but he had learned to silent cry.

When her hands moved, he flinched away, then he saw the hurt in her eyes and he leaned closer. Clare would not hurt him. She pulled herself down to the ground and threw her arms around him so they were locked in a tight embrace. Neither of them knew what to say, but both could feel what the other was thinking. Clare was damning herself for not sending the order a day sooner and Cassius was mourning the loss of a boy who reminded him of his childhood self, desperate for friendship, desperate for a brother that didn't exist.

Neither of them knew how long they sat there on the cold floor, but it felt like eternity. As each one of his tears fell onto her skin, it told her a part of his story. The abuse, the loneliness, the desire to impress. After years of silence, he told her about his past. She collected every tear and every story, placing it carefully in the front of her brain. He was fragile. Glass that she had managed to shatter a million times. She promised herself that she wouldn't break him again. His heart was in her hands and she would protect it with her life.

THE SECOND RED FLAME

Clare's birthday was on the fourteenth of February. Leading up to that day, her and Cassius spent their days arranging plans to help the village. Though the snow piles were lower, there was still a snow storm every other day. Just like Cruz had suggested, they put together food bags for each family. All members of the Pax family worked on the food packages. When shipment to the palace arrived, they would ration it.

Sage would start by opening the bag and attaching the royal letter, she would then pass it to Antoine, who put in the vegetables. Antoine would pass it to Cassius, who put in the crackers and cheese and then he would pass it onto Gracielle, who would put in the bread and fruit. Finally the basket would go to Clare, she would tie the bag with ribbon and take it to the guards who were on delivery duty. While the guards were at the village, they were instructed to inspect each home that they delivered food to. If there was something broken that was easily mendable with the tool boxes that they carried, they were instructed to fix it. With their efforts all throughout the beginning of February, there were less hungry faces and more warm spirits.

Clare's birthday was different from Sage's. With Antoine's current circumstances there was no way that she was going to be able to enjoy a grand event, but she was still secretly hoping that something special would happen to her on her birthday. She woke up on her birthday to Cassius standing over her. She jolted up from her slumber and scanned over him, once she registered that he wasn't hurt or sad, she relaxed.

He smiled and held out a bouquet of roses that he had collected from the garden. "I wanted to be the first one to wish you happy birthday," he said. "I'm sure that Sage might be a little jealous, but that's not the reason behind my action. I just wanted to see your beautiful face, both sleepy and happy at the same time." He extended the flowers out to her, there was a thick wrap of cotton around the stems so that she wouldn't hurt her hands by touching the thorns. She inhaled the sweet scent of the roses and placed them on her bedside table.

"Thank you, I love them." She slid out of bed and let her feet hit the cold floor.

He swooped her up in his arms so that she wouldn't have to shiver. Their eyes met and Cassius looked both hesitant and regretful, scared that she would be mad at him for picking her up. But she wasn't mad, she leaned up to his face and for the first time, she placed a gentle kiss on his lips. If his skin were light enough for a blush to appear, he would have been bright red. His cheeks were hot and his eyes were wide, but he forced himself to focus on the moment and return the kiss.

The kiss only lasted a moment before they both pulled away. This was supposed to be Clare's birthday, not Cassius's, but he felt as if he had gotten the best gift in the world. Kissing her was different. Not only was it grand, but there was an emotion behind their kiss that wasn't lust and it frightened Cassius. He wasn't used to that odd feeling.

Neither of them spoke about the kiss, he set her back down on the bed and went into her closet. "What would you like to wear?" His voice was a little shaky and he stomped his foot on the floor to regain his composure.

"You choose," she hummed.

Cassius was hesitant to take on such a big task. A few months ago, Cassius would have picked out something tight and something dark, but he knew now that wasn't her taste and he wanted her to feel comfortable on her special day. He cursed himself for being an arse a few months back, as he thumbed through the clothes in her closet. Eventually he found something fitting. There was no need for a ball gown because they weren't going to be having any more guests today. Instead, he picked out a long maroon dress with three black buttons down the middle. It had thin sleeves that stopped at her wrist and the dress itself trailed down to the floor.

"I haven't seen you wear this dress and it's close to your favorite color, that is why I picked it. I think you'd look even more gorgeous in it, if that is even possible." He handed her the dress and she slid off the bed to examine it.

"Thank you Cassius, I love it, you did a good job. I'll meet you downstairs after I've changed, could you put my roses in a vase?"

"Of course, I'm glad you like them."

When Cassius went out of the room with the roses in his hands, Phoebe came in with a bucket of new makeup. She helped Clare into her dress and tied her hair into a twist. "Your hair is getting long, it is almost to your sides," she said as she started to pin her hair up with clips. "I'm going to hurry and finish getting you ready. I can already tell there is an argument taking place downstairs between Cassius and Sage because he saw you first on your birthday and she's always seen you first," Phoebe said.

Once Clare's hair was finished, she helped her put on a pair of pearl earrings and then dusted her face with rosy pink blush. "You're all set, put on some shoes and get down there!" she exclaimed happily.

Clare thanked Phoebe and then hurriedly headed down the stairs in a matching pair of maroon flats. She was surprised to see them all standing there in a row. They were dressed up just like she had been. 'Had she really not noticed Cassius wearing that handsome black suit?'

Sage reached in front of Cassius to give her sister a hug. "We are only a year apart, for now," she smirked as she pulled back and gave her an orange box. "Since you're magical now, I got these for you from the market. I hope you like them.

" Clare let out a soft laugh and popped open the lid to the box. A beaded bracelet of rose quartz.

"I was reading the book mum forced me to analyze and I found out that if you accumulate more jewelry of the stone chosen for your magic, it helps with control. I don't know, it could all be a bunch of rubbish and if it is, I hope you at least think it looks pretty."

"That is so sweet Sage, it is beautiful, thank you." She slipped the bracelet on her arm, even though it didn't match her dress. She had left her quartz necklace in the room, she had rushed and forgot to put it on.

Antoine stepped forward when Sage stepped back. "For you, happy birthday." He handed her a small silver box. Inside were two more necklaces, a thin gold chain and a shiny black one. Along with the necklace chains there were two rings, each with a place to hold a gem. One was silver and the other was bronze. "I thought that you might want to switch things up when you're wearing your stone. You're into fashion, one small chain can't do the trick forever can it?" She embraced him tightly and he stumbled back a bit. He held onto her for a few moments, not wanting to let go, he had missed holding her like this, especially at night. The heat of Cassius's gaze made him let go. "I also wrote you a little story. It's on the shelf in the library. I thought it would be fun if you found it."

"Thank you," she said happily. "I can not wait to find your book."

Gracielle, a tad annoyed that she was practically last in line, pulled her daughter in close. "You are so old and grown up! You make me feel like an old, old, woman."

Clare pulled away from her grasp and set the boxes she was holding down so that she could accept her mother's gift. When she looked inside of the black box her mum had given her, her face lit up red and she shoved the lid back on top. A lace garter. "Seriously?!" she whispered.

"Just thought it was something that you might want," Gracielle said.

Clare put the box down next to the others, not bothering to announce to everyone else what she had just received. Phoebe took the boxes to her room.

They stood with her in the hallway for a moment and Wade watched them from a distance. He clung to the ceiling so that she would not see him. He had made it home just in time. Clare was unaware why he had taken so long and she had lost all hope that he was coming home, but he had a few stops to attend along the way. He wouldn't linger forever, but he'd remain in the palace for her special day. He would come back when his spirit was needed again.

They enjoyed a large breakfast and dinner that day. Antoine took her to the library in the afternoon to find his book. She had practically memorized the titles of all the romance books in the library from their time spent together. She could tell from the colors of the spines which section they were in. She started in the fantasy section which was a good guess. As she moved down the row of books, she eventually found his book among the author's whose first names started with A. "Well you made that very easy," she teased as she pulled out the book. It was written in a journal that he had painted a water color blue. There were magic swirls of green on the cover and the spine. He had painted the paper gold.

"It's gorgeous," she told him as she flipped through the pages. There must have been over two hundred. "How long have you been working on this?"

"For a bit. During the night mostly, but also in the day when you were busy. It's a story about a girl who reminds me of flames. Don't worry her name isn't Clare, but some might say they look and   act alike."

"Does she end up with the servant in the end?" Clare asked.

"No," he shook his head. "She ends up with the Prince like she is supposed to and they live happily ever after," he said as he stared at her frown.

"Why wouldn't you write the ending you want?" she asked him.

"Because that is not the ending you want, not anymore. I thought about writing it that way, but you're happy with him and you should be. I can't stay hidden here with you forever Clare. I miss home. The switch must happen soon."

"But you can't leave now, you have to wait until the snow clears."

"I know," he kissed her fingertips and pushed his glasses up. "This book isn't about you remember? It's about a girl who's impact spreads across the world like fire and as far as I'm aware, you haven't changed the world, at least not yet."

Clare smiled, "right, so if the girl who reminds you of fire wanted to end up with the servant after the story ended ... if she changed her mind?"

"If she changed her mind then the servant would gladly be with her. Would you read me a chapter please?"

They read the first chapter and then the next. Eventually afternoon turned into evening and Cassius was at the library door.

"I was just wondering if I could sit in and listen."

So he did and together they read the book until they got halfway through. The protagonist had just discovered her magic was meant to save the world. Too tired to continue reading and a little obligated to go spend time with everyone else, the three of them left the library to spend time with Gracielle and Sage. Though there wasn't a ball and there weren't very many guests in their home, Clare was happy to spend quality time with the people that she loved. A cool breeze swept through the room and made her shiver. Clare looked up and around in hopes to see Wade, but he was not in her line of vision. He was hiding behind the fireplace. Though she couldn't see him, she knew her father was here, it felt just like old times.

POISONOUS SUN

During the rest of February the three of them finished Antoine's book together. In the end, the protagonist had ended all war and she ruled the world with a dark haired prince as her lover, a fiery girl as her sister and a blonde boy as her friend. Clare kept the book in her room from then on, re reading it at night. She was afraid that if she let it out of her sight, the library might swallow it whole.

The same routine was starting to bore them all, but Antoine felt the most trapped.

As the beginning of March rolled around and the blizzards had stopped, he was itching to feel the sun on his skin. It was still cold outside, but there was no snow on the ground and the sun was shining bright. He was supposed to travel back to Deus in another week, but he couldn't wait any longer. Clare and Cassius were in the gardens together, Sage was napping and Gracielle was in the war room. Antoine felt the need to step into the light and feel human again. The guards would never let him out under Gracielle's strict orders, especially when she was around, but Antoine thought that he might be able to convince them today. He dressed a bit warmer that day, knowing he'd be able to finally feel the frost in the air. Confidently, he made his way up to a guard. He had put a large hat on and a thick blue scarf around his neck in hopes to conceal his identity. "I'd like to go outside please," he told the man at the front door. He was expecting a fight, but the guard was new and he had been too sleepy to recognize that this was Antoine, the man that they were under strict orders to keep safe. The guard let the door open. Glory awaited the servant.

The leaves crunched underneath his boots. He spread out his arms like a bird in the sky and relaxed as the sunshine bathed him. It engulfed him, swallowed him whole. When his skin was finally sick of it, he moved, he moved across the yard until he was at the front gate. 'How bad would it be to peer out and see the world?' His hand carefully grabbed the handle, silently pushing it open. When he stepped out of the gate, they were waiting for him. His mouth made no noise and a hand snatched him and pulled him to the other side of the gate.

The slouching guard's eyes swam around the perimeter. 'Oh no,' he thought. Antoine was gone. The guard by the door was called to full attention by the guards outside of the gate. They were trying to reach Antoine and bring him back, but the men had already caught him and threw him in the back of a black carriage.

"Call the queen immediately!" One of the guards shouted in a panic. The guard who knew he would be losing his job, tried to save it, by running as fast as possible. He bumped into Clare on his way to the queen. "Sorry princess."

"What is it? What is going on?" she asked urgently. She had heard the commotion outside and Antoine was nowhere to be seen.

"They've captured Antoine."

Clare's mouth fell open. She stood there frozen in time, until Cassius grabbed her arm and pulled her forward. He had dragged her out of the door before Gracielle had even been alerted. "A CARRIAGE NOW!" He shouted at the top of his lungs. There was no more nice Cassius, no more mercy. He had to save a boy that his father had doomed to his death.

A shiny white carriage arrived at once. "Someone tell the queen I can handle this," he shouted as he helped Clare into the carriage, adjusting her dress to fit. She was too shocked to move. The carriage took off before he could even shut the door. As the door slammed shut, he noticed tears in her eyes. He couldn't promise anything, but he would try his best to fix this and make it right. "We are going to try and get him back Clare, if my father is at the sight, then maybe I can fix this."

The carriage was flying down the gravel, they bounced up and down, twisting and turning at unpleasant angles.

She still wasn't responding, but there was an unpleasant crease in her eyebrows, her fists were curled.

Cassius looked to her neck. No necklace. He looked at her hand. No bracelet, no ring. "No magic okay? It's been awhile since you've practiced it." His voice was firm and hard, though he was trying to comfort her, his voice sounded like he was scolding her.

"Don't tell me what to do," she snarled at him.

It felt like the longest carriage ride that she had ever taken.

LOST SOULS

King Erebus stood at the end of his balcony on the third floor of the castle. He had a perfect view of Excidium's town square. His people were gathered in masses, sickeningly curious about the day's event. Public executions did not happen often, the king preferred to keep his killing away from the eyes of the people, but today's victim was an exception.

Queen Adria appeared from behind the double doors, her eyes sharp. "What are you doing?" she asked frantically as she rushed to where he stood on the balcony. She placed her hands on the railing and leaned over to get a good look. "Call it off now, I did not give you permission to kill him!" She placed a hand over her mouth when she saw the guards move a handcuffed figure out from a black carriage. "I SAID I DID NOT GIVE YOU PERMISSION TO KILL HIM!" Adria screamed out loud. She had not screamed this loud in years, her voice was hot, hurt and damaged.

King Erebus turned to her and placed his hand over her mouth. "Oh shut it, if you know what is best for you, you will stay quiet. We all know you are too scared to truly defy me."

Her eyes were swollen with tears. "GUARDS CALL IT OFF!" She screamed as if they could hear her, but she was one voice drowned out amongst thousands. Erebus sat down on his black velvet chair that he had brought out to watch the execution. "Shut the fuck up and let me watch in peace. I'll deal with you later," he growled.

Adria turned away from him, ready to leave, but he grabbed her wrist and pulled her down onto his lap. "Oh no, you stay here. The guards won't help you anymore. They're on my side now." He licked his lips and then pushed her off of his chair.

She sat down next to him on the floor, afraid of what would happen if she left. "I can't believe you're doing this," she said, her eyes were wet with tears. "Do you really think that this will make

Clare love Cassius? It will not, you fool, you've clearly never been in love."

"You are right, I haven't," he said as he glared at her. "This isn't for that stupid boy. I'm ready to start a war and this is my opportunity to do it. Don't act like a servant deserves rights Adria, you're lucky I don't publicly humiliate him first."

The town square in the kingdom of Excidium was packed with people of all classes and genders. Families, friends and couples gathered near the center of the square. At the center of the square there was a large platform. On top of the platform was a large frame with a noose hanging from it. Dug into the ground was a trap door that was now open. It went five feet down into the dirt. This was not always present in the square, normally there was a barrel of the kingdom's famous black moon flowers over the trap door and a list of the past kings and queens, but now there was a death trap. A line of carriages maneuvered their way through the crowds. The first held the prisoner. When the door was opened, a boy with white blonde hair was shoved out and kicked to his feet. He was crying, his face was wet and stained with tears. His hands were cuffed behind his back, his feet shackled, he was being dragged through the crowd. A white carriage was slowing to a stop when a girl with bright ginger hair clambered out. She was tearing through the crowd at a fast pace, there were tears falling from her eyes. "Stop this! Stop this! Please he didn't do anything wrong!" Clare called out to the guards.

A few murmurs followed her, 'princess? Why is the princess here?'

Cassius was right on her heels. He was visibly angry, but it wasn't Clare who he was angry with. He darted through the crowd and was quick to reach a guard. "I command you to stop this!" he shouted, his finger only a few inches from the guards face. The guard shrugged. "You are only a prince, I am sorry, but King Erebus was adamant about this. I'm sorry, but he didn't come down to watch, so we can't stop this."

Cassius's panicked eyes scanned over the scene, his teeth gritted. "My mum would have never agreed to this. You are fools!" he shouted at the guards as he backed away. 'Was there really nothing he could do?' Antoine hadn't been his favorite at first, but now they were mates and his death would hurt so many people. So what if Clare loved Antoine and she was happier when she was with him. If

Cassius had to suffer so that she could smile, he'd happily do it as long as there could be a scowl upon on his face. Cassius thought that he didn't deserve someone as good as Clare. He was a prince who once slept around and took out his anger on those he loved, he came from a background of twisted politics and insane rulers. Clare was a kind soul and she was gentle, too gentle, too breakable and there was nothing he could do to stop her from shattering to pieces in front of him, in front of everyone. He was once the glass, but she had took his place and he was her breaker. Human souls were fragile and they were often stomped on and broken by other humans. Prince Cassius felt as if any other prince in the world could defeat him, that any other prince could stop this. He was helpless.

Cisily rushed to his side, her burnt orange dress gathered up in her hands. "Cassius, Theo is rushing up to your parents right now. He is going to try and stop them. It's going to be okay Cass, Cass it's going to be okay." She grabbed his hand which was frozen like stone, her eyes scanned over his rigid body. "You just stay here okay? I'm going to grab Clare."

For the first time in a long time, she saw tears coming to the surface of his eyes. "No … these are my parents. I can't be a coward anymore. Just let me handle it, just let me handle it." He let go of her hand and moved to the front of the platform. He ignored the confused whispers and let his sunken, broken eyes move to Clare. She was keeping up pace with Antoine, whispering words of love into his ear. She was breaking, falling apart piece by piece and Cassius could do nothing but watch.

Clare crouched down to Antoine's height as he was dragged on the floor, she tried to quiet her sobs so that he could hear her clearly. "I'm so sorry, I promised I would bring you back alive, this is all my fault, I should have stayed away from you. I should've kept you at the Demetrias's, you would've been safer there. They never would have hurt you there, oh I was so selfish. I am so selfish. I will visit your family, I promise, they'll have a life inside of our palace walls, I am so sorry Antoine." As he was dragged to the front of the platform where Cassius stood, Clare crawled toward him and held onto his bound hands.

The guards were about to yank her away, but Cassius had drawn his sword and held it above Antoine and Clare's heads.

243

"No. Don't touch them you bastards. Give them a minute." Cassius's eyes searched for Theo somewhere in the crowd.

Cisily looked over her cousin's shoulder. "He should be back by now, he left an hour ago."

Antoine and Clare had their foreheads pressed together, their noses were pushed up against one another and their lips were barely touching. "I love you Antoine," she cried. "I am so sorry that my love has killed you."

His lips pushed against her's and gasps filled the crowd as the two shared one last delicate and sweet kiss. His lips still brushed against hers, his hair in her face. "You let me feel what no servant gets to feel in his lifetime, so loved. I'm sorry I have to say goodbye to you." He pressed his lips to her ear. "You can see spirits, you'll always see me princess. I won't leave you alone. I'll be by your side for as long as you want me to be."

Cassius lifted his sword and the guards took Antoine by his arms and dragged him up to the noose.

Clare was doubled over crying on the floor, her twisted face covered by her ginger waves. Cassius sheathed his sword and threw himself on the ground, his arms held onto Clare. As they placed Antoine's neck in the noose, Clare looked up and she read his lips. "I'm so scared."

"NO STOP, STOP!" she screamed out, pushing tight in hopes to break free of Cassius's grip. He was stroking the back of her hair with his hand, whispering something in her ear. He was crying.

As Antoine felt the noose around his neck tighten he locked eyes with Clare. "CLARE, CLARE!" he shouted out between gasps. The life slowly drained from his eyes. The trap door opened and he plummeted below. Normally the neck broke off, but the guards hadn't fastened the noose tight enough. Antoine suffered from suffocation, until his soul left his body. While he lost his breath, he thought of Clare's lips against his. He thought of all their snuggles and laughs, he thought through all of his memories with her and his family, until his heart stopped.

Clare's fingers were burning, twitching, she felt an overwhelming heat leave her body. Cassius let go of her in pain, the heat burned him. When she saw Antoine's body fall, she screamed so loud that the world shook. She managed to stand herself up, her body lit up in a mess of green flames, her eyes bright and menacing.   A burst of heat rushed across the crowd and the people hissed in pain. As her heat spread across the world, she crashed down to the ground, her eyes closed in defeat. Cisily came running, she pulled Clare back by her dress and let the dying flames burn her.   "Get her back to the palace," Cisily demanded.

Cassius shook his head. "No, you get her back to the palace. I have some things to take care of. Go with her Cis." His tears were gone and his hands curled into fists, "GUARDS! Retrieve Antoine's body and take him back to the Pax Palace, now. NOW!" Cassius commanded the Paxonian guards, who had followed him and Clare to the execution. His voice was cracked and his eyes were wet for Antoine, an unexpected companion he thought he would never have. That he thought he would never lose.

"Did you see her turn green? Cassius is going to marry a witch. She should be burned at the stakes." Rumors and comments began to spread through that crowd as fast as Clare's heat had.

Once the flames had disappeared and Clare's body wasn't as hot, Cisily with the help of another guard, laid Clare down in the back of the carriage. Cisily climbed into the seat opposite of her. The door of the carriage slammed shut.

Once Antoine's body was successfully transported into the second carriage, the two carriages hurried off towards the Pax palace. Cassius shouldered through the crowd. His eyes narrowed, his shoulders squared. "SHUT IT!" he told a group of murmuring adults as he passed them, his sword pointed towards them. The air was five degrees hotter than it had been and a few citizens had light burn marks on their arms. Cassius's own arm was as hot as lava, but he didn't look down. 'Natalia didn't say anything about this,' he thought to himself as he climbed onto the nearest horse and rode off to the castle that he once called home.

King Erebus turned to Adria after the execution, his eyebrows raised. "What a dramatic show. In fact quite spectacular. Magic in our very home and we didn't even notice." He laughed cynically, his voice was deep and unnerving. His eyes turned to his wife, she stood from the floor. She moved her lips to speak, to lash out, but he had drawn his sword. Before she managed to speak, he swung at her throat and in one swift motion he had slit it open. Blood rushed out in deep crimson pools. Her eyes widened and she crumpled to the floor, blood stained the wolf fur that lined the collar of her black leather dress. "You always spoke out of turn. Poor Adria, committed suicide." He wiped his blade clean with the fabric on her dress, watching as the life quickly drained from her eyes. "How ... tragic. Oh dear, you can't stop the war when you're dead." He took the dagger from her belt and placed it in the gaping hole in her throat. "You look prettier dead." He spun on his heels and was about to open the door, when someone beat him to it. Theo. "Oh Theodore, Adria just killed herself," he said solemnly.

Theo's mouth was wide, he turned around, ready to run, to sprint and tell someone what he had seen, but a hand grabbed him and pulled him back. "Poor boy, I'm so sorry that you had to see this. A secret like this is best kept and dead people are the best at keeping secrets." Erebus drove his sword into the boys back and then pushed him off of the sword. "Oh, what a blood bath." He wiped the blood off of his hands and onto the boys clothes. "This won't look too good, so I suppose I'll have to take you to the infirmary."

He picked the poor boy up into his arms and carried him down the stairs, pretending to rush his steps. The king stopped when he heard the front door slam shut and a familiar voice call out in anger.

"How foolish are you? I know mum didn't give you permission and I know that you've brainwashed these guards into believing your cruel antics." Then the sound of a sword and screams.

One.

Two.

Three.

Four.

King Erebus set Theo down in a hidden corner at the top of the stairs and slowly walked down the staircase, his cloak dragging behind him. His hands were soaked in half dried, half wet blood. His son was standing over four dead guards, his clothes covered in blood, his face splattered with it. "So you have taken to killing," Erebus mused as he stared at his son's heaving shoulders. "We finally have something in common. Don't be mad, you know that I had to kill Antoine for the greater good of Excidium. I had to start a war."

"A war that I will not side with you on," Cassius cried out, his eyes stared at the bodies in horror.

"Foolish boy, you have to side with me. You are destined to take over this kingdom one day, you can not run away from it."

"I'll abandon Excidium until you're dead, you sick, cruel, bastard. And if the people hate me, I don't give a damn. I'll treat them better upon my return than you ever have."

"And what makes you so much better than me? You're standing there with blood on your face and your clothes aren't you?"

"I am. I guess I'm not sure what makes us different. I'm a monster when I'm angry and it seems you are too. Do you care to explain why you're also covered in blood?"

"Oh, well I suppose you should know. I know you don't want to hear this my son, but your mother is gone."

Cassius went still. Beneath the blood that covered him, his skin dulled. His teeth gritted together, he shook his head and held out his hand in front of him. "No, no. She wouldn't abandon her kingdom, so where did she go then? Did she go to the Pax family to clean up your mess?" He lowered his hand and moved through the puddles of blood, so he was standing closer to his father.

"No," the king said solemnly, pretending to be terribly upset by the words that came out of his mouth. "She killed herself." Though his words were quick, in Cassius's mind they were slow and drawn out, falling off of his tongue at the same speed as an item moved along a conveyor belt. Cassius stumbled back. "What? No." He shook his head and clipped his blood drenched sword back onto to his belt, not thinking to wipe it off. "You're lying. She was fine the last time that I saw her, she was smiling, she might have not told you, but she damn well would have told me if she was upset! Even when I wrote to her, she assured me that she was fine, so stop lying to me you bastard!" As he continued speaking, he started to become louder, his tone aggressive.

"Well if you don't believe me, then you'll just have to see for yourself." His act of sadness had quickly faded. His son didn't believe a bit of it and there was no convincing him otherwise, there was no trust between the two.

Cassius flicked his hand to get some of the liquid off and forcefully brushed past his father who was pointing up the stairs. He walked too quickly to see Theo in the small corner. When he reached the balcony that his mother and father often hung out at, he opened the door and gasped. His mother was lying in a puddle of her own blood and it was no suicide, the stupid man had forgotten to shut her wide and desperate eyes. He rushed to her side and sat down in the pool of her blood, uncaring of how filthy and disastrous his clothes now were. He lifted her weight onto his lap. He was too shocked to cry, too numb to feel. He was a killer, he had succumbed to killing just like his father and he had lost Antoine only a few moments before. The boy with those kind doe eyes and his little nervous ticks. The boy who made him smile was gone and his mother was dead on the floor.

It took his brain a moment to process that she was truly gone. He would never ask Clare to fix her, they had learned that performing a revival spell would turn one's magic dark. Antoine ... oh Antoine, he had spilled the news about Julius's little secret when they were sleeping by the campfire that night. He had murmured it in his sleep. Cassius wouldn't wish that on his mother, forgetting her life, clumsy, confused, living her life again with his father. His mind began to go back to when he was little. After his father hit him, punched him, he could hear his mum screaming at his father for an hour in their bedroom. Cassius would curl up in his room and wait for the storm to pass with Cisily by his side. She would attempt to clean his wounds and after a little while, his mother would come. Cisily would leave and Adria would sit by his side. She would ask if she could hug her son and when he agreed, she would pull him in close, cover him in blankets and read to him until he was asleep. She never stopped, even when he got older, she had done it the day that they got back from the Pax's after Sage's birthday, when his father had hit him for not behaving up to his standards. They shared happier memories as well. On Sunday's they would have tea in the library, discuss fictional characters and gossip about Cassius's love life. The tears began to fall when he realized that he would never be able to share another moment like that with his mother.

Cassius spent a few moments looking down at her body. She wouldn't be at his wedding, she wouldn't get to be a good grandmother to his children, she wouldn't be there to finally come around and tell Clare that she loved her. He knew that she did. She had told him that in her most recent letter. 'I do like her a lot, Cassius. In fact I love her. I just can't show it around your father. I'm afraid of what he would do to me. 'What had she possibly done to deserve this?' In his heart, Cassius knew nothing she did could deserve this, but his father and him did not think alike, they were not alike, he knew this now. He wiped his fingers on the last clean part of his skin. He grabbed a handkerchief from the inside of his black vest. Surprisingly, it was clean. He wiped what blood that he could off of Adria's arms and face and then messily tucked the handkerchief away. He shut her eyes with shaking fingers. He turned his attention to his father, who stood at the doorway. He held protectively onto his mother. The emotion had hit him, his sobs turned violent. "YOU LIAR!" Cassius screamed out into the air. "She didn't deserve this. You do, but she didn't," he yelled between sobs.

Erebus curled his lips into a pout. His beard had grown out from the last time that Cassius had seen him, it did no justice to his sharp features. Cassius was glad that the only resemblance between them was their skin, a shade golden like honey. Erebus stepped out of the shadows. "Well it is too bad that no one is going to believe the word of a delusional prince over a king who is now in charge of an entire kingdom. I hope you'll make it to my coronation day. You'll be a good addition by my side. A push over like your mother, easy to control."

Cassius gently lowered Adria back onto the floor. His tears were quieting, but he was still hiccuping through his words. "I won't argue with you anymore, especially not in front of her. You're an awful man, but at least take care of her body. If you ever loved her in any way, then could you at least do her a service and call the nurses?"

Erebus cleared his throat. There was hardly any heart left inside his body, but he worshiped Mallory and therefore he had to respect the dead. "Fine. I'll call them. Walk with me down stairs, I'm sure we can sort this out." He stared at his son who was unwilling to move. "If you don't move, I'll throw her off the side of the castle." Cassius stood, his pink eyes appalled. The blood he had been sitting in dripped off of him like water as he walked. The remaining liquid was beginning to stain the pavement. He didn't take his eyes off of his mother until she was out of his sight. "I promise we won't sort this out," he said.

Erebus shrugged. "What are you going to do then?"

Cassius gritted his teeth, his eyes peering past his father, "I'm going to live with the Pax's. I don't want to be here anymore."

"Well good luck with that. I don't plan on going anywhere, but if the throne ever falls into your hands, the people will hate you for abandoning them. Don't even bother trying to let the people know what I did, you would be dead before you could finish your sentence."

Cassius turned away from his father, his hand clutched the sword attached to his belt. "Then let them hate me. I'll treat them better than you did these past few years. I'll be back for the funeral, but if I have to see your face after that day, I will not hesitate to slit your throat."

Erebus chuckled, his throat dry, his tone hollow, "what are you going to do? Murder some more people? I wouldn't bother putting me on that list. You wouldn't succeed."

Cassius felt his lip quiver, he was ready to cry, to break down again. He could get angry instead, dig up his emotions and go on another killing spree, but he didn't want to resemble the man standing beside him. "No I'm going home." He marched down the stairs and went into his old room. He washed off his arms in the bath and then grabbed a gray bag. He shoved a few photo albums and a pair of fresh clothes inside. He couldn't believe that he was doing this, but he'd have to head to the Demetrias's first. Clare needed to grieve alone ad so did he. He also had to tell both Maximus and Julius that he was sorry, he had to explain to them that his mother never had any ill will towards their parents and that it had only been his father. A strong rush surged through his stomach. As the smell of iron seeped through his pores, he bolted to the tub and vomited. It didn't stop until there was nothing left in his stomach. Disgusted with himself, Cassius wiped his mouth and let his sobs fill the room.

Once he had collected himself, cleaned his mess and found some mint gum to chew on, he went downstairs and hiccuped as he called for a carriage.

The guards were hesitant, ready to refuse him, but the king just nodded his head. He was eager to see his son off. He truly didn't need him by his side. He was better alone, where he could plot in peace.

The guard didn't converse with him. Normally when he rode, the designated coachman would chat with him before he got inside and stop occasionally to see if he needed anything, but that was not the case this time. There was no guard willing to sit with him on the inside of the now ruined carriage interior and the coachman was quiet. The time alone gave him the opportunity to process all of his grief. But it didn't feel real, any of it. There was a tiny piece of him that truly believed that if he shut his eyes tight and opened them again in a few hours, the storm would be reversed. Antoine would still be alive, Clare wouldn't have exposed herself and his mother would still be here. 'How were so many people dying? Who was next?' He hadn't even seen Theo and now that he thought about it, he was supposed to check on the boy for Cisily. He'd ask the coachman on his way out of the carriage and hope for an answer. He didn't allow himself anymore tears, not at this moment. He felt hollow and numb, his head was filled with guilt. In his anger he had killed four guards. Maybe they weren't innocent, they had killed people for the king, but they didn't deserve to die. He had never seen himself become so monstrous. He knew he could be cruel and stone cold, but he hadn't ever felt the urge to kill, not until his world came crashing down and swallowed him whole.

He had always been scared to become that monster, someone who resembled his father, but he had become that person in an instant. All those years of pushing down his anger and his pain, had resulted in death. There was only so much pain a human could take, but others handled their pain better than he did. Sage was angry, she was always so angry, 'but had she ever killed?' In Cassius's mind, Clare was incomparable to any human, she was kind by nature, she was not a part of the despicable human race, she was a flower in a beautiful garden. What she had done today was an accident, a mistake and Cassius was sure that she had felt so horrible for hurting others, even though she had been deeply wounded herself. In his mind, he didn't deserve her. 'And what about Julius? Surely there was no way that he had ever taken a life, but it was probable that Maximus had. Would Maximus be able to help him through his pain or empathize with him?' Balancing his immense amount of grief and guilt made him nauseous and the sickening smell of iron did not help his cause. As for the blood, he was still covered in it, but it was mostly all dried. He looked as if he had taken a bath in red paint and it had stained his skin.

Cassius did what he did best, he quieted his brain and pushed all of his emotions down until he could swallow them. He wouldn't think about his day anymore until he got to the Demetrias's and had to explain everything. Cassius let himself become numb. He was reluctant to the idea of turning on his own people before, but now that his mother was gone, Cassius was ready to go to war and he would not fight for Excidium.

The Demetrias's hadn't been expecting Cassius's arrival, so there was no one outside to greet him. As he stepped out of the carriage, he approached the coachman, who was eager to drive off. "Did you happen to see Theodore?"

The guard was in no obligation to respond to him, but when he saw that far off look in his eyes and the blood on his pants, he began to panic. "I mean I did … I did, but he … he didn't look good."

"What do you mean he didn't look good?" Cassius raised his eyebrows, his stern voice pressed for more information. The coachman panicked and reached for the reigns. Cassius placed a firm hand on them. "Tell me, what happened to him?" Sure Cassius had never been as close to Theo as he had Cisily, but they were family and he loved him dearly.

"He's dead." The coachman pushed Cassius's hand away and hurriedly rode off as quickly as possible so that way the prince wouldn't be able to take off after him.

Cassius stood there stunned. 'Dead? Surely he was lying.' He hadn't seen Theo anywhere when he arrived, but maybe that was the point. He thought about Cisily and how distraught she would be. No, no, Theo wasn't dead. He refused to believe that man's lies. He crossed the bridge lining the moat, his heart hammering in his chest. It was too late to turn around.

The guards at the door dipped their heads. "Prince Cassius, now is not a good time," the one on the right said. The one on the left stepped back, trying to get away from the smell of blood. The guard on the right looked him up and down.

"I have nowhere else to go," Cassius murmured. The guard considered this and then stepped aside pulling open the door. "This does seem like an emergency."

Cassius wasn't sure what he had been expecting, but what he saw wasn't it. Maximus was throwing a glass vase against the wall when he walked in. The glass shattered into a million pieces and the king was shouting in a language that Cassius couldn't understand. There were a few staff members attempting to calm him down, even his boyfriend was by his side, but the king wasn't listening. Maybe Cassius could help. Well probably not, considering how much Maximus seemed to dislike him. He cleared his throat and Maximus turned his head. His curled fists released and he tilted his head in confusion. "Cassius, get out of my home," he said, but then he looked him up and down. "I'm just joking, you look hideous. Please stay inside of my home."

Cassius took a few steps in and awkwardly surveyed the shattered glass. "Looks expensive," he commented. The staff fled at the sight of him. Stellan, was the only one who stuck around.

"It was expensive. Now why are you here?"

"I'm here because," he gulped, "I'm here for a lot of reasons actually."

Maximus stepped away from the broken glass. He kissed his boyfriend on the cheek, whispered something in his ear and then Stellan walked away.

Cassius shuffled his feet.

"Sit," the ginger commanded as he pointed to the floor. Cassius wrinkled his nose when he was told to sit on the floor, only to seat himself without complaint when he remembered the state of his body. 'How had he forgotten?'

Maximus sat down as well, his legs crossed.

"Where is Julius?" Cassius pondered. He wanted to apologize to him as well.

"Upset and crying. I'm sure he will come down later, we just got the news about an hour ago." Maximus seemed bothered when he spoke, not by Cassius, but upset about his brother. In fact, Cassius's presence didn't even seem to upset him anymore. Maybe he needed a distraction.

"Well, you can go ahead and start by explaining why you're covered in dried blood, then once I know, feel free to take a bath and change. Do you have a bag?"

He thought he had forgotten his bag inside of the carriage, that was until a guard came in, set it on the floor and then abruptly left. He hadn't left it in the carriage, he had set it on the floor when he went to talk to the coachman.

The two of them moved on from the question because it had been silently answered. Instead, Cassius was faced with re explaining his mother's death. "As you know after the," the word was stuck in his throat. It felt disrespectful to say it so soon after Antoine was gone, but Maximus understood and nodded for him to continue. "I went to go visit my parents. I was angry, mostly at my father because

253

I know my mother would never sentence anyone to death … she'd never do that. I don't know what overtook me, a monster perhaps, but I killed. I killed four of our guards quickly, I don't even remember the details. I'm in a bit of shock. I just know that I did it quickly and brutally." He looked away from Maximus's eyes. "Then, my father came down the stairs. He said some things and then told me," he felt his breath lock in his throat, it took everything in him not to let the numbness fade and instead break down again, "that my mother had killed herself."

An audible gasp came from Maximus, his eyes darkened with sadness.

"I knew that this wasn't true. I went up the stairs and she was," the last word barely left his throat, his voice was vibrating, cracking, "gone."

Before he could stop himself, the tears returned to his eyes and he sobbed, burying his head into his stained fingers.

Maximus hesitated, before moving forward and wrapping his arms around Cassius.

Eventually, the prince of Excidium quieted.

There was a comforting silence between them, but Cassius quickly broke it as he wiped his tears and pulled away from the king's embrace. "She would not have done that to herself. It was my father, he practically admitted it. And as an added bonus when I got here, I was told that my cousin is dead, but I'm not sure that's true because I haven't seen it with my own eyes," his lip was quivering, his eyes started to fill with tears, he couldn't keep numb for as long as he wanted to.

Maximus debated for a moment. After a few seconds of hesitation, he opened his arms once more to invite Cassius in for a second hug. The prince fell into the young king's arms, he shivered and let a few more tears fall onto the others lap.

"I am so sorry Cassius. Losing three people in the span of a few hours must not be easy to handle or process. I remember what I felt when my parents died. Well, when my mum died. Her body disappeared so I can never be sure, but she hasn't come back, so we assumed she died and the invaders took her away out of spite. Like you, I wasn't fond of my father, his death didn't affect me in an emotional sense. My mother on the other hand, she was kind and gentle. Her and Adria always got along well." He placed a hand on the other's back and sighed. "I'm sorry for treating you poorly. You were not responsible for her death. I know this because if you were truly like your father, you wouldn't have come here, you wouldn't have helped Clare, you wouldn't have tried to stop what they did to Antoine. I've killed, Cassius, it is a part of life. Something we don't want to do, but sometimes we must and though there were other ways to relieve your anger, I've made the same mistake. I've killed in my fury."

Cassius didn't bother to look up. Maximus's kind words had melted him. Maximus didn't blame him anymore, he was nice to him, he too had been in a similar situation. Cassius was curious if his mother's death had provoked his killings as well, but he didn't ask him. "I wanted to apologize as well. I'm sorry about your mother, she didn't deserve that," Cassius said as he sat up again.

"Neither did yours. I still feel my mother with me, if you pray, maybe it'll be the same for you." Maximus tilted his chin up and then looked back down. "I better go check on Julius and tell him that you've arrived. Will you let me show you to a bath? That's the most blood that I've ever seen on any person who's still alive," Maximus said.

Cassius awkwardly lifted himself up from the floor and wiped his eyes with his stained fingers. His head hung in shame at how vulnerable he had been.

He felt Maximus's long arm brush his shoulder. "Chin up, it's okay to cry."

That was all the two of them had said. Cassius was quiet as Maximus walked him to somewhere that he could bathe. Maximus brought him to a guest bedroom with a bath inside. He set down Cassius's bag and stepped out of the room. "I'm going to have the servants prepare you a meal. Would you like someone to assist you?"

"No, it's okay," he whispered, "thank you Maximus."

The king nodded and headed out the door, gently closing it behind him.

After he had helped Cassius fix a bath, Maximus headed over to Julius's room and opened the door. His twin brother's face was stuffed into a pillow, the fabric hid his tears. Maximus sat on the edge of the bed, his face solemn. The anger had faded and sadness took its place. "Julius," he whispered softly.

His twin brother took his face out of his pillow and pouted, his eyes were red. Julius leaned into his brother who held him close to his chest, Maximus's clothes reeked of death, they smelt like Cassius. "I promise that I'll get back at Erebus for what he did. I'm going to declare war on Excidium soon. It is about time that Erebus pays for his actions. He wants a war and I'm going to give it to him. Except, we are going to win this war. I promise that Antoine will not have died in vain."

"What did they do with Antoine's body and why do you smell like that?" Julius hiccuped, ignoring his brother's previous statement.

"They took his body back to the Pax palace and I think it's best that you head there. Go see Sage and grieve with him near. They'll probably have the funeral in their kingdom as long as it's alright with his family. I'll send a letter to his family at once to inform them of the news and I shall provide them with monthly payments. As much as I want to be there for you, you need to be there, with the Pax's. I'll be too busy here to help you grieve. And there's something else that I need to tell you. Cassius is here right now, it explains the smell."

Julius shot up from where he was laying and wiped his tears, "what? Why would he come here and show his face?"

Maximus exhaled, "he was never a part of this. You know that his father did this, his mother and him were not a part of Antoine's death. Cassius is here because he's alone. His mother died tonight. Erebus, that cruel man, killed her. He thinks that his cousin died tonight too, but he's not positive. Cassius was covered in blood when he arrived. His mother's blood. He's washing up right now, but he wanted to apologize to you. Really we should all be apologizing for how harshly we have treated one another."

"You're right. We have all witnessed death, we should be cheering for one another, not tearing one another down. You're right, him and I have to go to the Pax family at once even if we don't want to."

Maximus adjusted his position, "I hope you don't blame Clare or yourself for any part of Antoine's death."

"Why would I do that?"

"Because I can sense it. You know in your heart that if you never let Antoine travel with Clare and Clare had never been engaged to Cassius, that Antoine would still be here. I don't want you to think that way. He loved her, he did not regret traveling with her."

"How do you know that?" Julius asked.

"Because he wrote poems about her. When we change out his quarters, you can take his book, I think he would be okay with you reading it."

"Right," Julius said, "must we leave now?"

"I think you should. Pack a bag. I'll see you soon, you should come back home when you feel a bit better."

It was the longest bath that Cassius had taken in a long time and he had cried through every moment of it. He hadn't remembered the last time that he had shed so many tears. He had to scrub every inch of his body with the sponge, some places harder than others in attempts to get all the blood off. He felt sick watching the once clear water turn a murky red. As soon as he had got all of the blood off of his skin and cleaned himself with a bar of soap, he washed his hair and then got out of the bath. His tears seemed to stop and he hoped he had emptied himself of them so that he could finally breathe. He was quick to dry himself off with a towel and pull on a pair of loose pants and a big, clean shirt. He had a feeling sleep wouldn't come tonight or the night after and he doubted he'd be staying here. He had to go see Clare. It would be hard to face her, but he had to go. He slipped on the pair of slippers he had brought and stared at himself in the mirror, his lips curled in disgust. He felt the most human that he had felt in the past few months, so vulnerable and so full of emotions. He felt wicked and vile, just like how he believed humans were at their core. 'I won't do it again,' he thought as he stared at himself in the mirror. He ripped his face away from the glass, unable to look at himself any longer.

He met Julius at the front of the castle, they were both in comfortable clothes and held small bags.

"I'm sorry," Cassius said loudly, attempting to make up for all his years of silence.

Julius shook his head. "I'm sorry as well. I hope we can mend our feud now, if that's alright. It was wrong of us to treat you poorly when you had already been hurting so much."

"I returned the same hatred, I wasn't any better, but yes, maybe we will be good mates someday." Cassius turned to Maximus, who shook his hand and then gave his brother a hug.

"The carriage is ready for you two. You'll arrive late in the night, so remember your manners," he joked.

"I'm sure no one will be sleeping soundly," Cassius mumbled.

"Right," Julius agreed. "If you'd like to eat before we head out, there is a plate waiting for you."

"I appreciate it, but I feel too sick to eat right now," Cassius said.

Inside of the carriage, Julius ended up falling asleep. Cassius wasn't sure how, but he didn't want to judge, perhaps this was his way of burying his emotions. Cassius on the other hand was rehearsing what he was going to say to Clare. Each sentence was awkward and he scrapped about a dozen of them. He wanted to know if she was okay, but that was a stupid question in itself, of course she wasn't okay and neither was he. He wanted to protect her. She was now a wanted woman and there would be people storming the outside of the palace in hopes to catch a glimpse of magic. He wanted to run away with her, but she was a princess who couldn't run forever. Nonetheless, he was the prince who fled. Surely they could work something out. He thought he might be able to avoid her, but Clare would never avoid him, so that plan would not work. Pondering the situation was beginning to stress him out. His fingers picked at the edges of his shirt.

He didn't have any more time to think because the carriage arrived at the palace and a hundred people stood outside with torches and angry stares. He couldn't even believe that he thought of avoiding her after seeing this. A small, almost non existent portion of him wanted to slaughter all of those people and give into the monster that he was becoming, but no they didn't deserve that and he truly didn't want to kill them. He just wanted them all gone. He wanted to shout at them and scream, but Clare wouldn't want that.

Julius had opened his eyes, he peered out the window and murmured, "oh my."

"I know," Cassius mumbled.

The two of them had to push their way through the crowds. There were people yelling at them, telling them that it was unsafe to go inside. They were yelling questions at Cassius, wondering whether he knew if Clare truly had magic. He ignored them all. He wasn't wearing his crown and he wished that for one second, they could treat him like a human being and not some royal doll. The door was pulled open by the guards who had been expecting him.

Cassius barely got a chance to step inside the door, Cisily ran towards him with her arms open. He embraced her and she inhaled the sweet scent of his usual cologne that he had put on before he got in the carriage.

"How is Theo? Did he come with you?"

Cassius bit down on his lip. 'How was he supposed to greet her?' He couldn't say that her brother might be dead, right in front of everyone. He refused to deliver the news that way. "I think he's alright, we will talk about him soon. I just need a minute."

"Right, I'm sure there are much more pressing matters," Cisily said.

Cassius shook his head. "A little, but only selfishly so. I need to see Clare and Gracielle and make sure that they are alive and well. I hate to brush you off Cis, but I am engaged to Clare and I have a duty to make sure that she is alright."

"I understand. They're all in the dining area drinking tea. Go ahead and go see them," she said.

Cassius let his eyes flicker to Julius who was already heading that way. "No, I'm not going without you. Why aren't you in there with them Cis? You're a guest. Is it because they excluded you?"

"Oh no, of course not, I was waiting here for you," she linked her arm with his and he led her down the hallway. "It's been a bonkers day, but I knew you'd be here soon and I didn't want to leave you without a greeting from your cousin."

Cassius walked with her down the hall. Cisily seemed to be holding up well. She didn't know Antoine so she wasn't aching, but she had to watch a murder and though it wasn't her first, they never got easier. He didn't want his uncertain news to ruin her calm aura, but it would have to, not now, but later, in private. He'd never publicly humiliate her, she didn't deserve that. Cassius sucked in a breath as they rounded the corner to the dining area. Clare was the first thing on his mind. Sure he was hurting, but Clare was too and he cared more about her than he did himself. He had learned to love her, his heart grew for her, it burned for her. Cisily let go of his arm just before they entered the room. Cassius kicked off his slippers and then stepped into the room, suddenly in view, on display for the grieving family. Julius had already joined Sage, they were leaning up against one another, their eyes closed. Gracielle had a comforting hand on Clare's shoulder. Clare looked defeated, there were tear streaks on her red face, her clothes were the same as they had been earlier and her eyes were sunken. She opened her mouth to speak to him, but no words came out. 'Could she tell he was upset? Could she see Adria's ghost? What had she felt? Was there nothing to say? Did she know it all already?'

He spoke first. "Clare," he whispered, his eyes locked on her as if she were the only one in the room.

She stood from her chair and gravitated towards him like a moth to a flame. Before he knew it, she was in his arms, a ball of sweet warmth.

"How are you holding up?" he choked out. The smell of fresh roses was gone, she was withering, her heart slowly breaking. She placed her hand over his heart, she was scared that his would stop beating too. She rested her head on top of his chest where his heart lay and took in his scent like she always did. 'Was her love for Antoine suddenly gone, or had she always loved him too?' "Antoine told me about Adria," her voice was soft and hushed, broken and damaged, the sweetness that normally consumed it was replaced by tiredness.

He bit his lip and felt his eyes cloud. "Antoine is here?"

"He is, I can speak to his ghost. He knows that we still need him."

"Where is he now?" Cassius asked quietly.

"In the corner." She looked over her shoulder and smiled softly, then she turned back to Cassius. "He wants us to be happy, but that's beside the point. What happened to your mum? All he knows is that she's not living because someone, he won't tell me who, told him that she entered the spirit world.

'How could he tell her without crying in front of everyone?' Surely Sage was still judgmental and he didn't want Gracielle, to lose the image of the strong boy that she had envisioned in her head. Luckily Julius got the hint, he must have been in this same situation before. Normally someone speaking for him would have bothered him, but it did not bother him now.

"Erebus killed Adria," there was a new anger in his voice. Clare looked up to Cassius's face, about to burst into tears for him. She was upset for him, no one had ever been this upset for him before. He gently stroked her hair.

"Is it true?" she whispered against his chest.

He felt her wet tear roll down his shirt. He nodded and screwed his eyes tight, refusing to break down again.

Sage straightened, for the first time, she felt as if he were worth her sympathy, "I'm so sorry Cassius," she said.

He didn't want to push Clare away, but the attention was starting to get to him and his cheeks went hot. He gently stepped back from her and her hands fell. "Can we talk later?" he whispered. She nodded. They would talk later, but for now, they sat at the table. "The preparations for Antoine must be expensive, let me pay for them. I am sorry for my father's stupidity," Cassius said.

"We will split the cost with the Demetrias's, do not worry about pitching in. It's getting late, it's been a long day. Why doesn't everyone just try and head to bed," Gracielle said.

Cassius could feel the emotional exhaustion creeping over him, but he refused to let himself fall into sleep. "Thank you, Gracielle. I'll be with you in a second Clare, I need to talk to Cisily."

Clare made it hard for him to leave, but he did. He walked to Cisily who was waiting for him in the corner, her eyes were wet with tears, her aunt had just passed away. "Let's go to the gardens," he suggested. He walked with her to the gardens and together they sat on the bench surrounded by nature. The smell of Earth filled the crisp, clean air.

"What was it that you wanted to talk to me about? Was it about Aunt Adria? I'm so sorry for your loss, Cass."

He gulped, shaking his head, "It is your loss too, but no, that's not it. Before I came here, I went to the Demetrias's. When I got out of the carriage, the coachman told me that," he stopped. 'How was he going to break this to her, he didn't even know if it was true or if it was just some scheme that was made in order to get into his head.' "Theo had passed, but I'm not sure if it's true so please don't panic until we know!"

Cisily's lips parted. Oddly enough, she wasn't crying, she didn't crumble and break down, she didn't even panic. She re adjusted the way that she had been sitting and instead cleared her throat. There was worry in her eyes, but beyond that, she was cool and calm, calmer then she should have been.

Cassius tilted his head slightly. Leave it to Cisily to stay hopeful.

"I'm not sure if I believe you," her words were coated with worry and they felt strangled in her throat. "Tomorrow morning, I'll take a carriage home at once to go see. You've had a bit of a traumatic night." She stood from her place on the bench and gathered her dress in her hands.

'Is this what she was? Offended? Did she think that he had gone mad and made the situation up?' "I have, but Cis, I'm not making this up."

She shook her head, her lips bent in a frown. "I'm sure you're not Cassius, this just isn't good news to hear."

Before he could converse with her any further, she left the garden and headed down the hallway, surely she'd want to speak to Clare. He wanted to give them alone time, but he had to follow her. He couldn't lie any longer, to two very important women in his life. They were more respectable than he'd ever be. They deserved honesty.

He hurried along after Cisily. She was walking faster than him on purpose, but he had longer legs, so it was easy for him to catch up. "Can you give me a bit of privacy please?" she said.

"I would, but … there's something that I need to tell you, well and Clare, I figured you were going to go see her. Were you not?"

"I was," she huffed, glaring at him from the corner of her eye. "Is this news just as shocking and nerve wracking?"

"Maybe a bit shocking, but I don't know about nerve wracking," he said as he followed her.

When they reached Clare's bedroom, they were greeted by Phoebe, who was coming out of the room carrying a tray. She greeted Cassius and Cisily with a smile, before moving out of their way and heading down the hall. Clare was sitting on her bed, flipping through a book, her eyes were watering, she hadn't been expecting their company. She looked up and quickly blinked away her tears. She hadn't been expecting Cassius so soon, but she hadn't been expecting Cisily at all. She waved them both in and forced a smile. "What are you doing here Cisily? I'm delighted, but a little concerned," Clare said as she looked over to Cassius.

"Cassius, has something that he wants to tell the both of us," Cisily said. Her voice was cold, her tears had gone and she had shut down.

Cisily took a seat next to Clare on her bed.

Cassius stood awkwardly. "I don't really know how to tell you this." He wasn't that kind of person. Normally he knew exactly how to tell someone something and he never did it lightly. Protecting someone's feelings normally wasn't his first priority. If he didn't care so much about Clare and Cisily, he would have said it bluntly and then he would have walked away, not allowing them to ask questions. "I murdered four people," he said. His tone wasn't regretful, just monotone and blank.

Both girls stared at him with wide eyes, this was not the news that they had been expecting.

"You murdered four people just now or you've been murdering people?" Cisily asked, her tone was rather rough. She was annoyed with her cousin.

"Just now, after the execution." He cleared his throat. He forced his eyes to shift to Clare, who still seemed too shocked to respond. They made eye contact until she spoke.

"Because you were angry, or because they deserved it?" Clare asked.

"Both."

"Who?" both girls asked at the same time.

"A few of my father's guards. They turned on me and they're only loyal to him now. They didn't stop Antoine's execution and they knew about my father's cruel plan to murder my mum and they stayed. Maybe they didn't deserve to be slaughtered, but they deserved my rage. It's not reversible, so it doesn't matter what they deserved. I'm unchangeable. I've killed and not because I had to. I understand if you're furious with me."

Clare laughed and Cassius froze. 'Was she in shock from what she had heard? This wasn't something funny. Was she slowly going insane from the events of the day?'

"Sorry," she pressed a hand to her mouth. "I just think it's funny that this entire day is going to shit. I mean, I can't blame you for what you did. I don't want you to murder anyone else again and I do wish you hadn't done that, but I just exposed my magic and I am on the top of the most wanted list, everyone is dying and," she threw her hands up in the air, "and I'm sure a war will be declared tomorrow. So your crime, is not the worst thing to have happened tonight." She laid back on her bed in defeat and Cisily joined her. The girl's held hands and Cisily whispered something low and comforting to her.

"A lot has happened in the past few hours. I don't think anyone's in a clear head space," Cisily said. This time she didn't glare at her cousin, she just forced a smile and pointed it towards the girl she had grown to care for. "I came in here because I wanted to tell you that I'm leaving tomorrow morning."

"But you just got here Cis and I haven't seen you in so long," Clare protested.

"Now that I think about it, it's not safe for you to go back to Excidium, Cis. I won't allow it," Cassius said.

Cisily sat up from the bed, her lip curled in anger. "You're not the boss of me Cassius, you don't get to decide where I'm allowed to go."

"You're right, I'm not the boss of you and I don't get to decide, but I get to have an input. You could leave now, but let's say what happened to Theo is true, you would be next Cis. Let's just write a letter to confirm it."

"But what if he won't confirm it? What if alive or dead, I never see my brother again," she cried.

Cassius thought about this, his father wouldn't want Theo's death to look like his doing, so he'd let Cisily see the body. This way she'd be able to see Theo and he'd be safe. "You won't have to worry about that, I promise," Cassius said. He looked to Clare for help, but she didn't meet his eyes, she was too busy looking up at the ceiling. To his surprise, she spoke anyway.

Her eyes broke away from the ceiling and landed on Cisily. She squeezed her hand tighter. "I don't want anything to happen to you Cis, Cassius is right. Please stay here with me."

Cisily thought this over, but ultimately agreed. "Alright, only if it's not too much trouble. I'll stay here, but only after I go check on my brother." She broke away from the girl's touch. "I should get to sleep. I'm quite tired."

Cisily didn't look at Cassius as she exited the room. Phoebe met her outside and took her down the long hallway to a guest bedroom. When the door closed again, Clare sat up.

"Why is she mad at you?"

Cassius shrugged as he sat down beside her. "I'm not sure. Maybe she thinks I have something to do with this. I told her that I killed and then I told her that her brother might be dead all in the span of a few moments. I assure you, I would never do such a thing. I will be mortified if Theo is truly dead, but I do hope that is not the case." He drew in a breath and crawled over Clare to the other side of the bed where he would be sleeping. He always slept closest to the door when they were together. "Do you want to change out of that dress?" He threw her a sideways glance. He could tell she was too tired to bathe and although it was needed, he wouldn't press. When she said nothing and stared off into the distance, he took matters into his own hands. He would do anything to distract him from the pain that he was currently feeling and he would do anything to prolong their much needed conversation. He got up and pulled from her closet, the first nightgown that he saw, it was mint green with teal ribbons on the neckline. "How about this one?" he asked her. Snapping her out of her trance. She nodded.

He set it down on the bed and then went to her vanity. He grabbed a gray cloth and soaked it with water, he wrung it out and then grabbed a dry cloth.

She stared at him, confused "What are you doing?" she murmured, her mind clearly elsewhere.

"I'm taking care of you because you won't take care of yourself. May I take off your makeup?"

She nodded, "Cassius, are you taking care of yourself? I mean I lost Antoine, but you lost Antoine and your mother. I can not pretend to imagine the pain that you must be going through."

He lifted her chin up with his right hand, so her eyes were looking up at the ceiling. He could feel the tears rising at her concern, but he choked them down. "It's not a contest, but yes, I am doing my best to take care of myself, I came here after all." He grabbed the wet cloth and began to press it in circles on her face, he was gentle, applying pressure, but never too much. Her makeup began to come off in smudges. He switched rags, still holding her chin and then wiped the smudged makeup off with the dry towel until her face was clean. "Are you really just going to move on from what I did?" he asked her

"Yes I am. You remind me of a soldier, like my father, like Jesse. I think those guards might have attacked you if you didn't get rid of them first and even if they would not have attacked you, they were in full support of your father." She pressed a few pale fingers to her rosy cheeks and let out a soothing sigh at how refreshed her skin felt. She looked down to the night gown and balled the fabric up in her hands. "Would you do the honors?

Cassius swallowed hard and he shook his head. "No Clare, you still have feelings for Antoine. I don't want to do something that you are going to regret asking me to do because you were sad. I don't want to be that bloke. There's no need to start this now."

After a few moments of silence, Cassius turned his body to give her privacy, but he felt a tug on his wrist and she whirled him around. His lips parted, but no words came out.

She got closer to him until she was almost sitting on his lap. "I love both of you. I always would've ended up spending the rest of my life with you, a man I loved, but there was something drawing me into Antoine. I know it was wrong to love Antoine, but there was a connection and I did, I mean, I do love him too."

Cassius took a minute to process this information, he put an arm around her waist and pulled her in closer. "You love me too?" He couldn't think of a reason why she would love him. He couldn't write poems and he wasn't one to talk about books, he would rather throw knives or go horseback riding.'

"I always wanted what I couldn't have and I knew that I could have you, so for the longest time I made myself despise you. At first you were mean and cold, but soon I discovered that was just because of the facade your father had made you put on. Your walls slowly started to crack. I love how hard you try for me Cassius. Those dates you put together and how you took my makeup off without me asking or how you always put another blanket around me when I'm cold, or how you share your food with me when I don't like mine. Under all of those scowls and anger, there is a man that I love,"

"   Clare, please, I'm a monster, you deserve someone like Antoine and you're right, though you can not have him … you deserved him over me. Of course I'm in love with you," he said as he let out a hot breath. "You're the only reason I hold back from my darkest demons, you're the only reason that I'm a slightly better person now. If I had to search through hell and back to find you and your soul then I would. Your wish is my command. But I'm a monster of a human. You should not want me. I should only want you." He stopped talking when she placed a finger to his lips.

"Do not tell me what I should want."

When she lifted her finger, he spoke again. "Are you sure about this Clare? Is Antoine in here?"

She shook her head, "Antoine isn't in here and him and I have never had sex Cassius, if that's what you thought. I kissed him, but I never did anything of that sort. I shouldn't have even kissed him because you said you would try to be faithful to me and I should have tried harder to be faithful to you. My heart still holds love for the both of you, but I need you now more than ever. Though I may grieve, for a long, long time, I'm ready to start giving my heart to you fully. Cassius, my heart aches for you."

He was too stunned to speak, but when she leaned in and stopped, waiting for his reaction, he nodded and closed his eyes. Their lips pressed together in unison and moved at a similar speed. Her right hand was wound in the back of his deep black hair, her left hand pressed on his chest as she leaned against him. She pushed him down onto the bed and laid on top of him, kissing both of his cheeks. He kissed her lips once more and then rolled out from underneath her. Though he wished to keep kissing her, their emotions were high, things were different, he didn't want her to regret any of her decisions. So they settled on spending the rest of the night together, cuddled up. Cassius had always assumed he would hate to cuddle, but he was wrong, when Clare was in his arms, there was nothing he liked more.

Their last moments of peace before war were fleeting. After Clare changed into her nightgown, they held each other close all night, their legs entangled, their hands melded together. Clare fell asleep, but Cassius did not. Though it was odd to think that she was finally his, he felt guilty that to get here, Antoine had to die. 'Would she have chosen him over Antoine if he had lived? Was she ready to start a life with him before Antoine had gone? Or would she have chosen Antonine and broke off their engagement in the end?' His thoughts moved from this, to the execution and then to his mother's death. He spent all night thinking and wishing that things could be both different and the same, all at once.

SYMPATHY

Sage felt horrible. The sympathy that she felt for her sister was the strongest that it had ever been and the three people she loved the most were hurting. Her mother was upset because Clare was hurting and she had lost a boy that she'd grown to love. Clare and Julius were upset because they both had lost someone close to them. Though she too was hurting as Antoine had lived inside of her home and was like a brother that she never had, she felt guilty that she was escaping the worst of this tragedy. Her relationship with him was not as deep as Clare's or Gracielle's or Julius's. She didn't know what to do with her emotions. She couldn't disappear and sulk with her sword because she had to be there for the people that she loved the most. Julius was sitting next to her at the dining room table, everyone else had left the room. "How are you holding up?" she whispered. Comforting people wasn't her specialty, but she'd try her best to make him feel at home.

He rubbed his face, scrubbed it hard and then put his head on the table. "Not very well."

She sighed at his response, she was shit at consoling people. She placed a hand on his shoulder. "Would it make you feel better to employ the rest of his family?"

"No. It would put them in more danger, plus it would be a constant reminder, money will suffice," he groaned.

Sage was horrible at this, she felt as if anything she suggested would upset him. Though deep down she knew he wasn't upset at her, she couldn't shake the feeling that she was just making things worse.

She pondered what might make him feel better. "You know that I will kill that mother fucker, right?" she said to him. Though she was trying to joke around, there was no light heartedness to her voice. While she said the words, she realized that she was a bit serious. Cassius was annoying, but he was nothing like his father. She was finally warming up to him. Antoine was gone and Cassius was the closest person that Clare had to hang onto besides her mother and Sage. Cassius would always be second to Sage no matter how hard that he tried. Sage's frown turned into a smile when she realized that Julius was laughing. She grasped his hands tightly and kissed them, hoping this unusual display of affection would lift his spirits.   "Do you think you'll be able to sleep tonight?" she asked him.

"I think so. Oddly enough, that is my way of coping with things. Some people can't sleep because they will have nightmares, but my brain likes to drown things out. Ever since I came back from the, uh, dead, I haven't really dreamt much. I guess you can say that he missed that part of my revival."

"Well if you can get some sleep, then you should."

She stood up from the chair and helped him up, she had no trouble with his weight. Even though he was an average guy, not thin enough to be skinny, not thick enough to be fat, she could easily hold his weight and she didn't mind helping him. Sage linked arms with him and practically dragged him through the halls until she got to her room. Esmeralda frowned when she saw Julius, but she didn't scurry away like usual.

"I am so sorry Julius, I have lost and I am sorry that you must go through it too. I could not imagine losing Sage and I am sure that she could not imagine losing me either." She brushed past them and gave them their privacy.

Julius's eyes were too puffy and red to produce more tears. He threw himself on the bed and buried his head into the pillow. He was not up for conversation, he was ready to sleep the pain away. Sage walked to the other side of the bed, blew out the candles and helped him get under the covers. "Goodnight Julius." She planned to let him sleep as long as he needed.

"Night," he murmured lazily, his eyes closing shut.

While he was asleep, she stayed up throughout the night to make sure that he was safe and sound.

ALL HAIL THE KING

Though King Erebus already held a royal position in Excidium, he had never been the one who had the power to make decisions. The morning after Antoine's death, this changed. He had to convince Adria while she was alive, to be his puppet, in order to make his moves for him, but now that she was gone, there was no one to convince. Normally when a new person came into power, the people cheered and screamed, but the citizens of Excidium were silent. They watched with unblinking eyes as the new decision maker gave his speech.

He told them of Adria's tragic 'suicide.' He then went on to announce that traitors would not be tolerated and that there would be a new curfew at sundown. Military officers would be stationed in the streets and if anyone spoke badly about Excidium, or spoke out of line, they would go to prison or worse they would be executed. He told them as long as they obeyed his rules, then they would be fine. He told them of Cassius's betrayal and how his son had run off, he pretended to be devastated.

He promised there would be no war unless someone else declared it first. While he tried to make himself look like the brightest leader in Europe, he came off as cruel and frightening.

A few cries broke through the silence as he took off his old crown and placed a new one on top of his head.

WAR

Chaos erupted in Deus the same morning. King Maximus was dressed in a ruby red suit, a gold cloak hung from his neck and dragged behind him. He stood on his balcony and addressed his people. To some it may have looked like a young boy declaring war, but to others the sight looked like a strong man fighting for his people.

He declared war the same day as Erebus's coronation, which happened to be the morning after Antoine's death.

After announcing Antoine's death to the public, he called for his allies, Pax et Lux, to help aid him in the fight between good and evil. He went on to paint King Erebus as a cruel and cunning man. He claimed that he would not stop fighting this war until Erebus was dead. He wanted his head on a silver platter.

After the news had reached Gracielle, she too stood on the highest platform in her home. She addressed her half of Europe, while wearing a stunning white dress. She hadn't had to do this in a long time. She was hesitant on the decision, she talked it over with her daughters and the two agreed that war was necessary. Not only did he take Antoine, a boy everyone had grown to love, but Erebus also took Adria, his own wife, the ruler of Excidium. Now Erebus was free to control and torment his people however he liked and he had to be stopped.

When Gracielle spoke, Europe went silent. When the peaceful queen declared war, the world would change forever.

Soldiers from each kingdom were deployed. They fought each other in the streets. Spies roamed the villages. Each one looming, hoping to kill the other one's leader.

A TOUGH DECISION

Antoine's funeral was held a few days later in private. If Excidium found out that the Pax family was properly sending off a man who had been publicly executed, then they would have been outraged and the last thing that the Pax's wanted was to give Erebus more motivation.

The funeral was held in the back of the Pax palace, outside by the infirmary. Antoine's body had been cremated, that was the wish of his family. Instead of a casket, there was a foldable table adorned in Deus's colors. His ashes sat on top of the table in a bright yellow urn, carved on the vase was the symbol of the working dog.

There were three rows of chairs for the mourners. His mother and father along with his brother and sister were in the front row, then Clare, Julius, Maximus and Sage were seated in the second row. Gracielle sat in the back row with Cassius. A few of the servants from the Pax family came to observe, standing by the large back doors, their heads dipped in respect.

Standing at the front by the table, was Mary, the family nurse that had healed Cassius, she was holding a book about death in her hands, it featured both the Goddess, Evangeline and the Goddess, Mallory on the cover. "Today we are sadly gathered here to mourn the death of Antoine Paige. He was taken wrongfully from this world for crimes that he did not commit. His family and friends have gathered here today, to pay their respects to him. His honor will live on forever."

Clare had her face buried in her hands, attempting to hide her tears. She couldn't help but feel a tad responsible for his death. In her mind, if it wasn't for her foolish feelings for him, then he would have been sitting right here with her and instead of a funeral, they would have been a wedding or a party. She looked up from her hands and forced herself to watch.

That's when she caught him. He was still here. The cremation hadn't killed his soul. A wave of cold washed over her, she looked to her right and was comforted by a gentle and warm voice, one that she knew well.

'It wasn't your fault Clare,' he told her, his voice breaking. 'Remember you made me feel alive. One day something in this cruel world would have killed a servant. Erebus just got to me first. Please remind my mum that I love her.' Her eyes gazed into his spirit and she collapsed against her sister in tears.

"I will," she whispered quietly so that no one would hear her. She wasn't the only one in tears, Antoine's mother was sobbing and her children were clinging to her sadly. Antoine's father was still, his knuckles were clutching tightly onto the seat that he sat in.

"The Goddesses have spoken. Their presence is around us. Today we find out if Evangeline will take him up to the mansions of rest or if Mallory will drag him down with her." The pages of the book began to fly open and flip. The page that the flip through landed on was a picture of Evangeline the Goddess of Heaven. "He will rest with Evangeline when his soul leaves us," Mary said.

The tears quieted in relief.

Antoine smiled crookedly. If only he was brave enough to leave these people be and join Evangeline, in the sky. He wasn't. He didn't feel okay leaving them. He felt as if they all still needed his presence, so he decided against joining the glorious after life and stayed. He watched as each person went up to his urn and whispered their goodbyes. It was painful to watch his family mourn, but they were in good hands. The Pax's and the Demetrias's would make sure that they were alright. It pained him to see Clare, shivering over his ashes. She would never forgive herself for this, no matter how many times he told her that she had given him the best months of his life. Cassius was another painful interaction to watch. The entire time he was murmuring, 'sorry.' 'When would he realize that he wasn't his father?' Antoine thought. The respectful goodbyes stopped and his mother was given his urn.

He was curious to see the interactions Clare would have with his family. He watched from a distance as she approached them. The color black did not suit her well. Though she looked gorgeous in any dress she wore, the dull fabric made her look solemn. Antoine couldn't imagine a life where Clare had to live with the Antias family, constantly dressed in black, at least Cassius was willing to save her from that fate.

Clare stopped right in front of his mother and was greeted by the woman with a hug, something she hadn't been expecting. So Clare, continued the hugs, she gave one to his father and then one to each of his siblings. As he had expected, the first thing that she did was apologize. "I'm so sorry, I was foolish. Don't forgive me because I'm royalty. If it wasn't for me, none of this would have ever happened," she said.

"If my son chose you, then he must have been happy," the kind woman said as she pushed a strand of hair behind Clare's ear. "We have been sad ever since we heard the news. Today we want to celebrate his life with you and we want to get to know the girl who he loved so much." She offered her hand to the girl. "Come on, let's go inside. He wouldn't want you to freeze." She moved Clare inside and Antoine followed.

His mother was right, he would never want her to freeze.

"He loves you very much," Clare told Angelique on her way inside.

The woman, solemnly nodded.

Cassius stayed far away from Clare that day. Though the jealousy in his heart swelled, he wouldn't let it take over. In fact, he left the castle and went to go visit Cisily for Adria's funeral. He hadn't heard from her and he was beginning to think the rumors about Theo were true. He didn't trust his father to be alone with Cisily for too long and he had to go say his final goodbye to his mum. Antoine watched as Cassius left without saying goodbye, as he had already told the Pax's in the morning that he would be leaving.

Antoine took no offense. If the roles were reversed, Antoine would have done the same thing. If any of his siblings were possibly in trouble, he would have been there within minutes. If he was the one alive and he had to see Clare mourning over Cassius, he would've been sad, but he also would have felt a deep jealousy. In fact, he had heard Clare talk about the kiss she and Cassius had and he cringed. She was hurt, he reminded himself, but she had always loved him too and he had to accept that. 'She lost you, let her have this,' he thought to himself.

He directed his thoughts away from Cassius and instead drifted back inside of the palace. Clare had taken a seat on one of the sofas and his family sat across from her.

"What was your favorite thing about Antoine?" his mother asked.

"He was so kind," she said. The smile that he loved was coming back onto her lips, "we had a lot of the same interests. Art and literature. I felt very safe with him. He made me feel at home wherever I was." Clare made his soul melt.

"You know he wrote to us," his sister said, her mouth twisted up into a mischievous smile, "he was very very fond of you. He always talked about how gorgeous your hair was and how you were always so nice to be around, your bubbly disposition and such. He talked about how you made him a painting. You really did make him happy."

Clare's smile got brighter and so did his and if he could blush, his face would have been bright red.

"He told us about your magic too," the brother said. "I didn't want to ask this of you, but is it possible to revive him?"

Clare froze, her mouth opened to speak, but no words came out.

The boy's father hit him on the side of his arm and he winced.

"What? I was just asking?"

"I could, I could, but my magic would turn dark and all of Europe already knows that he is dead and they'll think that I'm some sort of monster," she said hesitantly.

Antoine frowned at her panic. Though it would be nice to become like Julius and be back in their lives, 'how was that possible?' He was already ash and Clare was right, too many people knew that he was dead for him to come back. He'd have to talk to her about this later. He didn't want her to do anything that she would regret. He winced as his mother handed over his ashes to Clare, just in case she wanted to bring him back. If he could speak to them, he would have scolded them for putting her in such an uncomfortable position.

"I'll look into it," she said and he could tell that her words were honest. She would think about bringing him back.

As soon as Clare was alone, Antoine found her. She was staring at his urn in her bedroom and Julius was by her side. "What do you think I should do? Should I try it? Are you glad that you're back to life? Would you wish this for Antoine? You know him well. Would he like it? He will just lie to me if I speak to him. He will tell me whatever I want to hear, be honest with me," she pleaded.

"Clare, take a deep breath," Julius said as he took one himself. He placed a hand on her shoulder. "Breathe. I don't know if I would want you to do this. I do think Antoine would enjoy being alive again, but that's only if he could be with you. You'd have to constantly battle between him and Cassius and you'd have to keep Antoine out of the public eye. Your magic would turn dark. So my answer is no, but who knows what the Goddesses would want you to do, maybe you can pray and hope for some answers," he suggested.

"I suppose that I could pray. I didn't even remember that this was possible, I didn't even consider bringing him back." She bit down on her lip. "Cassius would be devastated, he believes that I would choose Antoine over him. But if I am being quite honest, I don't know what I would do." She tapped her fingers against her leg. "I don't think I can do it, not yet." She stared at the urn. "Maybe ... maybe if he asks me to revive him, then I'll consider it, but for now, my life needs to stay how it is. There's a war going on, I can't add anymore chaos to anyone's lives. Everyone's fate is going to have to be final until I get some clarity. I feel like I'm suffocating, nothing in my life is constant because there's always some new magical change."

Julius frowned, he removed his hand off of her shoulder as she stood up from the bed. "I agree with you Clare, it's too much to ask of you, especially right now. Life keeps changing for me too, in fact this morning, Gracielle asked me if Sage and I would be willing to get married in a week."

"What?" Clare whispered. "Why didn't Sage tell me?"

"She found out this morning as well and today isn't a very happy day. She didn't want to make things about her and she's a bit nervous too, she doesn't want to get married yet, it wasn't her vision, but war makes things move quicker."

"I'll have to talk to her tonight," she mumbled. "Well thank you for everything, Julius. Go back to Sage and tell her that I'll talk to her shortly." She glanced to the corner. "I have a ghost to talk to and it's odd to talk to him when I'm not alone."

"I understand, I'll tell her to expect you and hello Antoine," he said as he waved to a random corner.

He shut the door. Clare was left alone with a ghost.

Antoine came through the door and pretended to seat himself on Clare's bed. "Please don't listen to my mom or my brother. Julius is right. Though I wouldn't mind coming back, I won't do it at your expense. If there was another magic user who could do it, I'd consider it, but I'm not that selfish. I want you and Cassius to be happy."

"I love you Antoine, but if you want Cassius and I to be happy then you can't continue to linger. You're just going to hurt yourself and Cassius feels uncomfortable when he sees me talking to you. He's trying to be accepting, about the whole talking to spirits thing, but it's a lot for people to comprehend and when it's you, I'm sure you can imagine the pain and guilt that he feels."

"I'll do my best to keep my distance then, though I'll always be near. I know you still need me so I won't disappear, but I'll give you your space. Please tell Cassius that he doesn't have to feel bad because I don't blame him."

"He knows that deep down, but he's always been told that everything has been his fault. He'll get there eventually. Do I tell your mum that I can see your spirit or do I keep that to myself?" she frowned.

Antoine debated for a few moments. "No do not tell her today, she has enough stress on her shoulders. Once again, I'm sorry that my brother asked this of you."

"Don't worry about it, he had every right to ask." Clare stood from the bed and smoothed out her dress. "I need to go now."

"I know, do your best to smile for me."

"Of course," she grinned. "Stay as positive as you can and maybe step away for a moment, it must be hard to see people mourn over you, especially Julius."

"Of course," he said, "I'll do my best to stay away. Please tell Julius that I said hello back and that I love him dearly."

"I will, goodbye Antoine." Clare quickly walked out of the room and refused to look back.

HOME IS WHERE THE HEART IS

Cassius arrived back at Excidium after hours of travel. Though he felt bad that he couldn't be there for Clare, he had to get out of the suffocating atmosphere of Antoine's funeral. He was positive that Sage would do a good job at consoling Clare while he was away. Although he was truly starting to care for all of the new people in his life, he had important personal matters of his own to attend to. When he approached the castle, he was stopped by the guards. "Like it or not you have to let me inside of my own castle, you idiots," he said as the guards continued to refuse his entrance. Eventually, a booming voice told the guards to step aside and allow his arrival

. With a roll of his eyes, Cassius stepped inside, his eyes landing on his father.

"So you've decided to come back and join our side of the fight. What a pity we have to be so divided because your best mates wanted to declare war," Erebus teased.

"You know that's not why I'm here," he said, his tone harsh. "And these mates that you're talking about had a good reason to declare war. Don't play dumb, this is what you wanted, you want to conquer."

"Enough of your bull shit. Cisily's upstairs. Make your visit quick, your presence disturbs me, the funeral will be held shortly in the courtyard."

"Right, I love standing near the same place where you murdered my mother. I know when the funeral is." He quickly stalked up the stairs and knocked on Cisily's door.

The call was quickly answered, but what he was met with shocked him.

Cisily stood there in a tattered dress, her hair messy and unbrushed. She had bruises on her neck, her eyes were sunken and her lips were swollen. She opened her mouth to speak, but she couldn't get out a word.

Cassius's arms were protectively around her and she leaned into them, letting her swollen eyes shut as she teared up against his shoulder. He let go of her, slammed the door and then guided her to the bed, sitting her down. "What the hell did he do to you?" It reminded him of the worst of one his beatings, but since she was a girl, he worried something else might have happened. "Cisily please, please tell me he didn't violate you."

"No!" she blurted out. "But you were right, Theo didn't make it," she cried. "I knew he did it, so I tried to stand up to him and he beat me. He hasn't been feeding me, he's kept me locked up in here with nothing but my thoughts. I think he was waiting for you to come get me," she whispered sadly, wiping her tears away with her sleeve.

"I should've come sooner!" he cried out. "I'm so sorry, I'll take you back to the Pax's with me, you can live there. Clare adores you, they won't mind. There is so much space there. I'll help you pack your things and we will leave immediately." He breathed in deeply and slowed his words down. "I'm sorry about Theo. I'm going to miss him. You didn't deserve to have him taken away from you."

Cisily looked away from him, "I know I didn't. If Clare doesn't mind then I'll come with you. Let's leave after the funeral. I want to get out of here and I'm starving."

Cisily stood up from the bed and went into her walk-in closet. She shut the door and changed into a long sleeve black dress that stopped at her ankles. After angrily brushing out her hair, she exited the closet and got out a large bag. She stuffed some of her favorite clothes, her childhood stuffed animals, some pictures and her toiletries inside. Afterwards, she piled up her pillows on top and shoved in her sketchbook.

"Since when did you start drawing?" he questioned as he handed her the two pillows and grabbed her bag.

"Clare might have inspired that," she admitted. She refused to glance   at herself in the mirror as she walked with her cousin down the stairs of the castle.

Erebus was by the front doors, his eyebrows raised. "I am so lucky that your parents are guarding the island across the sea and can not see you now. I could take it away from your mother, but it would seem suspicious on my part and I wouldn't want her to question me. I'm so glad that she doesn't have to see her children suffer. Have fun informing her of the news," he pouted, before waving to the two of them. "I suppose I won't see you again, I'll just hear of your deaths once I win the war. You'll regret leaving."

"I'm sure we'd both rather die than spend another hour with you," Cassius said, hurriedly dragging Cisily out of the door and into the courtyard.

The funeral was private and was only held for the royal family and staff that lived inside of the castle. Erebus was afraid that if he had a public funeral, the citizens might sniff out his lie and rebel against him. This was the only safe option. Though Adria was lying in the casket, it was closed. Cassius was sure that wherever she was now, she felt more at ease than she did living with Erebus. After everyone got a chance to say their respects, Cassius went up. He felt sick when his brain reminded him of the night that she died. "I'm glad you're finally able to rest," he whispered to her. "I love you," he said it three times before he went back to the mourning crowd. He watched with angry and teary eyes as they placed her casket in the ground for burial. 'Why must she be buried here?' he thought. If he had a say, he would have taken her far from this wicked place, but he had no voice here. This was no longer his home.

After the funeral, the two cousins called for a carriage in order to head back to Pax et Lux. "You have to be so glad to finally escape that place," Cassius said dully.

"I am, I've never liked it, but I never had to go through what you did, not until now, I'm sorry that was your childhood."

"Spare me the pity, it's alright." He placed her bag and pillows on the floor of the carriage and helped her in so they were sitting across from one another. "You should consider moving across the sea, with your parents. I'm sure they'd be glad to have you back. You would be treated like a real princess there. I doubt you'd even face much of the war on the island," he suggested as the carriage took off.

"You know, it's a good idea Cassius, but it's been so long, that we've lost our relationship, so I'd have to rebuild it first. I couldn't send her a lot of letters because of Erebus, but I suppose I could start now. I don't understand Erebus, his logic is so flawed. He abused me and locked me up, just to free me as soon as you showed up. He never even gave Theo the proper funeral that he deserved. I have his ashes in my bag, the woman who works at the lowest level of the hospital was kind enough to give them to me as we were leaving. I just don't know what to do with him, I don't want to keep him forever, that is just odd. I want him to be free, but I can't necessarily remember a place that he loved." She wiped off the flakes of makeup that had smudged on her face. "Do you have any ideas, Cass?"

He thought about it for a moment, "he loved books, but I wouldn't want him at our library, I don't want him anywhere near my father. Maybe try another library or an outside scenery. You could always bring him back home to your parents. I'm not sure … I mean, I can ask Clare if she knows anything."

"What would she know?" Cisily asked curiously.

"Oh right. Ugh. I'm still comprehending it myself, but I guess Clare can see spirits, spirits that she is close to. She didn't really know Theo, but maybe since she knows of him, she can see him and ask him what he wants. But don't get your hopes up Cis, maybe she can't see him, she couldn't see Adria."

"That's so cool, I've always admired Clare. I hope she can get in contact with him," she smiled at the idea and finished wiping her eyes on her sleeve. "How is your love for her coming along?"

"Complicated. I don't mean to put it this way, but now that Antoine is gone … we might have a chance at love. Ugh I'm such an ass," he put his head in his hands. "I just want her to be happy. I never really deserved happiness anyways, but she does."

"Don't say that, you do deserve happiness. And I'm sure that you two will be very happy someday. Wounds just hurt worse when they're fresh."

Though the day was slowly turning into evening, neither of them could take a nap and Cisily couldn't stand silence, so she filled the quiet with stories of her and Theo as children. Cassius listened attentively, responding with either giggles, tears or frowns. Listening was the least that he could do for her given the fact that she never had a chance to grieve properly at a funeral for her brother. Her stories didn't fill up enough time and soon she shifted the topic to something he needed to discuss, but dreaded. "How are you processing everything with your mum? Are you coping alright?" She was worried for him, Theo and Adria had died on the same night and he had just been faced with her casket. Though Cisily had found out more recently about Theo, both of their deaths were still new.

Cassius took a deep breath and gazed out the window. Part of him wanted to give her the one word answer that he gave to most people, 'fine,' but she didn't deserve that and if anything, she needed someone to grieve with.

"I don't know. I've been pushing it all down. I've just been trying to be there for Clare because of Antoine. It's hard." He took a deep breath and decided to continue, it was nice to finally get the words out. "My mum is in my dreams a lot. I have nightmares of killing those men and sometimes I have nightmares about finding her body. I don't really make much noise, I just get up and leave. If you want to know how to handle it, I don't know how, I'm not very good at it. I pretend that nothing happened at all and I constantly distract myself so I hardly have a moment with my own thoughts." He thought back to last night when he woke up startled from a nightmare. Clare was safe and sound, not moving a muscle, so he went down the stairs to get a glass of water and Sage was there. She didn't glare at him, her eyes softened and she thought about saying something, she opened her mouth, but he fled quickly before she had the chance to do so. He shivered at the close call. "Just do better than I do Cis."

Cisily folded her hands neatly in her lap. She wanted to reach out to him and hug him like a big sister would to a little brother, but she restrained herself. Cassius was not in the mood for hugs. She nodded in silent agreement that she would do better. "You know Cass, I have a question. Do you regret um … killing those people?" Her voice was tight and restrained, the question had slipped out and she was mentally cursing herself for asking such a thing.

"Yes. I should've taken my anger out on something else. Why do you ask?" His voice was hot and heavy, the question had made him furious, not at her, but at himself.

"Because when I knew Theo died, there was shock and then a terrible sadness and then I was just so angry. I thought I could slaughter everyone in sight, it was such a scary feeling, you know I'm not like that Cass. I thought about murdering uncle, but I knew I would stand no match. I'm sure you saw that he doubled the security after what you did. Instead I sat down and wrote a letter to my parents to inform them of Theo's death. Sure their duties give them no time to sail across the sea, but they deserve to know what happened to their son. When uncle saw, he snatched the letter and tore it to shreds. That is when he hurt me because I had put the real cause of Theo's death. I should've lied and said that it was some crazy accident, I know now to lie. I wished in that very moment that I had chosen to live with my parents, that we could have lived on that tiny island, the forgotten part of our kingdom. I told him this and things got worse. There was enough flame and adrenaline inside of me to kill him, but I didn't. Isn't that so awful of me?"

"No," Cassius's voice was hard and sure. "I would kill that man in a heartbeat. Sure I'd have to take the throne, it would be complicated, but I hate him so much that I could easily torture him or burn him. He deserves that, the men following him out of fear do not. Don't compare yourself to me Cis. We are nothing alike. You couldn't hurt the cruelest soul, nor should you. Leave that twisted man to me. I'd prefer to be the one who kills him." His voice was monotone, he was slowly beginning to lose himself and he wasn't sure even the prettiest of roses could save him.

Cassius and Cisily arrived at the palace as the sun went down. The guests were currently enjoying Antoine's favorite meal in the dining hall. When the carriages arrived, Clare excused herself from the table and met them outside. With security doubled, no more civilians stood outraged outside the palace gates, in fact they had given up entirely and gone home. The citizens were starting to question what they had really heard. They hadn't even been at the execution. They had only believed what they had heard from Deus civilians and with a war, they were not sure what they had heard was true anymore. There were no more screams and shouts outside, just the peaceful chirping of birds and the sound of the wind.

Cisily stepped out of the carriage first. Without hesitation, Clare ran to her as fast as she could and wrapped her arms around the girl. Cisily held her close, her hands running through Clare's ginger hair.

"What's happened to you?" Clare exclaimed. She pulled back to get a better look at her bruised face. Cassius stepped out of the carriage holding his cousin's bag and pillows.

"My father happened," Cassius said in irritation as he observed the two girls embrace.

Cisily could only nod in confirmation, she did not feel like telling the story, the physical and mental pain was too much to bear. "If it is alright with you Clare, I would like to live here. Only if there is space and I won't be bothering anyone."

"Of course you can live here!" Clare shouted, faster than what was polite. She gave the girl another quick hug before pulling away. "You look like you need something to eat. They're serving dinner now, but I'm not sure if you want to meet new people like this. I can have Phoebe draw you a bath and I'll bring you up a plate after they're gone. How does that sound?" she offered.

"It sounds great."

Though Clare acknowledged Cassius, she didn't take his hand until Cisily was escorted to her room and safe. "I'm glad you're back home," she told him as she gently squeezed his hand on their way back to the dining hall. If Erebus had done this to Cisily, she couldn't imagine what he had done to Cassius throughout the years.

'Home,' Cassius thought. It was a strong word, but it was fitting. His home would never be in Excidium, not anymore, at least not until his father was gone. Instead he would feel at home in the kingdom of Pax et Lux or anywhere the Pax's were near. He squeezed her hand back, afraid that if he spoke, he might start to cry.

They sat down at the dinner table and his plate was filled. He wasn't too hungry, but he ate it all out of respect. It felt awful to see Antoine's parents and siblings, the people that Antoine used to speak so dearly about. He tried to avoid their eyes and focus on Julius instead, but he couldn't avoid them forever. "Your father had no right to kill a man who wasn't even his own citizen, no he killed a boy! That should be illegal," Angelique said as she finally bursted.

"I know mam," he tried to think of what else to say, but Gracielle jumped in to save him just like his mother would any day.

"Don't take your anger out on the boy. I know you're upset, but he didn't have a part in this," the queen said. "Though what happened was awful, it was technically lawful. He wasn't in the Demetrias's kingdom, he was in ours, if he had been in his home kingdom, it would've been illegal to seize him, but unfortunately he was with us. So if you want to blame anyone, blame me."

Maximus who usually enjoyed drama, didn't like how heavy this scene was getting so he changed the subject. "Cassius and Clare, I have been meaning to tell you that I'm going to explain Clare's little outburst of magic to my people soon. I'm going to say that it was a prophecy from the Goddesses and that the heat that they felt had nothing to do with Clare, that she was just in the middle of the storm that they sent down to Earth. I'm going to say that they sent me an image explaining this. They'll listen to me as kings are known to be able to speak to the Goddesses. We all know that this is not true, but they believe it. In the meantime I think it is best that you two retreat to the royal territory as soon as possible. There are assassination threats looming out there for both of you. I think it's best that you hide until I clear Clare's name and people forget about this," he frowned as he looked at Antoine's family. "We won't forget his death, but ordinary civilians will."

"Good, we will leave tomorrow," Cassius said a little too quickly. He wouldn't be upset, to finally get away from all of this mayhem. In the midst of war at least both of them would be safe. The royal territory was a place for all three kingdoms to send their royalty, for vacation or for safety. Though Erebus had access, there was a very small chance that he would hear about this and show up himself.

"What about Cisily, she just got here?" Clare frowned.

"'I'll stay with her, make sure she's got company," Sage assured. "You two need to go and make sure that you're safe, even though I'll miss you," Sage said as she glanced over at Clare.

Antoine's family left shortly after that conversation. They had finished their meal and had to head back to their kingdom. Julius and Maximus would be leaving with them. Julius left with a kiss from Sage, promising that he would see her very soon for their wedding and that after they were married, they could spend as much time as they liked together. Maximus was sent off with a hug from the Pax's and a firm handshake from Cassius. Clare was the only one to give a final goodbye hug to Antoine's family, the solemn feeling returning. She offered to give his ashes back to his mother and she simply shook her head, "I can't have the reminder. If you don't change your mind, I'm sure you'll know where he would like to be spread." She headed off into the night without another word.

"What was all that about?" Cassius asked furiously when both carriages left and they were standing in the sitting room.

Sage and Gracielle were on the sofa, listening curiously to the conversation, Sage was ready to insert herself at any moment.

"His brother and mother, they want me to bring Antoine back to life."

Everyone in the room gasped.

Cassius grabbed her wrist a bit too tightly and when he saw Sage's glare over Clare's shoulder, he let go. "I won't let you do that. Not because I'd be jealous, but because I care about you. Your magic will turn dark if you do that. You should have shoved his ashes back into her hand. Crikey! Where are we going to put them? Doesn't she realize that we have enough stress," he shouted, clearly melting.

Sage stood up and crossed her arms over her chest, "I don't like his attitude," she hissed, "but I agree with him, I don't really want you to revive anyone either."

Gracielle stood, "me neither love, please, don't do it."

Clare felt like lashing out and telling them all that they didn't have a say in her actions and that she would do what she wanted to, but she didn't. "I'm not going to," she gulped. "It wouldn't be good for anyone. I'll miss him, but this isn't the solution. Maybe it was the solution for Julius, but it's not the solution for Antoine. I wouldn't want to bring him into a life of war anyways. I'll give Julius his ashes back after the wedding, he can spread them at Deus." She bit her lip and slowly backed away from Cassius. "Now if you'll excuse me, I have a meal to deliver."

Her feet went as fast as they could take her. The chefs were starting to put the leftovers away when she ordered another plate. They made her a plate as fast as they could and then she was on her way to the bedroom where Cisily would be staying. She knocked on the door and Phoebe answered.

"Hi princess," she said happily. "Cisily, just finished her bath and is expecting you. May I do anything else?"

Clare was silent, of course everyone was meant to address her as princess, but hardly anyone she was close to did. Besides Antoine, she felt her heart throb, ready to explode. "No thank you," she whispered, before moving inside of the room.

Cisily was sitting on the bed in a long sleeve, forest green night gown covered with lighter green polka dots. Her hair was combed and gelled back and her skin was clean, but the bruises remained.

Clare handed her the plate of food and sat down beside her. "Was your bath alright?"

"Yes everything was perfect, thank you for the food," she immediately began to dig in. "Are you alright? You seem tense," Cisily questioned through a mouthful of food.

"I'm fine, life is just stressful, I'm sure that you know this. We have to leave tomorrow. Cassius and I. I'm so sorry, but I promise you that Sage is good company."

"I believe you," Cisily gave the girl a confident smile and then went back to eating. She knew better than to ask if Clare had seen Theo, she'd heard the yelling from downstairs.

Clare knew Cisily didn't like silence, so while she ate, she answered her questions for her. She told her how she could see spirits, how she saw her father and Antoine and how she was ashamed that she hadn't told her mum and Sage about Wade, but how there hadn't been a good time. She finally explained that Cassius had told her about Theo and that she hadn't seen his spirit yet. She explained that this could be because his spirit had already entered heaven or because he was stuck at the castle in Excidium
. She noticed Cisily's shoulders relax, the girl took comfort in knowing that her brother might already be resting peacefully in the land above. She knew well in her heart that he would be with Evangeline for he had never hurt a soul.

After dinner, Cisily explained that she would love to talk more, but she hadn't been sleeping and needed some rest. While this was partially true, she could tell that Cassius and Clare needed to talk. The two girls embraced one more time before Clare left the room and promised to say goodbye to her in the morning.

On her way back to her bedroom, Clare ran into Sage. As the two collided, Sage gently pushed her sister off. "Hey, watch where you are going clumsy," she teased. "I'm not ganging up against you by the way, I just care about you. I know your life has gotten carried away with boys, but I hope I'm still prevalent enough to listen to," Sage said.

"I know you care about me. I'm so sorry that is how all of this has made you feel. Trust me, if I could step away from boys and just hang out with you all day, I would. I'd drop it all in a heartbeat, but I'm engaged to one."

"And if you want to make yourself happy, you have to spend time with him." Sage finished her sentence for her.

"Right. I promise you when the war calms down, then we can finally hang out just with one another. I could really really use that," she said almost desperately.

"I could use it too," Sage said as she embraced her sister in a hug and whispered the words, "I miss you and I love you."

"I miss you and I love you too," Clare whispered back. "And I'm happy for you, I heard about the wedding, Julius let it slip."

"Right," Sage blushed. "Thank you. I'm sorry that I didn't tell you. I wanted to be the one to tell you, but there wasn't a good time. Now go ahead and go talk to Mr. Grump," Sage teased, smiling brighter when Clare rolled her eyes.

"Don't apologize, just know that I'm happy for you. Goodnight Sage."

"Goodnight Clare."

Clare kept walking until she got to Cassius's bedroom, where he was waiting for her. He was sitting on the floor with a blanket sprawled out in front of him and two sketchbooks. "I thought we could do this again, it seemed to relieve a lot of our worries," his voice was soft and sincere. He picked up a paint brush and dipped it in paint, sending messy strokes onto his page.

Clare melted instantly. She practically ran towards the sketchbook, the door slamming behind her. She sat and crossed her legs. She picked up a brush and dipped it in green paint, her hand started moving. "You have great ideas," she told him happily. "What are you going to paint?" She peaked over at his canvas and this time he let her look.

"Some flowers, it's the only thing that I can paint well," he admitted as he continued moving his brush. "How do you feel about going away tomorrow?"

"I'd prefer to stay here, but if it's for our safety, then of course I will go with no complaints."

"I think it could be a nice get away," he admitted. "I'll be sure to set up little things like this."

"Well then I look forward to it," she said honestly. "You're not mad at me are you?"

"No, no. I just got mad that his family would expect that from you. I can tell that you're drained."

"And I can tell you are too, you don't tell me, but I sense it. You are grieving too and that's okay. You know I think you need to loosen up a little and I think I do too."

"So what's your grand plan?" he asked her.

She didn't think about it much before she did it. She dipped a large glob of paint onto her brush and hurled it at his face. He gasped as the paint hit him square in the forehead, his shocked mouth twisting into a smile.

He dipped his paint in red and flicked it at her neck, it splattered messily against her skin.

Neither of them cared very much for the black funeral clothes that they were wearing, in fact neither of them wanted to fully remember this day.

Globs and globs of paint were waisted as their brushes dipped into the liquid and were flicked at the other person. At one point they began to dodge each other's attempts and the paint splattered against the furniture and the cold floor.

Within a few minutes, they were both covered in a rainbow of paint, the paint stained their clothes and clung to their skin and hair.

When Clare first met Cassius, she would have never guessed that he could be so silly, so free, but she was glad that he had changed in this way.

Eventually they had used up a good amount of the paint and Clare collapsed onto his lap, laughing as she reached up to touch his paint stained face. He was smiling down at her, locks of his black hair now pink and yellow.

"I could fall asleep like this," Clare hummed as she shut her eyes.

"You could, but I think a bath might be beneficial," he kissed the top of her forehead, blue paint stained his lips.

"Will you take a bath with me?" she asked him.

His eyes lit up and for a second he almost refused her, but his heart compelled him to say yes, "of course I will."

'Why did this have to be a vulnerable experience? He had slept with his fair share of people before Clare came into the picture. Why was stepping into a tub without clothing suddenly so nerve-racking? Was it because there were feelings involved and he actually cared about what she thought of him and his body?'

Clare was also not as confident as she should've been. The two of them helped each other undress, their eyes lingered for just a moment before they both got into the bath and began to wash off all of the paint.

There was no need for words, their gazes were enough. The simple touches when they handed off the bar of soap or when their knees bumped together was enough.

Once they were out of the bath, they both dried off and changed. Cassius, who slept hot, was just in his boxers and a shirt despite the cold air. Clare who preferred a bit more fabric, dressed in a white long sleeve nightgown and white knee-high socks. The two of them climbed into bed and he held her silently against his chest, his arms wrapped protectively around her.

Sleep came quickly for the both of them, neither of them had nightmares for the first time in a few days.

When the morning came, Clare was still wrapped up in his arms, she had barely moved from her original position. She gently tapped him and since he was already stirring, he woke up. "Can I go into the carriage like this?" she asked sleepily as she kissed the base of his neck.

"I don't see anything wrong with that," he admitted. "I will put on an outfit of course."

Cassius dressed in his normal black attire and the two of them made their way downstairs, not bothering to pack as the royal territory palace was stocked with clothes and food.

Cassius hugged Gracielle and Cisily goodbye and waved to Sage.

Clare hugged them all and took a plate of food for them to share on the ride there.

The carriage rolled away before the clock struck nine.

UNBREAKABLE BOND

It was the day of Sage's wedding with Julius. A cold afternoon during the first week of March. Though the trees were beginning to grow back their leaves, the ground was covered in a thin layer of snow on this particular day. Sage wasn't a romantic or a dreamer so the scenery didn't bother her, it just hadn't been what she was expecting for her wedding. She always envisioned it in the summer, warm, but not too hot, with a clear and bright sky. But this was an arranged marriage and of course things were subject to change, especially in times of war. Their marriage needed to be solidified so the people could see that the Demetrias's and the Pax's were united and that they would be both a powerful and united force.

"I wasn't expecting this day to come so soon," Sage said, squinting at herself in the mirror.

They were in the palace at the royal territory where Clare and Cassius had been staying. The territory was hidden away from the ordinary citizens, this land belonged to all three kingdoms, but Erebus made it clear he would not be in attendance. They could have their little show to themselves.

Clare stood behind her sister and rubbed her shoulders. "I wasn't expecting you to be wed so soon either, but you're ready to be married to him aren't you? You have been in love with Julius for years, though you both still don't like to say the words," she laughed. Clare stepped back from her sister and clapped her hands together in excitement. "You look so gorgeous!" she squealed.

Sage smiled, "yes of course I'm ready to marry him, I'm chuffed to bits actually because this means that he will get to come to live with us. It'll be an odd change, but an exciting one. Though I don't want to rip him away from Maximus, I don't want him to get lonely," she frowned. "And thank you for the compliment, I do feel rather pretty."

"Of course! You deserve it. And Maximus will be alright, he has a lover now and Julius isn't imprisoned, so he can leave the palace whenever he wants to go see him," Clare said.

"I suppose that's true," Sage responded.

Sage wasn't one to wear frills or lace. Her wedding gown was a solid white with no jewels or beads, except for one emerald brooch, clipped to the middle of the cropped, white suit jacket on top of her dress. The brooch had been her mother's, Gracielle had worn it on her wedding day and now, Sage would wear it on hers. The material of the dress was made out of shiny, thick cloth that was suitable for the chilly weather. The dress was long and fit tight around her hips, but became loose at her thighs and then descended into a long train that stretched out a few feet behind her. Underneath her dress was a pair of white boots. Her hair was too short to style, but it was brushed out to perfection. On the top of her head, she wore her regular silver crown and clipped to the crown, was a sheer veil. Tucked underneath the collar of her dress, she wore her elephant necklace that she had refused to part with. Her sword was sitting across the room.

"You may not wear your sword to the ceremony," Gracielle said from the chair in the corner. Gracielle and Clare were gathered in a room to get Sage ready and hide her from Julius's eyes.

"I think it would be rather on brand if I wore my sword and since it's my wedding," Sage beamed, "I think I should be allowed to." She glanced to Clare for support.

"I also think that she should be allowed to wear her sword," Clare said.

Gracielle sighed and moved across the room. She picked up a new olive green weapons belt and clipped it around her daughters waist.

"I had this made for the occasion. I was hoping that I wouldn't have to give it to you until after the wedding, but … you are the bride and the bride should always get her way." Once the belt was fastened around Sage's hips, Gracielle handed Amicus to her daughter.

Sage happily clipped the sword on to her belt and kissed her mother on the cheek.

"Thank you, I love it mum, but enough about me. You two look gorgeous."

Clare shook her head with a smile on her face, her sister couldn't stand all of the attention.

The colors of the wedding were royal blue and emerald green. Sage had convinced her mother to tweak their family colors just a bit. Those on Sage's side of the wedding party wore emerald green while those on Julius's side of the wedding party wore royal blue.

Clare wore a loose emerald green dress. The fabric was made of soft cotton and had no lace or extra material. The neckline was cut in a v and the sleeves were puffy, long and flowing. The dress itself went past her ankles, so the smallest bit of fabric dragged on the floor. Along with her dress, Clare wore her rose quartz necklace, her crown and her engagement ring. She also wore emerald green boots dyed just for the occasion. Her hair was twisted into a crown braid on the back of her head, two pieces of wavy ginger hair framed her face. Her makeup was light and natural, while her sisters was more pronounced.

"It will be funny to see Cassius in emerald green, considering he usually picks black," Clare laughed.

Sage rolled her eyes, "I still don't know how I feel about him being on my side of the wedding party, but I suppose he's grown on me." She looked over to her mother who was putting the last bobby pin in Clare's hair.

"He's family now," Gracielle reminded Sage.

Gracielle's dress was simple. She wore an emerald green dress with long sleeves that clung to her skin, the neckline was high and covered her entire neck. The dress itself was long and straight, spilling to her ankles and then stopping, her emerald green boots that were identical to Clare's were exposed. She had put her hair in a bun on the top of her head and had finished her outfit with silver jewelry, emerald green gloves and a white jacket for the cold. The queen wouldn't sacrifice her comfort for fashion. Clare had done her mother's makeup just as lightly as her own.

"It's almost time isn't it," Gracielle said. "I'll be right back, take some deep breaths, I'm going to gather the rest of your wedding party."

Clare was the maid of honor and Gracielle would walk Sage down the aisle. Her other bridesmaids were Cisily, who she had taken a liking to, Phoebe, Esmeralda and Julius's cousin, Diana.

Julius's best man was Maximus and his groomsmen were Cassius, Stellan and Antoine, as Clare had told him that he had promised to be there in spirit.

Both Julius and Sage had agreed that both the flower "girl" and ring bearer would be the same person, Italus.

The wedding party gathered in the doorway in the back of the palace ready to exit to the garden where the wedding was going to be held. Sage took a deep breath and looked to Clare.

"You can do this," Clare assured as she took her sister's hand and guided her out of the room. "I know you don't like attention, but it's just one day and you know everyone here. There is no pressure."

The two sisters made their way down the stairs, a gasp came from the group of people gathered in the hallway when they saw the beauty of the bride.

"Julius is going to faint!" Diana, his cousin squealed.

Italus came running over to her and gave her calves a hug. "You look so pretty," he said.

A blush spread across her cheeks at all of the compliments. "Thank you," she smiled. Her eyes turned to her mother, who was now frantically hustling around the hallway in order to make sure that everything and everyone was in the right place.

"The music will begin shortly, everyone get into your places," Gracielle commanded.

A soothing instrumental melody on the harp began to play accompanied by a high and serene sound on the flute. The doors of the palace opened and Clare and Maximus were the first to walk out into the chilly air. Their arms were linked and their chins were up. They rounded the corner out into the gardens. Clare was shivering and Maximus looked over to her with a silly grin.

"Should've worn a jacket," he teased, plastering a smile on his face once the small crowd came into view. The crowd mostly consisted of the two kingdom's staff and family.

"Don't worry, the ceremony won't last that long. Do you know that our fiancé is giving me the death glare?" Maximus asked.

"Oh hush, he knows I'm not your type," she laughed.

Upon reaching the long stretch of royal blue silk carpet, the two stopped talking. Once they got to the altar decorated in olive leaves, they split, Maximus on the left and Clare on the right.

The rest of the wedding party followed them down the carpet. Stellan was paired with Cisily, Cassius was paired with Diana and Phoebe was paired with Esmeralda. Italus came down the carpet next, he was dressed in a royal blue suit with a pink rose attached to it, in his hands, he had a small woven basket filled with olive green and pink flowers. He skipped down the aisle and smiled at Julius who was nervously standing at the front of the altar. Julius was wearing a deep royal blue suit that was a velvet material, along with shiny black shoes and his metal leaf crown. He was wearing a soft blue and light brown eyeshadow look and his brown hair was neatly combed onto his forehead.

He smiled at Italus and did his best to relax his shoulders. He was about to see one of the most beautiful girls in the world in one of the most beautiful settings, in front of people that he loved. He bit down on his lip and gazed nervously at Maximus who affirmed that he would be okay with a nod of his head.

The music slowed to a soft and gentle pace and another girl joined the ensemble. She began to sing a song about everlasting love.

Sage rounded the corner, her arms linked with her mother. Wade's spirit was drifting a few inches away from her. He would have held her arm, but he was afraid the cold would startle her as she made her way down the aisle. Gracielle had her head tilted against her daughter's head as they walked. The guests of the wedding stood up at the sight of Sage and a few audible gasps could be heard.

Sage met eyes with Julius and grinned. He was so handsome, so vulnerable. She could see the tears spilling out of his eyes and she wished that she could pick up the pace to wipe them for him. He always looked perfect to her, today didn't change this, but it changed many other things.

Her mother let go of her at the altar and Sage stepped up to where Julius stood. She took his shaking hands in her own and whispered something to him that only he could hear.

"How did I get to marry someone so perfect?" he whispered back, laughing through his happy tears.

She reached a hand up to wipe his tears and when she was done, she placed her hand back in his. "I'm wondering the same thing."

Her eyes flickered to the brown podium behind them. Standing there, was a woman dressed in the bright colors of Oralee, gold and teal. The woman placed her hands on top of the podium and gestured for everyone to sit. "Please be seated." She turned to Sage and Julius, her heart full of warmth, she radiated kindness. "I was asked to go to the temple and when I was there, Oralee gave me her blessing to go through with this wedding." She basked in the cheers from the crowd. "The goddess claims that she will visit you two tonight," she looked directly at Sage who was trying to push away her look of skepticism. "Marriage is a special bond, where two people love each other and join in union. Though this pair of lovers was married for the sake of politics, their love blossomed long before their engagement, as they grew up with one another in their childhood. They shared toys and play fought. This couple has been together through death and pain, yet they are still standing strong. Today they will solidify their love and promise to be loyal to one another for eternity as Oralee rarely approves of a marriage where the two partners will fall out of love. She only endorses unbreakable bonds. Before Sage and Julius can be joined in union, they must tell Oralee why they are so in love. Sage, please go first."

Julius's hand squeezed Sage's tightly. He inhaled deeply and then exhaled and gestured for her to do the same, to calm the nerves that he knew were surging through her body.

She took a deep breath and then began to speak, her voice shaky. She tried to block out everyone else, but the nerves didn't go away. Her and Julius weren't romantics, they were awkward and clumsy, rash and sometimes harsh, she didn't often confess such sweet things to him.

"Julius, I have not met another man or woman who understands me the way that you do. Well, besides Clare," she joked. "I love that you love every bit about me. You understand and appreciate all of the time that I take training with a sword and you've never judged the amount of food that I eat on a daily basis. You've never scolded me for being lazy. You understand everything that I do. I love you for that and I love you … because you're you. You're awkward and funny, clumsy and sweet. You've never made me feel inferior or uncomfortable. You've always made me feel at home. I'm not really sure what else to say, so I hope that Oralee is satisfied," she said nervously.

The woman nodded because Oralee, was indeed satisfied. Sage had been looking down the entire time that she spoke. When she looked up nervously to meet Julius's gaze, he was smiling that same crooked and funny smile that he made when he was overwhelmed with joy.

Julius bounced a few times on his heels. Once the woman gestured for him to begin, he did.

"I'm not good with words or speeches either, in fact, I'm worse," he admitted. A reassuring squeeze from her hand kept him going. His short term memory wasn't great either and he didn't remember what he was going to say, so he had to make it up on the spot. "My love for you does not die. I could be gone into oblivion and my heart would still love you, it would still find its way back to you. In fact it has and I know that it sounds cheesy, but it's true. I don't think there could have been a better match for me. I also don't think that there could have been a couple out there that is worse than us at this. I'm really glad that I get to start a new chapter with you. You're a fierce woman who's taught me a lot of things about courage. I've learned from you and I hope to keep learning. I love you Sage," he said confidently, his cheeks going hot as the crowd awed.

"I think Oralee will be very pleased with those comments." The woman began to speak about marriage and the strong ties that it created. After about five minutes of talking, she presented them with the most crucial part of the ceremony. She grabbed a small oak bowl filled with water from Oralee's temple and stepped closer to them. "Julius, under Oralee, do you accept Sage to be your wife?"

"I do," he said confidently, his smile wide.

"Sage, under Oralee, do you accept Julius to be your husband?"

"I do," she said just as confidently. They technically didn't have a choice, but it felt as if they did.

The woman poured the water over their intertwined hands and a spark of blue flew up in the air. "Oralee approves," she said joyously. If no spark arose, then they would have had to try for marriage another day if they wanted to stay on the Goddesses good side, but this hardly happened, most couples did not try for marriage if they did not think that their Goddess would approve. The woman stepped back, "you may seal the marriage with a kiss."

Julius and Sage had both agreed that they didn't feel comfortable putting their full affections on display, so their kiss was short. Julius moved his lips to meet hers and their lips quickly joined before pulling away. Sage gave him a wink, a promise that there would be more to come later.

They both awkwardly shrugged their shoulders at all of the cheers.

Italus approached them with a small black box. Julius thanked him as he took the box from his hand. He opened it up and took out their matching silver wedding bands. Plain, just like Sage had requested.

He placed her ring on her finger and then she placed his ring on his. The ceremony was over.

"I suppose we have a party to attend now. One day of peace in a time of war," Sage said.

Though that was how it felt, that was not reality. Back at Pax et Lux, the guards were doubled and the palace flag was raised to make it seem like the royalty had never left. While they danced and drank, soldiers were sent off to their deaths and innocent children inside of Excidium, were locked away from their families because of their opinions. After the wedding, Clare and Cassius would continue to stay at the royal territory in hiding until the public finally forgot Clare's accident. Gracielle and the others would return home immediately. In times of war, there was no honeymoon.

Sage leaned her head against Julius as they walked down the aisle and back into the palace. She was happy to go inside because the wind was picking up, blowing the snow around outside. The sky was also getting cloudy. If she guessed correctly, then a storm would be on its way. Julius pulled her in tight to his body, he wasn't as warm as a normal human would be, but he did the trick.

"I'm so lucky and happy to be married to you, but I am also glad we got that over with," he told her, drowning out everything else around him. He knew that his brother was probably right behind his heels, but Maximus wasn't the most important person right now, Sage was.

As soon as they stepped into the warm hall, Julius quickly shut the door behind him. He leaned down to give Sage a more passionate kiss, his hands held onto the sides of her cheeks. She melted into his touch and kissed back, breaking away from him when the door swung open again.

"I feel the same," she told him in response to his earlier statement.

Maximus and Clare were the first pair to enter. Maximus went to hug Julius and Clare hugged Sage. Maximus pulled away from his brother to hug Sage and Clare followed his lead and gave a hug to Julius.

"Congratulations you two," Maximus congratulated. "I would love to drink all night at your party, but unfortunately our bastard father died and left me as king, so now I must go be an adult because Mr. Erebus wanted to start a war." He stomped his foot on the ground for dramatic affect. "Please enjoy your special night and have a drink for me," he told the three of them. He gave Clare a hug on his way out, "If you need me, write to me. You will be okay, the people will forget about this soon, we are going to release the statement as soon as I get back home and the morning comes."

He kissed her cheek and then hurriedly strode towards his carriage. At the news of their departure, Stellan ran quickly though the doors to congratulate the married couple before heading back to the carriage.

Cassius came next, he was glad to be free of Diana, who was talking his ear off as if he didn't have a fiancé. He rolled his eyes in exasperation and then fixed his expression at the sight of the newly wed couple.

"Congratulations," he told them both. He wasn't sure if he should give them a hug or a handshake, so he just stood back. "I'm glad that something good could come out of such hard times," he added. Julius took his hand and shook it. Sage hesitated, but she caught a glance at her sister who was staring hopefully at her, so she moved forward and gave Cassius a quick side hug before pulling away.

"I'll see you two in the reception hall. I've got to be there before all of the guests arrive so that I may greet everyone. Weddings sadly require a lot of attention," Sage said as her and Julius linked arms and headed down the hall.

The reception would be held in the ballroom. Natalia had not been at the ceremony, but she had been invited to the reception and she had come with Jesse. The two of them matched in emerald green and black attire. Fran had come by herself, but was hanging around her sister and Jesse who seemed relatively happy to be at the wedding. The guest list was relatively small, but there was a woman who came to the ceremony uninvited She was a tall woman with long legs and a chiseled jawline. Her skin was a warm shade of cream and sparkled under the lights. Her eyes were the brightest, crystal diamond blue and her smile was warm. Her blonde hair fell in loose curls just below her shoulder. She wasn't dressed for a wedding, or the cold, but her outfit was magnificent. A dress that perfectly matched the color of her eyes flowed against her body in magnificent waves as if she had just stepped out of one of the world's clearest oceans. The large puffed sleeves on her dress were sheer and thin, swallowing her toned arms. The neckline of her dress plunged in the outline of a v, revealing the sides of her breasts. The sheer fabric got thicker as it cascaded down, leaving slits for her legs. She walked barefoot against the cold stone and hardly shivered. She had disguised herself during the ceremony, but her act was over, Oralee had attended their wedding.

The Goddesses were real.

She met the shocked and bewildered stares with a gentle smile and gracefully moved as if she were floating, down the hall and to the newly married couple.

"Congratulations you two," her tone was warm and full, but a bit tired as if she had spent her whole day at the beach.

While Sage and Julius tried to form the words to talk, she went instead.

"I would like to talk to Julius," she stared down at him like she had known him her whole life and he too felt an instant connection.

"May Sage come? Anything I know will flow back to her and I don't want to leave her alone on her wedding night."

"Of course, where is Maximus? Can you bring his carriage back?" she asked.

"I'll send someone for him," Julius said.

Oralee, Julius, Sage and Maximus all stood together in one of the guest bedrooms of the palace. At first Maximus was angry that he had been called back, but when he saw the reason, he quieted himself. Home could wait a few more moments. None of the young royals knew what to say in the presence of a Goddess, Europe's Goddess, so they waited for her to speak.

"Once again, congratulations. I am aware that I did crash the wedding, my apologies," she grinned. "But it was time I came forward. It has been long enough and though I was going to hide it from you, I will not do so any longer. Maximus and Julius, I am your mother."

She scanned their faces and when she was met with two looks of horrific shock, she quickly continued. "I know, you must be thinking that I look nothing like your mother, one of the powers of any Goddess is that we can change our appearance at will. I could flick my fingers and in an instant I would be in her warm brown hair and soft colored eyes, but I won't scare you. I chose this form because I think it suits my personality well. The people also love to paint me in this form. But never mind that, let me explain how I am your mother. I slept with Augustus because I knew he was not a good man. He had to become a father, he had to have children next in line to his throne and I knew that kids with my genes would grow up to be great people. I was expecting one child, but then I had two and I am so grateful for the both of you. It was me all those years, just in disguise so you wouldn't know that I was Oralee. I disappeared the night when Augustus was killed, when you thought I died. I had worked closely with Mallory. Since the Antias family heavily believed in her, I had her send them signs and hints that they should kill Augustus. I knew I had to get rid of him, but I did not know that Julius was going to die as well and if I would have known, I would have not gone through with the plan. I still curse myself for it. After that incident, I knew that I had to return full time to my duties as a Goddess and that Deus would be in good hands. I bargained again with Mallory. She agreed to let one of her followers bring Julius back to life. Ever since then, I have been watching over you, but I have not been present. I couldn't miss a big day like this and … I had to reveal myself because of the girl, Clare."

Oralee could have continued, but she paused, waiting for her sons to absorb the information.

She set her eyes on Sage, who was comfortingly holding Julius against her waist. Oralee's eyes melted at the sight of her daughter in law, she was so glad that her son was happy.

While Julius seemed fearful of what this might mean, Maximus looked rather angry. Though it made sense in his brain, he was having a rather hard time accepting it in his heart, "please just continue," his voice was heavy. He gestured toward her politely, she was still a Goddess after all.

"The Goddesses chose Clare when she was born. Evangilene, who can see versions of the future, saw that Clare was destined to do great things. It is currently time for those great things to happen. I didn't think that Clare would cross paths with you two so heavily, but it seems that she has. If she has ever felt a pull towards you, it is because you have the blood of the Goddesses in you. Of course you could never be a God, there are no male deities and you are only half divine … but you are special. This is why some may have described you as perfect or serene, but it does not look like you have inherited any abilities and if you have, they haven't surfaced yet." She looked over towards Sage who was holding her breath, her face red.

"Shouldn't you help guide my sister?" she asked. "Or will you lie to her too?"

"Don't worry Sage, I was planning on talking to her eventually." Oralee wasn't surprised by Sage's attitude, she remembered the girl from Julius's childhood. She always seemed to have something to say. The Goddess looked back to her sons. "Please tell me that you forgive me."

Julius was the first to speak. Though Maximus and Julius had both preferred their mother over their father, Julius had always clung onto her tighter than Maximus had. Julius was sensitive and kind, so when someone asked for forgiveness, he was usually the first to give it. He let go of Sage and walked towards his mother, his eyes watery and his hands outstretched in hopes that she would hug him. She did. When he felt her embrace it was all the confirmation that he needed to know that this was his mother. Hugging her was comforting and made his heart slow into a melodic tune. She smelled like she always had, of fresh salt and coconut.

She opened the hug and looked to Maximus in hopes that he would join them. Maximus was hesitant, but as he remembered the years of comfort that she had given him when his father was so cruel, he joined their embrace and rested his head on her shoulder.

"I forgive you," Maximus whispered as his anger subsided. He looked up at her, his eyes scared. "Do you know about Stellan?"

"I do, from what I have seen I love him already, but please introduce me before you go." She ran a hand through her sons ginger hair.

Her eyes shifted to Sage, who was standing alone in the corner, she seemed a bit awkward, she was looking over the blade of her sword.

Oralee smiled at her. "Please, you are family now."

Sage wasn't one for hugs from anyone, but this was Julius's mother, this was Oralee. She joined the embrace and was glad that it was quickly over.

When the three of them split from the hug, Sage was sure that she had seen tears of joy in Julius's eyes, but they were gone as quick as they had come. "I'm not going to hold you from your guests any longer, please go to your reception! I'm going to walk Max out to his carriage, but I'll be back," she promised them.

While the two of them walked to the ballroom, Oralee took Maximus's hand and walked with him outside.

"How are you not cold?" he asked her as they went outside.

"It's in my blood, I am protected from the heat and the cold. Let me ask you something, do you really feel cold at the moment?" She smiled at her son's expression. There was a clap of thunder. It was going to rain soon.

"I'm a bit chilly, but not as cold as I should be, I have always dressed warmly because that is what I have been told to do, not because I feel like I need to. Good observation," he said. "Though I'm a bit sad that you don't look like the woman I once knew, I'm glad that you are her and I am glad that you are alive. You won't stay around long will you?" He noticed her frown in response to his question.

"I'll try to be there for you two whenever I can, but I won't be a constant presence in your life. The future that is coming is intense. I need to sort things out with the other Goddesses and with Clare, to keep everyone safe."

"I am scared for Clare, please tell me that your plan is not to use her as a weapon because if it is you'd be better off using Sage," Maximus teased.

Oralee's frown deepened. "I'm afraid that Clare will be a large part of this new future."

"And you're not going to tell me what that future is are you?"

"I'm sorry Max, I can't."

Upon reaching the carriage, the two of them were greeted by Stellan. He was smiling goofily, pulling a pair of white silk gloves over his hands.

"Hello darling," he said to Maximus. His eyes broke away from Maximus when he noticed who was standing beside him. He bowed his head to Oralee.

"Love, I'm sure that you are aware of Oralee. Remember when I mentioned my mother? Well, this is her. I suppose that she didn't actually die, but instead, she fled. My mum has always been Oralee, she was just disguised. I apologize that your bonkers life with me just keeps getting more strange, but I promise I haven't been keeping secrets. I just found this information out myself." Maximus's expression was soft, his eyes were truly apologetic.

"Don't be silly, I love life with you even if it is a little bonkers at times. I just wish that you would tell the people about us, but I know right now isn't the time for that conversation. Other than that, I'm perfectly content, even with the magic and the Goddesses." Stellan placed a kiss on Maximus's forehead and then turned to Oralee. He had taken this so well because he had always believed that the Goddesses were real.

"It's nice to meet you Stellan, I look forward to getting to know you more in the future, but I am aware that you have to leave and I am not quite done here." She took his gloved hand and gave it a solid shake before pulling away.

"I'll tell the people about you soon, I promise," Maximus said. He was happy to see his mother and his boyfriend getting along so well. He wished that he could continue this blissful reunion at the reception, but he had a kingdom to attend to. "Come back to the castle please, as soon as you can," Maximus said desperately, taking her image in, in case he never saw her again.

"I'll be there as soon as time allows. How does that sound?"

"It sounds delightful. I could use another break from war," Maximus said.

"Well then it's a deal. Goodbye Max, goodbye Stellan," she waved.

"Bye Oralee!" Stellan shouted.

"Bye … mum," Maximus said.

Oralee watched the two of them climb into the carriage and headed inside once they were out of sight. It began to rain.

Back at the reception, the food had just been served. Sage, Julius, Gracielle, Clare and Cassius all sat together, with one empty chair open for Oralee. The Goddess arrived quickly and took the empty seat in hopes that it was for her. She didn't want to interrupt their conversation, but upon her arrival they all looked to her.

"Can you please tell Clare whatever you want to tell her. I don't want to be rude, but I'd like to get on with the rest of my night without another plot twist," Sage said as she took a bite of her mashed potatoes, her eyebrows raised in annoyance.

"Right, I'm so sorry. Clare, I'm sure that Julius has filled you in," once she their heads nod, she smiled and began. "I wanted to talk to you Clare. I guess I can just say it here, it's a safe space. The Goddesses chose you for your magic, they saw something special in you and some special things that you might be able to do in your future. You've felt a strange pull towards my sons because I am their mother and while they share my blood, you share some of my magic. You're not related to me in a familial way, but since I chose you to have magic, it makes sense for you to feel closely connected to them. I just wanted to share that to you and clear up some confusion. Special people run in your family, that's why you found another person with magic in your family, but that doesn't mean magic is passed down by blood. The Goddesses chose you."

Clare swallowed the piece of meat that she was chewing on, her eyes were terrified. "I am not sure why you chose me to posses magic, but nonetheless I am honored. Your explanation helped to clear up my confusion, so thank you for talking to me. Am I in debt to you? Am I supposed to go to you for guidance?"

"You are not in debt to me, but it would be appreciated if you complied to my wishes in the future. You can come to me for magic guidance if you are having a hard time with control and judging by your outburst at the town center, I assume you are struggling. Anything other than that, no, we will come to you. It will become clear to you what you are meant to do someday soon."

Oralee looked back at Julius and frowned, "I have some important business to attend to. Let's talk now and then I promise I will leave you be," she said. Julius looked to Sage for her permission and when she agreed, he stood and walked with Oralee out into the hall.

"What is it that you want to know? Though we have missed you, it hasn't been too long since you have been gone and I get the feeling that you've been watching."

"I just want to know how you've been ... how life has been for you after you came back," she whispered.

"Well ... when I first came back I was very confused and I was weak. All the muscle that I had gained in the previous years had practically disappeared. As you can tell, I don't have much of it left. I had most of my memories when I woke up, but some of them were gone entirely. I tripped over my feet a lot and I had forgotten how to do some things. Maximus had to coach me through them again. But eventually life was almost normal, I just can't remember much from my younger years. Sage has been a gift. I regret not telling her about my accident sooner, but I was afraid that I'd lose her. I really do love her and I wouldn't have needed an arranged marriage to marry her."

"I'm glad that you've been doing well and that you found her and I'm sorry that I left."

"I would have left too. You did the right thing, Europe needed you more than we did," he smiled.

"Thank you," she said.

"I don't mean to be rude, but I have a wife I need to get back to. I'll talk with you another time, please make sure to stick around, especially with the war, we are going to need you."

"Of course I will, I love you Julius."

"Love you mum," he embraced her in a gentle hug. He stayed there in her arms for a minute before he pulled away and walked out of her sight.

Sage had finished her meal by the time that Julius came back. Sage was typically always hungry and she was unafraid to eat seconds and thirds even on her wedding night. Julius sat next to her and squeezed her hand under the table. He attempted to finish his food quickly so that they could get on with the festivities. Though he was fond of the idea of consuming a ton of alcohol, he didn't want to ruin the sweet night he'd be able to spend with her. Instead, he kept filling up Cassius and Clare's glasses, knowing the two of them could use a good stress reliever. They didn't object, in fact they downed drink after drink, clinking their glasses and getting closer to one another with each one.

Gracielle, had left the table to dance around the ballroom and when Sage and Julius came back from making their rounds and partaking in a few dances themselves, they found the couple slumped against one another. Cassius was playing with her hair and Clare was gazing up at him, giggling. It was a sight that Julius found pure and a sight that Sage found revolting.

Jesse and Gracielle had reunited. Though their talk was awkward and forced at first, throughout the evening they got well acquainted with one another. Gracielle had also taken a liking to Fran and Natalia and had promised that they could come to the palace anytime that they liked. While the queen danced, she kept her eye on Clare who had one too many glasses of wine and was flirting with Cassius, brushing her fingers against his face. He was too out of it to truly react,

306

instead he just held her close, his eyes half open. She'd need to put the two of them to bed soon.

"Jesse, I'm so sorry, please know that you are welcome at our home anytime. I really shouldn't have cut you out of my life for all of those years." Gracielle was holding onto him in a slow dance. He had forgotten how to Waltz, so she led the way.

"I forgive you Gracielle, but only because Wade would have wanted me to." His eyes flickered over to where Clare was sitting. "And because I want to be there for your daughters, they deserve me back in their lives. So I think, if it'll be alright, I'll stay in the palace. I'm sure there are plenty of guest bedrooms."

"Yes there are plenty, you can travel home with us. Though both of my girls might take a moment to warm up to you, I'm sure they'll both appreciate your presence."

"I hope so, I'm not the happiest person, but I will learn to smile around them."

"Don't punish yourself for what you've been through. It's okay not to be bubbly when life gives you no reason to be," Gracielle whispered.

"You have always been so kind," Jesse told her.

"I wouldn't say that, I pushed you away."

"You had just as much of a right to grieve as I did. I could have always come back and asked how you were, but I didn't. If I did, you would have accepted me back."

"I would've."

"Then there's my point."

"Where are Sage and Julius?" Gracielle asked, changing the subject.

"Oh they've left."

Sage and Julius traveled in the rain to a carriage that took them to the small cottage across from the palace. The rain was starting to pound against the floor, but the carriage was still able to continue. It was only a five minute ride to the small cottage where they would stay for the night. Sage wasn't full of lust, but she was filled with the need to spend some time alone with her husband. The coachman left the two of them with a singular wave and they dashed inside of the warm and cozy cottage, removing their boots and placing them at the door.

The home was filled with warm lighting from lanterns and various candles, a sofa and large bookshelves filled with books of all colors and sizes. Around the corner was a bedroom and inside were their things that had already been placed there early in the day.

Sage smiled as she took off the white coat that had been over her wedding dress. "I can't wait to get out of this thing. Did you get one last good look?"

Julius paused and placed a hand on his chin, he scratched his nonexistent stubble and then grinned from ear to ear. "I think I did, let me fetch you what you've packed."

Sage unzipped the back of her dress to the best of her abilities and then slipped out of it. She caught his blush as he turned around to hand her the pair of night clothes from her suitcase.

"Naked women still fluster you?"

"Not necessarily, just your beauty and you're technically not naked." He turned back around and gestured to the undergarments that she was still wearing. He wasn't phased when she pulled off her brassiere, it would be more comfortable for her without it. "I'll never get enough of you."

"And I will never get enough of you," Sage said. "You know, a normal married couple would be participating in a very scandalous act right now."

"Did … did you want?" he stuttered.

"No silly, not right now. Maybe another night."

"Oh okay," he said with a satisfied smile on his face. His company was enough for her and that made him beam with joy.

Sage grinned at his smile and took the clothes from his hand. She pulled on a loose long sleeve t-shirt and a pair of silk pants. She slipped into a pair of socks that were fuzzy and warm. She went to the vanity to take off her makeup while he stripped off his suit.

"I feel more comfortable around you now that you know the truth. Lying to you about my scar didn't feel right," Julius said. He turned around to face her, hoping that she would glance at him. Sage might have known that she was beautiful, but Julius was still unconfident with the way that he looked and though he knew that there was no one else she'd rather be with, he often let his thoughts focus on his insecurities. He often wondered if she was pleased with his body and though he knew that the answer was yes in his heart, his brain made him wonder if the answer was no.

Sage had just finished wiping the makeup off of her face with a wet cloth, she turned around expecting to see Julius clothed, but he was standing there in his boxers.

"Are you trying to make me faint?" she asked. She stood up from the chair. "I know you have got to be freezing." She walked over to him and rested her warm hands against his chest.

"Just a little bit," he whispered.

"Are you hinting at something?" she whispered back, her fingers gently trailed down his stomach. "Because you're very handsome and I'm delighted to be with you," she kissed the crook of his neck.

Relief flooded his stomach and he felt himself relax. "I would just like to spend tonight with you like this."

"With hardly any clothes?"

"Yes," he laughed. "There are plenty of blankets to warm me up."

Sage dropped her hand to meet his and guided him to bed. She crawled underneath the heavy comforter with him and pressed herself up against him. He wasn't as warm as he used to be and she loved to provide him with what he couldn't have. With her head against his chest, she placed both of her hands on his stomach, "I love you. I don't say it enough, I don't know why it's so hard, but it feels a bit easier now that I know you absolutely feel the same. Just know that I love you."

"I love you too Sage," he kissed the top of her head and closed his eyes. "That was a good wedding. A bit odd considering a Goddess who is apparently my mum was in attendance, but since when could we escape the abnormal?"

"Strangeness follows us, but yes a good wedding. Hopefully Clare and Cassius got upstairs alright. Did you see them?"

"I did, they were still in the ballroom when we left, but your mum had an eye on them. They've both been through it, so I don't blame them for indulging."

"Me neither, but I found it a bit funny. Clare hasn't ever drank that much. Not that I know of anyways."

"Well there is a first time for everything, but don't worry about it, your mums got it. I'm glad that she got to see Jesse again. Did you ever get to meet him?"

"Oh Oralee, I totally forgot to go introduce myself further. He said congratulations, but that was about all I exchanged with him. I'll be sure to chat with him some more tomorrow, I'm sure he spent the night at the royal palace like most of the guests."

"I'm sure he did, you'll be alright. And I think that we might have to find a new saying that does not include Oralee, it's a bit strange now," he admitted. His hands ran down her arms.

"Oh right, my bad. I'll figure something out," she said. She broke away from him and told him that she would be right back. When she came back, she brought a clean wet cloth. "You're not supposed to sleep with makeup on, Julius," she told him. Crawling back onto the bed, she held the cloth up to his face and when he nodded, she began to gently move the rag in circles until she got all of the makeup off. She laughed at how pink his face was from the cloth and kissed his lips before tossing the cloth on the floor and rolling to lay down next to him.

"So tonight, are you going to be tried enough to sleep?" he asked her curiously. Though he might be able to go to bed, he had this idea in his head, he wanted to spend the entire night talking with her.

"I could sleep, but I don't have to sleep tonight if that's what you're asking. What exactly did you have in mind?" she questioned.

"I just wanted to spend as much time with you as possible. I want to ask you questions, read to you and enjoy your company before reality sets back in."

"That sounds delightful to me."

They did exactly that. Julius asked Sage every question that he could possibly think of. He learned that her favorite season was summer and that if she had to pick a favorite book, even though she hated them, it would be *The History of European* Wars. He learned that she could spend hours under the stars and that if she could only walk the world at night and sleep during the day, she would.

She learned that he truly had no favorite season and that his favorite book was, *A Tale of Love*. He told her that if he could have a different path in life he would prefer not to have a high status, he wanted to be one with the people, he wanted others to only see his heart and not his money.

Later that night, he read to her, she much preferred stories when Julius told them to her.

They fell asleep when the sun came up and were woken up a few hours later by a knock on the door.

"Sage, wake up, your carriage leaves soon," Clare shouted from outside of the door. Though Clare wouldn't be coming home just yet,

Sage had to leave to perform her duties. Clare looked a mess, her hair was sticking up, her eyes were puffy, she had a massive headache and her shirt was on backwards.

Sage leapt out of bed at the sound of her sister's voice and opened the door. When she took in the sight of her, she raised her eyebrows. "I'm not even going to ask what happened to you or what you might have done, but we will be ready soon, in fact, I need to go see Jesse before he leaves, so tell mum I'll be down shortly." She waited for Clare to nod and once she did, she shut the door and ran back to her room.

Julius woke up, lazily rubbing the sleepiness out of his eyes. "It's breakfast time already isn't it?" He looked over to Sage who was already stripping off her night clothes and looking for something new to wear. She wasn't going to bathe here, he was already well aware of that. He stood from the bed and got dressed in a pair of comfortable pants and a knitted cream sweater. He pulled his boots on and quickly ran a brush through his hair.

For her outfit, Sage had chosen a pair of olive green pants and a white long sleeve turtleneck. She put her new weapons belt around her waist and clipped her sword onto to it.

"It is breakfast time." She took the brush from him and ran it through her short straight hair before tossing it into her bag. "You kept us up late, remember," she winked, messily throwing everything else, including her wedding dress into the bag. Once she zipped it up, Julius came by her side and swung the bag over his shoulders. Sage was completely capable, in fact, she seemed annoyed that he was carrying it, but he wanted to be polite.

Breakfast was made and on the table by the time that they had arrived. All of the guests had departed aside from Jesse and Natalia who had come as dates and of course Gracielle, who reluctantly had stayed the night in order to keep an eye on her hungover daughter. But the queen had Cisily now to help her and she sent the young girl home the night before with Phoebe and Esmeralda, so that they could all keep an eye on the palace. Cassius and Clare were also in attendance at breakfast, they both looked extremely tired, but they had gotten out of bed to share a meal with the newly wed couple.

Sage sat down at the end of the table, rubbing her head, she too had a headache, but not for the same reason.

Julius set both of their bags down and sat happily by her side. "Good morning," he greeted. His eyes shifted to Cassius who looked more like a zombie than a man. Him and Clare seemed happier than they had been a few weeks prior and judging by their disheveled appearances, they had been up to something themselves. At least Clare finally had her shirt on correctly.

"Good morning," Gracielle greeted as she started to load up her plate. "Jesse and Natalia, I'd like you to formally meet Julius and of course you know Sage, you just haven't seen her in a while," she said as she poured some coffee into Jesse's mug.

"Nice to meet you kid, you seem like a gentle fellow and nice to see you Sage." He smiled sadly at her, she was a married woman, 'where had the time gone?'

"It's good to see you again Jesse and it's nice to meet you Natalia," Sage said.

"Where's the blonde kid?" Jesse asked curiously as he took a bite of his food.

Silence filled the space, Julius's heart sank in his chest and Clare recoiled uncomfortably.

Gracielle was the first one to speak in hopes to make Jesse feel better. 'How would he take the news that someone died?' He had only known him briefly, but Antoine was very young. "Jesse, he was executed. He's no longer with us," Gracielle said.

Clare looked up from the fruit she was eating, "actually he is," she whispered softly, looking to a far off corner. Antoine stood awkwardly, he was still too scared to go to the afterlife, but this time, there was someone waiting for him, ready to disappear with him when it was time. Wade stood by Antoine's side, a hand on his shoulder. The two of them were still watching over the Pax family. When it was their time to leave their loved ones behind, Wade promised Clare that he would take care of Antoine in the afterlife.

"What the hell are you talking about?" Sage growled. Though she had just become aware that the Goddesses were real yesterday, she had no faith in spirits, she had once heard Clare talking to an absent figure, but she thought it was just her sister grieving. She had never heard Cassius and Clare's conversation the night of the execution. She wanted to believe her sister, but it all felt so fake that she finally burst.

Clare folded her arms across her chest and rolled her eyes. "Seriously Sage? Believe it or not, but I can see spirits. Antoine has been staying around and well … recently so has Wade."

"What?" Sage and Gracielle said simultaneously.

"Since when? Why didn't you tell me? You selfish fool!" Sage snapped.

"I didn't tell you because the few times that I have seen him, there was never an appropriate moment to bring it up. Forgive me for just wanting you to be happy," she retorted, sharing only half of the truth to make her sister feel better. She angrily took a bite of her eggs.

"I've seen it," Cassius reassured. "Well, I can't see the spirits, but I've seen her talk to them and I trust her and so should you. If she says Antoine and Wade are here then I believe her."

"Wade is here?" Gracielle whispered, her heart thumping against her chest.

Clare nodded and promised that she would translate for Wade later so the two of them could talk, but they both agreed that it couldn't be today. They had to get back to their kingdoms and assure that there had been no new attacks.

As Clare walked with her mother, Sage, Julius, Natalia and Jesse to their carriages, she gave them each a hug, before turning to Julius. "Do you know when this will all be cleared up so I can come home?" she asked him. She knew Erebus would not clear her name, but Maximus had promised to explain her outburst of magic to the people.

"Maximus has got it covered, you should be able to come back to your home within the next week. Once he delivers his message, your mother can back it and if Cassius backs it, that clears it for all three kingdoms. Don't stress about it okay? One day everything is going to be alright again."

He gave her another hug before he pulled away and stepped into the carriage that Sage was in.

"We'll see you soon, I promise!" he shouted, before shutting the door.

She said goodbye to her mother and thanked her for staying the night.

She finally she said goodbye to Natalia and Jesse. "When you're at the palace and you are ready, I promise that I'll have Wade speak to you again. Well you'll speak to me and I'll translate what he says to you. Is that alright?"

"Yeah, that would be okay," Jesse murmured. He gave her a thankful pat on the back.

Once Natalia had embraced both Cassius and Clare, she left with Jesse.

The carriages rolled off, leaving Cassius and Clare alone.

A PERMANENT DECISION

Three days later, Clare and Cassius were allowed to return home. There were no angry citizens near the palace and when they walked through the town, people stared, but no one was mad at the princess. Gracielle and Maximus had done a good job creating an explanation for what had happened. They stuck to the original story that Maximus had proposed. There were a few citizens who didn't believe this story and still thought that she had magic, but they weren't loud and they weren't angry like they had been before.

Cassius was not able to speak to his people, but instead he spoke to the people of Pax et Lux and confirmed Gracielle and Maximus's story. He assured that since he was engaged to Clare, he would know if she had magic. Erebus did not speak upon the matter. Though he did not agree with their claims, he did not come out against them. No one would believe him if he did, his kingdom was already in unrest. His citizens were angry that their queen was gone and they were angry at him for killing a man who did nothing but love. His citizens were burning down statues and buildings, demanding that their prince come back and take the throne, but Erebus would never step down willingly and Cassius was not in the right headspace to challenge him.

Gracielle, was ready to step down. She welcomed Clare and Cassius home with open arms. Cisily embraced them as well, but Sage was not at the door.

"Where is she?" Clare asked curiously as the guard dropped their bags. She peaked her head around the hallway, her hand dropped from Cassius's.

"She's upset with me," Gracielle said. "Julius is with her. They're trying to make a decision."

"Why would she be upset with you and why does she need to make a decision?" Clare asked curiously.

"I'm done, I don't have it in me anymore Clare, I'm old and I'm alone. The people will get bored of me. They need a young voice to

315

lead them through war. I've trained her well and I want Sage to take the throne with Julius by her side."

Disregarding her manners, Clare ran down the hallway and up the stairs to Sage's room. She burst through the doors and found her sister sitting on the floor, clutching her elephant necklace. Julius was holding her tight. He'd have to become the king if she agreed to become the queen. He wouldn't have any true power, but he would stand by her decisions and help her make them if she needed assistance.

"Sage," Clare called, hoping that her sister would look up from her lap. "You can do this. I want you to do this. If I'm at all any part of the reason why you're holding back, please tell me. I promise that you will not be alone. I will help you. If you can not make a decision or write a speech, I will do it for you. Just be our voice. Mum doesn't have the strength for another war. It'll kill her." She kept her distance in hopes that Sage would listen and not respond angrily. She then looked to Julius. "And I know you would do good too. I trust you, my mum trusts you. Prince of Deus and King of Pax et Lux. You will be able to manage them both. I believe in you Julius, just as much as I believe in Sage."

Cassius had followed Clare up to Sage's room, he stood by the cracked open door. He thought about turning away, but instead he squeezed inside. "I believe in you two as well and I am not lying." He wasn't sure he liked the idea of Sage running a kingdom, she had a short temper and was not great with her words, but if Clare trusted her, then he would trust her too. Even if he still wanted to hate her, for punching him in the face and beating him at all of those fights. As for Julius, his dislike towards him had faded. He'd be perfectly okay with him as king. Not that Cassius had a say in any of this, he just liked to believe that he did.

Sage looked up from the floor, she dropped the necklace that had been in her fingers. "You are not holding me back Clare. I am holding myself back. Is papa here?" she asked her sister. Sage's eyes were sunken, she did not to believe in herself. "I would like to get his opinion on the matter, if you will translate his words for me. Mum said she wasn't ready to talk to him and that she needed time to go over what she would say. I'm sorry for what I said earlier, but just know that I believe you now."

316

"It's alright Sage. I think papa is here. I just got home, so I'm not really sure. If he is, I'll translate for you."

Clare held out her hand for her sister to take. Sage grasped it firmly.

Cassius and Julius acknowledged that they needed to give the two girls some space and and exited the room.

Clare and Sage followed the cold. They found Wade's spirit in the library.

He looked thrilled to see the two of them together. "Sage, Clare!" he exclaimed, though he knew only one of his daughters could see and hear him.

"He's right here," Clare said, she gestured to the back left corner of the library. "I hope you trust me." She pointed Sage to the back of the room. "Look this way. He can talk to you. I'll translate. Go ahead and talk to papa. He will respond to you. Just trust me."

"Talk to the wall … no talk to Papa. I trust you Clare," Sage said whispered.

Sage sat down on the floor and did her best to look straight ahead, but she found herself looking down at her lap. "Hi papa," she whispered. "I miss you and I have an important question for you. I don't know if I can be queen. Please be honest with me. Can I do this? If not, tell me no. I don't want to ruin mum's great work," she hesitantly looked over to Clare.

"He wants to know if he can stand closer to you. Oh he wants to know if he can kneel down by your side," Clare said.

When her sister nodded, Wade's spirit rushed towards her and Sage was hit with an icy cold blast. She shivered as he knelt by her side.

" Of course you can do this. You're my daughter," Wade said. "I trust you with this kingdom and this kingdom will trust you, they'll come to love you." As he said each word, Clare regurgitated it back to Sage.

"And if I mess up? If they hate me?"

"Then you fix your mistake and there are many people around you who will help guide you in the right direction. They'll support you and so will I. If you girls aren't ready for me to leave, then I won't leave. I'll stay."

"Please stay," Sage begged after she heard his words from Clare.

The conversation didn't last much longer. Sage told Clare that she was good after the two exchanged temporary goodbyes. Wade had left the library to give them space.

"So what are you going to tell mum?" Clare asked.

"I'm going to tell her yes, but promise me that you are going to help me."

"Of course," Clare smiled. "I'll be right by your side."

THE GODDESSES THRONE

An announcement spread throughout Pax et Lux that evening. The people were informed that Gracielle would step down from her position in a weeks time and that Sage would take her place.

During that week, Gracielle took the time to locate all of the important files, codes, commands and keys that she would need to transfer to Sage. She spent day and night preparing the girl to lead, following up on their lessons about manners and history and adding in lessons about how to command during a time of war.

The day of Sage's coronation had arrived. Sage was dressed in the largest olive green ball gown that her mother could find. Her short, chin length hair had been brushed until it was pin straight. Julius stood by her side in a matching olive green suit. His hair was not shaggy like usual, but instead gelled up into a swoop on the right side of his head. A new crown had been made for him. It was pointed and silver, with both metal leaves and flowers twisted together on the crown's rim. Diamonds and sapphire jewels alternated throughout the points of the crown.

Sage was still wearing her old crown, she'd have a new hand made crown given to her shortly.

The two of them stood on the palace rooftop that overlooked the city. They could see people lined up for miles and miles, trying to get a glimpse of the ceremony that would be written in the newspapers. The royal family was far enough away where no one could directly attack them, but close enough to the people where they could hear their shouts.

The ceremony was supposed to be short. Gracielle would take the crown off of Sage's head, put the new one on her daughter and then the Goddesses would send a sign of approval.

The mother took off her daughter's princess crown and set it aside. Gracielle placed the new crown on top of her daughter's head.

It was a round crown with intricate loops rising from the base and a diamond dangling down from every oval. White and olive green metal flowers lined the side of the crown.

Before Gracielle could speak, there was an arrow. Enemy soldiers were nearby and the arrow flew straight towards Sage's heart. Gasps, screams and the look of shock on the future queens face would be frozen in time.

Clare, who had been standing at the entrance to the rooftop, linking arms with Cassius, let go of him and sprinted forward. She threw off her rose quartz necklace and tossed it to Cassius. She stepped in front of her sister, her heart pounding, her belly on fire. Her palms opened and a big green blast spread for miles and miles. When the blast subsided, a green haze lingered in the air. When Clare looked to assess the damage, her jaw opened wide.

Sage stood, her eyes wide and unblinking, her hand out. Gracielle was leaned forward, Cassius's hand clutched her necklace, but they were all frozen still. She looked for the spirit of Antoine and Wade who had been standing beside her and Cassius. They were not frozen.

A loud clap of thunder sounded, even though the sky was sunny and bright.

Eight Goddesses touched down onto the Earth. They were a mess of beauty wrapped in magnificent dresses.

Olive, of North America, was a short woman, she was pale and had freckles all over her face and her skin. Her chestnut hair was wavy and was kept to the side in a braid that stopped just below her breast. She had wispy bangs that covered her forehead and stopped just above her hazel eyes. She wore a bright orange dress with long sheer sleeves, the dress cascaded in a train behind her bare feet. Abilene, the Goddess of Asia, was even shorter. She had brown skin and pin straight black hair that cut off at her shoulders. She had deep brown eyes and perfectly clear skin. Her dress cut across her shoulders and was a pastel purple with light pink swirls, there was a slit in her dress at her thighs that exposed her skin and her bright pink heels.

Jenara, of Antarctica, towered over Abilene. Her hair was pitch black and fell down to her waist in wispy curls, her hair was full of volume and parted to the right. Her eyes were bright blue, her skin a light shade of brown. She wore a pure white dress with white pearls and shiny, pastel blue shoes.

Visola, of Africa, was a bit shorter than Jenara. Her skin was the shade of the night sky and her brown hair was bunched up in tight curls at the top of her head. Her eyes were brown and framed by her winged eyeliner and thick eyelashes. She wore a tight ruby red dress, gold bracelets and ruby red heels.

Next to Visola, was Mallory, of South America, more widely known as the Goddess of death. She was not too short, but not too tall and had a smug look on her face, her light hazel eyes glared around the space. Her hair was wavy and ebony black, she had it pinned back with a skull clip. Her dress spilled over her tan skin and was pitch black and sheer, it cascaded down to her ankles that were covered by black boots.

Kalani, of Oceania, who was the same height as Visola, stood right by Mallory's side. Kalani had dark brown curly hair that went down to her shoulders and light brown eyes. She wore a red skirt that cascaded down to her ankles and a brown blouse.

The last Goddess stood at the front with Oralee, her name was Evangeline and she was the Goddess of Australia and the Goddess of life. She was the tallest out of the group. Her hair was wavy, bright blonde and fell to her lower back. She wore a golden dress that draped across her cream skin and crossed in all different directions, she also wore tall golden shoes. Her bright yellow eyes fixed onto Clare.

"That wasn't you," Evangeline told her. "We stopped time. It's time that we talk to you Clare. You and your family are going to help us change the world."

ABOUT THE AUTHOR

A. Kingsley grew up in Arizona and has been writing since she was a little girl. She is currently a teenager with a lot more life to live. *The Goddesses Throne* is her first novel. She plans to continue the *Two Red Flames* series and share her love of writing with the world.

Made in the USA
Las Vegas, NV
22 January 2021